Exeter

Ken Arthur

Round Table Publishing

ISBN: 978-0-9801808-0-0

Library of Congress Control Number: 2008940757

Round Table Publishing
1011 Surrey Lane
Bldg 200, Suite 200
Flower Mound, TX 75022

****

Other Books By Ken Arthur

Overtime—The Bonus Years
with Ben E. Dickerson, Ph.D.
and
Brothers and Sisters—For Better Or Worse
with Ben E. Dickerson, Ph.D. and Derrel Watkins, Ph.D.

Both available from KenArthurBooks.com

****

Cover design by
Suzanne Parada
Indianapolis, IN
s_parada@sbcglobal.net

Dedication

To Mary – for making my life a joy;
To Kristi – for being a lady I'm always proud of;
To Kevin – for being the kind of man I wish I were;
To Celia – for being a daughter-in-law from Heaven;
To Rob – for being a great son-in-law… you did it right;
To Mom – for living your years with grace and raising us right;
To Mom Campbell – for loving a son-in-law as a son;
To Terry, Granny, Aunt Jim, Dad Campbell, Sandra,
& the victims of September 11, 2001 -
Requiescat in Pace.

Foreword

September 11, 2001 was a tragedy not only for America, but also for all free people around the world. The cowardly attacks against the United States forever changed the way we viewed our world.

Exeter was a completed manuscript long before the events of 9-11. On that terrible day, this book was in the hands of prospective publishers being reviewed. The day after the attack, I called my agent in Boston and instructed him to remove *Exeter* from the market. The thought of publishing a book whose premise was a potential terrorist attack on the United States was unthinkable at the time.

Now—seven years later—at the encouragement of family and friends, I have decided it is time to publish this book.

While *Exeter* is fiction, the agencies from around the world profiled in the book are real and are dedicated to keeping us safe from those who would destroy our way of life. We owe them a debt of gratitude.

KMA
September 2008

It is in the shelter of each other that the people live.
Irish Proverb

A ship in harbor is safe, but that's not what ships are built for.
Albert Einstein

One

The New World - September 1544

Manuel Ortiz had led his men into a trap. As he stared into the campfire outside his tent, the same thoughts returned again and again. Ortiz was a soldier and these feelings of imminent doom were foreign to him. Never before had he struggled with such doubts. Ortiz commanded the finest conquistadors in the empire, and his authority came from the King himself. No man, no situation could possibly stand in his way.

Here though, completely surrounded by dense forest and undergrowth, he felt trapped and vulnerable. The forest, which was so beautiful and peaceful during the day, now seemed menacing and foreboding. Every sound from the darkness, even the quiet night breeze, was somehow amplified. Ortiz felt as if every one of his senses was warning him of danger. Even though no enemy had revealed himself, Ortiz could almost feel the eyes that monitored his movements. Those eyes were hidden and invisible, but were there nonetheless.

Ortiz and his army had been sent to this new land at the command of King Phillip II of Spain. Two years before, an expedition led by Francisco de Coronado had returned to Spain with tales of entire cities made of gold. He also told of a tribe of warriors in the new land. Some questioned the accuracy of both reports, but de Coronado steadfastly stood by his accounts.

The controversy mattered little to King Phillip II. He saw this tribe, if it did exist, as a threat to his absolute rule over the newly claimed territory. If there were warriors in his land, the king wanted them quashed. To that end, Ortiz was to search the region. If a tribe were found, he was to crush them.

For three months, the expedition had explored and charted the land. Traveling north, they had recently crossed one small mountain range and entered a massive basin of radiant white desert sand extending as far as the eye could see. The intense light of the sun reflecting off the dunes had temporarily blinded several of his men. One man had died as the result of snakebite, and another was seriously ill for two days after being stung by a scorpion.

The dunes seemed to continue forever, but Ortiz's advance scouts had reported changing terrain ahead. To the distant west was a barren mountain range, which seemed devoid of any vegetation. Farther north and east was the beginnings of another range. This one had an emerald cascade of color with evergreen trees decorating its sides.

The weeks of painfully slow exploration had revealed no indication the mysterious tribe existed at all. Ortiz's soldiers had been joking about their phantom adversary. Most of them believed that any army hidden in this desolate parcel of land deserved to live here. The temperature during the day was incredibly hot, while the nights dropped to near freezing. It seemed that nothing could long survive in this environment, nor would want to.

Finally the army had reached the easterly mountain range that rose out of the flatness and reached toward the sky. The men could now easily discern the forests that covered the mountain. Patches of white betrayed the early autumn snows that had fallen at higher elevations.

The men's spirits had risen considerably when they could finally see new and changing terrain, even if it meant almost certainly a more difficult climb through the mountain passes. Doggedly they continued until finally they were well into the mountains. Campsites were pitched under tall pine trees where they slept far more comfortably with pine needles beneath their bedrolls instead of the hot sand.

However, since entering the region's dense mountain woodlands, it had seemed that the journey was damned. Several pack horses had disappeared mysteriously, a third of the food supply was also missing, and much of the stored water had been contaminated somehow. In light of the supply problems, the mission was in danger of failing. Water was hard to find in the mountains, and game was impossible to shoot in enough quantity to feed the army. Soon, the expedition would be forced to shorten their quest. Manual Ortiz sat in his tent and pondered the future. He wondered when his men would face the unknown.

Hand-picked for their ruthless ability to handle danger, his soldiers were the best in the Spanish empire. Some had been with Francisco Pizarro six years earlier when he conquered the mighty Inca civilization. Each man was capable of killing without remorse. Now, however, they were restless, frustrated, and ready to fight whatever hidden demon had cursed their mission. Little did they know how soon their wish would be answered, and how tragic that response would be.

Humbarto de la Vaca, Ortiz's lieutenant and second-in-command, had come to his superior's tent to urge him to abandon the excursion and return to Spain. "God has not blessed this trip. He has cursed it and us. We must leave before He kills us for disobeying!"

"Enough!" Ortiz's eyes flashed with anger. "Another word and God will have nothing to do with your death! I will kill you myself. We will not return in disgrace to face the Crown." Then softening his tone, he continued, "Barto, you've been my friend for many years. We have never run from a battle before and now we must continue. The men will fight at our command. No one can defeat us."

Suddenly their discussion was interrupted by a warning shout. A perimeter guard had found the body of another sentry and raised the alarm. His shout was immediately silenced as an arrow, shot from the shadows, tore through his neck. Panic at the sudden pain rapidly turned to disbelief as he felt blood cascading down the front of his battle dress. Sinking to his knees the man was suddenly hit in rapid succession by three more arrows. He died without ever seeing his assailants.

Pandemonium broke out as sergeants, drawn from sleep in their tents, attempted to rally the soldiers to battle. Their shouts of orders were lost in the cries of pain and cursing from their troops. Many of the men in desperation fired their weapons into the darkness. The majority never got a chance to reload as a barrage of incoming arrows dropped them almost instantly.

"Madre de Dios!" de la Vaca yelled. "We are cursed by the devil himself. He comes in the darkness invisible, and attacks us from the shadows. We cannot stand up to him. Retreat now, I beg you!"

Drawing his sword, Ortiz looked hard at his lieutenant. "You cannot believe such lies. Cowardice is a curse of the weak. Leave now before your fear affects my men."

Manual Ortiz turned to face the battle. From the rustle of the tent behind him, he knew that his old friend had indeed run away. There was no time to consider the cowardly actions of his second-in-command, nor would he ever know that Humbarto de la Vaca was dead fifteen seconds after he left the tent.

Ortiz immediately ran to the center of the compound. Drawing the remaining conquistadors around him, he established two concentric circles of defense. Using this mutual protection, the guards believed they could repel any further assaults from the invisible army in the shadows.

Suddenly the attack stopped and an eerie silence swept over the camp. From the darkness a voice spoke, "Invaders of our land, lay down your weapons, and we will harm you no more!"

A quiet fear crept through the soldiers. The mysterious voice spoke in flawless Castilian Spanish. Ortiz, struggling to sound firm and in control responded, "We will not negotiate with the darkness. Reveal yourself and we will speak."

Like a ghost appearing from nothingness, a man emerged. The flickering campfires revealed little about this specter. He was almost six feet tall with a broad muscular build. Shoulder length hair surrounded a strong chiseled face. His powerful voice and proud demeanor communicated immediately that he was a man accustomed to being obeyed.

As the man spoke and fully entered the light, he raised his hands to show he was unarmed. Moving slowly toward the soldiers, he spoke firmly, "You must leave here. We have tried to make you turn back for the past several weeks, and yet you continued. Now you have driven us to defend our homes and families. All we want is for you to leave us in peace and never again enter our land. With this promise, no further harm will come to you."

"We are here in the name of King Phillip of Spain. Your people live in his domain and are under his rule. I, Manuel Ortiz, the King's servant, order you to surrender your weapons and live within his protection."

A new hardness entered the lone spokesman's voice. "I am king here and my people serve only me."

Without warning, one of the soldiers elected to act alone. Silently drawing up his weapon, he fired at the tribal king. His musket, fired in haste, nonetheless found its mark. The lead ball entered the warrior's chest just above the right breast and exited out his back leaving the victim mortally wounded. Death, though inevitable, was not immediate.

Stumbling backwards into the shadows, the king was already beginning to lose consciousness. Seemingly from nowhere, hands began to reach for him. One face in particular appeared. "Father," it spoke gently, "I'm here."

The dying man felt a surprising calmness as he looked up at his son. He answered softly, "You, Micha, will soon be king. There was much I wanted to tell you before this day, but now there is little time. Listen carefully to my words and obey my last commands. You are to rule our people with compassion. Listen to the Elders. Their counsel through the years has given me much wisdom. You, too, will need their advice and insight." Breathing deeply the King continued, "Now I give you my last and most difficult command. We have been great warriors, and no army has ever defeated us, but our people are tired of war. Lead them away from here. Find a home so remote that outsiders will never again trouble them. In this new land, hide yourselves away. But remember, be strong and always keep the Protectors learning."

A flash of pain momentarily quieted the King. Knowing his strength was nearly spent, the man repeated, "My son, live apart, but always keep the Protectors learning."

"I will, Father. I will do as you have commanded." The King took a long look at his son, smiled for a moment, and then his eyes went blank.

Even as the new king was laying his father's body down, warriors hidden throughout the forest were beginning to exact revenge.

Manuel Ortiz watched in horror as his soldiers were slaughtered before him. Man after man fell, their bodies struck simultaneously by arrows from every direction. So devastating was the attack that it was over in less than thirty seconds.

Every man was dead. No cries of pain or movement came from any soldier. The expedition commander stood unscathed, surrounded by the bodies of those who were to protect him.

Terrified, he screamed into the darkness, "Kill me, as well! Don't leave me with the souls of these men. Kill me!"

Another voice came from the shadows. It was the sound of a young man, but carried an air of authority. "You will not die by our arrows. It is my command that you return to your king and tell him that we wish only to live in peace. We will leave this land and he can have it for his domain. But, tell him that we give it – he has not conquered it. It will soon be sunrise. Leave here as soon as you can. Take two animals and whatever provisions you require. Do not worry about your soldiers. I give you my word that they will be buried with the dignity and honor we give our own warriors."

That was the last sound Ortiz heard from his unseen enemy. In a daze of shock and disbelief he packed a mule with provisions. The sun was just cresting the mountain ridge as Ortiz rode from his camp.

* * * * *

Within two months, he had returned to the Spanish settlement his expedition had left. Shortly afterwards, he was on a ship sailing to Spain. Manuel Ortiz had expected to return a hero. Instead he was the sole survivor of his army, and as such, was accused of cowardice and fleeing his men.

The only ones who listened to his story of the battle were the scholars. Many of them had studied ancient manuscripts and learned that the early Greek and Roman armies had also faced a tribe of seemingly indestructible warriors. Most believed these stories to be simply legends, but other scholars believed that there might be a connection.

Ortiz never got a chance to find out for sure. Four months after returning from his expedition, he took his own life. His troubled mind was finally at rest.

The fallen king's last command to his son was carried out. His people lived in peace and remained in hiding for four hundred and sixty-four years.

Two

Santa Fe, New Mexico - October 16, 2009

Maria Rodriguez-O'Leary walked slowly around the Palace of the Governors with a pace that was more a result of concentration than of her advanced years. Her gray hair was pulled tightly back into a bun and framed a face that was once beautiful, but was now wrinkled and weathered. She walked slightly stooped. Even though her body was showing signs of age, her mind was still excellent.

Mrs. Rodriguez-O'Leary's peculiar name came from her marriage to an Irish architect named Sean O'Leary. His love for Spanish design had brought him to study in Santa Fe at the end of World War II. After completing his research in New Mexico, Sean had planned to return to Ireland and introduce his native country to the beauty of this region's homes and buildings.

He had grandiose plans for large estates of homes all built in this style. He could visualize, as only a dreamer could, hundreds of buildings designed in the stark walls of covered adobe brick or stucco.

Sean was confident he would create this architectural masterpiece, but he also knew some Irish "purists" would initially rebel as he built block creations in the rolling green hills around Dublin. He was sure they would eventually grow to love the simple line and angles of his designs. They would come to appreciate the joy of large, open rooms instead of the small cramped spaces that described traditional houses. Sean Michael O'Leary would be the one to bring this beauty to them. There was no doubt in his mind about that fact.

His dream for Ireland seemed far away. First he had to learn the style, and for that he had come to Santa Fe.

As many young architects do, Sean enjoyed walking and looking at old buildings. He always took a note pad to sketch any unusual design he happened to notice. To his friends, he laughingly explained this habit by saying, "You never know when a transient moment of genius might strike me. I want this pad available to record that event for posterity."

One old house in particular often caught his eye and he had sketched it several times during his walks. The split-level home was on a street near the boarding house where he lived, so he passed there regularly. Something about the place kept bringing Sean back, but he never could quite put his finger on it. Sean had attempted to capture the design on his note pad from every possible direction. *What I wouldn't give to see the inside of that house.* The same thought went through his mind constantly, but he couldn't bring himself to ask the owners for permission to examine their floor plan. That, after all, was not how it was done in Ireland. A stranger would never be so intrusive. So Sean was sure he would have to be content only to imagine how the inside looked.

One afternoon, as he stood and studied the house, a young lady walked by. She stopped long enough to check out the stranger.

"Are you looking for a specific address?" she asked cautiously.

Sean, suddenly feeling very conspicuous and a bit foolish, smiled sheepishly. "Thanks, no. I suppose I do look a wee bit lost out here. But I'm just enjoying looking at that house." The young lady's eyebrow went up in a request for more information, and she listened without comment as for the next few minutes he explained the nature of his study.

"I know the people who live here," she commented. "Would you like me to introduce you? I'm sure they will let you look around the inside of the house." With a coy smile she added, "By the way, my name is Maria."

"Sean Michael O'Leary, at your service." A quaint bow accompanied the name. Maria was entranced by the Irish accent and the manners of this man.

As he followed her up the walkway, Sean couldn't help but wonder how old Maria was. She's eighteen, maybe nineteen ... not that it matters. I've precious little time for girls, and I won't be here that much longer—still she is a beauty.

Walking up to the impressive mahogany door, Maria knocked loudly. Within a few moments a matronly Mexican woman answered and for a moment looked perplexed. "Señorita Maria, come in, come in."

"Sylvia, this is my friend Mr. Sean O'Leary. Is Doctor Rodriguez in?"

"Sí, Señorita. He's in his study. Do you wish me to tell him you are here?"

"No, we'll go on back. Thank you."

The two young people walked toward the rear of the house. Sean's head was on a swivel as he looked around. The ornate cornices particularly fascinated him. He was trying to absorb every detail when Maria stopped in front of a door. Reaching into her purse, she removed a rubber band. Pulling her long dark hair off her shoulders and back into a ponytail, she used the band to hold it there. "He prefers it this way," she explained.

Her quiet knock brought an immediate booming, "What is it?"

Maria opened the door just wide enough to peek around the side. "Are you busy?"

"Never too busy for you. Come on inside here."

Behind the desk sat a massive man. Sean guessed he easily weighed two hundred and fifty pounds. He didn't appear to have an ounce of fat on him; he was just huge. His eyebrows raised noticeably when Sean walked in. "Papa, I want you to meet Mr. Sean O'Leary. He's a guest in our area." She went on to give an abbreviated version of his study and his plans. The doctor listened silently, occasionally looking over the young man. Sean hardly paid any attention. He was still struck by the word, Papa.

Doctor Rodriguez asked to see some of Sean's drawings. He nodded appreciatively as he perused the notebook. Finally, he got up and walked around to Sean with his enormous hand outstretched. "Mi casa es su casa. You are welcome in my home. Now, you two get out of here. I have work to do." As they turned to leave, the old man looked up from his desk again. "Maria, don't wait until right outside my door to pull your hair back. Remember, a beautiful face should not be hidden by hair."

"Yes, Papa. I love you, too." The father's eyes sparkled with delight. He was a man who obviously cherished his daughter.

Sean could barely contain his excitement. He spent the next three hours exploring the house. He sketched and measured nearly every room. He traced the hand-carved moldings that capped the walls and surrounded the door jams. Throughout the process, Maria regaled him with stories of family events that had occurred in each alcove. She seemed to be having as much fun as he was.

Over the next seven months Maria and Sean spent many hours together walking Santa Fe streets examining old houses. Maria had a good eye for detail and often discovered things that had escaped Sean's attention. Slowly the two discovered they had more in common than just architecture, and within a year they were married.

From the beginning, they made an unlikely pair. His ruddy complexion and flaming red hair was a contrast to her dark brown skin and black hair. Her strong Spanish nature and his Irish temper had generated some loud explosive arguments, but they had loved with a passion and had adored each other.

* * * * *

Sean never returned to Ireland. He and Maria stayed in Santa Fe and his architectural firm became one of the most prosperous in New Mexico. His death two years before had left her devastated.

Maria continued to live in the expansive house she and Sean had built. It was far bigger than she needed, but she could not bring herself to sell it. He had left her wealthy, but alone. Recently, her twenty-one year old granddaughter, Deidre, had come to live with her. The old woman was grateful for the companionship, but Sean had been her life and even now she desperately missed him.

* * * * *

Chamber of Commerce pamphlets had long touted that Santa Fe was founded in 1610 as the capital of the Spanish colony of New Mexico. Therefore, it was the oldest seat of government in the United States. Such hype meant nothing to Maria. All she cared about was the joy of being here and enjoying her memories.

When she was especially lonely, Maria would often walk through the Palace of the Governors because this had been one of Sean's favorite places, and she felt especially close to him here. Four centuries before, the original Spanish Governors had allowed local Indians and peasants to sell wares around the Palace. This custom continues, although tourists are now the primary customers. Around the courtyard square or plaza, as it is called, local vendors line the walkway to sell handicrafts, Indian blankets, turquoise jewelry, pottery, and souvenirs of every description.

The day had been unbearably hot. Even now, with the sun dropping behind the Sanger de Christi Mountains, the high cirrus clouds appeared to be on fire. Their wispy feather-like appearance blazed with an orange-red color that was impossible to ignore.

Maria had spent the past hour admiring the work of various merchants. She enjoyed encouraging these young craftsmen and had helped several financially as they started their businesses. Her patronage had allowed many of these artisans to create their beautiful artwork on a large enough scale to provide a livable wage.

In one area of the plaza was a crippled man who was carving crucifix from small scraps of wood. As Maria stooped to pick up one of the crosses, a flash of motion startled her. The old woman realized too late that her bag was being torn off her arm. By reflex alone, she attempted to cling to the strap and yell for help.

The young thief saw his plan for a quick grab and escape down the nearby alley evaporating. In desperation, he hit the old woman. As she fell, he turned to run. The man believed that his speed and the element of surprise would confound the startled onlookers long enough for him to evade capture down a narrow alleyway.

The thug was wrong. From the crowd one man moved to a point directly between the robber and the alley and blocked the only viable escape route. The youth was trapped and became desperate. He pulled a five-inch switchblade from his back pocket, and with a practiced menacing motion, flicked out the blade. He looked for a reaction from his would-be captor and was surprised when he found there was none. Holding the knife carefully, the hoodlum was ready to slash his way by the young man who now blocked his only escape.

"Get out of my way, man. I swear I'll cut you. Go on! It's none of your business." The thug's inflection was hard and ominous, but there was confusion in his mind. He was well familiar with violence, and experience told him that most people would back off when confronted with a knife. This man was different. Instead of showing fear, his brown eyes went suddenly cold and hard. The robber had never seen anyone so calm in the face of danger.

In a quiet voice the man spoke, "You made it my business when you hit the old woman. Now put down the knife and I won't hurt you. Otherwise, give it your best shot. Perhaps you'll find me harder to handle than she was." The man's controlled, slow tone unnerved the mugger even more, and he frantically began to slice the air with the switchblade in a feeble attempt to hurt Maria's defender. One of his slashes nicked the man's forearm.

Instantly, the stranger sidestepped. With carefully aimed chops, he struck the thug on opposite sides of the wrist. The blows momentarily stunned the nerves in the boy's hand causing the knife to drop free. The mugger stared at his now empty hand in total surprise. Before he could move, the rescuer unleashed two lightning jabs: one to the solar plexus, and another to the jaw.

The young thug woke up several minutes later as a Santa Fe policeman was handcuffing him.

Once the drama had ended, the young defender stepped to Maria. While dazed and frightened, she was otherwise unharmed. Her granddaughter was there and already helping her up.

Smiling, the rescuer reached down, easily picked up the elderly frame and set her carefully on a park bench. Maria noticed the gentleness with which he carried her, but her granddaughter noticed more. He was handsome, with long brown hair that went almost to his shoulders and dark brown eyes set in a smooth, tan face. She guessed he stood around five foot ten, maybe eleven inches tall, and was about twenty-five years old. She also observed the absence of a ring on his left hand.

Maria spoke first. "Thank you for your help."

"Por nada, Señora. I hope you're okay."

"Yes, I'm fine, just a little shaken. That boy—I was afraid he would kill you."

The smile returned. "It will be a while before he hurts anyone again."

Deidre, who until now had been quiet, pleaded softly, "Grandmother, please let me take you to see the doctor. This has been too much excitement for you."

"No. All I need is to go home and rest. Besides all the doctor would do is fuss at me, and treat me like an old woman. I certainly don't need that!"

Realizing that she had lost the argument, Deidre addressed the man. "Thank you for helping. My grandmother was right however, you could have been killed."

"Where I was raised, our old people are treated with respect. Striking an elder would never go unpunished. Besides, he was a bully. Such people are only dangerous if they have the upper hand." He didn't continue. The implication was obvious.

Noticing his injury for the first time, Maria reached into her purse and removed a handkerchief. "Here. Please let us take you to the hospital to have that checked. You might need sutures."

"The cut isn't deep. Besides, I have something in my hotel room that will take care of it."

"Hotel? Then you're not from Santa Fe?" Deidre's voice betrayed her disappointment.

"No, I'm just visiting here."

"Well then, perhaps we can repay your kindness with a home cooked meal." Deidre suddenly went silent. She realized the invitation might be out of line. Then apologizing, she continued, "I guess that's a bit forward, Mr. ..."

"Isha. My friends just call me Isha." The warmth and charm in his voice cut through the awkwardness of the moment. "And yes, a meal with two lovely ladies would indeed be a treat."

Three

"The meal was delicious, Mrs. O'Leary." Isha focused his attention on Deidre and smiled. "My compliments to the chef. I must confess I was really tired of fast food." His plate was empty for the third time.

"Well you're most welcome, and I'm glad you enjoyed it." It wasn't often Deidre cooked a big meal, and even more rare when it was for a man. She had especially enjoyed cooking for this one.

All evening she had noticed his subtle incongruities. Isha had the poise and confidence of a surgeon, but dressed like a farm hand. He had been so gentle and kind when addressing Maria, and yet as she had seen firsthand, he could handle himself in a fight. Above all, he had a boyish charm and easy smile that she found irresistible.

"Isha, what brings you to Santa Fe?" Deidre asked, "Are you here on business?"

"No, I'm just doing some research here in Santa Fe. My father had an old friend from here. All my life I've heard stories about the region, so I decided to learn a little about it myself first-hand."

Isha had a simple bandage covering the cut from his fight. "Did you have a doctor check that?"

"No, I treated it with something my grandfather taught me. He was a strong believer in using natural medicines. I think he probably had a salve, elixir, lotion, or balm for just about every possible problem, and I don't think he ever saw a medical doctor in his life. But, since he lived to be ninety-four years old, and was still hunting and fishing a week before he died, I guess his remedies were pretty good."

After dinner, while Deidre cleared the table, Maria took Isha on a tour of the house. "Sean and I planned this place for years. Being an architect, he wanted it to be just perfect. Neither of us would have been happy in the city, so we built it out here in the mountains. It gave us privacy from neighbors, and freedom to do pretty much what we wanted. Sean enjoyed entertaining, so he built a place where our friends would feel welcome. Most of all, because our family grew up here, it's been more than just a house; it's been our home. I have memories in each room that are special. Not even getting old can take those away."

"Mrs. O'Leary, old age is a state of mind not of years. You are in many ways younger than some people my age." Isha smiled at the wrinkled face before him. "Now, show me this beautiful house."

The old woman gently took the young man's arm and led him into a large game room. A carved mahogany six-foot by twelve-foot snooker table occupied the center of the space. It had fifteen red balls and six colored balls placed carefully in a very specific pattern on its bed. "Sean was a snooker champion in his Irish county. He wanted me to learn the game, but I never could master the cue." Maria gently touched the table and for a moment was lost in thought. "John—he was Deidre's father—used to play his father long tournaments in here. I could often hear them laughing all the way into the family room. Those two were a competitive pair, and it didn't matter what they were doing, they always tried to best the other one. Anyway, since no one around here knows how to play snooker anymore, it just stays set up."

At the end of a long hallway was the media room. In the center of the space was a well-used, overstuffed, leather recliner facing a wall-sized cabinet. Built into the arm of the chair was what appeared to be a remote control unit. Its unusual design and large number of buttons caught Isha's eye. "I don't think I've ever seen a remote like this one before."

"You haven't seen one before because Sean designed and built it himself. My husband was something of an inventor who never created anything really useful ... just things he wanted to see or use." Maria reached down and pushed a button on the remote. The cabinet doors retracted into the wall revealing a hidden television set. Shortly afterwards, the television screen showed a gentle warm-up glow that was replaced by the familiar face of the Fox News Channel anchor. "Being one of the early big screen TVs, it was difficult to see the picture when there was much sunlight in the room. So, he could sit here in his chair, and take care of that problem." She pushed another button. From recessed panels above the windows, heavy shades lowered and totally darkened the room. "With this little gadget of his, he could sit here and watch TV on the brightest day. He used to say all he needed was some invention to bring his beer while he watched football. However, there was no need for such an invention because bringing Sean his beer was my responsibility."

As the tour continued, Maria pointed out some bronze western statues in the hallway. She was most proud of the authentic Remington sculpture that occupied the entrance to the library. In this room were floor-to-ceiling cases that contained books of every description. The deep-red mahogany panel and bookcases exuded masculinity. An old, red leather chair was located in a bay window that looked out to the mountains. Its worn and cracked cover revealed the amount of wear it had received over the years. "My Sean read incessantly. If he was supposed to be out working in the yard or doing some other chore, I could almost always find him in here instead."

As they wandered through the house, Maria showed her guest Sean's study where the architectural drafting table and ink drawing pens still sat. She explained, "Sean left computer designing to his younger associates. He refused to use anything but his old pens and ink."

As the tour progressed, Maria even took Isha into the back yard to see the "fort" Sean had built John for his tenth birthday. It was an eight-foot by eight-foot room with a simple shingle roof. The place had been constructed on legs that put it almost five feet above the ground. Looking under the platform, Isha saw that a trap door was the only entrance.

"I can still see John and his father out here sawing and hammering on this place. They were funny to watch. Here was this little boy explaining to his father, in no uncertain terms, exactly how he wanted his fort built. During the summer, I guess he spent more nights sleeping in here than in his own bedroom. The last person to play in here probably was Deidre when she was a little girl and visiting us during the summers. I still have it painted every few years and have a handyman who makes little repairs on it so that my great grandchildren can play here someday."

Finally, after Isha was convinced he had seen every possible room, Maria stopped before a closed door. "Sean loved this house, but this room was his favorite. It reminded him of Ireland, and the family and friends he left behind." Maria opened the door and turned on the lights.

Isha walked in, and for a moment couldn't believe what he was seeing. It was as if he had been instantly transported half way around the world to Dublin. Sean had created a picture perfect Irish pub. The rough-hewn timber walls were covered with football banners from various soccer clubs. The shelves were still stocked with whiskey bottles and glasses. Authentic Guinness and Fosters draught beer dispensers were mounted in the center of the bar. In the corner, hung a regulation five feet eight inches above the floor, was the mandatory dartboard. Bar towels of every description were on small tables throughout the room.

It was evident to Isha that this had been a place of refuge for Sean. Here, with the doors closed and the rowdy music playing, he was again a young man in Dublin.

Turning to Maria, Isha saw the silent tears in her eyes. "Mrs. O'Leary, your husband was a remarkable man. He was blessed with the gift to design and build a house that was more than just shelter from the elements; it was shelter from the world. And he was doubly blessed to have a loving wife with whom to share it. I am honored you allowed me to see this."

"Sean would have liked you, Isha. For protecting me today, he would have wanted you to have this." Maria removed a gold neck chain from the pocket of her blazer. She stood on her tiptoes, and placed the chain around Isha's neck. Sensing that he was about to protest, Maria quickly added, "It brings me great joy to see you wear it."

"Then I accept this gift from you – and from Sean. I will wear it with pride."

Closing the door to the pub, the old woman took Isha back to the dining room where Deidre was cutting a cake still warm from the oven.

Maria raised her hand in mock horror. "No cake for me. At my age, the calories go straight to the thighs. Besides, this day has been a bit too long and eventful. I'm going to bed." She took Isha's hand and then spontaneously kissed him on the cheek. "Thank you again for today. If you are in Santa Fe again, there is always a room here for you." She smiled at the two young people, turned, and left.

After Maria was gone, Deidre noticed the chain around her guest's neck. "My grandfather wore that necklace for years. I thought it had been lost. She must think you very special." Deidre took Isha's hand, "My grandmother showed you the house. Let me show you the grounds."

In typical Spanish style, the house had a courtyard beyond which lay a well-manicured flower garden. Fifty yards away was a small lake with a fishing pier. Its depths were constantly replenished by mountain streams and were clear and cold. A light breeze was all that disturbed the tranquil water as it created the tiniest ripples on the otherwise mirror-like surface. The reflection of a full moon reflected of the water and provided more than enough light for Isha and Deidre to clearly see each other.

The two young people walked out on the pier. Several seconds of total silence passed as the couple watched the wandering light. It was obvious Deidre was struggling with how to say—or whether to say—what she was feeling. She had known this man for only a few hours and yet she felt totally safe with him. There was no doubt he had touched feelings in her that had been dormant for some time.

Finally, Deidre turned and looked at Isha. "My parents were killed in a car accident eleven months ago. I had just graduated from college, and didn't really know what to do or where to go. My grandmother was lonely and we both were hurting, so we decided we needed each other, and I came to live here. I love my grandmother, but I miss being with someone my own age. Having you here tonight has been great." Deidre was thankful that the moonlight was not enough to reveal her blush.

Isha looked into Deidre's eyes and almost unconsciously cupped her face with his hands. As she looked into his eyes expectantly, for a moment she felt like an awkward schoolgirl out on a first date. With incredible tenderness, he leaned forward and kissed her.

Deidre felt her knees weaken. The warmth of Isha's lips and the touch of his hand were enough to start an instant and powerful craving in Deidre. The passion between them grew quickly as their kiss became more intense. Isha slowly took his hand from Deidre's face and moved it down. The young woman breathed deeply as he gently touched her. Without a word, Isha effortlessly lifted Deidre and carried her into the shadows near the lake. The darkness enveloped the two as excitement and desire took control.

An hour later, Deidre and Isha walked hand-in-hand back to the house. The young people laughed and spoke quietly to each other.

Knowing that the evening was soon ending, Isha stopped at the front door. "Thank you, Deidre for a wonderful time." He smiled boyishly. "Would you by chance be free for a movie tomorrow night?"

Deidre answered immediately, "I would love to see a movie with you!"

Isha kissed Deidre good night. As she closed the door, Deidre suddenly realized that the man was walking away into the woods. For the first time she realized that he had not driven to Maria's house, but before she could yell at him, Isha disappeared into the darkness.

Four

Morning was Deidre's time of the day, and she loved to get up early and run before breakfast. During her first few weeks in Santa Fe, the 6,100-foot altitude had left her winded and able to run only short distances. Now, acclimated to the high altitude, Deidre could easily go several miles. She could even handle the steepest mountain roads. Not bad for someone who a year ago couldn't even climb a flight of stairs without stopping to catch her breath, she often thought.

Deidre's standard outfit was a purple jogging pants with a matching top and a headband to keep her hair back and out of her eyes. Her athletic figure and extraordinary looks were a pleasant distraction for the drivers along the highway. More than one early morning commuter had slowed his car down to enjoy watching her run along Interstate 25. Deidre never really noticed the attention as she enjoyed her solitary run. In her private thoughts, she felt watching the sun rising through the mountain passes gave her an advantage over others. Deidre figured it was a small game of one-upmanship with the majority of humanity. They were, after all, still asleep in their beds while she was awake and alive.

Today, however, there would be no run. Deidre didn't want to risk being gone even for a short time in case Isha called. As she lay there, Deidre wondered if he was still asleep in his hotel room.

I wonder if he's dreaming of me? Deidre laughed at herself for asking such a childish question. Still within her, there was an overwhelming desire to remember every detail of him. She wanted to be able to recall each moment of their time together by the lake. Unconsciously she smiled to herself and felt deliciously decadent.

The morning was already alive with sounds from outside and Deidre, who loved the beauty of this land, looked out of her window towards the western hills. Stretching and yawning, Deidre reluctantly got out of her bed and went in to her bathroom for a long shower.

Every day for the past several months, Deidre had prepared her grandmother's breakfast. The routine was easy, and almost without variation. She always had two slices of toast with orange marmalade, and a small bowl of oatmeal. On the side was hot tea with cream (a habit she acquired from Sean's Irish background). Deidre actually looked forward each day to this small duty. It was a wonderful way to spend a few private minutes with Maria. Often they would sit on the terrace and talk about changes in the world.

Maria liked to lament the fast pace of today and recall with fondness her slower, simpler life as a young lady of Deidre's age. Not that everything was perfect back then. The world was still recovering from World War II. Lives were being rebuilt, and a glimmer of hope for the future was just beginning to develop again.

Maria's gift of storytelling and her wonderful memory combined to bring the past alive for her granddaughter. She especially enjoyed sharing tales of Deidre's father, John, as a young boy. She could make him seem in one moment as mischief personified, and then chuckle in recalling some tender moment. He had climbed every mountain peak in the area, knew each arroyo by heart, and had hiked over almost every square mile of forest around. He had loved Santa Fe. Growing up with the mountains in his back yard had helped him develop a love for nature. Camping and hiking in those secluded areas had given him confidence to handle himself in unfamiliar surroundings. It had been a great place to grow up.

Maria loved to tell stories about her only son, and Deidre loved to hear them all.

Today, there were no stories. Maria seemed to be enjoying her private thoughts this morning. She sat on the back patio and ate her breakfast. Occasionally she would stop and take a deep breath of mountain air. Deidre hardly noticed. She was lost in her own thoughts for the moment. Finally, after she finished her breakfast, Maria asked Deidre to take a walk with her.

There was a path that began at the wood line beside the lake and meandered through Maria's estate. The path wove among the pine trees in a gradual, easy slope that ended about half way up the mountain. Because of the moderate incline, Maria had little difficulty hiking the path. Besides, she knew every step of the trail.

After the two women were some distance from the house, Maria stopped suddenly. There, in a clearing was a doe with her yearling. The young one stayed close to his mother as she cautiously sniffed the air. After several moments of watching silently, Maria and Deidre moved on.

Maria seemed preoccupied with her walk today. She pointed out with genuine delight the various birds they encountered. Surrounded by the woods, they could no longer hear any sounds of civilization. Even the interstate highway was far enough away to be muffled by the forest. Finally, Maria sat down on a large flat rock to rest. Deidre stood for a moment, and then chose a spot by her grandmother to sit. They looked out over the valley below. The shades of green seemed endless. Timber roads snaked their way up the mountains in the distance. At the base of the mountain, the woman could make out their house, although the surrounding trees hid most of it. Maria's lake was the only easily discernible feature.

After several seconds Maria broke the silence. "This is one of my favorite places in the world. Your grandfather and I would often sit here and watch the sunset. He loved it, but the walk home afterwards in the dark would terrify me. Somehow holding on to his arm made it all ok. The sounds and shadows were never as frightening when I was with him. He made me feel secure and protected, and most of all, loved. I remember feeling that way with him from the first moment we met. I didn't understand it, and couldn't explain it, but I knew it." Turning to face Deidre, the old woman continued, "Everyone needs to be loved like that. Don't be afraid of caring for someone, my child. Remember, there is always a danger that you will be hurt, but love is worth that risk."

"Well, when I meet the right man I'm sure I won't have any doubts about that."

"Don't be so sure. The unknown always makes a person uncomfortable." Shifting her weight around to look at Deidre, the next words seemed to flow very slowly. "For instance, how did you feel around Isha last night?"

"Oh, he's...nice." Deidre answered suspiciously. "Why do you ask?"

"Because I liked him. And at my age, I rarely second guess my initial opinions about someone. Over the years, I've decided that my gut feelings are usually fairly accurate. Anyway, if you're interested, and if it matters, you have my blessings to see him again."

Deidre was confused, but pleased with her grandmother's words, and sat quietly for a moment. Her mind replayed the last evening. Without realizing it, she started to smile. "I did enjoy his company." Looking carefully for a response from Maria, she continued, "We have a date to see a movie tonight. Would you like to come along? I'm sure he would not mind at all."

A wrinkled smile erupted from the old woman's face. "Thank you dear, but no. You children don't need me along as a chaperon. One thing I would remind you, however. Enjoy your time together, but please remember, my bedroom window overlooks the lake."

As Deidre's face suddenly went beet red, she turned to see her grandmother give her an impish smile and wink.

Five

Patience had never been Deidre's strong suit. She tried everything to make the hours pass quickly, but to no avail. Nothing worked. Finally, just as the sun was setting, the sound of a car in their driveway brought Deidre and Maria to the front door. They stood there in disbelief at the sight before them. A chauffeur driven Mercedes-Benz limousine was just coming to a stop. The driver opened the door and Isha stepped out. That can't be the same man who was here for dinner, Deidre thought.

Tonight he wore no jeans and sneakers. Instead, Isha looked like a model in a men's wear catalog. He was wearing gray plaid wool slacks, oxford shirt, and a cashmere sweater. "He's gorgeous," Deidre whispered. All she heard was a subtle laugh from her grandmother.

Both women were speechless as Isha walked up to the door. He was carrying two yellow roses. They realized at the same moment that they were staring. "Good evening, ladies. I hope I'm not late." His smile seemed even more engaging, and his charm even more entrancing than it was the previous evening. He gave each lady a rose.

"No, you're right on time," replied Deidre. "Funny, but this isn't exactly the way we expected you. Didn't you say you were a student? No student I've ever known has had a car like this one – not to mention a driver."

"Well, my father serves in a position that has a few concomitant perks. And Tomás, my driver, is also my friend. He's been my companion and mentor since I was a child. And before me, he was my father's counselor. He doesn't say much, but he's very loyal to my family." He smiled again at Deidre, "We had better hurry."

Tomás opened the door as the young couple approached. He was a man of about seventy, but still looked solidly built. He had a shock of silver hair, and gray eyes that were intense and appeared to examine everything. Just being near Tomás, Deidre felt an aura of tranquility, which he seemed to wear like a mantle.

Watching them drive off, Maria kept searching her memory. I know that I've met Tomás somewhere, but I just can't remember. She quickly dismissed the idea as ridiculous.

Inside the car, Deidre was quiet. These trappings of wealth were foreign to her, but Isha also seemed uncomfortable. "Deidre, I guess I owe you an explanation." Taking a deep breath, and choosing his words carefully, Isha continued. "My father is head of a rather large group of people. I'm a student, just like I told you, but I work for my community. My research has a direct result on the people in our organization. We have thirty-five scholars, just like me, scattered all over the world that study different cultures and report back to the organization. That's about all I can tell you. The nature of our work is private. It's nothing sinister, but it is confidential. Try to understand."

Resigning herself to being puzzled Deidre finally responded, "I don't understand, Isha, but I'm not going to let that upset our date." Trying to change the subject, Deidre ignored the myriad of questions rambling around in her mind. "What movie are we going to see?"

Isha, relieved that she was not going to press for more information, answered, "The choice is all yours. I haven't been to the cinema in so long that anything will be great."

"How about that latest Meryl Streep movie? I've heard it's terrific."

"Sounds good to me. Let's see where it's showing." Reaching into a seat back pocket, Isha pulled out a morning edition of the Santa Fe daily newspaper and referred to the entertainment section. Pressing a button, the glass partition to the driver lowered, and Isha gave instructions to Tomás.

A nod from Tomás was all that acknowledged the request.

The movie was everything Deidre expected. Streep gave her normal superlative performance. Deidre enjoyed crying on Isha's shoulder. He seemed to take it all in stride. Even Tomás, who discretely sat a few rows behind the couple, was smiling when they left the theater. It was the most emotion Deidre had detected from him all evening.

After the movie, Isha and Deidre walked slowly to the car. Anyone passing by would hardly have noticed the young couple, or Tomás trailing several feet behind. Hand in hand, the two young people seemed lost in conversation. As they reached the car, Tomás smoothly moved ahead to open the door. Deidre smiled at the old man, "Thank you, Tomás. You are most kind."

He paused for a moment, and looked intently at her. Instantly his demeanor changed, and he smiled quickly. "My lady, it is an honor to be with someone as lovely as yourself."

Isha good-naturedly chided his driver, "Old friend, she is my date tonight. Quit using your charms on her."

"I beg your forgiveness, sir. I was momentarily overwhelmed by her beauty."

"Using that as an excuse, I have no choice but to pardon you. Now, since the hour is still early, please take us for a drive into the mountains."

"As you wish, Sire."

After they were moving, Deidre looked squarely at Isha. "Ok, what gives here? Tomás keeps calling you Sir or Sire, and he treats you with such deference. He isn't just your driver, is he?"

"Like I said before, Tomás is my mentor and my friend. He and I have been together since I was four years old. He was my father's teacher forty years ago. They studied in Santa Fe long before you or I was around. So now, he uses his experience and memories to color what I learn here."

It was obvious to Isha that his date neither understood nor accepted his explanation at face value. She did however allow the subject to die, for which he was grateful. I've already told her more than I should without the

Elder's approval, Isha thought. He was torn by what to tell her. Isha stared at the back of his driver's head. He knew that the glass partition separating them had prevented Tomás from hearing the conversation. Isha wondered what Tomás would say in this situation, especially considering who Deidre's father had been. Did his special place give her the right to know more than other Outworlders? Did she have the same dispensation the Elders had given her father? He decided in the final analysis he could not make those determinations alone. Frustration welled within Isha's thoughts. Just when I need my teacher most, I can't even talk to him!

Before long, Tomás had the car outside the city and north on US Highway 84. He left the main road and got on the Old Taos Highway. His turbocharged Mercedes engine easily handled the steep road grades and cruised through the tree lined mountain passes. Deidre seemed lost in the beauty of the scenery. Her mind was really somewhere else. Why is he so mysterious? He never gives me a straight answer about his family or his home. It scares me that I feel so comfortable with him and really know so little. In a moment of frustration Deidre hit the armrest of the car. Isha looked at her in surprise. She couldn't take the suspense any longer. "Why won't you just tell me the truth? No one is this secretive unless they are doing something illegal. Now either you come straight with me, or take me home right now!"

"Deidre, last night I had a wonderful time with you. Tonight I wanted to let you know how special that was to me. I must leave soon. It will do you no good to fret over a man you will likely not see again." Deidre started to speak, but Isha stopped her, "All I can tell you about my family is that we are part of a very unique community. I'm sorry I can't tell you more." Disappointment was evident in Isha's voice. "I'll have Tomás take you home."

"No, let's drive a little longer. I'm crazy for trusting you, but my grandmother says sometimes you have to believe in your gut level feelings. Ok, I'll rely on mine." She looked out at the landscape, now veiled in darkness. She wasn't aware of her reflection in the window, but Isha was. He moved his hand over and held hers. Nothing else about the family or Isha's work was mentioned.

Shortly after midnight, Tomás stopped the car in front of the Rodriguez-O'Leary home. He stayed in his seat looking straight ahead. In the rear compartment, the young couple was still not ready to leave.

"Isha, thanks for a wonderful evening. Can you come in for a while?"

"No. I must leave. Tomorrow, Tomás and I are returning home. I didn't want to tell you until now, because I didn't want to spoil the evening for us."

"Deidre tried to smile back at her date, but she couldn't. The brave facade was rapidly failing. "I'll miss you. I ... I haven't enjoyed anyone else's company in a long time." She looked out the window trying to gain control of her emotions. "Will you ever get back here?"

"Perhaps, but I promise you will never be far from my thoughts. When I think of you, I will remember what one of my favorite poets from home wrote:

We are of one heart, you and I,
And nothing can ever end
The feelings that bind us.

I'd like to believe that he wrote those words for people like us."

Taking her in his arms, Isha gently kissed Deidre. The tears that she had been controlling now flowed. "Why do you have to leave just when we're getting close? Is there no way you can stay longer?"

"No, my work here is complete." Searching for something to say that might comfort her, he went on. "I know how you love Shakespeare. I think I understand how Romeo felt when he said, 'I've more care to stay than will to go.'"

"Remember that he and Juliet had just spent the night together when he whispered those words."

Isha touched a button on his armrest. Tomás noted the light flash on his dash panel, and got out to open the rear door. He looked towards the house and momentarily froze. Isha saw, or perhaps sensed the change in his driver. The old man quickly opened the door, but stopped Isha from getting out. "Sire, she needs to stay here in the car."

Deidre couldn't see anything, but Isha didn't ask for an explanation. He spoke quietly, "Stay in the car, Deidre. Don't get out until I come back."

"Isha, what is it? I'm frightened."

"Just stay here. You'll be safe, and I'll be right back." Isha closed the door and listened to hear Deidre push the lock down.

Isha and Tomás slowly approached the house. "Sire, the front door has been forced. Do you see how the wooden jam has been broken? I am certain it was not that way when we left this evening."

"You are as observant today as when my father was a young protector. Stay with the car."

"You or John's mother may need me."

"All right Tomás. On that side of the house is another entrance. Go there and wait. I'll signal you if I'm in trouble. Be careful."

Isha moved quietly into the shadows. He was thankful that clouds now covered the full moon from the previous night. Next he removed his shoes and socks. Using skills practiced since his childhood, Isha could now move silently through the darkness. Within minutes, he had completely circled the house. Approaching the side entrance, Isha let out a low whistle. Tomás materialized out of the blackness. "Tomás, I've found lights in almost every room, but I can't see past the closed curtains. I'm going inside. You are to stay and protect Deidre."

The old man started to object, but Isha stopped him. "Listen, I'll be fine. You have taught me well. Now I want you to protect Deidre. These are my orders."

Surrendering to Isha's will, he simply said, "Be careful then, Isha." There was no reason to say more.

Tomás moved slowly back into the darkness. Isha was certain within seconds his friend would be back at the car. He also knew Tomás would protect Deidre with his life if necessary, but he pitied anyone who underestimated the warrior abilities of the old man.

The front door was ajar, and Isha slowly inched it open using his shoulder. He didn't want to disturb any fingerprints that might be present.

The entry way was empty. Slowly Isha moved into the family room. The entire area was completely destroyed. Furniture was overturned, lamps broken, and even pictures torn off the wall. It was obvious that whoever had done this was in a hurry and whatever they were looking for they had not found. Isha had to control an overwhelming desire to rush through the house in search of Maria. Getting myself killed foolishly would serve no one, he realized.

Moving in total silence, Isha looked for Maria. Each room was in the same total disarray. Finally, he stood outside Sean's Pub. From inside, Isha heard talking. Slowly he pushed the door open an inch, then two. Looking through the crack, he could see across the room and into a mirror on the opposite wall.

What he saw made his blood run cold. Maria, still dressed in bedclothes, was sitting on a stool at the bar. Her arms were outstretched, and her hands were tied to the brass railing attached to the front of the bar. Two men, one on either side of her, were talking in hushed tones. "Look here old woman, we know you've got money in this house. You always pay your workers in cash. Don't lie to us and say you don't have a little coin around!"

Mrs. O'Leary, her face badly bruised, was barely able to answer, "Pablo, I helped you when you needed a job. I paid you cash because you didn't have a bank. I helped you. Why do you do this to me?"

The man Maria had called "Pablo" kept up his banter. His speech was slow and deliberate, as if to terrorize her with each word. "Lady, I need the money. If you'll just give it to me, I can get a fix and leave town. You'll never see me again. Now, give me the money!" To emphasize his command, the man savagely slapped Maria across the face. It was the last act of violence he ever committed.

Isha threw open the door and covered the distance between himself and the men in two running steps. The junkie who had just hit Maria turned at the unexpected noise. He was immediately smashed against the wall as Isha leaped and struck him with a flying sidekick.

The perfectly executed attack smashed Pablo in the middle of his chest. The force of the kick crushed his breastbone and instantly stopped his heart.

Pablo fell heavily to the floor. His eyes, though sightless in death, were wide open in surprise.

Isha turned to meet the second man. With time to react, he had grabbed a gun from his belt, and quickly pulled on the trigger for a point blank shot at Isha.

In his haste and panic, the man had neglected to release the safety. The half-second it took him to slide the switch forward into the armed position was all it required for Isha to move.

He jumped straight up and snapped his right foot out at an inhuman speed. Isha's foot impacted the thug's arm half way between the wrist and elbow. There was a noticeable snap as the man's ulna shattered and the gun was propelled across the room. Isha then quickly pivoted on his right foot, twisted, and swung his left leg upwards. This rapid three hundred-sixty degree motion drove Isha's foot squarely into the side of the man's head. His kick was perfectly placed for its desired effect. As a result, there was no pain revealed on the man's face, because his top vertebra had been crushed and his spinal cord severed. Lying on the floor completely paralyzed, he tried to speak, but no sound escaped. He died quickly from asphyxiation.

The entire confrontation had lasted less than ten seconds.

As Isha quickly untied Maria's swollen hands, he looked intently at her face. The right pupil was much larger than the left. She had bruises on both cheeks and a cut under the right eye and on her bottom lip.

"Maria, it's Isha. Talk to me!" His rough commands had a gentle purpose; to determine how badly she was hurt. With Maria now leaning on him for support, Isha touched the crown on his watch four times in rapid succession.

Outside at the limo, Tomás stiffened as four quick beeps sounded from his wrist. "Miss, it's safe to enter the house now, but Isha needs us. Stay close behind me."

Deidre needed no further encouragement. She rushed to follow the old man inside. He hardly appeared to notice the destruction in the room. "Isha, where are you?" he yelled.

From the back hallway the young warrior appeared carrying Maria. She was barely conscious. "Tomás get on the phone. Use my code and contact the Elders directly. Tell them I am bringing Maria O'Leary to the pasture entrance for medical help. Have them dispatch our best neurologist immediately. I suspect she may have bleeding inside her skull. Deidre, you go ahead of me and open the car door."

"Who did this?" she asked in a frightened voice, "Why did they hurt my grandmother?"

"Some junkies looking for drug money. They will never again hurt anyone." There was no hint of remorse in Isha's voice.

He carried Maria easily in his arms out to the Mercedes. Deidre had the door open and helped him place her grandmother in the back seat. They were just finishing when Tomás came out of the house.

"Isha, the Elders have given permission, but only for Mrs. O'Leary to enter – no one else." He stole a glance at Deidre.

Isha ignored the statement, and as he got into the back seat with the two women, he said, "Start driving towards the entrance." He stopped for a moment then quietly added, "Tomás, use all your skills. Time is not on our side."

The mentor looked solemnly at Maria's bruised face now resting in her granddaughter's lap. "I will, Sir. You know, I still remember her kindness even after all these years." Deidre looked up at that comment, but said nothing.

Within seconds, Tomás had the car moving at better than ninety-five miles per hour down the highway. Fortunately, there were no late night traffic or highway patrolmen to impede their progress. The Mercedes was performing like a thoroughbred: its turbo working at peak efficiency.

In the back seat, Deidre cradled Maria's head. She was bent over and whispering encouraging words to the injured woman. Isha continued to check her pulse, respiration, and pupils. Using a flashlight, he tested her eyes for light sensitivity. The left pupil retracted when he flashed the light into it, while the right one remained dilated.

Isha picked up the car phone and quickly pushed seven buttons. After hearing a connection tone, he pressed several more and waited. Almost immediately he spoke, "This is Prince Isha. Connect me with my father." Deidre sat in stunned silence. Within moments he continued, "Father, have you spoken to the Elders? Good. John's mother is very ill. I'll explain everything at the cavern." He looked directly into Deidre's fawn eyes. "Sir, the Elders only approved Mrs. O'Leary, but I have also brought her granddaughter, Deidre. There was no protection at the house, and she is caring for your friend. Please explain to them that as a Protector, I felt the move was justified." He listened for a short while then responded, "Thank you, Father. We will be there shortly."

As he hung up the phone, Isha put his other hand on Deidre's arm. The initial shock of the experience was beginning to wear off, and she was ready to start asking questions. "Why aren't we headed into Santa Fe? There aren't any doctors or hospitals this direction."

"Your grandmother will soon have the finest medical care available anywhere. I promise."

Her fear came out as anger. "Who were you talking to? And why do you keep referring to my grandmother in relation to my father? What does he have to do with all this? He's been dead almost a year!"

Isha looked squarely into Deidre's face. He spoke slowly, carefully choosing each word. "Yes, I know he's dead. I knew it the day after the accident. Your father and my father were friends, and had been since they were thirteen years old. When John O'Leary died, I saw my father weep for the first time in my life. Please trust me. You will understand it all soon. We're almost there."

As if on cue, Tomás radically slowed the car and exited the interstate on to a nondescript mountain lane. The car bounced with each rut in the dirt grooves that constituted the road here. Each strain on the car's struts caused a moan from Maria. Isha leaned over and whispered into her ear, "Hold on Mrs. O'Leary. We'll be stopping in a few minutes."

About that time, the limo approached a cattle guard and a metal gate. There was nothing about this gate to make it appear different from the thousand similar gates in the area. It was unique, however. Tomás touched a button on his center console, and the gate opened. Once he drove through, it immediately closed behind.

Since leaving the main highway, the car had been observed by hidden sensors and cameras. No one could approach that entrance undetected.

A hundred yards beyond the fence, Tomás drove into a rustic cattle barn. From all appearances, the building would fall down at any moment. However, once inside, Tomás stopped the car, and turned off the lights.

Deidre screamed as suddenly the car began to sink into the ground.

Six

"It's ok." Isha's calm voice cut through Deidre's initial startled fear. She looked at him and by reflex grabbed his hand. "We're safe here. In a few moments we'll be in my home."

There was not even a whisper of sound as the car sank. Though the barn was unlit, and the car was dark, Deidre's senses were working overtime and she seemed to notice every detail of the descent. The straw covered flooring had given way, and the limousine was dropping in what appeared to be a giant elevator. They disappeared into a pit that had smooth concrete walls. As they plunged lower, a tranquil glow began to surround them from everywhere, almost like an artificial sunlight. The light was different; not stark like incandescent, or flickering like fluorescent. Instead, it was a soothing, almost warm light. The walls themselves appeared to be producing the glow.

Every elevator Deidre had ever ridden had that characteristic bumpiness and sway as it moved up or down on cables and pulleys. This one was different. Only the sinking feeling in the pit of her stomach let Deidre know that in fact she was rapidly dropping into the Earth. There was not even the hint of any sounds of machinery. Seconds later, the descent stopped and Tomás restarted the engine.

After going so far underground, Deidre was expecting to end up in a cave of some sort. She had been to Carlsbad Caverns and knew how large the subterranean rooms could be. However, she was not prepared for what lay before them. Instead of a rock chamber, she was looking at what appeared to be a modern building's entry hall. It seemed that Tomás had driven the car into the lobby of some Manhattan skyscraper. The area had smooth marble walls and floors. Looking straight ahead, the room continued for as far as Deidre could see.

As the car pulled off the ramp, the elevator instantly started rising. Within a couple of seconds, it had retreated into the concrete shaft and was gone from view.

People were converging on the car from every direction. There were several men in lab coats who were standing by with a stretcher.

Even before Tomás had the engine off, Isha jumped out and motioned to the medical team. They smoothly eased into the back seat to examine Maria before they moved her. The old woman's face, still cradled in her granddaughter's lap, was swollen and beginning to blacken.

From outside, Isha watched. His attention was drawn from the doctor to Deidre. She looked so frightened, her complexion pale, and her eyes empty. The senior doctor on the medical team got out of the car and moved to Isha. The nametag on his chest identified him as Lawrence Roberts, M.D. His assistants were gently lifting their patient on to a backboard.

"She definitely has a concussion, Sire. We'll know shortly how severe her injuries are."

"Do everything you can. She is very precious to the King."

"I will." Looking at the stretcher, the doctor nodded towards Deidre. "Would you like the young lady to accompany us to the trauma center?"

"No. I'll attend to her. We'll follow shortly. Thank you."

Maria was now secure on the transportation gurney, and the team was rolling her quickly in the direction of the door. Deidre was holding her grandmother's hand and having to run to keep up. As the team slowed to enter the door, Isha stopped her. "They will give her excellent care, I promise. Come with me for now, and I'll take you to my father's house to rest."

Deidre was in too much shock to protest. She felt drained and weak. The movie she and Isha had attended seemed a distant memory. Now the events of the past hour were beginning to have their effect. Without warning, her knees buckled. She felt Isha's arm slip under her as he effortlessly lifted her weakened body. Almost immediately, Deidre lost her battle with fatigue and shock as unconsciousness fell over her.

* * * * *

The sound of quiet music began to filter into Deidre's awakening mind. She opened her eyes slowly, almost fearfully, but saw nothing except a pale green light that seemed far away. There was nothing for her eyes to focus upon. The soothing sound of strings seemed to surround her, gently bringing her back into awareness. Despite her confusion, Deidre felt a peace that was wonderful. Then Isha's voice was there, "Good morning. How do you like our beds?"

"Where are you? For that matter, where the hell am I?"

"A gentle laugh seemed to enter her mind. "Just a second – I'll get you...." A moment later, the music faded away and a dim white light slowly replaced the green glow. A slight click and the raising of a dome that covered the bed followed that. For the first time Deidre realized that she had been inside a cocoon shaped module. Standing beside her was Isha. He no longer was wearing the clothes from their date. Instead, he was dressed in a brown robe that tied in the front. "The monitor let me know you were rested and ready to wake up, so I decided you might want a familiar voice first thing. I trust you slept well."

"Yeah, I haven't felt this good in a long time. What kind of bed is this?"

"It's our sleep chamber. When someone is ill or deeply depressed, they sleep here until their body has time to refresh itself. What do you remember about REM, or rapid eye movement sleep?"

"Um, as I recall, it's the stage where dreams occur. I'm not sure, because I never dream."

"Well, you get an A+ on your biology grade, but an F on your own sleep physiology. According to the chamber, you've been dreaming almost constantly for the past ten hours."

Deidre shook her head slowly. "No way. I remember enough college psychology courses to know that the longest REM sleep lasts in an adult is about an hour."

"Normally, that's true. But also remember that babies can spend up to half their sleep time there. Our research has shown that the body can recharge itself in REM sleep far faster than otherwise. Basically what this chamber does is establish your own alpha brain waves to fool the body into that level of sleep you require. Once there, it can keep you resting almost indefinitely without the use of any drugs."

"I've never heard of such a device. You can't tell me that I wouldn't have at least seen it in Reader's Digest for goodness sake!"

"Well, don't be too concerned that it's new to you. In about two years a researcher at Kings College in Cambridge, England will discover the process." With that revelation, Isha reached over, took Deidre's hand, and helped her out of the chamber.

* * * * *

About the same moment, Maria opened her eyes in the medical chamber. She gingerly touched the bandages that covered most of her head. As her eyes focused and cleared, she became aware of a figure standing beside her bed. It took several seconds of concentration to see him clearly.

The man, tall and imposing, was looking down at her. His eyes were touched at the edges by wrinkles that furrowed deeply when he smiled. His hair mixed brown and gray almost equally and was combed casually back. His hand rested on hers gently, almost comfortingly. When he spoke, the words were soft. "Mrs. O'Leary, how do you feel?"

Weakly Maria summoned a response. "I won't be dancing tonight. My head is throbbing."

"I'm afraid you were hurt pretty badly. But don't worry, before long, I'll personally take you to a dance."

The memories of the previous evening began to cascade into the old woman's mind. "Oh, those men! How did I get away from those cruel men?"

The gentleman carefully avoided giving Maria details of her rescue. "The main thing now is to get your strength back. So rest. I'll be near by if you need me."

"Thank you. Are you my doctor?"

The man shook his head no, but he continued to hold Maria's hand.

"Well, if you're not my physician, who are you? Why are you in my room? Where is my granddaughter?"

A spontaneous smile returned to the man's face. "My son, Isha, found you and brought you here. He and Deidre will arrive soon. Right now, she is resting at my home. And to answer your other question, my name is Annu, and I'm here because I want to be."

Maria frowned beneath her bandages as she pondered the man's unique name. "Annu ... what a unique name. My son knew a boy named Annu many years ago. They were inseparable as children; playing, camping, fishing, hiking."

Hearing those words, the man patted Mrs. O'Leary's hand. As she continued to look at his face, the years melted away, "Was that boy you?"

"Yes. I have wonderful memories of those days that even the passage of many years cannot diminish. Your son and I had a special bond of friendship. He kept a covenant with my people and me throughout his life that is cherished even today. Now, while you are here, you are my guest. Nothing you need or desire will be denied you."

"Here? Aren't I in the hospital in Santa Fe?

"No, you're not in Santa Fe, but you are in a hospital. It will be easier to explain after you are stronger. For now you need to rest. I promise, I will not be far." With that, he was gone. From somewhere, quiet music began playing and Maria O'Leary suddenly felt sleepy.

Seven

From inside the royal tram, Isha and Deidre observed the wonders of his kingdom. "This place is called Exeter. My people have lived here for more than four hundred years. It's very special to us because this was the first area our forefathers ever settled. They once lived above but were driven into these chambers by the onslaught of others. After centuries of almost constant war, our tribes came to believe that they could live in peace only by living apart. They began what you see today; a civilization that is completely isolated. We live here on our own terms." Isha's pride in Exeter was evident by the tone of his comments. He was animate in pointing out his favorite places to Deidre as they traveled. Tubes, similar to subway tunnels, seemed to crisscross in every direction connecting mammoth rooms. "Exeter is basically several clusters of colonies. Our carrier trams connect these caverns. Actually, the areas are part of the same system of caves that make up Carlsbad Caverns."

"I've been there. I remember the guide saying there are hundreds of miles of unexplored caves, but I didn't know they reached this far north. And none of Carlsbad Caverns I saw look anything like this."

"Well, we've made some improvements through the centuries," Isha said in an obvious understatement.

The tram came to a smooth, but rapid stop. There were several distinguished looking men waiting. One stepped forward. "Prince Isha, welcome home. We've missed you during your travels. Your Elders await you." The remaining men all made a slight bow at these words.

There was a barely perceptible change in Isha's face as he thanked the men. Then turning to Deidre he introduced her to them. The man who had originally greeted Isha gently took her hand and kissed it. Deidre felt a little embarrassed by this, but quickly recovered. The Chief Elder continued, "Miss O'Leary, our council welcomes you and we pray for the swift recovery of your grandmother. While you slept, Prince Isha told us about the senseless events that led to you being here. We completely condone his actions. Also, belatedly accept our sorrow at the loss of your parents. Your father was a true friend to Exeter."

Deidre was now becoming accustomed to surprises and questions so simply thanked them. One thing kept gnawing at her however—her father had known about this place all her life, and yet had never even hinted at its existence.

Movement of a man coming out of a door caught Deidre's eye. He was much younger than the Elders—around Isha's age. She figured he was about five feet ten inches tall with an extremely athletic and muscular build. He had short brown hair and deep-set green eyes. The man leaned against a wall behind the Elders until they moved away into their chamber. Isha glared almost viciously at the man as he approached, then with a serious face said, "All right you beggar, come forward and tremble before your prince."

"Tremble? You're lucky I found time to come see you at all. I had important duties to perform today. However, since your summons was so urgent, I assumed some matter of intense importance required my attention."

Ignoring the young man's insults Isha turned to Deidre. As he spoke to Deidre the Prince's words seemed harsh, "Miss O'Leary, allow me to introduce you to Kevin. He's the only man in Exeter who treats me with no respect whatsoever. In fact, the only reason I tolerate him is because without my almost constant attention, he would no doubt come to some terrible end, and I don't want that on my conscience."

"Please forgive Prince Isha's ill manners, my lady." Kevin's eyes never left Isha. "It stems from his early days when I gave him the thrashing of his life. He has never forgiven me, even though I have graciously avoided reminding His Highness of that ignominious day."

The facade fell as the men laughed and hugged each other warmly. "How have you been, my friend?" the Prince asked.

"I've been well, Isha. Welcome home. And Miss O'Leary, it really is a pleasure to meet you."

"Thank you." Deidre was relieved to find the belligerence was feigned.

"Deidre, I have to meet with the Elders for a few hours, so I've asked Kevin to escort you to the hospital. After that, he'll take you anywhere else you wish to go. I'll be able to rejoin you later."

The Prince walked them back to the tram. As they entered, Isha waved, turned, and entered the Elder's chamber. "Hospital, please," Kevin spoke. The tram immediately moved out and was soon moving rapidly through the tubes.

"So, what's this about the thrashing you gave Isha? Was that just a joke or what?"

Kevin laughed. "Well, it started when we were eight. Prince Isha was in training to be a Protector. Even though I wasn't selected to be one, it was still my dream. Anyway, everyday I slipped into the school and watched from a hidden area.

Each young Protector has a mentor or instructor who teaches everything. Usually, a child who is selected enters training around four or five years of age, and finish when they are twenty. Much of what they learn is known only to the Protectors, so naturally their education is private. In my room at night I would practice the skills I had seen that day. One day, Prince Isha found me. Instead of turning me in, he started helping me. We practiced in secret every night. We did that for almost three years until the King found out. I guess he should have been furious with Isha for revealing secrets only Protectors should know. But, instead he said someone who wanted it as bad as I did deserved a chance." Kevin seemed to be enjoying his memories. "To prove my skills as a warrior, I had to fight the best man in training. That, of course, was Prince Isha. We had never fought each other; practiced and sparred, but never really fought. Isha was on his honor to fight with all his skill despite our friendship. Our protectors learn many ways of defending themselves. Some, like karate and other martial arts, you would recognize. But, like I said, other things are known only to Protectors. Anyway, on my eleventh birthday, we met before the King, the Protectors, and their mentors. There was never any serious doubt about who would be victorious. After all, Isha had studied under Tomás for almost seven years. But I had learned well from the Prince. Anyway, every punch or kick I threw, Isha was able to block. I was doing pretty well, too, until he got a jab in and broke my nose." Kevin chuckled to himself. "The pain wasn't all that bad, but it started bleeding badly. I mean the whole area got quiet. I'm not really sure if Isha was surprised by the hit or shocked by the amount of blood that was pouring out of my nose, but for just a second, he dropped his guard. I got through with what had to be the luckiest hit of my life, and knocked Isha out cold. For the entire bout he had clobbered me, but I won because of a lucky shot."

"Well, what happened?" Deidre couldn't hold her curiosity any longer. "Did you get to be a Protector?"

"Obviously I was sure all hell would break loose. Here I was this upstart with no official mentor trying to become a Protector – and I'd just knocked out the King's only son. Yep, I figured it was all over. The King came down and checked with Isha to make sure he was okay, and then he took me aside. Before I could tell him I was sorry, he put his arm around me. He asked if I would put the same discipline into learning with a real teacher as I had with Isha. All I could do was nod my head. I was appointed a mentor, and on my twenty-third birthday the King himself anointed me as a Protector. It took me three extra years to make up for starting late. But it was the proudest moment of my life. Prince Isha was the reason I was able to reach that goal. He's a remarkable man. He has never once demanded special attention because of his position. Our people love him for that."

The two sat quietly looking out of the car for several seconds. Finally, the silence was overpowering. Deidre was too full of wonder and questions to remain quiet. "How is it that we have light, but I don't see any source? There aren't any street lamps or spotlights at all. It looks like sunlight, but obviously that's not possible."

"I'm not an engineer, but as I understand it, the interior walls are impregnated with a substance that gives off light when an electrical charge is passed through it. All the walls have minute wires that are part of the matrix. So at 'sunrise' a small current is begun and as our day passes, the charge is increased and light increases. Later the process is reversed and we enter 'night'."

Deidre tried unsuccessfully to consider the technology that could produce such advanced environmental control. "How did you ever come to build such an amazing place?"

Kevin knew the story as well as any child raised in Exeter. "Several hundred years ago, we had a trio of scientists who were brilliant even by today's standards. They were the embodiment of Galileo, Leonardo da Vinci, Einstein, and a hundred other geniuses you would know. They had theories of light and power generation, magnetic propulsion, and even food production that have not been conceived in your society even today. These three men were so far ahead of their time that Exeter was able to create our home when those above were still living in log cabins with fireplaces for heating and cooking. In the centuries since, our scientists have continued to build on those revolutionary concepts. That's how we've been able to do what you see here."

Deidre still struggled to grasp what she was seeing. "It seems that Exeter is designed to appear very much like any large city above."

Kevin thought for a second before answering. "Regardless of how long we have lived in these caverns, we are still humans. God designed us to survive and grow in your world. So through the centuries, we've made refinements to Exeter. We do try and emulate the outside world as much as possible. Our climate system even has programs to allow for occasional thunderstorms. Of course no actual rain falls, but cool humid air is fed into the area. It charges the air with positive ions to produce the same effect that causes the air to seem so fresh after a storm passes. They even have distant thunder sounds that permeate the rooms. The effect is refreshing and prevents our climate control from being too predictable. Even perfect weather is boring if that's all you ever have."

"Yeah, I suppose it would be." Deidre was lost in thought when the tram pulled into the hospital chamber. As they exited, the car almost immediately pulled out of the area. For the first time she realized that there was no driver. "How did the tram know where to take us? When we left Isha – I mean Prince Isha, you told someone to take us to the hospital."

"Sure. I told the car. Our cars have a voice recognition computer that processes our destination request and determines the quickest path to that location. It takes into consideration all the possible conflicts between cars and makes changes as necessary to prevent traffic jams or accidents. I like using Prince Isha's tram since it has priority handling." Kevin gave Deidre a playful wink.

Within minutes the two were approaching the hospital chamber. There was a neurosurgeon waiting for them. He explained to Deidre that her grandmother had suffered a concussion. "Basically," he began, "her brain is bruised and possibly swelling inside the skull. I've given her medication to minimize that, but she is very ill. For a younger person this type of injury is generally not serious, but at Mrs. O'Leary's age, there can be complications. The next twenty-four to forty-eight hours are the most critical. If there are any problems I'll get with you immediately. In the mean time, there isn't really anything you can do."

For the next day and a half, Deidre rarely left the hospital. Maria was kept sedated and in the sleep chamber. On the second day, she awoke and told the doctors she was ready to leave. While there was no way the physicians would actually allow her to go, especially since it was four in the morning, they were now confident she was going to be all right. She would have an awful headache for a few days, but that would pass. The doctors knew even with their skill as healers, they could not take full credit for her recovery. She was a tough lady.

When the crisis had passed, Deidre was able to leave the hospital for the first time. Isha took the opportunity to show her the beauty of his father's kingdom. Life for him, while complicated by Deidre's presence, was full. He was happy.

Half a world away.... .

Eight

London, England - October 20, 2009

Geoffrey Singer was bored. His office in the basement level of a gaudy government building next to the River Thames was as dreary as the October London weather outside. He looked around the bare gray walls for the thousandth time in hopes of seeing something remotely interesting to stare at. There was nothing. Singer's mind began wandering back two months earlier to his summer holiday on Spain's Southern coast. Five days of nothing but sleeping on the Andalusia province's white beaches under a hot sun, with the royal blue Mediterranean Sea and a bevy of European and Scandinavian women as distractions. There had been no pressures, no impossible deadlines, and no crisis to handle.

He spent his days wind surfing, swimming, dozing, and admiring the view of beautiful ladies working on their all-over tans. At night the pace sped up considerably. Singer had become actively involved with the nightlife of Algeciras, a small town near his favorite beach. Dinner was usually around 10:00 p.m. Dancing at one of the many clubs followed and continued until three or four in the morning. Things never really got going until midnight. Most American tourists had a difficult time adjusting to the fact that restaurants in Spain didn't even open until after eight o'clock at night.

Geoffrey was used to that because his work in London often made him dine late anyway. This holiday, Geoffrey decided, would be completely tied to research. He wanted to discover which beer complimented girls from each country. To his way of thinking, it was a noble quest of the heart for a hard working public servant. Before his vacation was complete, he had personally tasted nine different beers, and three different women. He made a promise that this research would be a lifelong study.

In reality, Singer spent his days researching other people's research. His title as Deputy Director for Intelligence Assessment was, as he called it, another bureaucratic case of calling a sow's ear a silk purse. He saw himself as a tiny cog in DI6 (once known as MI6), the British Secret Intelligence Service, which is responsible for espionage outside Great Britain. On rare occasions he dealt with interesting or even important information, but the past three days had been dull.

Glancing at his watch, Singer decided he could slip out for an early lunch. Knowing October was not a high tourist month, he decided to risk a meal at his favorite spot, a pub right around the corner from Buckingham Palace. During the spring and summer, the crowds made it impossible to eat there unless you had some time to spare. Today the wait wouldn't be too bad and Singer wanted some pub food.

A devious thought evolved in his brain. Singer picked up the receiver for his secure telephone line and referred to the small black notebook he kept in his inside coat pocket. He then dialed the number beside the listing *Centre Court Pub*. The phone was answered on the first ring. "United States Embassy, message room, Staff Sergeant Green speaking. This is a secure line, may I help you, sir?"

"Yes, this is Geoffrey Singer calling secure line. I must speak to Mr. Colin Johnson. It is a matter of some importance."

"Please stand by, sir." Sergeant Green quickly began the Embassy internal page system to locate Johnson. Secure line meant the voice transmissions going both directions were electronically encoded and scrambled to prevent unauthorized monitoring. It was reserved for phone calls where sensitive information was discussed.

Colin Johnson was in a meeting with Richard Nail, who served as the Protocol Chief for the American Ambassador to the Court of Saint James. Also present was an advance agent for the US Secret Service. Vice President Roy Dickerson was to visit England the following week, and the three men were discussing the final details. Johnson, who served as the Embassy Intelligence Chief, was to be the primary liaison for security with the local authorities. The meeting, which had already lasted almost four hours, had covered every possible subject and showed no signs of ending. Johnson felt it had already been about two hours too long.

When the intercom on his desk buzzed, Nail immediately pushed the button, "Janet," he growled, "I told you not to disturb us!" Johnson noticed with slight amusement that the vein in the other man's neck bulged when he was provoked. It bulged often.

His secretary's voice cracked slightly as she answered, "Yes sir, but Mr. Johnson has a Code One phone call. I thought it must be important enough to interrupt."

Nail released the button without any comment or apology. "Colin, use my line, but this damn well better be crucial!"

The intel officer pealed his lanky six-foot frame out of the leather chair. His stiff legs were grateful for the stretch. He turned the phone around, pushed the yellow button farthest to the right, and punched in two numbers. "This is Johnson. Go ahead and patch me through."

A second later, a man with an unmistakable Suffolk accent came on the line. "Colin, old chap, how about taking a fellow spy out for dinner and a couple of pints at the Swan Pub?"

Without so much as a blink of the eye in reaction, Johnson replied, "Ok, but is the intelligence source valid? I don't want any mistakes on this. Understand?"

Singer laughed and continued, "Wonderful! How about in thirty minutes then?"

"All right, but hold the material until I can personally review it. Stick it in an eyes only folder with my name on the cover."

"Smashing! See you in half an hour then. Cheers."

Allowing a deep sigh to escape, Johnson looked at the other two men. "Something's come up that I've got to look over. How about we get back together in a couple of hours?"

Nail was obviously angered. "What's going on here, Colin?"

"Probably nothing, sir," he replied cryptically. Stealing a glance at the Secret Service Agent for effect, he went on. "I'll fill you in later if I find anything." He walked out before Nail had a chance to ask more.

As Johnson walked by Nail's secretary's work station, he stopped for a moment and straightened the mahogany and brass name tag on the young lady's desk. *Janet Kay* was engraved into the brass with expressive cursive lettering. Colin gave the attractive brunette a quick kiss on her cheek and smiled down at her. Janet was one of those people who was popular with everyone who knew her, except Richard Nail. "You know, JMo, I don't think even the man's mother liked him. He just can't help being an ass."

"Thank you, Colin," she replied demurely.

Janet watched Johnson leave the office. He was the only one on the executive staff who treated the support personnel as equals. He was also the only one who paid enough attention to know Janet's friends called her *J Mo*. She recognized he had no real designs on her, but he always flirted with her without breaking any unspoken boundaries. Janet had heard he was dating a young British lady, but she recognized office rumors were often notoriously inaccurate about such things. Besides, Janet didn't have time to encourage Colin Johnson. She was too busy juggling the two suitors who were making her dating life both exciting and a little risky. One man was a six-foot tall British soccer player and the other was the only son of a senior aide on the Prime Minister's staff. Up to now neither knew about the other and Janet planned on keeping it that way a bit longer. She was having fun with her game of "playing the field". For Janet, the after hours activities made her day-to-day job of working for Richard Nail bearable.

* * * * *

Both Johnson and Singer left their offices at about the same time. Singer hailed a black taxicab. It took him northwest across the Thames and up Vauxhall Bridge Road. Repair on a broken water main on Grosvenor Place required the cab to take a more round about route to the pub. Instead of going left on Grosvenor Place, they turned right onto Buckingham Place Road which brought them around the front of the Queen's residence. The flag, or standard, flying above Buckingham Palace's central balcony signified that Queen Elizabeth was in residence. There were dozens of tourists standing in front of the tall metal fence to have their picture taken with Buckingham Palace in the background. Singer's cab went past the Queen Victoria Memorial and up Constitution Hill. With only a right turn on Piccadilly to go, he could already see the brick and stone front to the Swan Pub.

Johnson, on the other hand, had decided to walk the three-quarters of a mile from the Embassy. As Johnson left, he and the Marine guard on duty, a Texan, had a quick bull session about how the their favorite NFL teams were doing. For the hundredth time this football season, they both decided that not getting to see American football games on TV was the worst thing about their time in London.

Johnson took long strides as he walked down South Audley. Passing South Street, he could see the flag flying above the Egyptian Embassy. He made a mental note to check into taking a trip to Cairo. He knew he probably wouldn't, but every time he went this way, he made that promise. Within fifteen minutes, he was cutting across a parking lot and rounding the corner from Park Street. Just then he saw Geoffrey Singer getting out of his cab.

"Geoff, old boy. I owe you this meal for getting my butt out of the longest meeting of my life."

"Glad to oblige. Let's try and get inside and eat before Her Majesty's Government decides she must have me back in my cell."

It took almost fifteen minutes to get seated, but both men passed the time in casual conversation. Never did the topic of work surface. Even countries as philosophically and politically close as America and Great Britain had information they chose not to share. It was an unspoken agreement between the two men that it was just easier to leave their occupations out of their discussions. While most men would find this difficult, these two enjoyed having a respite from the demands of security. Besides, there were too many other areas that they enjoyed together.

Sitting on the upper tier of the pub, they spent several minutes looking around the walls at the football banners and beer advertisements. Wonder how old this place is?", Johnson asked.

"Who knows. This area is almost all from the same era and Buckingham Place has been the royal residence since 1837, but it was around on a much smaller scale from the late 1700s."

"Well, we Americans have difficulty understanding that you Brits don't tear things down and rebuild them. You just keep repairing and adding on. I've been here a long time and it still amazes me that I can eat a hamburger in a 250 year old building."

Just as the hamburgers were brought to the table Singer noticed a vibration on his hip. "Blast it! I hate mobile phones! I can't get away from the buggers any more at all." Sliding out of the booth, he looked squarely at Johnson. "Colin, don't touch my food. Friendship only goes so far. If so much as one sesame seed is missing, I'll hunt you down and hurt you. Understand?"

"I'll guard it with my life, Geoff. Trust me."

Singer spied an open area across the restaurant where no one was nearby. He answered his cell phone. "This is Singer."

On the other end was the familiar voice of his secretary. "Sir, I was just told to locate you. Lord Baldwin has ordered a meeting. He said to tell you it was an Excalibur."

Singer didn't wait for more. "On my way. Please ask my staff to wait in the assembly area until I get there." Excalibur! Damn it all to hell!

Nine

Geoffrey Singer came straight back to the table, and looked longingly at his hamburger, then to Johnson. "Sorry, old boy. Something's come up. I've got to get back straight away. Please ask the young waitress to wrap this hamburger. Tell her I'll pick it up at her flat after work."

Johnson laughed. "Ok. But, she's not your type. I detect she has brains to go with the rest of her equipment." With his best imitation cockney accent, the American waved Singer away. "Begone ye vermin. I 'ave a meal to be consumed in peace."

"Right. We'll do this again soon, Colin. Sorry for leaving before we got to eat—especially since you have to pay the check now. Later, my friend."

Colin Johnson watched Geoff leave. Even the lighthearted kidding that marked his departure did not hide the deep concern in Geoff's eyes. What ever had required his presence on such short notice was serious.

Once outside, Geoffrey Singer quickly caught a taxi. He showed the cabbie his government ID and told him to ignore any police or traffic signal. Singer also promised an extra ten-pound note if they could reach his office in less than ten minutes.

Taking this challenge as carte blanche to drive as he wanted, the man sped off with reckless abandon.

In the back seat Geoffrey Singer tried to prepare himself for what was ahead. Excalibur was a code term that came from the ancient English legend of King Arthur and his sword in the stone. At DI6, the word was used as a code to mobilize certain key members of the agency. It was a signal applied in only dangerous or disastrous events. The Director General himself could call it, no one else. It was this level of involvement that concerned Geoffrey Singer the most.

Lord Patrick Baldwin was not one to call a code word meeting lightly. His appointment as DG came after serving many years in the intelligence community. He was recognized on both sides of the Atlantic Ocean as a brilliant man who reacted coolly in challenging situations.

Surprisingly, the CIA, Israeli Mossad, and KGB probably knew the DG better than the man on the street in London. Because of Britain's Official Secrets Act, for years it had been illegal even to disclose his name to the press. Parliament had eased the restrictions in 1991, but the man's position and biography were still very protected.

Geoffrey Singer was a crucial member of the crisis team formed to handle international emergencies. He had a mind trained to sort seemingly unrelated details into a coherent pattern, and had earned a reputation for developing some of the most complex counterintelligence scenarios in the agency. No terrorist threat was too far-fetched for Singer. Part of his success came from a belief that if he could conceive of the plan, then someone else could do so also. Geoff also believed that if he could develop the terrorist plot, he could also plan a defense to defeat it.

From the back seat of the cab as it crossed the Vauxhall Bridge, Singer looked at the imposing building that housed DI6. Architecturally, it seemed totally incongruous to the buildings around it. The multi-story concrete and green glass structure was completed in 1994, and looked more like a United States Fortune 500 corporate headquarters than a British governmental intelligence agency. The numerous balconies and convoluted shapes on the building made it eye-catching. Not surprisingly, it was designed with an impressive protection system in place. Each side of the building was safeguarded with twenty-four closed-circuit television cameras. A pedestrian walking by would probably notice a few obvious security cameras mounted on the building. The majority, however, were invisible, camouflaged in light fixtures and along walk paths. Security around the building, while incredibly tight, was almost totally inconspicuous.

The taxi driver easily earned his promised ten pound bonus by speeding across the Thames and pulling up to the Vauxhall Cross address seven minutes after leaving the Swan Pub. Three totally ignored red traffic lights and several startled pedestrians marked the path they had driven.

Waiting curbside was Singer's assistant, Rimi. She started talking as soon as they were out of earshot of the cabby. "This isn't a regular operation, Geoff. The Director has called a level-one department head briefing in The Centre in twelve minutes. I haven't seen Lord Baldwin pull everyone together like this quickly before."

"Not to worry, Love. The ol' boy has probably finally learned how to work his intercom system and wanted to play with it."

Rimi wasn't fooled. While she did not have a clearance to know the meaning of Excalibur, she did know her boss. She could tell when he was concerned, and that was what bothered her.

"Listen, get my staff together. I'll find out what's happening, and see where we're headed. Just tell everyone to stay close for a while. Ok?"

"Yes, sir." Rimi turned and was gone before Singer had a chance to say more. *Damn, she's too efficient. I planned on having her order some lunch for me,* he thought.

Geoffrey Singer pushed through the revolving doors and entered the building. He ignored the cameras on both sides of the entryway that monitored every arrival and departure. Instead he nodded at the two uniformed guards sitting in an enclosure to his left. The solid panel of the booth's bottom half was in reality a veneer over Kevlar sheets that could stop the bullets from any assault weapon. The booth's bulletproof tempered glass upper half was one and a quarter inches thick.

Singer waved at the first guard. The man had served at the same post for nine years. "Mr. Singer," the guard's metallic voice came over the intercom, "will you be able to join a few of us boys for a pub crawl next Friday? It's a good-bye party for Paddy O'Donnell. He's finally giving in to his Missus and moving to the Dales to raise sheep – or so he claims. Anyway, we figure to start out around six o'clock at the Judes's Ferry Pub, and end up someplace else much, much later." Pub crawls were the traditional way to say hello or good-bye to someone. During the evening, the group would go to several different pubs. This would continue until they were crawling to the last one – hence the name.

Geoffrey chuckled. "A pub crawl. I haven't been a part of one in years. Tell Paddy I would be proud to drink a few pints in his honor. Plan on it. The first round of drinks will be on me."

"Well, sir, that's kind. But to be honest, at your salary, we'd already planned several rounds on you."

Geoffrey Singer was still smiling as he stepped up to one of the six cylindrical glass and metal booths in the entryway. The capsules were about six and a half feet high, and large enough for only one person inside. The surrounding wall, which separated the entrance area from the rest of the building, was made of clear Plexiglas. The only way into the facility was through one of the six capsules. Entry required a redundant security procedure.

At the right hand side of each enclosure was a keypad and card reader. Geoffrey slid his ID card through the slot and then typed 052171, his personal code, into the keypad. Once both his reader card and ID number were verified, the front half of the cylinder quickly rotated open. Singer stepped in, and the door closed rapidly behind him. Being slightly claustrophobic, Singer hated the brief moment he was sealed inside the tiny booth. But as soon the front half of the cylinder was locked securely closed, the back half opened and the Deputy Director of Intelligence Assessment of British DI6 stepped into his world.

He walked quickly and entered the lift, or elevator, as the Yanks called it. Once the door closed, he took the key he kept on a chain around his neck and inserted it in a lock at the top of the control panel. Turning it, the compartment started moving quickly, but not up. Instead, it started down into a bombproof shelter called The Centre deep beneath the building.

It seemed the movement would never end. Finally, the door opened, and Singer was faced by a very serious looking young Royal Marine guard.

"Sir, your ID, please." The DIA handed the young man his card, and stood silently as the Marine carefully checked the picture. "Sir, it says here that you have a scar on your left wrist. May I see it please?"

Geoff pulled up the cuff from his shirt. "The result of a rather nasty motorcycle accident in my younger days."

The guard ignored the small talk. After examining the scar and the ID again, the man then opened the door to the command center.

Several of Lord Baldwin's top staff was already present. "Geoff, any idea why we're here?" The question came from Richard Chatwick, an expert on Middle East affairs.

"No idea. I read all the classified message traffic this morning, but there wasn't anything special. The customs lads at Gatwick broke up an arms shipment ... they're not sure who the final recipients were supposed to be, and there were a couple of gun shots taken at a U.S. Senator late last night as he left his mistress' apartment. That one probably won't get too much public attention. The Senator is rich, and the mistress is the nineteen-year-old daughter of a Cabinet member. Nasty stuff that Washington night life."

Everyone laughed, but stopped abruptly as Lord Baldwin entered the room. The men all stood, but he waved them back into their seats immediately.

"Gentlemen, a most disturbing bit of information has just reached me. It appears that our old friend, Azmud Salomi has recently purchased a rather nasty nuclear device. As all of you know, when he eliminated the militant faction who was ravaging and raping his country, we were hopeful he would be a stabilizing force in the region. Richard, your people did a smashing job of seeing through his public relations press releases, and calling for close attention to be paid to his actions. He has been dreadfully quiet of late. The Mossad has discovered why." Lord Baldwin took a moment to look at the men sitting before him. "It seems when Mr. Gorbachev's policy of perestroika failed, and he and Yeltsin allowed the USSR to split up, they did a less than satisfactory inventory of the warheads in a few of the newly independent states. Our initial indications are that a group of scientists in either Latvia or Estonia may have used their positions to acquire and sell a fifty kiloton warhead right under the noses of both the military and civil authorities. According to our source, Salomi plans on holding the world hostage with his new toy."

"Excuse me, Lord Baldwin," this from Chatwick, "but as powerful as Salomi is, he lacks the vehicle to launch a warhead. Supposedly all of his scud missiles were dismantled. And even if one was to have survived, the best he could do was attempt a scud missile attack on Israel. We all know that is possible because of the Persian Gulf war, but Salomi knows that the Israeli government would immediately retaliate with a full nuclear strike. One fifty kiloton bomb would destroy the best part of any modern city, but the response would absolutely destroy the region. Not even a madman like Salomi would call down that kind of destruction. He knows he would not survive."

Lord Baldwin nodded thoughtfully. "That's my thinking, too. Now, what could be his aims?" Moving to a wall map of the Persian Gulf area, he stared at it for a moment. Then without removing eyes from the area he continued, "He obviously wants to increase his stature in the Middle East. He needs to further the radical faction of his coalition. He definitely wants to embarrass the United Nations and certainly the United States for their dismantling of Iraq's military. Finally, he wants to be remembered as the leader who restored Iraq to what he considers its proper place of dominance in the region. With all those obvious agenda items, and God only knows what other ones fill that perverted mind of his, what could Salomi use a single nuclear warhead to accomplish? And remember, he doesn't have any viable delivery system."

"Yes sir, he does." Geoffrey Singer almost painfully got out of his chair and walked to the wall map. "The early atomic weapons were huge. The atomic bomb dubbed Little Boy that was carried on the Enola Gay and dropped on Hiroshima weighed four and a half tons, and was ten feet long. The one dropped three days later on Nagasaki was called Fat Boy and was even bigger. However, today's nuclear weapons have been, shall we say, improved significantly. You could easily place a modern warhead, and all the equipment required to arm it, inside any minivan. If he could get it into England, he could simply place it inside a small lorry and drive it right up any motorway. So, my guess is that our friend has no plans to attach the warhead to a scud missile. I'm willing to wager that he plans on sending it special delivery, either by train, ship, or lorry."

The room sat in silence for a moment. "Dear Mother of God...," someone finally whispered.

Ten

Exeter - October 20, 2009

Isha and Annu were sitting on opposite sides of a table in their home. The King's chambers had a spartan appearance with gray walls that were virtually devoid of artwork or pictures. The furniture was made of handcrafted oak with carefully waxed surfaces to show the intricacies of the wood's beautiful grain. A ceremonial sword hanging by a golden cord and accented by a recessed spotlight was the only remembrance of the older man's days as a Protector. On a credenza behind the King's desk, in a silver frame, was a picture of two boys sitting in a fort behind a Spanish style house. It had been there for as long as Isha could remember. A year earlier, the picture had been draped with a black scarf for three days.

Annu had assumed the role of king at the death of his father twenty-three years earlier. The monarchy followed a similar path to that of the British royalty except that the leadership of the tribe descended to the eldest child regardless of gender. There had been two queens in the past one hundred years. Annu's paternal grandmother had been the last. She had ruled for almost forty years, and was regarded as one of the finest warriors to sit on the throne.

Annu, as the tribe's monarch, also differed from the British sovereign in that he actually ruled instead of holding a purely ceremonial role. In place of a Parliament, however were the Elders of the Tribe. These men and women were elected from the different colonies in Exeter. They were primarily advisors to the king, but exercised great control over the day-to-day operation of the dominion. Rarely did any conflict develop between the Crown and the Elders that could not be settled through compromise. Over a thousand years ago, the earliest warriors had agreed that the monarch's power was absolute and overriding of the Elders. No record could be found to suggest that any king or queen had ever exercised that right. A spirit of unity permeated the relationship between the Ruler and the Elders, and both honored and respected the other.

Enjoying their rare private time together, Annu and Isha had a chessboard between them that was the center of their attention. The men were concentrating on a match that had already consumed two hours. Between moves, neither man neither spoke nor dared to interrupt the strategic planning of the other person, unless it appeared they might be losing the match.

Annu had taught his son chess in these very chambers when the boy was six. It was a traditional thing for the warrior fathers to do. Anyone who aspired to be a Protector was expected to hone their mental agility by being skilled in strategy games.

"Interesting move, Isha."

"It wouldn't work against anyone except you, Father," Isha responded. The lighthearted answer reflected the fact that neither of the men was particularly interested in the game.

Deidre was staying with her grandmother in the hospital. Mrs. Rodriguez-O'Leary had been moved into a suite with an extra room to accommodate Deidre. It had only been three days since the attack in her home, but the old woman was quickly regaining strength, and soon would be strong enough to leave the medical chambers.

A decision had to be made shortly as to the best way to explain Exeter to her. All Maria knew was that she was not in Santa Fe. Most of the confusion in her mind she attributed to her injuries and the pain medication. Annu felt that when Maria was stronger he could show her his world. He wanted her to see first hand the vast civilization that had thrived completely hidden only a few miles from her home. He had already searched through his collection to find pictures of her son and himself playing in the recesses of the chambers. The King wanted Maria to know how special her son had been to the tribe.

The day after Isha brought the women to the cavern, a team of workers had gone to Maria's house. They completely eradicated any evidence of the previous night's events. The bodies of the men who had terrorized Mrs. Rodriguez-O'Leary were buried in the tribe's cemetery. Maria's doctors had told the Elders that her shock would prevent her from remembering most of the details of the attack. Having the house returned to normal before her return would lessen the trauma of coming home. There would be few physical indications to remind her of that night. Also, the King wanted nothing to be visible in case someone should decide to visit Maria and stumble on the crime.

Late in the afternoon, Deidre returned to the chambers. Her eyes were bright for the first time since the attack. Isha immediately knew she bore good news. "My grandmother woke up this morning and is acting like her old feisty self. She asked the nurse why there was no TV in the room. Seems she's afraid one of her soap operas might have something significant happen, and she'll miss it." Deidre paused for a moment and walked to Annu. Kissing him gently on the cheek, she continued, "Sir, I haven't really had the time to thank you for all that's been done for my grandmother. The doctors told me that she was very close to death when we arrived. I also know you had to approve us being allowed down here, and so I owe you for her life. I promise that I will keep your secret."

Annu smiled. "Approving your admittance was easy. I made that decision long ago. Wait a moment here. I have some things to show you." Isha nodded at his father knowingly. The older man left the room, and a few moments later returned wearing an ornate purple robe with gold trim. "I apologize for the quick change, but where we're going, I must wear a bit more formal clothing."

Annu, Isha and Deidre were soon in the tram. The King took the opportunity to begin explaining. "I want you to see some things about your father that I doubt you've ever known. He and I met long ago in the mountains near Mrs. O'Leary's home. I was twelve or thirteen, and in training to be a Protector. Anyway, I had been outside Exeter without permission from my mentor, Tomás. He was much younger then", the King added as a private joke. "It wasn't the first time I had left without permission, but usually I got away with it. Late in the day, I was rock climbing when a ledge broke loose under my weight. I fell about twenty feet and was hurt pretty badly. I probably would have died there. Your father was also in the mountains that day. He heard my cries and soon found me. He recognized how bad the situation was, but he didn't panic. Instead he covered me with his jacket and treated me for shock. John knew that I would not last long in the mountains. Before I lost consciousness, I told him about a cave nearby and the hidden passage that I used to come and go. To this day I don't know why he believed my almost incoherent words, but he ran to the spot and began yelling. One of our sentries heard his shouts, and sent a mentor to investigate.

Shortly after, I was in Exeter's medical chambers. In the excitement of saving the King's only son, my rescuers assumed that John was also from here, and allowed him to enter with them. After the mistake was discovered, my father took John to our chambers and tried to explain how sacred our secret was. Right then your father promised to keep it. He was no older than I, but he showed maturity well beyond his years."

The tram slowed and stopped before a large chamber. "This is the museum chamber." Isha's words betrayed awe at the place. "Our history is essentially stored here. I think you will find it interesting."

The party entered the chamber and was immediately met by the head curator, William Macomber. "Sire, I was told your tram was here. Is there any way I may be of service?"

"Thank you, Bill I want to see my coronation visuals."

"As you wish, sir. It will take a few minutes. The studio is right this way."

"We'll be there in fifteen minutes. I want to show my guests around the area first."

"The studio will be ready when you are, Sire." Macomber left the group to prepare the King's request.

The walls of this chamber reminded Deidre of the British Museum in London. Floor-to-ceiling display cases, some fourteen feet tall, were everywhere. "This area is for our more recent history. Here they store artifacts from the past five hundred years. Farther back are chambers with older exhibits. Before our tribe settled in Exeter, we were a nomadic people. Our ancestors believed that to know oneself, you must know your history. So, our history was carried by storytellers who told the legends and tales from the past. Micha, the king who established Exeter, decreed this chamber as the first official room. That's why we have an unbroken collection for our study. There are samples of our clothing, weapons, tools, implements, and even medicines."

Deidre paused in amazement. "You mean before your tribe created homes, or schools, or hospitals, they made this place?"

"Sure. All those other things already existed for us. We carried them with us all the time." Isha looked proudly around him. "This chamber was something that we could never have before. It's a very special place for every member of Exeter because it chronicles who we were as a people, and why we came to live here."

In the center of the chamber was a display case that caught Deidre's attention. It was spotlighted from every direction, and seemed to be the main focus of the entire area. Walking closer, she found the glass capsule held a single lead ball. "This was the musket ball that killed King Micha's father. It was his last command to Micha that began the search for these caves."

Macomber returned and caught the King's eye. "Sire, the room is ready."

Annu shook the man's hand. "Thank you. I appreciate your helpfulness. Have you ever seen these views?"

"No, sir. I haven't. I remember my father telling me about being there. He's the one who took most of the scenes."

"I remember your father well. He was a remarkable curator, and he passed his gift to you. The museum has never looked better. Do you have time to watch these with us?"

William Macomber had heard that King Annu had a remarkable memory, but was still amazed that the King actually recalled his father. He was even more astounded that the King had noticed his work. "Thank you, Sire. I would be honored."

The four people walked into the viewing room. It was a circular area that was thirty-five feet across. The center area was a fifteen-foot wide metal platform or stage. Around the platform was an elevated ring with chairs. The King had Deidre sit to his left with Isha on the right. Macomber was about to sit in the next row back, but Annu stopped him. "When I asked you to join us, I didn't expect you to sit behind us. You are a member of my party. Please, sit beside my son."

"I'm sorry, Sire. I just did not want to seem presumptuous."

"Don't let it bother you. Your family has served these hallowed chambers for many years. You deserve to sit with the King and his family within these walls. Now, relax. You are among friends."

Within moments, the lamps dimmed. The central area of the room was bathed in a very dim light. Then, almost magically, a holographic image of a man appeared on the platform. The image was about eighteen inches tall, but otherwise looked 100% solid and real. He was holding a rolled parchment, and began reading "By the last command of our King Edward, we today impart his continuing reign to Annu. King Annu shall rule Exeter from this day until he, too, joins his ancestors. Stand tall, all people of our tribe ... today is a great day for our land."

The herald faded out and in his place stood a young Annu. He appeared to be about twenty years old, but already he had the look of a ruler. The platform rotated until Deidre could see over the shoulder of the holographic image of Annu. From this angle, she could see a crowd of people. There seemed to be no end to the multitude. They were all peering intently up at their new king.

"My people, I stand before you as a man saddened at the death of our King and my father. He ruled you for many years, and you knew he loved you beyond words. Know now that I will try and be the same kind of king. God has blessed this tribe, and we bow before Him to ask humbly for wisdom in the coming days. I ask for your prayers."

The people watched as Annu bowed and a crown was placed upon his head. He then stood and the same robe he was now wearing was draped over his shoulders. The newly crowned King turned to kiss his mother Queen Catherine on the cheek. She stepped back from her son, and the platform once again rotated, and Deidre now knew what she had been brought to see. There, standing beside King Annu, was her father. Annu pressed a button on his chair, and the image froze. Another button, and the image enlarged to where he was nearly full size.

"Daddy? Is that really my father?" Seeing him so clearly and so vividly, Deidre felt the tears well up in her eyes. "I can't believe it. He looks so close."

Annu's hand reached over and took hers. "Your father is the only outsider to ever be a part of a coronation. He was at my right side when I was crowned. It was my choice to have him in that spot of honor. By the time of my coronation, your father had been my best friend for almost ten years. He had proven his faithfulness to our secret many times. He was a symbol to our people that perhaps someday we could again live with those above." Annu stopped and stared at John's image. "I, too, miss your father. He was the brother I never had. He was my confidant. When I married Isha's mother, he was my best man. When she died, he was my comforter. John O'Leary was a special man. I am not the least bit surprised you knew nothing of this place. When he was twelve, he promised my father never to reveal our secret. To him that was a sacred promise, and he never once broke it – not even to you or your mother."

Deidre felt the tears rolling down her cheeks. She knew that Annu and Isha were trusting her with the same secret. She also knew she too would keep it until her death. "Thank you, your Highness, for showing me this."

"From this day forward, you are to address me as Annu. Your father and I were like brothers. You now are a member of our tribe." The King let out an audible sigh. "Well, I'm sorry to leave this happy moment, but I have some work to accomplish. Isha, if you'll please take care of Deidre I would appreciate it. And Bill, again thanks for your help." Everyone stood as Annu left.

Eleven

London

Number 10 Downing Street sits just off a broad avenue named Whitehall, which runs through the West End of London in what was formally the City of Westminster. It is a five-minute walk from the Houses of Parliament, Westminster Abby, and Big Ben. Tourists who daily make that stroll are usually somewhat amazed at how little of the Prime Minister's residence can be seen. It faces at a ninety-degree angle to Whitehall, and the door to the house is mere inches from the pavement.

Two constables stand guard at the approach to Downing Street. This afternoon they were more than normally wary of the tourists who stood behind the ornate ten-foot iron fence trying to photograph the British Prime Minister's address one hundred fifty meters away. These two men and this fence were only the first veneer of protection for the Prime Minister.

Several closed circuit cameras were also trained on the area with a security agent constantly monitoring the crowds below as well as the flow of traffic down Whitehall. Any vehicle with official business on Downing Street would have two-way radio communication with this agent, and would notify him as it approached. The agent would then pass the word to the constables on the street to open the barriers. This had to be orchestrated carefully to avoid having the street entrance open too long.

The fence would never stop any determined attempt to enter the street by a potential assassin in a car or truck. That possibility was met by a two-foot high armor barricade that was raised across the entire width of the street thirty feet inside the fence. For vehicles on official business, the barricade would be retracted into the street to allow them to drive over, then immediately raised again to block the access. If necessary to protect the Prime Minister, this barricade had the power to raise a ten-ton lorry off its wheels. With the threat of terrorist activity always a possibility, security was never lax.

The American and Japanese tour groups standing at the access were gently but firmly moved by one of the constables as a black limo slowed and turned onto Downing Street. The darkened windows almost hid the lone occupant of the back seat. Just in case it was someone important, the Americans waved animatedly at the car. Sir Patrick Baldwin was too lost in thought to take notice.

As the car stopped in front of 10 Downing Street, a plain-clothes security guard opened the door to the car. He blocked the exit until he was certain the DI6 Director General was ready to leave the car. The black mahogany door to the residence opened. The agent scanned the area quickly then almost imperceptibly nodded at the older man in the back seat. Baldwin walked the few paces while the agent smoothly stayed along side to shield the DG with his own body.

Inside, Sir Patrick was escorted immediately to a conference room where Prime Minister Donald Norman was reading. Norman was a career politician from the Conservative Party. His tenure had already survived a no-confidence vote in Parliament, and appeared to be even stronger now that the United Kingdom's economy was on the rise. He was also known as a man who actually appreciated the insights of his intelligence gathering services. "Sir Patrick, it's good of you to come. I felt it best to discuss the situation face to face instead of over the phone. Even secure lines bother me when subjects such as this are discussed."

"It was no problem, Prime Minister." Getting right to the subject was a trademark of the DG. "Sir, I'm afraid my DDI has proposed a most uncomfortable scenario for the current situation. He's convinced us that Salomi can easily transport the device and arming mechanism inside a standard shipping container." He paused a moment to light his pipe. "This situation is such that I believe we must alert the Americans and perhaps the French."

Prime Minister Norman sat almost totally still for thirty seconds. "I want this handled carefully. If those buggers on Fleet Street hear of this they'll have it splashed all over the papers before we can stop it. I want absolute discretion. No sense having the entire country in a panic until we know for sure our fears are substantiated." The Prime Minister rubbed his tired eyes. He felt much older than his fifty-eight years. The tone of his voice betrayed his concern. He and the DG had been close friends for many years. The formality of British titles was not appropriate to him at the moment. "Patrick, if you really feel this mad man has a nuclear device, the means to detonate it, and a method to transport it, then yes, inform the Americans. However, I do not want to advise the French government. France has sold technology and weapons to virtually every Arab nation. Their surface-to-air missiles and radar technology has been used against the West in every conflict for as long as I can remember. There is no reason to believe the Salomi would ever attack the country that has seen fit to betray the rest of the world's safety for the sake of a few military sales. France is safe. You can believe me. Besides, if we tell the French government what we know or suspect, Salomi will have that same information within a few hours."

Sir Patrick Baldwin knew the Prime Minister was right. "Sir, I'll set up a meeting with the US Intelligence Chief immediately. Perhaps you should send a simultaneous message to the President."

* * * * *

Fifteen minutes later, Geoffrey Singer was again on a secure phone call with his friend at the American Embassy. "Colin, we have a situation that may well affect the United States. I really need to discuss it face to face. Any chance you could be here in an hour?"

"I'll be there, Geoff. Obviously this is something you want to keep between us for now, but I need to justify my absence to that pain-in-the-ass protocol chief. Any suggestions?"

"Yes, old boy, first of all, it's pain-in-the-arse ... not ass. Secondly, tell that pain-in-the-arse there are more important things in the world besides what color napkins are placed beside the Ambassador's teacup this afternoon. Cheers." With that, Singer hung up.

"Thanks." Johnson said to the dial tone.

Fortunately for Johnson, Richard Nail was busy with the Secret Service detail and couldn't be disturbed. This gave him the opportunity to leave the Embassy without explanation.

Deciding against using a high profile staff car, Colin Johnson took a cab to 85 Vauxhall Cross. He pulled up in front of the government office building twenty minutes later. Singer's assistant was waiting for him. He smiled at seeing her. They had dated off and on for the past two years. Based on years in government service, Colin had long ago decided that there was some unwritten rule stating only overweight middle-aged matronly women with sagging breasts could be assistants. Rimi was the exception to this rule – an oversight Colin was glad existed. He enjoyed the company of this young lady from the Yorkshire Dales of central England. He loved the way she slightly exaggerated her accent for his enjoyment. She started doing so shortly after they met when he told her that her voice was the soundtrack of his dreams.

"'Ello, Colin. Bloody hell of a way to meet isn't it? I can't believe I have to escort you to the conference room instead of to my flat."

"All good things in their time."

"Whatever is happening, will you try and find time to have dinner with me soon? I've missed you."

Colin Johnson winked at her. "I promise nothing would make me happier. Plan on next Friday. I'll pick you up at 6:30. We'll take a walk through the maze at Hampton Court; have a candle lit dinner for two at the establishment of your choice; and take a leisurely drive through the country. We might even find a nice B&B for the evening."

A bed and breakfast had not been something Rimi had expected, but the thought of it made her hope the weekend could start immediately.

"Deal! You Yanks are such romantics. Now you tell Mr. Singer that no matter what the crisis, you have to have it settled before Friday. That gives you seventy-two hours. Get busy!" With that she quickly stood on her tiptoes and kissed Colin on the cheek. That brief show of affection as all Rimi had time to do as they walked through the rotating door of the building and into the vestibule.

Rimi walked Johnson to the enclosed booth on their left. One of the guards operated a switch on the console in front of him. A metal tray, similar to those used at drive thru bank stations, opened from the front of the booth. Colin placed his United States Embassy ID card into the tray that closed immediately and slid back into the wall.

The guards inside the booth both verified Johnson's identity by closely checking his ID card. They had been expecting him since Geoffrey Singer had called the security desk and told them to prepare for Johnson's arrival.

While they were examining the ID, one of the men conversationally said to Rimi, "Have you been staying busy, Miss?"

"No, everything has been a little slow in our office lately," she replied carefully. It was the correct response.

The guard smiled and nodded back. That short dialogue was in fact a duress code. Duress codes were a way to prevent someone using some kind of threat to force their way into DI6. The procedure was simple. If an unauthorized group were trying to force Rimi into getting one of their people inside DI6, the conversation would have had a different twist. When the guard asked the seemingly innocuous question, she would have said that she had been very busy lately. The guard would have made no immediate or overt response, but he would have known that the stranger in front of him was dangerous. Some excuse would have been made to prevent the person from gaining access to the secure part of the building. Another series of coded questions would have informed the guards what kind of duress they were under. Just by having an apparently normal conversation, the two DI6 employees could be giving each other a great deal of information. That, today, was not the case.

Satisfied that Colin Johnson was who he said he was, the guard pressed a code into a panel before him. One of the six enclosures opened, and Colin entered.

On the other side of the capsule, Geoffrey Singer was waiting. As the second door opened, he shook Johnson's hand. "Colin, thanks for coming on such short notice. Our security desk called and said you were here. I'll need to escort you to the meeting area. Rimi, thanks for taking care of our guest. We'll be a while. If you want, you can go ahead and leave for the day. However, carry your mobile phone. Please make sure it has a charged battery this time. It's possible we may need you later."

"Yes, sir, Mister Singer." She tried to sound professional as she continued, "Mister Johnson, it was a pleasure seeing you again. Remember what I told you!" The emphasis on the "mister" did not escape Singer.

Once in the elevator and on the way down to the underground conference center, Geoff laughed softly. "Does Rimi really think I don't know about you two? She practically drools whenever you're in the office. No wonder she never got clearance to do field work. Her face tells everything, and she can't even lie well. But, she is a wonderful assistant, the best I've ever had. Be careful with her, Colin."

With feigned innocence, Johnson replied, "Geoff, I can't begin to imagine what you're talking about. She and I have a professional relationship. That's all."

"I understand, 'ol boy." Taking his handkerchief out with a flourish, Singer handed it to Johnson. "Now, would you be so kind as to wipe her lipstick off your cheek before Sir Patrick sees it. I would be grateful."

The elevator door opened to the Royal Marine. It took almost two minutes to clear Johnson through to the conference area. Once inside, Singer began his explanation of the day's events. He quickly covered the facts and fears of the council as well as their desire to keep the matter low-key for the moment. "The Prime Minister is calling your President as we speak. The CIA will probably be getting the same information within the hour. The DG wanted to have you involved at this level until we can come up with a plan of action between our countries."

"I understand. Geoff. What was the initial source of the intelligence?"

"I'll have to let the Director go into that, but I assure you, the source is credible. We have placed the reliability at around 80%. Considering the nature of the situation, we're not taking any chances."

At that moment Sir Patrick Baldwin came into the room. Both men stood as he entered. Singer spoke first. "Sir, may I present Mr. Colin Johnson."

"A pleasure, Mr. Johnson."

"Thank you, sir. Your DDI here has given me the basic information on our current situation. I was wondering if the source of your data could be revealed?"

"No doubt you're considering verifying it from another source, eh? All right. We got the preliminary information from the Mossad. They have a mole working in the Estonian storage facility where the device was kept. There is very little chance the details were confused. It appears the bomb components were shipped by way of rail through Latvia and into Germany. We surmise, but cannot yet confirm, a fundamentalist faction of the Islamic Revolutionary Guard or IRG handled that

. The IRG is a relatively new coalition of several rather nasty groups of terrorist organizations all tied in one way or the other to Azmud Salomi."

"Yes I'm familiar with the IRG. They're the ones who hit the oil storage facilities in northern Israel last summer. They are quite capable of handling something this difficult. And Salomi has the bankroll to fund such an undertaking. He's been too quiet for a while. I guess this explains why."

"The Mossad believes the weapon was shipped in a packing crate to Munich. We got this information too late to stop the train en route, but shortly after it arrived, we told the German government that the train was carrying a large quantity of high-grade narcotics. They were most helpful in rounding up everyone who had any contact with the train in the Munich station. No one can remember seeing any unusual individuals or cargo. But by then, the crate could have been anywhere."

Johnson considered the DG for a moment. "How did the Mossad get the information?"

"How the information was received is not something I can discuss. I am, however, unprepared to ignore it."

"Sir Patrick, how do you want the US Embassy here in London involved? No doubt you are aware that we cannot become concerned directly. The CIA works with your DI6, but as a State Department employee, I can't see where I fit in."

A knowing smile wrinkled its way across the old man's face. "Come, come, my dear Colin. Perhaps you've heard of General Jace Pellicone."

Momentarily Johnson was confused. "Yes sir, he's a retired Marine general who is now serving as the CIA Director."

"He's also one of my oldest and dearest friends. Jace and his wife, Marsey, just spent a week with my wife and I at our Scottish country home. He often sends me interesting material to read. For example, during the last year I've read several of your Middle East assessments. They have been most insightful."

"Sir, I'm not sure what you're talking about. I work for the State Department."

"Rest easy, young man. Jace told me you're one of the bright stars in his organization. You have nothing to fear from me. I assure you that Jace and I communicate clearly on each other's in-country associates. Baldwin continued, "The Director wants you to be my CIA liaison here in the United Kingdom. I suspect as we speak Richard Nail is getting a rather terse telex informing him of your temporary detachment to New Scotland Yard. It will appear to him that they are using your security experience, when in reality it will be your intelligence background DI6 is using. I assume Nail does not know who you really work for. Is that correct?"

"No sir. He thinks I'm a State Department security analyst. That's all."

"We'll let him continue thinking that way. In the meantime, on the basis of Jace Pellicone's recommendation, I'll see that you have clearance to any intelligence information dealing with this current situation. Based on the information we have, we may need every bit of genius in each of us. Thank you gentlemen."

Sir Patrick Baldwin got to his feet from the high-back leather chair. As he left the conference room, he turned to the two men. "One last thing, the Prime Minister wants me to brief him twice a day on our progress. Please try and hypothesize some possible scenarios for me. I was never very good at those things. I would appreciate it, gentlemen."

Geoffrey Singer laughed as the door was closed. "Never good at those things? Bull! That old man has a sixth sense about possible scenarios. I've studied every case he had during his early years in the intelligence community. He's broken just about every rule and solved nearly 100% of the cases he's investigated for the past forty years. My guess is that he already has a hunch on what Salomi has planned for that nuclear bomb, but he wants to see how we'll handle it."

"All right, Geoff. Let's see where we're headed." Walking to the map that covered the entire twelve-foot wall, Johnson continued, "We need a list of possible targets for the weapon. Does Salomi intend to get it out of Europe – can he hit England – is Israel a valid target knowing they would certainly retaliate with their own weapons?"

Both men knew they had more questions than answers. It was going to be a long night.

Twelve

Washington, D.C.

President Thomas Rogers was sitting in the small study that connected to his more formal oval office. Before him was a folder with Eyes of the President Only embossed on the cover. Inside was material England's Prime Minister Norman had sent through secure telemetry to the White House message center. The report detailed information gathered since the President had talked with the Prime Minister the previous day. The Mossad's discovery that a nuclear warhead allegedly had been stolen had not come as a surprise to him. For weeks the daily Central Intelligence Agency (CIA), National Security Agency (NSA), and the Defense Intelligence Agency (DIA), had all been using their individual sources to monitor Azmud Salomi. For the most part, they had credited him with having the usual Middle East flair for rhetoric and threats, but no substance. They did recognize that of all the Middle East dictators, Salomi was potentially the most dangerous. He was considered pathologically unstable and capable of violent, unpredictable behavior.

The President had no choice but to increase surveillance in the region. Silently he cursed Congress for cutting the new Skyminder satellites from the budget. NASA had had six Shuttle launches eliminated from the schedule. One of those missions was ostensibly to place an earth resources satellite into geosynchronous, or stationary, orbit. This research module was in reality to have been the Skyminder, capable of intercepting telephone and microwave transmissions, as well as provide photographic telemetry. This would have given the intelligence community virtually instantaneous information over the entire region.

A sour thought crossed the President's mind. He didn't believe for a moment that his primary information agencies would share their data with each other and come to a unified conclusion that he could use. The CIA, DIA, NSA, and probably ten or fifteen smaller government agencies would put their parochial interests of justifying enormous budgets ahead of providing coordinated information to the Executive Branch. For the thousandth time since taking office, the President of the United States was angry because the very people he depended upon cared more for their own interests than for the country.

He was in the first half of his administration and already feeling the pressure of public opinion. His popularity had started plummeting after several key aides were indicted for federal election law violations and obstruction of justice. He was counting the days until his term was completed and he could fade into the background as Ford, Carter, Nixon, and Bush had been able to do and Clinton had never tried to do.

The President pressed the intercom button. "Diane, please ask the Chief to come in here. Thanks."

"Yes, Mr. President."

Thirty seconds later there was a single knock on the door. Platte Janosek, the President's Chief of Staff entered without waiting. "Yes, sir."

"Platte, what's on the agenda for today? Is there any open time when I can work in a briefing?"

"Sir, at two o'clock you're scheduled to be measured for a couple of suits and get a haircut. Obviously those could be postponed without any trouble." Both men laughed at the joke. The President was nearly bald with just a fringe of gray hair around his head.

"Please take care of canceling those if you would, Platte. I just need some time to digest this material from the Prime Minister. Also, ask all the intelligence chiefs to have someone available around two o'clock in case I need any more information."

"I'll take care of it, Sir." Before walking out the door, Janosek looked over his shoulder. "Just a reminder, Mr. President, I'm going up on the Hill to meet with the Joint Budget Committee at noon. Unless I miss my guess, it should be over by two-thirty."

Platte Janosek rarely missed his guesses. He had been around Capitol Hill for better than twenty-five years. He knew every Senator, and almost every Congressman on a first-name basis. With very few exceptions, the legislators liked, or at least respected, him. Janosek was the perfect Chief of Staff for the President. Unlike many of his predecessors, Janosek did not believe in bullying his way through staff members or Congress. Instead, as a consummate artist at compromise, he maneuvered the President's programs and projects through the maze of committees and hearings with ease. It was unusual when he failed to achieve one of his objectives.

The President smiled, "Illegitimae Non Carborundum, Platte. Don't let the bastards wear you down."

"We'll get through this year's cuts all right. But I wouldn't place any major bets on next year."

"Thanks for the warm prediction. See you and Gale for dinner?"

"Yes sir, we'll be here." Platte Janosek quietly closed the door behind him.

Shifting easily in his leather chair, the President set his folder aside and looked over his typed appointments agenda for the day. In thirty minutes he was scheduled to meet with a group of professional athletes for a photo session encouraging student participation in sports. The engagement had already been quietly delayed once when a key player was suddenly banned for life from the NBA for substance abuse. What made the situation even more troublesome was the fact that this was the second time the player had been "banned for life". No wonder we have problems with credibility among our young people, President Rogers thought. Life in prison means serving five years and banned for life from sports - if you're an important player - means a season and a run through some drug rehab program. It angered the President when he allowed his cynicism to get the better of him.

* * * * *

At almost the same time, on a dock outside Le Havre, France, a crate labeled Automobile Parts was being loaded into the forward cargo hold of a Panamanian freighter named the Peligroso. While the dock was covered with crates and pallets waiting for workers to load them, this crate was singled out for special handling. The Peligroso was known as a general cargo ship, and weighed forty thousand tons. Underway, she could produce twenty-one knots in calm seas, and sixteen knots if in seven-foot swells. Her hull was designed to prevent water from splashing up onto the upper deck.

Dock manager Julien Gauthier had been paid a handsome bribe to ensure the cargo was loaded. All he knew was that someone from the Renault factory wanted these parts in the United States immediately. Furthermore, they did not want to suffer any bureaucratic red tape in getting it aboard the Peligroso. This happened occasionally, and Gauthier was always rewarded with a generous gift. He needed the money as he had a son about to enter a pharmacy school at the state university.

The individual who contacted Gauthier worked for several international companies. He was paid to intercede unofficially for the companies with dock managers at Calais, Boulogne sur Mer, Le Havre, Nantes, and Bordeaux. His work was to be sure that certain key shipments were expedited on to ships. The managers took him at his word when he assured them that never were drugs or contraband being shipped, just high-priority equipment or parts for industrial use. In Le Havre, Gauthier was told simply that the companies needed the material immediately. Gauthier rationalized his dishonesty by saying that no one got hurt; his involvement just streamlined the system to allow cargo on quickly.

Unfortunately, this time he was wrong. As Julien Gauthier left the office and walked to his Peugeot sedan six hours after supervising the loading of the ship, the businessman who had delivered the bribe approached him. The French manager had often dealt with the man, and smiled warmly as he approached.

"Bonsoir Monsieur Gauthier. I trust you have had a profitable day."

"Bonsoir. Yes, your shipment leaves with the tide. Everything has been taken care of. Within a few days, your auto parts will be in New York City. Why can't Renault get their parts distribution down where these kinds of emergency shipments are not required?"

"Who's to say? I simply see that the parts are loaded. I do not try and decipher motives. Tell me, old friend, you are certain everything was loaded exactly as prescribed?"

"Absolutely. I personally checked the tie down straps to assure the crate would not move regardless of sea conditions. You have my word on it."

"That is good to hear. Julien, I will see you soon, and thanks again for you help. A tout a'leure, mes copain"

"Au revoir."

Julien Gauthier got in his Peugeot and started the long drive through the French countryside to his mistress' home. There were few automobiles along the winding roads which allowed him to drive quickly. He downshifted into each turn and accelerated rapidly to near the engine's red line. The French countryside was a near blur as the car sped down the roads. Darkness came early this time of the year. It had already fallen, hiding the shades of the dark green forest.

Driving as rapidly as he was, Julien Gauthier knew he should have one hundred percent of his attention on the road. However, his wife was in Paris for several days, and the thought of his young mistress waiting kept invading his thoughts. She knows I'm driving over. Just now she's getting out of a long soaking bath. He smiled unconsciously. The thought of her perfect body, still wet from the bath, were clear in his mind's eye. She'll be wearing something that accentuates her – attributes, he thought, and she'll have just a touch of perfume on. Tonight will be beautiful. What the woman lacked in experience, she made up for in enthusiasm and her desire to please Gauthier. His wife had grown indifferent and unresponsive to him over the years, so he had no problems justifying to himself the expense of keeping his lover.

What Julien Gauthier did not know, would never know, was that a hole had been drilled into his exhaust system by an expert. No one would ever see it. A small wad of clay had been carefully placed into the tail pipe to constrict it partially. It was not enough to seriously affect performance, but just enough to cause the resulting back pressure to force carbon monoxide into the passenger compartment. Since leaving work, Gauthier had been slowly poisoned. His driving was almost imperceptibly becoming sluggish as his mind grew sleepy. Two times Gauthier's reaction to sharp turns was slowed to the point that his front wheel left the highway.

Just outside Lyons la Forêt, the highway made a ninety-degree left turn. The dock manager missed it completely and his powder blue Peugeot went straight into the trees. The car disintegrated around him as it impacted smaller saplings and bushes. Gauthier's dulled brain still comprehended the events as if in slow motion. He saw, rather than felt, the one tree branch that came through the windshield and impaled itself through his chest.

Several hours later, the accident was discovered. As Julien Gauthier's body was removed from the wreckage, his sightless eyes were still open. The coroner later decreed the accident was the result of careless driving. Since there was no odor of alcohol, and no evidence of drugs, he did not order an autopsy.

Julien Gauthier did not die as the result of an accident. He was murdered for his innocent part in the crime of the century.

Thirteen

Exeter

Deidre had very little free time. When she wasn't at the hospital, she was visiting many of the cultural and historical centers of Exeter. She was beginning to feel a part of the tribe. Wherever she toured, people would greet her warmly and personally. Several she met had known her father and told her of their experiences with him. Since her grandmother was now no longer in danger, Deidre felt more freedom to spend more time away from the hospital. It was also easier to avoid difficult questions that way.

While things were easier for Deidre, Maria was becoming more frustrated. Almost three days of staying in bed was enough for her. She was no longer kept in the special bed with the canopy and now she was in a regular hospital room. Even though the doctor felt she should stay in bed another day or two, she was not about to allow anyone to forbid her from getting around. Finally, the staff decided that she could walk in her room, but only with a nurse present. This, while a royal pain, was acceptable to Maria. She still had a throbbing headache, but the doctors assured her that this would pass within a day or two. The entire medical staff was amazed that not only had she not died, but also she seemed to be getting her strength back at an amazing speed.

Maria was up and walking when Isha and Deidre entered the hospital chamber. Deidre was wearing a gift from the Elders. It was a silken robe with golden striping. The nurse politely left the room when the Prince arrived. Deidre noticed that he always seemly slightly embarrassed when someone showed him special attention, but it was his place in the tribe, and he accepted it with grace.

"Mrs. O'Leary, how are you feeling?" Isha knew the old woman was still confused from the beating and the strange surroundings. However, she still had not asked about it. "I trust you are being treated well."

"Yes, except that I would love to trade this head in on a newer and less painful model. Plus, I can hardly wait to get into clothes that were not designed to fit both anorexic and maternity patients."

Deidre answered her. "Grandmother, Isha is taking me home to get some clothes. Is there anything special you want that I can bring you?"

"Yes, my own bed. This one has lumps in all the wrong places. Not that I'm complaining mind you. They finally brought me a TV so I can watch my soap operas."

"All right. We'll bring some comfortable clothes for you from home. See you in a few hours."

As the two young people left, the nurse returned. "Prince Isha and your granddaughter make a beautiful couple Mrs. O'Leary."

"Prince? You know that young man? Isn't he just a student here in Santa Fe? Tell me about him."

The nurse, realizing her error, attempted to correct herself quickly. "Now, Mrs. O'Leary, you've been doing too much. It's time to get back in bed and rest. If the doctors find out how long I've let you stay up, they will be all over me. Now you don't want me to get into trouble do you?"

"All right. But, you're going to have to start explaining things pretty soon. I know I'm old, but I'm not stupid."

The nurse laughed. "Mrs. O'Leary, no one around here could accuse you of that. It's just that for now your only job is to rest up and heal. Later, there will be time to answer all your questions. Remember, you've had a pretty tough time the past few days. It's natural to feel a little confused. That will pass."

Getting back into her hospital bed, Maria replied, "I suppose you're right. I am feeling a bit tired. But you have to promise me that we'll talk soon. I don't like thinking something is being hidden from me. It brings out my crotchety old nature."

"Ok, I promise. In fact, I'll tell the doctor just how curious you are. He's so much better at explaining things than I am." The nurse tucked the blanket in around her patient. "He'll be in shortly. Sleep well, Mrs. O'Leary."

* * * * *

In the tram, Isha and Deidre were talking about the immediate future. "Your grandmother will probably leave the hospital today or tomorrow. My father wants you both to stay with us until she is able to care for herself. Is there anything you can think of that will make your grandmother more comfortable?"

"I can't think of anything." Remembering something her grandmother said, Deidre suddenly asked, "How did you get her soap operas down here? That's the only thing she's complained about, and the next day she has a TV set and all the channels. You don't have TV reception in Exeter. In fact, I don't remember ever even seeing a TV set down here. How did that happen?"

"TV is considered a tremendous waste of time. Our children are not raised with the TV as a baby-sitter, and so they prefer to have a good book or game. It's all in what you set as priorities. But Mrs. O'Leary wanted her shows. It was a simple matter of intercepting satellite feeds and channeling them into her room. It was an easy solution to her isolation."

It took ten minutes to reach the royal chamber. Annu was waiting. He had received a call from the doctor asking for instructions as to what he should tell Maria about Exeter. It was decided that the King should be the one to explain the community to her. Isha did not envy his father's task. Maria was, after all, an intelligent feisty senior. She would have more questions than he would have answers.

* * * * *

After leaving the royal chambers, Isha and Deidre picked up Kevin and his wife, Celia. Kevin was wearing a robe identical to Isha's. Celia was dressed in what Deidre thought of as "church clothes". In the days prior, Kevin had talked to Deidre non-stop about Celia, but she had been away visiting friends in another colony of Exeter. It was obvious that Kevin and Celia were prefect for each other. She was intelligent, adventurous, and a beautiful lady with a warm smile.

"Deidre, I'm so glad to finally meet you." Celia said. "These guys have done nothing but talk about you. I'm used to Kevin going on and on, but our Prince is usually much more reserved. You must be someone special."

"Thanks, Celia. I can't tell you how glad I am to have another girl around. I've been getting a little tired of the testosterone festival that goes along with these two."

"Wait a minute guys." Deidre suddenly remembered the plan for the day, "You two are not dressed to go above."

"We have one more event to witness before we can leave Exeter."

"My legs are dead! I can't see another museum or concert or exhibition. Sorry fellows. I'm beat!"

Kevin laughed, "You've seen a lot, I'll grant you, but the best is yet to come. You have one more event to witness. I promise it will be special."

* * * * *

A short time later the two warriors escorted Deidre and Celia into a large chamber. An audience of several hundred stood when their prince entered. Isha and his three friends were escorted to a boxed area at the front of the crowd. Everyone remained standing until the Prince sat down. As the guests settled, the lights dimmed and a spot light bathed the solitary figure on the stage before them. "Your Highness, ladies and gentlemen, our Protectors are ready for their induction into the brotherhood. For the past fifteen years they have studied, practiced, and learned. Today their mentors declare them ready to defend Exeter."

At that moment eight men and six women entered the stage from the right. All were twenty years old and in perfect physical condition. None was exceptionally large or muscular, but each one stood tall and proud.

The first one, a young man named Cody, stepped forward. He had finished at the top of his class and was therefore spokesman for the group. "My fellow Protectors present ourselves to you."

The house lights came up slightly. Isha whispered to Deidre, "Stay here. We'll be back in a moment." Deidre nodded her understanding.

The Prince and Kevin stood, as did about fifty other people in the audience. Most of them were wearing identical robes. Those not in robes were most certainly the parents of the graduates.

Celia read Deidre's mind and whispered, "Those are graduation robes. This is the first time the new Protectors have been allowed to wear theirs, and it's a big deal for them ... kind of rite of passage."

The fourteen graduates knelt on the stage and those who joined from the audience surrounded them.

The voice of the announcer was heard again. "The Brotherhood of the Protectors continues. Each of those before you has vowed to one another with their sacred promise to keep their honor and Brotherhood pure. They have further promised to this tribe their lives as Protectors. Stand now and hear their words."

Everyone rose to their feet together. "We belong to each other," the fourteen began in unison. "We belong to each other because of our common calling to defend our beloved Exeter. We stand before you ready. We belong to each other."

From her vantage point Deidre could easily see the tears on the cheeks of almost everyone on the stage. This was clearly a significant moment in the lives of these young people, but it was also extremely important to those who had joined from the audience.

The announcer's resonate bass voice echoed through the hall, "Your Highness, ladies and gentlemen, I present your new Protectors!"

Applause and cheers erupted from the assembly. Isha was walking from person to person on stage. Each celebrant seemed to be in awe at being in the presence of the heir apparent to the throne. Isha leaned close to each individual and spoke quietly. Without exception, the Protector would immediately beam. As the last person was congratulated, Isha walked to the microphone.

"My friends, the King sends his personal congratulations to these graduates. He is proud of your accomplishment and your dedication to Exeter. As is his tradition, each of you will be spending a day with him soon." He looked around to the graduates behind him. "Hone up on your chess game." Polite laughter was heard from those who knew the Prince wasn't kidding.

Again, Isha looked back at the crowd on the stage and motioned to five people to come forward. He shook hands with the father, and three sons, and hugged the mother. "Ladies and gentlemen, today we celebrated a "first" in the history of Exeter, and I wanted to share it with you. This is David and Robin Marcus. David has been a Protector for almost thirty years and is one the King's best friends. He and Robin have brought three amazing men into this world, and as of this morning, all three of them are now Protectors.

Robert, his friends call him Robbie, has been a Protector six years. Jackson has been a Protector three years. And this morning Cody joined this band of warriors. As I said before, in the history of Exeter, there have never been four Protectors in one family."

From deep in the audience, a single clap of applause started what became a thunderous sound.

* * * * *

Isha and Kevin returned to Deidre and Celia, and escorted them from the chamber.

Once again in the familiar tram, Kevin explained a little about the ceremony. "The rest of the day these kids will have parties and celebrations going on. I remember how good it felt to finally be finished with my training."

Celia reached over and touched her husband's arm affectionately. "I remember your party, Kevin. That was the first time you ever kissed me."

"That explains why the ceremony was so short. I kept thinking that after all these years of training, they deserved more than just a half hour celebration." Deidre remembered something from the ceremony and asked what it was that Isha was saying that seemed to excite the celebrants. "Obviously this was an important day for the new Protectors, but whatever you were saying really seemed to top it off."

"Nothing. They were just glad that they are finally finished with their training."

Kevin interrupted, "That's bull, Isha. Deidre, my friend here is the de facto commander of all Protectors. He studies each of the students during training. They don't even know it, but he keeps up with them. So today, as he asked about these kid's parents and siblings by name, the Protectors realized just how much he really knew about them. That's pretty heady stuff for a twenty year old."

"To quote you, that's 'bull'. They just were happy that you wouldn't be giving them any more lectures on the latest sociopolitical upheaval somewhere in the world. Most of them would rather be in the gym acting as a practice dummy for karate kicks instead of struggling through your classes."

Kevin feigned a deep hurt. "Highness, those neophytes need to know as much about the problems they will encounter on trips as they know about defense. You're just jealous because they always slept through your sermons on how to wear the ceremonial swords at parades."

"Why do I let you hang around with me you insolent slob? Ceremony and protocol is just as important as the latest dictatorial uprising in Outer Mongolia or somewhere. And I'm not jealous of anyone who wasn't even given a ceremonial sword because everyone was afraid he would hurt himself with it!"

"Sticks and stones... ."

Deidre and Celia nodded their heads at each other in resignation as the two men continued to exchange barbs with each other. Deidre had long ago decided that Kevin was the only person Isha could totally be himself around. These two men shared a rare friendship. She really enjoyed their good-natured sparring and Celia seemed to take it all in stride.

The joking ended as the tram pulled to the royal quarters. It seemed a full day had already passed, but it was only 9:30 a.m. in Exeter.

* * * * *

Five minutes after entering the royal quarters, Isha came out wearing blue jeans and a denim shirt. It took Deidre longer to change back into her above ground clothes. Isha took the extra time to speak to the King about Maria's condition and comments. He had a suggestion that Annu liked. Deidre came in as the two men finished their conversation. "Good luck with Mrs. O'Leary, Father."

"Thank you, my children. I am sure that somehow Maria will get the better of me." Laughing, he said, "I do however have the final control. If I can't handle her questions, I can always order her put in the sleep chamber. That way she can rest until I am smart enough to deal with her."

"Sorry, Father. We don't have that kind of time. She'll always be one step ahead of us. Just tell her everything. I'm convinced that explaining Exeter and her son's relationship will be easier than you expect. She has a strong spirit."

"As did her son, and does her granddaughter. Be careful up there."

Isha and Deidre got off the tram at a new station. It was still under construction, but usable. "Where are we?"

"My father wanted a station here, and what he requests usually happens fairly quickly. Come on and I'll show you why." The couple climbed a series of steep ladders until they rested on a landing. "This will soon be an elevator shaft to the tram station. Come on, we have just a little farther to go." Taking Deidre's hand, Isha led her a few steps farther into the sunlight. A short distance below Deidre could see her grandmother's lake and home. "It seems this shaft has always been here. My father helped design the tram system to this part of the caverns. He figured someday your father would inherit Mrs. O'Leary's home, and he wanted to have a convenient passage for visits. When your father's accident ended that dream, my father ordered the tram station closed. Now he's having it completed. I guess he hopes that you and your grandmother might want to come to Exeter on occasion. I know that's my hope."

Deidre squeezed the hand that she held. "I can't think of anything I would want more."

The entrance to the tunnel the young couple left was hidden well by foliage. Isha knew that engineers would soon have a secret passage designed and in place that would be impossible to see if you walked just feet from it. Isha stopped Deidre as she came in the back door of the house. "There are a few changes to the house since you left. Here is one of them." A small touch pad was mounted on the wall next to the door. "We installed a complete security system into the house. It's monitored by the same control organization that protects all entrances to Exeter. If there were ever a need again, a whole army would be here in minutes. Now I don't have to worry about you and your grandmother being here alone."

Deidre put her arms around Isha's neck. Her eyes looked adoringly into his as she pulled his lips down to hers for a long tender kiss. Releasing her pressure just a little she whispered, "I can't imagine why you're so concerned about our safety."

"Because you're special to me. I hope sooner or later to prove that to you." Isha smiled at Deidre.

A naughty thought immediately formed in Deidre's mind. "You don't have to wait, your highness. How would it be if I took a few minutes of your valuable time to show you how special you are to me?"

"And just what do you have in mind?"

"I'll give you a hint." She paused for a moment then began unbuttoning her blouse. "Perhaps you can figure out what I'm thinking."

"I'm a fairly perceptive guy," he answered. With those words, Isha gently kissed Deidre. His hands moved down to finish the job she had begun.

* * * * *

Almost an hour later, as Deidre was modestly covering herself with a sheet, she watched Isha with unabashed fascination. He was standing next to the bed pulling on his shorts. The prince looked up to see her studying him. "Miss, weren't you ever taught it's not nice to stare?"

"Sorry, sir. I was really thinking if I could entice you to join me again?"

Isha laughed. "Tempting - really tempting." He glanced at his watch. "However, in about half an hour a team of workers will be stopping by. I really would rather meet them fully dressed. I'm funny like that."

"Workers? What kind of workers?"

"I'll explain later, but for now would you be kind enough to stop tempting me. Putting some clothes back on would be a good start."

"Yes, your highness. Your wish is my command." With that, she slowly pulled the sheet down.

Isha glanced again at his watch as he got back into the bed. "Hopefully, the team will be punctual, not early."

Fourteen

Isha and Deidre soon finished the task of getting everything they needed for staying in Exeter. Just as they were leaving, six men showed up. Isha took them into the house, stayed a moment and then returned to Deidre. The couple walked to the hidden passage and were on a tram within ten minutes of leaving the back door.

At noon, Deidre visited her grandmother in the hospital chamber to bring her the clothes from home. When she got there, the nurse told Deidre that Maria was in the library.

Deidre found the old woman sitting in a rocking chair, reading a romance novel. Maria looked up, obviously pleased, when the young lady walked up. "Deidre, look at what a young man just brought me. It's the book that I've been reading at home. It was on my bedside table. He just told me that Isha had sent it. How did he know I wanted my book?"

"He just seems to always know things like that." Deidre honestly couldn't remember Isha going into Maria's bedroom, but like so many other of his abilities, he just was able to accomplish anything he wanted.

Nothing else was said about the book.

Twenty minutes later, a doctor came to see Mrs. O'Leary. "Ma'am, the nurse told me you were in here. It's my opinion that you're strong enough to leave our hospital. I want you to take it very easy for the next week or so, and I want to see you in a week for some final checks before I turn you completely loose."

"Leave? I finally get to go home?" Maria was excited to hear that her hospital stay was ending.

"You're not exactly going home. We feel like you need another few days of care before you're ready to be alone. So, it's been decided..."

"It's been decided that you will come and stay with Isha and me for a few days." King Annu had walked up just in time to rescue the doctor from Mrs. O'Leary's famous cross-examination. The King had been to see Maria several times in the past few days. He had tactfully avoided almost all of her questions regarding where she was. After a while, Maria would ask about something, and then she would answer her own question by saying, "Yes, I know. We'll talk about that later." It had become a standing joke between them.

Now was the time for them to have that talk. Deidre tactfully left her grandmother and the King. Annu walked Maria to a settee. He was clearly nervous about the coming conversation, but looked Mrs. O'Leary in the eyes and started.

Over the next two hours, no one dared enter the library. King Annu began by telling the story of how John O'Leary saved his life. He then described in some detail how their friendship had developed over the years. Finally, he told Maria about Exeter. He had decided that she would probably not comprehend the immensity of the subterranean civilization. When Annu was finished, he waited. Maria had listened silently the entire time, never interrupting. Now he expected her to inundate him with questions. Instead, she said, "Take me to see this beautiful place," she paused, considering how to address Annu, and then finished, "your Highness." The old woman looked around the room. "I've thought for some time that things here were not as they seemed, but never would have conceived of anything as remarkable as Exeter sounds."

"My lady, those are the best words you could have chosen. My people have long waited to meet the mother of their favorite outsider. I believe you will be pleased with what you see. Also, everyone in Exeter calls me by my title except my family. I have already told Deidre, and now I tell you, I would consider it an honor if you would just call me Annu." The inferred adoption into the royal family was obvious.

* * * * *

The King's tram was seen throughout Exeter for the next several hours. Long before Maria gave out, Annu was ready to return to his chamber. He knew she was tiring. He also realized the doctor would not be happy if Maria returned in a less than fully rested condition. The King had assured the staff that Maria would be kept quiet and calm. He laughed when they said this because he was fully aware that they had been unable to keep her quiet and calm. He also was keenly mindful that the entire hospital staff had become protective of this plucky octogenarian.

It was approaching 6:00 p.m. when Isha and Deidre met the tram outside the royal chambers. Maria hugged the Prince and kissed her granddaughter on both cheeks. "Isha, why didn't you tell me about this wonderful place when we first met. I might have shooed Deidre away and tried to make a pass at you myself!" Everyone laughed.

"Mrs. O'Leary, you made me feel welcome in your home, and now it's my chance to repay your hospitality. Come on in. We've made some preparations for your arrival. I hope you enjoy your time with us."

The chamber was ready for Maria. She was escorted to the room where she was to sleep, but she stopped at the door. Every inch of the area had been transformed into her bedroom at home. Prince Isha escorted her in. "In the hospital, you said that the only thing you wanted was to sleep in your own bed. Well, here it is. And we decided that you might feel more comfortable in familiar surroundings, so we also decided to bring the rest of your furnishings here."

The room was complete down to the pictures on the wall. "This was Annu's and Isha's idea," Deidre said. "They wanted you to feel at home."

Silent tears rolled down the wrinkled cheeks. "It's so good to have a big family again." She hugged Annu. "You will never replace John. I miss him everyday. But, I know now that I again have a son. Thank you." The weariness in Maria's eyes revealed the depth of her fatigue. "If it's ok with you, I'd like to rest for a while. This has been a very eventful day for an old woman like me. Thank you again for all you've done for Deidre and me." Annu walked Maria into her chamber.

Isha was now completely sure that his decision to bring the ladies to Exeter that night was the correct one. It seemed weeks instead of just days ago, but so much had happened. Without consciously planning it, the Prince took Deidre's hand and squeezed it. Her squeeze in return almost startled him. He looked down at the young lady, and then put his arm around her shoulder. Nothing could possibly disturb the moment.

The Prince was wrong. Five minutes later, Maria was asleep. Shortly, the men and Deidre were talking in the living area when a messenger came to the chamber. "Sire, we believe that one of the Protectors has been killed in Germany." He handed the King a page of green tinted paper. Annu read it silently.

"It says here that the death is only assumed." There was more of a question in his voice than an accusation. "Get more definite information from our people over there, and get back to me."

Annu returned to the family area and asked Isha to join him for a minute. Once they were in the King's private chamber, Annu showed the note to his son, and asked, "Who do we have in that area?" Isha, realizing that the King's question was rhetorical, didn't answer.

In a corner of the King's room was a small alcove. Both men went in and closed the door. Annu opened a drawer in the table and removed his laptop computer. The older man opened the top and adjusted the attached micro-camera. He typed a password on the screen and waited. Five seconds later, the screen showed the computer was online. Annu consulted a worn leather notebook to find the name and secure URL address for the person he wanted to contact. As the king typed in the code, he mentally chastised himself. *There was a time when I knew every Protector anywhere in the world. Now I have to check a book!* He was still fussing at himself when a face appeared on the monitor. The woman appeared to have just awakened.

Without waiting, King Annu spoke, "Kristi, I'm sorry to waken you. But I have a problem here and may need your help."

A flawless young face peered back at Annu on the screen. "Your Highness, it's not a problem. How can I assist you, Sir?"

"Kristi, I've just been told one of our Protectors has had an accident in Germany. I know it's early there in Edinburgh, and I'm sorry to get you up, but we need to have someone standing by for contingency purposes."

"Sir, do you have any details?"

"Not yet. I'll have the communications section transmit everything to you. They'll have his cover and itinerary ready. I'll get back with you. Thanks."

The young woman's face could not hide a deep and instantaneous concern. It was obvious she wanted to ask more, but controlled herself. "Yes sir. As soon as I have the facts I'll be back with you. If something comes up, do you want me to use regular channels, or to use this mode?" "Call me direct. I'll be standing by. Thank you, again, Kristi." Annu shut down the machine, and closed the cover.

* * * * *

Annu would not get too far away from his chamber until there was more information on the loss of his man. Isha took the time to explain the situation to Deidre. "I know you've been wondering about our Protectors. In the ancient days, the Protectors were quite literally our first line of defense. They were the Green Berets, SEALS, and SAS of their day. Whenever an enemy was stalking us, they would meet the enemy far off and defeat them before there was a threat to the actual tribe. Now, since we have virtually no threat of invasion, when a Protector graduates he or she is sent out to live among the Outworlders. They all have skills and training that make them fit into the society where they live." Deidre had sat and listened attentively. Isha paused to give her a chance to ask a question or make a comment. She did neither, so he continued. "Now, our Protectors have a more subtle purpose. They still guard our homeland, but they also work in your world above to help there, too. At the risk of destroying some of your historical education, it has often been our Protectors who have made discoveries that you now take for granted. You might be surprised to know that many of the inventors whose discoveries you've studied since first grade were, in fact, our people working above."

"Do you mean inventions like the sleep chamber?" Deidre asked tentatively.

"Sure, and countless others that you use everyday. Our revelations to the Outworld never are meant to help just one country. We are, by tradition, non-aligned politically. For example, we never use Protectors to fight or defend other countries – not even the United States. It is our custom and heritage that we owe allegiance to no nation. Remember, we were here before the United States was."

"If Protectors live all around the world, how do you handle such things as passports, and customs, and a million other details? You just don't go and live in a foreign country without going through some sort of immigration process. How do you handle that problem?"

To answer the question the Prince walked over to a desk and sat down. He motioned for Deidre to sit beside him. "When and where were you born?" he asked.

"May 21, 1985 in Temple, Texas. My dad had finished medical school and was doing a surgical residency there."

Isha picked up a phone and dialed a number from memory. "Good evening," he said to whomever answered, "I need a birth certificate for Miss Deidre O'Leary, born May 21, 1985, in Temple, Texas." He paused, listening for a moment before continuing. "No, a copy will be fine. Thank you. Good night." He hung up the phone and motioned to Deidre to follow him to a laser printer. From the printer tray, Isha removed a piece of paper, and handed it to Deidre. "Miss O'Leary, I believe you'll find this to be a copy of your actual birth certificate from the State Bureau of Public Records in Austin. I could, if you wish, have an original here in a hour or so." He smiled at the look on the young woman's face.

"How can you forge something that quickly?"

"It's not a forgery. It is a true copy of your actual birth certificate. But to answer your question, we do it like everything in the world today. Computers. Not only can we retrieve information, but if we need to, we can create it. If a Protector needs to be from Nevada, or Nova Scotia, or a small country village in Suffolk, England, we can make it happen. Each Protector who leaves Exeter to live above does so with a complete "life". There are military records, college transcripts, job resumes, and even credit histories placed in appropriate computers. All the files are complete and cross-referenced. As far as the world above can tell, our Protectors were born, raised, educated, and have worked all their lives above; even if they just arrived yesterday."

Deidre sat amazed for a moment. Her mind struggled with what she was seeing. "Just when I think you couldn't do another thing to surprise me, you show me something like this." Suddenly her brow furrowed in thought. "Isn't it illegal to just create a person like that?"

"I suppose that it could be construed as illegal," Isha answered honestly, "but we believe our gifts to the above world more than make up for the slight bending of local laws."

Deidre decided that her concerns were probably unfounded. Who am I to question Exeter's methods, she thought. Her contemplation was interrupted when King Annu came into the room.

"Isha, I've just gotten word that Ron Warren has been confirmed murdered in Germany. He was traveling as a Russian student. Ron was able to call us before he died. Because his message was so confusing it took the communications team a while to figure it out. We also know that the hospital where he was taken contacted the Russian embassy right after Ron called us. That message has been intercepted and translated. There's a courier on his way here with a transcript of the Embassy call, and a tape of Ron's message. I've got to go and see his parents. I want you to stay here and take the transcript for me."

Isha nodded his understanding. He knew Ron was a new Protector, probably only twenty-four or five years old. He had lived in Russia for the past year, and was about to move to Germany. Suddenly a disturbing thought came to Isha. Ron was still "Russian", but had a new "German" identity also been established? That could be a real problem if someone did a little background inquiry on the murder victim. Isha called the computer section and determined that no new identity had been established. Isha told the specialists to do a quick check of Ron's files to make sure they would pass the check both the German and Russian investigations that were sure to follow. With that accomplished, Isha sat with Deidre until the messenger arrived.

Fifteen

It took a half hour for the courier to appear at the Royal Chambers. Isha noted that a Protector was carrying the paper. It was unusual to have such a messenger, but Isha knew why he was carrying the dispatch. The Brotherhood of Protectors was already mourning the loss of a fellow warrior. The tape with Ron's last phone call was also delivered. Isha first opened the written transcript of the Hospital to Embassy call.

....

Transcript of Conversation Between
Doctor Christoph Rausch & The Russian Embassy
in Bonn, Germany
RE: Protector Ron Warren (AKA Petrov Sergie)
20 October, 2009
Call Initiated 1007 UTC (0407 Local Exeter Time)
E = Embassy Personnel
CR = Doctor Christoph Rausch
(Translator's comments in parentheses)
(Translated by J.M. Parish 1406 UTC)

E -   Russian Embassy, Michola Gabonovich speaking. May I direct your call?

CR - This is Doctor Christoph Rausch calling from Ingolstadt. I have a male patient here who has been hurt badly. He is carrying a Russian passport and says he is from the Siberian frontier. He's lost a great deal of blood. To be honest, I do not expect him to survive his injuries. (Pause of four seconds)

E -   One moment Herr Doctor. (clicking sound - possibly from call transfer) (Pause of twenty-two seconds) (new voice) Herr Doctor, I am Vannest Valisostov, the Deputy Attaché for the Russian Ambassador. Would you be so kind as to tell me about your patient?

CR - His papers and picture identify him as Petrov Sergie. He has suffered two gunshot wounds. On a secondary level he also has numerous contusions, and abrasions. To be specific, one projectile entered the upper left quadrant of the torso and exited through the shoulder area. This caused a pneumothorax, or collapsed lung. It also started an internal hemorrhage. The second wound was to the lower right quadrant of the torso. This damaged the ascending colon and part of the small intestine. It appears that after he was shot, Mr. Sergie was thrown off a moving train and left for dead by his attackers. When he was brought here, Mr. Sergie was in hypovolemic shock. If the young man were not so healthy, he would not have survived this long.

E -   Excuse me Doctor. I must confess a certain ignorance as to the medical terms. You said he was hypo-something.

CR- My apologies – hypovolemic means he was suffering from extreme blood loss.

E - You also said that he is very critical. Can you tell me what his chances of survival are?

CR - He's now in surgery. I treated him initially in the emergency ward. Even though I was able to stabilize him initially, I honestly do not expect him to survive long. Perhaps if he had gotten to us sooner or not lost so much blood, we could have done more. I assure you we are doing all that is possible. The surgeon who is performing the work is one of the best. When I left the surgical theater, he was not optimistic. There is a great deal of injury.

E. - Herr Doctor, we certainly appreciate all you have done for our countryman. Please do not think that I am questioning your opinion or actions. I must merely consider what my superiors will need to know. Has he told you anything that would explain his injuries?

CR - I did not talk with him long before we had to operate. He was in a great deal of pain, and would only say he was a student traveling on the train to Munchen when two men shot him. His conversations were somewhat erratic. From what he said, I suspect he saw something he was not supposed to see. It appears he discovered someone trying to smuggle something into Germany.

E - Do you believe he knows who the assailants are?

CR - No. I am certain he does not know who shot him. One thing he most definitely is aware of, whatever he saw has him most agitated. He refused to tell me, but he kept saying, 'It's a complete system.' Does that mean anything to you?

E - Honestly, no it does not. Obviously, this is a matter for the local police. I will send a representative from the Embassy to you immediately, but I recommend you also call the authorities.

CR - I have already done so. A gunshot requires me to notify the police. Mr. Sergie is a remarkable young man. In spite of the blood loss and pain, he refused any surgery until we allowed him to speak by telephone with someone here in the area. He was most adamant. Normally, I would not have allowed it, but he became extremely belligerent. It was obvious the only way I would easily treat him was to give in, so I dialed the phone. I was nearby, but missed most of his short conversation. I did notice he spoke English. I imagine he will have a friend here soon.

E - English? You said Mr. Sergie was a student? He probably contacted another student. Please write down that phone number for us. It would help if we need to contact Mr. Sergie's friend.

CR - I noted the number in Mr. Sergie's medical record as a possible emergency contact. It will be available should you need it. If Mr. Sergie does not survive, after the authorities are complete, do you wish me to release his remains, or wait for your representative?

E - Please ask our German friends not to release Mr. Sergie's body. I will inquire of our passport control officer and see where his family is. We will need first to inform them of the tragedy. Doctor Rausch, our country appreciates the care you gave Mr. Sergie. I will be back in contact with you very soon. Good day, Herr Doctor.

CR - Good day, sir. (Break of contact)

Call Completed 1014 UTC (0414 Local Exeter Time)

....

Isha was certain that by now the authorities were investigating the homicide. German police had an earned reputation for being very thorough. They would not release Ron's body until they were finished with their initial inquiry. That meant it might be several days before someone from Exeter could pose as a relative and bring his body home. The Prince made a mental note to verify with the external security section that those arrangements were being made.

* * * * *

King Annu returned within a few hours to his home. The strain was evident upon his face. To Ron's family, the news of their only son's death was compounded by the fact that he had been murdered. Annu was there not as the King, but as a father who grieved with them. There was no attempt on the warrior's part to be regal. He knew the value of being with these people in their loss. It weighed on him, too.

Isha and his father sat down with a snifter of brandy and the tape of Ron's last phone call. They both knew he was probably aware his wounds were fatal, so expected the call to be difficult to hear. A file folder with Ron's picture, and resume were open before them. As the words began, Deidre took a sip of Isha's drink, winced, then got some wine, and joined the men on the couch.

"This is Petrov Sergie," the voice was weak and strained. "I have been hurt and am in a hospital in Ingolstadt. Please send a helper for me. There is a hard situation going on. I can't tell you what, but my best friend in training had a nickname for this. I...". The voice faded. Another voice was almost inaudible in the background. Ron was arguing with the person. "I have to make this call first, you can have me afterwards. Now leave me for one minute." There were several seconds of silence. Then the voice returned, this time stronger. "I am not sure if I will be able to go much longer. Please tell my parents that I love them. Don't let me die for nothing. Stop them before they can move it." There was a click followed by the dial tone.

The tape was silent for a moment and a new voice came on. "This is Reems. I received Ron's call at 0931 UTC. I've canceled this phone number in the telephone computer system to protect the safe area, and will await information on Ron's condition before acting. Let me know what you want me to do. I'll stand by."

Annu listened to the tape again, then a third time. "The communications section is still considering Ron's tape. Obviously the free text comment meant he did not feel he could directly say what he saw."

Isha exhaled audibly. He explained to Deidre, "We use the expression 'hard situation' to describe one that is dangerous." He sat there looking at the ceiling for a moment. "I can't remember. Who was Ron's best friend during Protector training?"

It was at this time that Kevin came to the chambers. He had already heard about the death of a fellow Protector.

"Kevin, do you remember who was Ron's mentor? I need to call him and find out who was Ron's best friend."

"You don't need to call him. I worked with that class for a few weeks at the end of training. He and Elise Diamond were pals."

"That's right! Elise! What did Ron mean by his best friend having a nickname for his situation?"

"Elise had an unfortunate history of breaking things in training. They nicknamed her 'Nuke, the Destroyer' as a joke."

The four people all reached the same realization at about the same time. Annu was the first to speak. "Would Ron recognize a nuclear weapon if he saw it? I know I wouldn't."

Kevin nodded. "Sire, the Protectors have seen samples of almost every kind of device they might encounter in the world. Some have worked in military nuclear areas. To answer your question, I can't be sure if Ron would recognize a weapon, but it would be my guess that he could."

"Father," Isha continued, "Ron obviously saw something. Maybe he just heard something. But there is no doubt that he believed a nuclear bomb was on that train. What do you think we need to do?"

"Wait until we hear from our people in Europe. They will have touched all the intelligence agencies files before calling us. Until then we rest."

Sixteen

Colin Johnson's face showed the strain of the past several days. London was his favorite city in the world, but this had not been a favorite assignment. His position in the Embassy had made his real job too difficult.

Johnson's work with the CIA had come about after two tours in the US Air Force Office of Special Investigations (OSI). He had a distinguished career with several outstanding decorations – all of them fictitious.

Colin Johnson was a Protector. The CIA had recruited him after his predecessor, also a Protector, retired. For the past twenty-five years, Exeter made sure they always had a Protector in a key position of The Company. It was a perfect way for Exeter to influence the intelligence community of the entire world.

An extensive background check on Johnson by the FBI had revealed one speeding ticket in New Jersey that had resulted in a $135 fine. He had no credit problems and appeared to live within his means. The investigation showed that his parents were both deceased, and he had no brothers or sisters.

In reality, his parents were both alive in Exeter and he had two younger sisters.

Despite the fact that his entire career was based on a fake computer generated history, Johnson had been an excellent intelligence officer for the CIA. His quick discerning mind was perfect for the job of taking minute bits of disjointed information and collating them into a logical pattern.

When he was first assigned to the American embassy, Johnson had been told that no one in London was to know he was really with the CIA. He argued vehemently with the Operations Director at Langley to allow him to divulge his CIA job to the embassy personnel. It made no sense to him that two government entities could possibly have secrets from each other, especially in a foreign country. The CIA Station Chief not so patiently explained to Johnson that it was not up to him to make policy. Johnson, however, continued to make his point-of-view known up the chain of command. Supervisor after supervisor refused to change the policy. Finally, the Deputy Director of Operations himself heard of this young agent who was being a nuisance by questioning standard procedures. The DDO called Colin to his office.

"Johnson," he asked, "just what the hell do you mean bothering everyone in the organization with your damn demands? Don't you think we've done this once or twice before?" The DDO's inflection and volume both got higher as he warmed to his ass chewing. "We tell who we want when we want about what we want. Is that clear? I've spent the past forty-five minutes looking through your file trying to figure out how we let a troublemaker into the ranks. Just where do you get off trying to change everything around here?"

"Sir, I just think I could be more effective if the embassy staff knew about my work with the CIA. I wouldn't have to always be looking over my shoulders."

The old man gave one of his famous grandfatherly looks. His tone was softened somewhat. "Colin, you've never had an assignment like this but an embassy has more leaks than a sieve. If you tell one bureaucrat something, they have to prove their importance by telling another bureaucrat. Pretty soon every one of the cretins knows, and their wives know, and their wives boyfriends know, and it just gets out of hand." The old man paused for a second and smiled benignly. "I've got to admit something to you, I like a man who stands his ground when he thinks something is right. Let me consider your proposal."

Just before Colin left for England, a decision was made that the American Ambassador to the Court of Saint James was to be informed about Johnson's CIA connection. Only the Ambassador was to know. Richard Nail was specifically excluded from the information. His reputation for being a difficult and self-important individual made the decision necessary.

Fortunately, Johnson's CIA work had been limited to making updated reports of current files on the many anti-American groups with ties to the United Kingdom. His position as Intelligence Chief in the Embassy had been a great front. Everyone expected him to keep abreast of current international events. No one, except the American Ambassador, knew to whom Johnson disseminated his information.

Colin Johnson had often laughed to himself about the irony of his situation. He was, in fact, living three, not two, lives. To some, he was a CIA operative, to others, a State Department employee, but in reality, he was a citizen of another civilization altogether. No one in the United States government would ever have imagined that possibility.

Colin Johnson and Geoffrey Singer were finishing a snack of traditional fish and chips in the subterranean bowels of DI6. The two had been working virtually non-stop for nine hours. It was just after midnight, and both men were exhausted. This was the first time they had even stopped to eat. Fatigue and frustration dogged both men. "Geoff," Colin said while taking a mouth full of chips, "Do you think this madman can really smuggle a weapon into the West?"

Geoffrey Singer thought carefully before answering. "With enough money, almost anything is possible. The one thing Azmud Salomi has is an almost limitless supply of oil money. I think we have to go on the assumption that he has the capability. Now, our biggest hurdle is determining how he will do it, not if he can do it."

"I know, but until we can get some more definitive information on how the device was smuggled, we won't be able to make valid assumptions."

"We'll just have to keep working until more details and intelligence comes in. That's all we can do. Do you need to check in with the Embassy?"

"That's the one bright spot in this situation," Johnson answered. "I got to tell Richard Nail that I wasn't going to be in for a few days. He had already been informed that I was transferred to New Scotland Yard, and man, was he ready to hit the roof. He demanded to know what I was doing."

"I hope you told him he could go sod himself?"

"I wasn't quite that colorful. No, all I said was that my attention was required with some intelligence material at New Scotland Yard. I told him that I was not at liberty to discuss it."

"That jackass hates being left out of anything because he's convinced that he is the epicenter of that Embassy. He's nothing but a bureaucratic bozo, and every diplomat in London knows it."

Colin smiled in spite of himself. He enjoyed it when Geoffrey Singer became passionate about a subject because his use of non-diplomatic expressions was far more eloquent. "Well," Colin finished, "there wasn't much the man could say. The Ambassador himself was the one who informed him. Sir Patrick must have called the CIA Director as soon as he left here, and someone at the State Department must have been called seconds later. Nothing in Washington happens that quickly." Both men laughed. Johnson continued, "I would have loved to hear Nail's arguments to the Ambassador about how important I was to the Vice President's visit. Just a month or so ago, Nail was trying to have me relieved because he said the Intelligence Chief job should be handled by his staff. I guess the Ambassador reminded him of that."

"I once had a friend who said that looking good is a full-time job. With people like your Mr. Nail, looking good is a full-time job of taking credit for other's work. But don't worry; you Yanks don't have the exclusive possession to those types of people. Her Majesty's government is also full of them."

Johnson stretched fully. "Listen, Geoff, I'm calling it a day, or is it night out there. I've lost track. Let's meet back here in eight hours."

"Agreed. I could use some sleep myself."

The two men entered the elevator for the ride up to the street level. As the door opened, Geoff and Colin found themselves facing five security agents instead of the usual three. Johnson realized there was a potential problem for later. "Will those gorillas out there let me near this elevator when I come back?"

"Yes. Sir Patrick has given you full access to anything in this area. There will be an ID card and personal code available for you at the entrance when you return. We've used our file on you for verification information. I hope all the lies I've told about you the past three years are at least remotely accurate."

"I'm sure your info on me is about as correct as mine is on you." The men both laughed. "If this situation wasn't so dangerous, it would be hilarious."

Colin seriously considered going to Rimi's flat, but decided he really needed sleep, not companionship for the evening. It was now approaching 1:00 a.m., and his body craved rest.

Colin slowly walked the four blocks to Vauxhall Tube Station. Just prior to descending the stairs to the lower levels, three strangers approached. Years of training as a Protector had honed the man's survival skills. Johnson knew immediately that he was in danger. He carefully backed up to a wall to prevent the men from getting behind him. Quickly the men fanned out in front of their intended victim. "Gentlemen," the American spoke softly, "you don't want to do this. It will not go the way you want it to."

"Looks like we got ourselves a bleeding Yank," the largest man laughed. He looked on either side to his two cohorts and then back at Colin. "We appreciate your concern for our safety, bloke, but what we really want is your wallet." The man's inflection hardened. "Now, let's have it."

Colin Johnson's voice became even quieter. "Let me see if I understand this. You three are officially robbing me? I mean when I talk about this later, I want to make sure of my story." There was a hint of humor in his tone.

"You're a cool one, Yank! But, trust me, I have every intention of spending your pound notes on several pints of bitter at some pub very shortly."

"Well, now that we have that settled, if you are going to have that beer tonight. You'll have to... ." Right in the middle of his sentence, Colin pulled his right foot up and kicked out into the knee of the man on his right. There was an audible snap as the man's knee was broken and displaced. The resulting pain was excruciating. As the thug fell, Johnson pivoted and struck him in the jaw with his left open palm.

Almost simultaneously, Colin rotated and kicked out with his left foot hitting the second man in the head twice in rapid succession. The two roundhouse kicks dropped the man like a stone.

Only one brute remained standing; the one who had done all the talking. He was now alone with his intended victim. The other two hoodlums were crumpled up on the sidewalk. Colin looked down at them then up. "All right, it's your turn. Do you still want my wallet, friend?"

As an answer, the robber lifted a four-foot long hickory stick that had been used as a cane. There was fury in his eyes. "Mate, I'll have your wallet or your blood."

"I was afraid you might say something like that. All right, but remember, I did give you the option."

"Damn it, give me your friggin wallet, Yank!" The stick was raised.

Before the cane reached its apogee, Johnson hit his opponent with an open palm into the middle of the sternum. A look of surprise registered on the face of the mugger. He only had that look for a moment. Johnson used the other open palm to strike the man point-blank into the jaw. The shock was enough to knock the man out cold.

The entire event had lasted less than thirty seconds. Colin Johnson stepped over the unconscious men and entered the Vauxhall Station. He found a bobby there and told him that three drunks were sleeping outside the station.

It took Johnson half an hour to get to his flat. It was in a quiet section of North London. He liked it that way. As he opened the front door, Colin checked that the alarm system was still armed, and punched the proper code to disarm it. Like most commercial home units, the alarm was essentially just a warning device. Colin knew that any criminal worth the name could easily defeat this security system. In reality, it was simply a smoke screen to cover a more sophisticated system. It took Colin a couple of seconds to disarm the secondary alarm pad that was concealed behind a hidden panel. Involved were infrared and motion detectors. If activated, they would flood the room with an instantaneous, but short-term, knockout gas, and use shielded phone lines to notify the police. Colin felt funny about having all this security when he never had classified material at the apartment, but it was normal procedure for CIA members stationed overseas.

Johnson had been home for several minutes when he remembered to check his answering machine. Man, I must be tired, he thought. Normally, checking his messages was the first thing he did after coming in.

"Colin, this is Kristi," a familiar voice spoke from the machine. "I really need to talk with you. It's important. Call me as soon as you can. I'm home."

There were several other messages, but the one from Kristi really caught Colin's attention. There was desperation to her voice that was unusual. Colin glanced at his watch and wondered whether or not it was too late to call. He was still deciding when the phone rang.

"Colin, I'm glad you're there." It was Kristi. "I've been talking with home, and we've had a tragedy. King Annu needs some information, and I think you may be in a position to help me."

The mention of the King's name set off mental alarms and made Johnson immediately halt the conversation. "Kristi, give me a few minutes. I'll call you back on the scrambler."

Colin Johnson went into his bedroom. His bedside table had a false front that opened to reveal a safe. Turning the dial three times, Colin worked the combination and released the heavy lugs securing the door. The first thing he removed from the safe was a small black box. Colin walked around the room with the box and noted an indicator that was on the front. Had any bugs, recording devices, or radio transmitters been present, their electromagnetic signatures would have been evident to Johnson. Certain the apartment was secure, Colin took a telephone from the safe and plugged it into a machine similar to the one on the secure line at the Embassy. Unlike the Embassy machine, this one, designed and manufactured in Exeter, was several times more efficient at producing transmissions that were protected from unauthorized listening. Colin dialed Kristi's number in Edinburgh. She answered on the first ring.

"Ok, we're free to talk now. The King called you? What's the problem?"

"Colin," Kristi was now choking back her tears, "we've lost a Protector in Germany. The communications section told me it was Ron Warren – he was murdered." Now that the words were out, Kristi allowed the emotion she had been controlling to finally come free.

Johnson didn't say anything for several seconds. Kristi was the only other Protector in the United Kingdom, and Colin was sure she probably knew the murdered man. He waited for her to speak.

"His Highness has asked me to get as much information as possible. Exeter is sending me the transcript of Ron's last call to our safe number, and a transcript of the phone call between some doctor in Germany and the Russian Embassy. It must concern Ron somehow. If you want, when I get them, I can send them to you over this line."

Colin Johnson thought for several seconds before answering. "Yeah, send them to me. I'll wait up." He again paused before continuing. "Are you ok, Kristi?"

"Ron, – we were engaged," she sobbed quietly. "We were together for the last two years of training, and were going to get married next year when he started his new work. Exeter had already given me permission to work in Germany with him. We would have been the first husband and wife Protector team!" The tears were flowing now. Johnson could hear her struggling to regain her composure over the phone.

"Kristi, does the King know about you and Ron?"

"No. I'm sure he would never have asked me to get the details of Ron's death if he had known."

Johnson made a quick decision. "Kristi, I want you to pack some clothes. You'll come and stay here for a few days. Anything that requires your attention can be accomplished from my place. You don't need to be alone."

The silence on the other end told Colin that she was wondering what to do. He continued, "Listen Kristi, you're my friend. Now, pack. It'll take me about two hours to get a plane up there."

"Thank you, Colin. It's kind of you. I don't know what to say." The softness of her voice exposed the pain she was feeling.

"We're Protectors. Remember? We belong to each other. Now get ready. I'll be there to pick you up soon."

Johnson broke the connection and then established a satellite link with the King's chamber. It only took a few moments for Annu to answer. Very briefly Colin explained the situation to his ruler. King Annu regretted the pain he had inadvertently brought Kristi. It bothered him that he had been unaware of their involvement. "Colin, thanks for taking care of Kristi."

"No problem, Sire. We have a plane at Luton Airport that ostensibly belongs to one of your companies over here. I'm going to take it to get her."

"That's a good plan. Let me know if I can help with anything."

"I will, Highness." The London Protector thought about protocol and decorum before continuing. "Sir, this is none of my business, but I know you regret telling Kristi about Ron. You shouldn't. There was no way you could have known, and Sir, she doesn't blame you."

"Well, thanks, Colin. I should have been aware of something as important as a wedding between two of my Protectors. Take care of her for me."

"I'll do that, Sir. Johnson out." The connection was immediately broken.

* * * * *

Colin napped as he was driven by taxi to the Luton Airport a few miles north of London. He had called a couple of local pilots for the trip. The flight plan had been filed, walk-around inspection on the plane accomplished, and pre-start checklist finished all before he arrived. This meant that they were taxiing for takeoff within five minutes of Johnson's arrival.

Colin had leased an eight passenger business jet for the trip. He was less interested in the luxurious seats in the cabin than he was the speed of the airplane. After a thirty-five minute flight, the pilots began their descent into the Edinburgh airport. Air traffic at this early hour was light, and it took just fifteen additional minutes until the main landing gear were touching down. The transient parking ramp was nearby and a night manager was waiting to meet the jet. Colin gave him quick instructions regarding the servicing of the plane, and then went into the hanger office to call Kristi.

Instead he found her waiting. Her chocolate brown eyes were swollen from crying, but she still smiled when Colin walked in. "Thanks for this, Colin."

"You're welcome, and don't worry about it. You can do your work in London just as well as you could here. Besides, I'll enjoy having your company."

By the time the pair returned to the plane, it had been refueled and a flight plan returning to London had been filed. The cruise back was uneventful. Kristi had her seat reclined back almost flat and was asleep right after takeoff.

Colin wished he could be sleeping, too, but his mind was too active. He knew within a few hours he would be back with Geoff Singer working on the nuclear warhead problem. Finally, Johnson forced himself to relax, and he fell into a light sleep.

The two protectors were at Colin's home by five fifteen in the morning. Almost before they were out of the Luton Airport, Colin had fallen asleep in the cab. Kristi had his head in her lap all the way to the flat.

Once inside, Colin took Kristi's luggage to his guest room and she went in to unpack her bags. Colin checked in on her a few minutes later and found the bags still full and Kristi sound asleep on the bed.

The emotional strain of the past several hours had worn out her out. Johnson wished they were in Exeter to make use of a sleep chamber for her. He knew she really needed to be home where she could deal with her grief surrounded by family and friends. It was Johnson's plan to have her on a plane to the United States as soon as possible.

The immediate demand on Colin was another hour and a half of sleep. He got undressed and set the alarm on his wristwatch for seven o'clock. Before getting into bed, Johnson considered just how tired he was. As an afterthought, he got out an old wind-up travel clock and set it to ring fifteen minutes after the first alarm. He knew if he slept through the gentle beeping from his watch, the loud bell of the second clock would definitely get him awake. It took less than thirty seconds for Colin to be asleep.

Seventeen

The beeping alarm gently brought Colin Johnson awake. He switched it off and then did the same for the travel clock. He lay there for almost a minute allowing his mind to fully rouse. He got out of bed and quietly moved to the bathroom to shower and shave. Coming out fifteen minutes later, he smelled the distinctive aroma of coffee and bacon. Kristi was in the kitchen and in the process of making breakfast. She looked fresh despite having just a couple hours sleep.

"Sorry I woke you up, Kristi. You should still be in bed." Colin gave her an affectionate hug.

Kristi stood on her tiptoes and kissed Colin on the cheek. "I heard you get up. I've always been a light sleeper. I thought you might like something to eat before you leave."

"Well, I've got to admit it's been awhile since I tasted good home cooking." Colin picked up an extra crisp slice of bacon and chewed it appreciatively. English bacon was usually cut in thick ham slices instead of strips as Americans preferred. Colin had a local butcher slice his into strips. It was one of the few things he did to remind him of home. "How did you know I loved my bacon this way?" he asked facetiously.

A cloud formed over Kristi's face. "That's the way Ron liked me to cook his." She looked immediately on the verge of tears. "He wouldn't eat it if it was what he called wimpy. I'm sorry, Colin. I promised myself I wouldn't be maudlin." She forced a smile on her face. "Anyway, this is the only way I know how to cook bacon. I put it in the skillet until it smells burnt, and then I serve it. Works every time." Her smile fooled neither herself nor Colin. She was hurting desperately, and wouldn't allow herself to grieve here. That would come later.

Colin made up his mind right then. Kristi would be on the next available flight to the United States. He would use his own money if necessary to get her a seat. "Listen, I wish I could skip out on work today, but there are some things I've got to do. Will you be all right here?"

"You know I will. I'll be busy. Annu has asked me to stand by to help him. That'll keep me occupied."

"Ok. Thanks for the breakfast." Colin got up and excused himself. He went into his room and closed the door. He didn't want Kristi to hear his conversation. It only took him a minute to open the bedside safe, connect his secure line to Exeter, and call King Annu. The King's face appeared on the screen after the second ring.

"I'm sorry to awaken you, your Highness. I want your permission to send Kristi to Exeter. She's having a hard time with Ron's death. I think she needs to be home with her family. I'd like to put her on a flight today if possible. American Airlines has a plane out of Gatwick late tonight. With connections in New York, she would reach Exeter by late tomorrow afternoon." Colin waited for the King to consider his answer.

It only took Annu a moment to come up with an alternative idea. "Colin, here's what I want you to do. It appears that we'll be able to recover Ron's body to Exeter by late tonight. I want Kristi here when that happens." The King thought for a second, deciding the best course of action. "I want you to charter a jet to fly her to New York's Kennedy Airport, then on to either Albuquerque or Santa Fe. Let me know when that's done. Use one of our companies to charter the plane. Just make sure she's here as soon as possible."

"I will, Sir. By the way, have we heard any more on how Ron was killed?"

Annu's face showed momentary confusion by the question. "That's right, you were picking up Kristi when we got the first information. It seems he was on a train to Munich. Whoever shot him threw his body off the train in the middle of nowhere. It appears they thought he was already dead, and no one would find the body immediately. A farmer discovered Ron and got him to a hospital. He regained consciousness and before he would let the doctors work on him, Ron made a phone call out to one of our safe areas. He couldn't speak freely, but we have interpreted his cryptic comments to mean that he somehow found or heard about a nuclear weapon on board the train, was caught, and shot. I know that sounds strange, but that's what we think."

Colin Johnson felt a chill run down his spine. For a second he just stared at the screen. Annu looked back with wonder. "Colin, what's the matter?"

"Sire, I need to get back to you. It is at least a possibility that I'm working on something here in London that's tied to Ron's killing. If that is the case, we have a situation that may be truly international."

Annu realized immediately the significance of his Protector's statement. "Keep me informed if you will, Colin."

"I will, and thank you for allowing Kristi to come home. I'll take care of the details of getting her there and report back."

"Kristi needs to be in Exeter. I appreciate you recognizing that fact and suggesting it. Good bye, Colin." The screen went blank. Johnson stared at it for several seconds.

Johnson sat in total silence as he considered King Annu's revelation. Is it possible Ron Warren's death is the common thread to solve the mystery he and Geoffrey Singer were struggling with? The thought kept going through his brain.

Colin put the secure telephone back in the safe, and then used the regular phone to call the Managing Director of a manufacturing firm north of London. He quickly informed the man of Annu's wishes. Colin knew the man would handle the chartering of a jet immediately. While the Managing Director was not a Protector, he was actually from Exeter. Everyone in his company thought he had been born in Mildenhall, Suffolk, raised in

Thetford, and educated at Kings College in Cambridge. Prior to arriving in England twenty years before, the Managing Director had never been to any of those places. Now he really felt at home anywhere in the United Kingdom. When Colin called, speaking for King Annu, the Managing Director immediately used his connections to schedule the newest business jet available. The charter service often flew executives on short notice, so this international flight was nothing special to them. All that mattered to Colin was that Kristi would be clearing customs in New York City before the scheduled commercial flight even took off from Gatwick Airport south of London. She would be in Santa Fe five hours later.

The jet that would fly Kristi home had only been in production since 2006, and cost thirty-one million dollars. The plane could be fitted for up to twenty passengers, but this one was configured to provide fourteen executives with plush surroundings as they flew. It would cruise up to 51,000 feet at almost nine-tenths the speed of sound. Its range of 6,500 nautical miles would easily allow the jet to fly Kristi from London to New York in about five and a half hours with plenty of reserve fuel upon landing. After customs and immigration were cleared, they would use a second set of pilots to fly the five-hour leg into Santa Fe, New Mexico.

Money was not a factor. Annu secretly owned companies in twelve countries. His assets were shrouded by several layers of consortiums and holding banks. Almost all of the companies were run by presidents and CEOs who had impeccable credentials and resumes, but were in reality from Exeter. They handled the day-to-day operations, but their King was the ultimate authority for the businesses.

If he were living above and taking credit for his companies, King Annu would be worth well over two hundred million dollars. Instead of accepting any personal wealth, he used the profits from the companies to send Protectors all over the world and to fund research. He chose instead to live a relatively simple life among his people.

There were times, like now, when Annu used his immense financial resources to help one of his subjects. Annu didn't care that his decision to charter a jet would cost him many times the price of a first class ticket on a scheduled airline. All he cared about was that one of his Protectors was hurting, and needed to be home as soon as possible without the hassles of flying commercially.

Protectors were, the King felt, the best gift Exeter could ever give to the outsiders. Because of their skills and abilities, Protectors had for centuries been pivotal figures in history. Many of the greatest medical and scientific discoveries through the ages had been made by Protectors while living in their assumed identities outside Exeter. The names of these Protectors were known to every school child above. Biographies of these men and women were in libraries around the world. To list just the Nobel Prize winners in the scientific community would have been a formidable task. No one would have ever imagined that these giants of science, medicine, literature, and technology were in fact citizens of another civilization called Exeter.

Generations ago, it had been easier to manage the task of infiltrating a civilization with a Protector. Word of mouth was the primary means of communication. People moved from place to place easily, and Protectors could assume any identity they desired. Today, the job was more difficult because of the computer. The technological sections of Exeter constantly had to develop new methods of incorporating Protectors into societies around the world with complete cross-referenced histories in computers. To be effective, these men and women had to have identities completely established.

Even though Protectors and other members of Exeter lived on every continent and in almost half of the countries of the world, never had one pseudo-identity been compromised. This was a remarkable accomplishment especially considering the sensitive areas many of these men and women worked in. They were involved all over the world with governmental, military and civilian intelligence agencies, scientific and military research and development departments, and even NASA. Knowing the Protector's assumed persona would receive the most complete background investigations made the establishment of identities all the more important. None had ever failed to be authentic in every detail. It was a source of great pride among those who were responsible for fabricating these fictitious lives. Evidence of this elite attitude was a hand painted sign in the work chambers that said:

Only God Can Create the Body, But We Can Create the Person.

The covert placement of these Protectors worldwide was quite possibly facing the closest scrutiny in the history of Exeter.

Eighteen

The Peligroso left the dock with the tide. She was one of nineteen ships from different countries to depart Le Havre that day. Many of them were destined for Mediterranean ports or South America. Six were arriving in the United States. The Peligroso was one of those six. She was scheduled to dock in New York City in eight days.

The fifty kiloton nuclear warhead in her hold was to be armed on that date. After it was armed, the device was programmed to detonate when the altitude sensor had detected one hundred vertical feet of movement. The plan was for the bomb to explode when the unloading crane lifted it from the cargo hold.

Azmud Salomi had selected the Peligroso to carry the warhead because of the particular dock scheduled to receive her in New York harbor. For the weapon to perform Salomi's gruesome effect, placement was crucial. Since most of the docks on Manhattan had long ago been demolished, the Peligroso's unloading facility was actually on the New Jersey shore at the entrance to the Hudson River.

That minor detail didn't really matter. The lower end of Manhattan Island was only a half-mile away, directly across the river. There would be nothing but open water to attenuate the full force of the nuclear blast hitting the city.

Salomi knew that the location of the explosion was crucial. His warhead was tiny in comparison to those aboard the old intercontinental ballistic missiles. This weapon was designed to be carried by a jet such as the Mikoyan/Gurevich MIG 27 (called the Flogger D by NATO), and employed in theater nuclear operations. During the cold war era, a few trusted Russian Generals were authorized to use these small yield weapons in wartime if it became apparent NATO forces were about to over-run a critical area.

Salomi also knew a bomb of this size wouldn't come close to destroying any significant part of Manhattan. It didn't need to. All that mattered to the terrorists was that most of the concrete and steel buildings on the lower several blocks would be destroyed. They would absorb the brunt of the blast and fireball, leaving most of the island untouched by the physical effects of the explosion. However, the entire New York City and Newark, New Jersey areas would be contaminated with radioactive fallout.

Wall Street, and the headquarters of a large number of Fortune 500 companies would be obliterated. Thousands would die instantly in the collapse of office and commercial buildings. Within a few weeks millions more would die or be sickened by the fallout. There was nothing in history to equal this type of terrorist destruction.

Azmud Salomi planned the detonation as retribution for what he perceived were the numerous assaults on his country by the United States. It had taken him almost three years to plan and execute the scheme. Three Estonian scientists had been carefully courted. Money and gifts had quietly found their way to the head of the weapons storage facilities. At the end of perestroika, these civilians had easily deceived the military leaders who were accountable for the nuclear weapons and their storage. The former Soviet military hierarchy had been trained to believe civilians lacked the ability to think independently. To them it was inconceivable these egg-headed technicians could be that clever.

Even the United Nations inspectors responsible for insuring that SALT I, SALT II, and SALT III treaties were complied with were thoroughly fooled. The theft of a nuclear warhead, while virtually impossible in the West, was painfully simple to execute in the confusion resulting from the break up of the former Soviet Union. Everyone involved merely wrote the loss of the weapon off as a bookkeeping error. Sadly, there were no civilian or military leaders in power to demand a more complete accounting.

A fifty kiloton nuclear weapon simply was shipped out of the country in a relatively small container. No one noticed. No one cared. The lives of millions would be destroyed because of a criminal lack of controls on the disbursement of the most dangerous weapons mankind could produce.

The tremendous civilian loss of life that would come from the detonation did not trouble Salomi in the least. He knew that an attack of this magnitude on the United States would solidify his leadership role in the Middle East. The Kings of Saudi Arabia and Jordan would be seen as weak for their close association with the American government. They would lose face, which would strengthen his position. Total domination of the Middle East would be within his grasp.

By eight-thirty in the morning, Colin Johnson was back with Geoffrey Singer in DI6. Kristi was to be picked up at his apartment and would be taking off for home around ten o'clock. She had cried when he told her about the King's generosity. Colin knew sending her home was the right choice. Now he hoped to make the right decision about his next conversation with Geoffrey. His plan was simple – he would tell Geoffrey the truth.

Singer considered his friend carefully. "You look like you didn't sleep at all last night, Colin. Take it from one who has burnt both ends of the candle most of his young and colorful life. You have to get at least a little rest every night. Otherwise you start to look like the picture of Dorian Gray."

"Well actually, ol' boy, last night I found some details that might explain a lot. I can't tell you my source, but I'm ninety-five percent sure of it. There was a young Russian university student named Petrov Sergie killed on the Riga to Munich train yesterday. Before the young man died, he reported to some friends his discovery of a nuclear warhead on the train."

Singer looked at Johnson with unconcealed skepticism. "Did you fall down and hit your head last night?" The pitch on his voice went up to nearly a high-pitched squeak. "Colin, a university student? Hell, I'm not even sure I'd recognize a nuclear bomb. How the world would a university student know one on sight? Just where did you find out about this young man?"

"Geoff, that's something you'll just have to trust me with. I'm certain that this Mr. Sergie knew what he saw. More importantly, he was murdered for his discovery. I've got an idea ... to me, the best course of action is to run a check of the passenger and cargo manifests to see if anything or anyone appears suspicious. Can you access that kind of info?"

"Probably not legally, but I have some friends in the Bundesnachrichtendienst who should be able to get that kind of information."

"I don't know what that is," Colin admitted.

"The Bundesnachrichtendienst or BND is the Secret Service for the German government. There are a few people over there that owe me a favor or two. If you're fairly certain of your source..."

"I am," Colin interrupted.

"Then I'll have the lists here before noon. In the meantime, let's try to figure out how Salomi could get a weapon off the train and transport it. Sir Patrick will be down here in a few hours. I'd like to be able to give him some concrete ideas."

Colin stretched. "Listen, Geoff. I need thirty or forty-five minutes of sleep. I know we're in a time bind, but I have to take at least that much or I'll be worthless. Is there somewhere to catch a little shut eye?"

"Sure. We have a conference room down the hall. There's a nice long couch there that's perfect for a quick nap. I've used it once or twice myself when slaving late night down here. While you take a nap, I'll get to work on that passenger and cargo list."

Colin nodded thanks and left the room. As he passed the SAS guard posted by the door he jokingly told the man to shoot anyone who tried to wake him. The unsmiling, unspoken response told Colin that humor was not this muscular man's strong suit.

Geoffrey was right. The couch was perfect and sleep came quickly.

Seemingly moments later, he was gently brought awake by a hand carefully groping him. "'Ello, love." Rimi's beautiful English accent stirred Colin from his slumber. "Mr. Singer asked me to come and awaken you."

"Well, you certainly did that. You make a very stimulating alarm clock. Sort of makes me want to press the snooze button and let you wake me up the same way in a few more minutes."

A deep throaty laugh was the only response. It was accompanied by a warm smile. Rimi's smile was both gorgeous and intoxicating. She had long dancer's legs and a taut figure. She realized she was attractive, and knew how to gain the attention of the opposite sex. Rimi dated other men, but she never allowed sex to enter the picture. She reserved that part of her life for Colin Johnson alone. There was no question in her mind that she loved this American. She planned on marrying him someday. The fact that he had never mentioned marriage did not worry her in the least. When the time was right, he would. In the meantime, she deeply enjoyed their time together.

"If you'll find time in your busy schedule, I'll have a steak ready to broil at my flat." Rimi winked at Johnson. "That is if you're willing to work me onto your agenda."

"I'll bring a bottle of wine." Colin reached behind Rimi's neck and pulled her down for another delicious kiss ... this one more passionate and compelling. "Thanks for waking me up, Rimi."

"'Twas my pleasure, Mr. Johnson." She glanced down. "Looks like I woke you all the way up. Sorry I have to leave you like this, but perhaps I can deal with the problem at my flat later." Trying to sound professional again, Rimi cleared her throat. "Now Mr. Singer is awaiting you in The Centre, so get your cute bum down there. He'll be wondering what's keeping you."

"I don't think he'll be wondering at all. Thanks again for the perfect wake up call."

It had been an hour since Johnson had left The Centre for his nap. During that time Singer had been busy. "I've got the passenger list from the train you mentioned. The cargo manifest should be along shortly. The BND with its typical Teutonic efficiency had the names here within forty-five minutes. I let you sleep an extra quarter hour."

"Thanks. I needed the rest. Oh, yeah, also thanks for the wake up service. I was most pleased to see your assistant."

"Colin, you surprise me. I am a gentleman. You make it sound as if I sent her down there with ulterior motives in mind. I never allow lascivious thoughts to enter my thinking. I am a man of pure spirit," Geoffrey Singer spoke piously.

"Yes, well, I appreciate the purity of your actions. And I again thank you."

"For what? Rimi is not cleared for entry into this room, and I couldn't just leave myself, so I called upstairs to ask her assistance." Singer paused for a moment, took a clean handkerchief from his jacket pocket, and handed it to Johnson. "Please be so kind as to wipe her lipstick off. You seem to have a problem remembering to do that."

"Blast it!" was all Colin could say.

Their conversation stopped when the door opened and Sir Patrick Baldwin entered. His tall, erect body, piercing blue eyes, gray hair, and tailored suit made Sir Patrick a formidable figure. He looked twenty years younger than his actual age of seventy-two.

"Gentleman. I have a meeting with the Prime Minister in two hours. Have you anything I can report?"

"Yes, sir, we have. It will be another few hours before anything concrete is ready, but we do have some theories to give you."

Over the next ten minutes, the two men described in as much detail as possible their thoughts and assumptions – including the link between the nuclear bomb and Petrov Sergie. Instead of deriding the possibility, Sir Patrick nodded thoughtfully.

"In the past, I've often known the most improbable scenarios to be the most fruitful," Sir Patrick said. He also concluded their plan to check the passenger list was a good one, but doubted the plan to trace cargo manifests would work. He encouraged them to try it anyway. "Keep up the good work, gentlemen. I'll be available if you need anything."

At one o'clock, Sir Patrick was at 10 Downing Street. Fifteen minutes after that, the Prime Minister was talking with the President of the United States.

Nineteen

The hours before dawn were the hardest for Annu. He stood before the mirror in his chamber and considered the man in the reflection. His face showed a lack of rest. Experience had taught him that soon his effectiveness would suffer, but time was limited. He couldn't even take the couple of hours in a sleep chamber it would require to recharge his body. There's too much to do right now. This afternoon, I'll take a long nap. That's all I need. A quick look at the mirror told Annu that he was lying to himself. The image looking back at Exeter's king was a stranger. He looked tired. Annu was a youthful forty-nine, but this man looked much older. The wrinkles around his eyes were deep and pronounced. His brow was furrowed.

Since the news of Ron Warren's death, there had been a series of official and personal actions that had required his attention. The most tedious was securing the recovery and return of Ron's body. This would have to be handled carefully since it involved both the Russian and German governments.

Exeter's security section had been monitoring the telephone and fax transmissions from the police station and the Russian consulate regarding Ron's murder. The Germans had officially decided that the crime had been committed outside their borders and therefore not a criminal case for their attention. With the political situation between the countries still mending after decades of strain, the Germans were happy to let the whole issue fall to the Russians. For their part, the Russians were felt lucky not to have an international situation arising from the episode.

Ron's body was to be released to the embassy authorities within the next twelve hours. From there it was to be returned to his "home" in Russia.

Because of Ron's covert identity, the Russians logically believed that one of their citizens had been murdered. Certainly an investigation would be required, but no one really expected to find the murderer. The train on which Petrov Sergie was traveling when he was shot had made several stops after he was thrown off. He had not been found in time for the authorities to stop the train and investigate those aboard. There would certainly be a cursory inquiry, but there were other high profile cases that had priority.

Even a superficial inquiry brought the danger that something would raise suspicions about Ron. Exeter's External Security Section had already performed a complete check on his life and identity as the Russian Petrov Sergie. They had determined that it was completely established, and there would be nothing about him that would arouse official attention. Once his body was returned to Russia, it would be a relatively easy matter to secretly bring Ron to Exeter for burial. Isha had already dispatched Kevin to Europe to handle this. The sooner Ron was in Exeter, the better for his family. The waiting was becoming unbearable for the young man's mother and father.

Knowing that Isha and Kevin were taking care of getting Ron's body home helped the King relax a bit. Annu was still trying to decide what to do about the possibility Ron had discovered a nuclear device on board the train. If there were in fact a bomb on board, where was its destination, and more ominous, what was its purpose?

It had been several years since Annu's wife, Queen Angela, had died. He remembered fondly her gift of being able to lie down and fall asleep anywhere within seconds. It had been a joke between them for years that if the King had romance on his mind, he had to entice her before her head hit the pillow. After that, it was too late. Right now, Annu wished for that gift. He couldn't sleep. His tormented mind was too troubled to quiet.

Maria was awakened by the sounds of King Annu in his chamber. She listened for a while to the muted noise in the next area as he moved about. The resilient old woman was rapidly regaining her strength. Slipping on a warm, brown, terry cloth robe, she walked around to the King's room. The door was ajar. She quietly pushed it open and cleared her throat to get Annu's attention. "You're up late aren't you?" she commented.

"Well actually, I'm up early. Some things refuse to wait until a civil hour." He gave Maria a wan smile. "Come in and sit a while. Would you care for something to eat or perhaps some coffee?"

"No, thank you." The old woman considered Annu. His shoulders were bent as if the weight of the world rested on them. "You know," she said gently, "when Sean died, what I missed most was our talks. I could be all flustered about something and he would just make some little comment that put everything in perspective. I guess he just had a gift for making my worries and problems seem so easily resolved. I miss that old goat." She moved close to the King and continued in her best grandmother voice, "Now, I'm not Sean, but I'm a pretty good listener."

Annu sat quietly for a moment and gathered his thoughts. The words came with difficulty. He weighed each expression carefully. "Sometimes, fortunately not often, but sometimes, I have to make a decision that affects the lives of hundreds or thousands of my people. On even more rare occasions, my decisions affect many lives of those who live above. Right now, I must determine a course of action that will concern literally millions. If I choose not to act, those millions may be faced with a man-made disaster. If I do act, my tribe will possibly be revealed to those above. That would certainly spell the end of our tribe." The furrows in the King's brow deepened as he thought hard. "The lives of your millions in exchange for the existence of our thousands."

"Is there no one above who can intercede for you without revealing Exeter?"

"Not in a way that can protect my people. At least not in a way that I can think of."

Maria got up from her chair and put an arm around the man who had adopted her into his family. In her finest motherly voice, Maria said, "Then, Your Highness, let's have that breakfast you offered me, and consider the problem together."

Twenty

President Thomas Rogers had his Chief of Staff with him listening to Prime Minister Norman on the secure communication link. Neither man could believe a dead college student was the catalyst behind such high level discussions. After their first communication the previous day, the President had held a discussion with representatives of all the intelligence gathering services. All of the agencies had heard some rumors of a stolen nuclear warhead, but none had placed any credence to the stories.

While international terrorism had become an asylum for every lunatic fringe group, most of these organizations lacked the knowledge, the financial backing, or the multi-national network to carry out an elaborate operation. This did not keep them from making threats against the United States, and every claim had to be checked out.

Determining which threats were credible was a labor-intensive process that kept a large number of agents constantly working. The United States government just couldn't afford to ignore any believable threats. That was why there had been so few actual terrorist activities carried out on United States soil. The general public had no idea how many plans were discovered and broken before they could be implemented.

The operative word was *believable*. Anything the analysts considered "not believable", was by definition not worth the man-hours required to do an investigation. It was a parochial mindset, but from these men's point-of-view, there was no other way of looking at it.

The Defense Intelligence Agency (DIA) was the President's main intelligence assessment department. Along with the CIA, FBI, and NSA, they had completely discounted the possibility of a stolen warhead. Every person at the meeting had given essentially the same response: Mr. President, we've examined the data and determined it is impossible Azmud Salomi (or anyone else for that matter) could have stolen a nuclear warhead and the arming apparatus required. Since it wasn't believable to these intelligence chiefs, it simply didn't justify an in-depth inquiry.

This would prove to be a costly, dangerous, and tragic miscalculation on their part.

The President had asked each agency to continue examining the data to see if anything new came in that changed their assessment. He knew he was spitting into the wind. No one in the intelligence field had the balls to disagree with anyone else. Independent thought was frowned upon. If someone's ideas proved false, that agent's credibility suffered. Almost worse was a notion that proved true and embarrassed everyone else. If that happened, an agent could expect to spend the rest of his career in an out of the way location doing nothing of consequence.

The President knew when they heard the British were naming a dead college student as a prime source, the American intelligence community would politely laugh out loud.

He wasn't far off. Chief of Staff, Platte Janosek, sat in on a meeting at 10:00 a.m. chaired by the Operations Director of the Central Intelligence Agency. The Ops Director had this meeting twice a day to discuss any significant intelligence message traffic that had come to the CIA's Langley facility. Since the volume of material was significant, the Station chief from each region decided what was to be discussed.

Normally, the President's Chief of Staff wasn't there, and the Ops Director made special note of it. "Mr. Janosek, how are you this bright and beautiful morning?" His cheery greeting fooled no one. The Ops Director did not like having a White House weenie at his meeting.

"Actually, I'm fine. Just happened to be in the neighborhood and thought I'd stop in for a cup of coffee. Someone said it was kept in here." Janosek's ingratiating smile also hid his real feeling. *Screw you! I don't really care that you don't like me being here. I go where the President tells me to go.* "Seriously, the President is interested in the DI6 report on the stolen nuclear warhead."

"The allegedly stolen warhead, Mr. Janosek." Everyone in the room stiffened at the icy tone from the Ops Director's voice. He was famous for his ability to intimidate even the most hardened agent with that tone. Platte Janosek didn't even appear to notice.

"Whatever you want to call it, Mr. Director. The President still wants to know what you've found out." Janosek paused for effect, "The British Prime Minister has convinced the President that the situation is significant. The President has gotten the feeling that you don't agree. With all due respect, Mr. Director, he has asked me to hang around to see the allegedly stolen warhead is being investigated."

"Damn it! We all know that it's a waste of time to chase this kind of flimsy lead." The Ops Director was almost literally yelling. His immense face was red with a huge vein bulging on his forehead. "The Prime Minister may have the resources to track down these ridiculous stories, but we do not! I've personally talked with my German counterpart. He agrees that there is no way a warhead could have been smuggled through his country undetected. That, Mr. Janosek, is that."

"I'll pass on to the President your personal assurance that the Germans see things your way. Now if you would be so kind as to tell me what you have learned from the British."

The CIA Ops Director sat there seething for several seconds. However, the first item on the agenda was a report from the British desk. The CIA bureau chief at the meeting shook his head sarcastically and commented he couldn't believe the Mossad would even have passed this rather worthless bullshit to the British. He didn't know the information about the university student had not come from the Israelis, but from an American named Colin Johnson who was a CIA employee on temporary duty with the British DI6.

Twenty-One

The Peligroso was four hours out on its seven-day trip. The ship was one of a new design with advanced electronic controls. Her five hundred twenty foot hull could be pushed along at almost twenty knots while carrying sixteen thousand tons of cargo.

Her crew of twenty-six had already settled into the familiar routine of life on board a cargo ship. Each member had well defined duties to accomplish. On board a cargo ship, each man's job, from the captain to the engine room crewman, is considered critical. There is no room for individuals who don't pull their weight – and they are not tolerated.

The Peligroso's captain, McLean Andrews had been raised in Montrose on the eastern seaboard of Scotland, and had gone to sea as a sixteen year old. He was a tall, silver-haired man with a weathered face, rough callused hands, and a rare intellect. In thirty years at sea, there was not an ocean he hadn't sailed, nor a continent he had not seen.

Andrews was known as a disciplined master of his ship. Despite a reputation for toughness, his crew respected him because of his fairness and the dignity he showed his men. In a profession known for its harsh and abusive captains, Andrews had a different philosophy. While he would not tolerate slackness or dereliction of duty, he never belittled or ridiculed his men, nor would he allow any of his officers to do so.

Captain Andrews was fiercely loyal to his crew. The company was reminded of that trait from time-to-time. The previous year, his second officer, Scott McQueen, had asked to fly home from a South American port when his wife, Beth, had gone into labor a month early. The managing director for the shipping line told the officer that he would be fired if he left the ship while it was on a voyage. Andrews interceded and told the manager that McQueen was a member of his crew, and only he would decide who was to be fired. When the company man still didn't agree, Captain Andrews then expressed his opinion in a loud and colorful conversation with the president of the shipping line. The president wisely agreed that it would be in the company's best interests if McQueen were allowed to fly home. After all, good captains were hard to find, and Andrews was among the best. Once permission was received, Captain Andrews went so far as to personally lend the man money for his trip.

Eight days later, Scott McQueen returned. He was the proud father of a healthy, if small, little boy. As soon as everything was okay, and Beth's mother had come to help the new mom, McQueen was on a plane to meet the ship in its next port. As he boarded the ship, Scott McQueen reported to the captain to express his appreciation.

Captain Andrews shrugged off any thanks from his officer. "You'd have been no use to me a worryin' here," he said. "We're glad to have you back,

Mr. McQueen. The mate's been standing your watch, and he'll appreciate the extra sleep he'll be a gettin'."

The young officer found out much later that the captain, not the first mate, had been pulling most of his watches. Nothing else was ever said about the matter, but the young man knew when he eventually was given command of a ship, he would remember how his captain had acted and try to emulate his leadership style.

This kind of loyalty permeated the entire crew. It was therefore surprising when, just hours before this voyage, Captain Andrews had had to quickly hire six seamen when his regular crew members failed to return from their shore leave. Replacing them had been no trouble. There were always seasoned seamen near the docks just waiting for the opportunity to get crew on a departing ship.

The six replacements were a strange group. They had come to the ship together immediately after Captain Andrews put the word out he was hiring. If he had been a suspicious man, the captain might have questioned them closer. As it was, he simply checked their maritime licenses and counted his blessings to have so easily replaced his absent crewmen.

The new men in actuality were only marginally qualified. None had worked on a ship for several years, although they professed to be completely current. Since very little time remained before they left port, the first mate had the men relieved of first watch and told them to get settled in and then report to him for assignments. When they got into their crew quarters, they quickly unpacked. Besides clothing and personal items, their baggage also contained automatic weapons and ammunition.

These men were part of Azmud Salomi's followers. Only one of the six, Lyndon Pearson, knew Salomi's true plan. The rest were only told to make sure that his shipment was delivered safely at any cost. Pearson would not tell the rest of his comrades the real purpose behind their mission. However between themselves, the five had decided that their Salomi was planning a major attack on some U.S. target. They believed the box in the cargo bay probably carried weapons, but their unsophisticated minds could not even conceive of the destruction they were transporting. None realized or suspected that neither Salomi nor Pearson expected them to survive his plan.

* * * * *

The Peligroso's departure from Le Havre had begun in a northeasterly direction towards England. Once in the middle of the English Channel, Captain Andrews then brought his ship to an almost due west heading. To the left, he could see the French shoreline and the indistinct outline of Cherbourg and the lighthouse at Cape de la Hogue. To his right, Andrews could see the southern English coast. Within the next few hours the cliffs of Britain's Lands End and the Isles of Scilly would pass off the starboard tail of the ship. Then the azure waters of the English Channel would give way to the Celtic or Irish Sea. By nightfall, they would be entering the Atlantic Ocean.

The openness of the ocean sea-lanes was hours away. The next several hours, however, were an uncomfortable part of a voyage for any captain in these waters. Within the first one hundred nautical miles of Le Havre, there were twelve different routes for ferries between the United Kingdom, France, and the Channel Islands. Added to these routes were the many small fishing boats that daily sailed these waters. Collisions between large cargo ships and ferry or fishing boats, while rare, still happened too often. Captain McLean Andrews was damn certain he was not going to have his career ended by an accident. He would breathe much easier when they were beyond this area. He hated being in the channel.

Soon the Atlantic shipping lanes would take her far from any land and nearer by the hour to her docking in New York City. Captain Andrews had sailed this exact route more times than he could remember. Two failed marriages marked the amount of time that he had spent at sea, and he had two grown children, neither one of who really knew their father.

His eldest child, Liddie, was an actress and singer. He had never seen her perform on stage, even though she had twice been in off Broadway productions in New York. She was still unmarried although he had heard she was living with an artist in an apartment in Manhattan.

Andrews' second child was a son, Nash. He had only recently finished his university degree in petroleum engineering and was employed on an offshore drilling rig near Aberdeen, Scotland.

The older he became, the more Andrews wished he had spent time with his children in their younger years. They were almost strangers to him. The rare times together at holidays were awkward for everyone. In recent years, he had begun making excuses to avoid even those occasional encounters.

* * * * *

Late in the afternoon, the Peligroso left the shores of England behind her. For the first time, Captain Andrews felt free to leave his bridge. He turned the ship over to his first officer and went to his cabin one level below. After changing into a fresh uniform, the captain, as was his custom, made his way to the main cargo holds deep in the bowels of the ship. This was always his earliest chance to see how well his first mate had supervised the loading and tie down of the cargo. Rarely did he ever have to have any changes or corrections made. His mate was a stickler for detail when it came to proper cargo stowage.

One box caught Andrews' eye. At first he wasn't sure why, but then he realized the discrepancy. The wooden shipping container was stamped in bright, freshly painted, red letters Auto Parts, but there was neither an attached manifest packet, nor a sender's address.

The manifest packet was in a sealed pouch usually stapled to the container. It would have to be found before the box could be unloaded, because the package contained information required by United States Customs Officials. They scrupulously checked the shipping manifests against the master shipping logs to assure that everything coming into the U.S. was allowed in and not subject to tariffs. It was a tedious chore, but it was made more difficult when a container lacked its shipping pouch.

Andrews made a mental note to ask his first mate about this container.

As he moved on through the cargo hold, the captain was totally unaware of a man hiding among the containers watching his every move. A nine-millimeter Parabellum Berretta Model 92FS was aimed at Captain Andrews' head until he was well down the cargo hold. This fifteen round semi-automatic aluminum alloy pistol had been machined to allow the assassin to screw on a highly effective silencer to the five-inch barrel.

Returning to his cabin, Captain Andrews soon became engrossed in completing his logs and reports. This was the part of his position that he hated the most. There was a single knock on his door.

"Come in." Andrews looked up to see Paxton Frame, his First Mate enter. "Mr. Frame, it's good to see you. I was actually going to ask you stop by later."

"Problem, sir?" Frame was still standing before his captain's desk. He shifted uncomfortably.

"No, no. Not a problem, Mr. Frame. Just a little thing I noticed this evening. There's a container in the forward hold that's missing its shipping slip. I would appreciate it if you would take a quick look around down there and see if you can find it. It'll save us a lot of time when we reach dock."

"Yes, sir. I don't know how it got by me. I apologize, sir."

"No apology necessary, Mr. Frame. Just a detail." The captain looked at his first mate for a moment then smiled. "Obviously you have something else on your mind? Have a seat and tell me how can I help you?"

Paxton Frame was hesitant to answer. "Captain, I came to discuss those men you hired in France, but it will wait until later."

"Go ahead. I have the time now. Tell me what's bothering you about these new men."

"It's nothing, sir. I'll handle it myself. I really should not have troubled you. I'll see to the cargo immediately." He got up and headed for the door. "Good night, sir."

"I don't like secrets on my ship when it comes to the crew, Mr. Frame. Now, what is it about these men?" Andrews' response was sharper than he had intended.

"Sir, they don't seem to know their way around a cargo vessel. I know it's just been a few hours, but they've found every excuse imaginable to avoid duty. I'll take care of these men myself. I shouldn't have troubled you, captain, but I wanted you to know."

"It is not a trouble when it involves my ship or my crew. Please keep me informed."

"Aye, sir. Good night. I'll see to the cargo in the forward hold."

As soon as Paxton Frame left his cabin, Captain Andrews sat there for a moment considering his first mate. If Frame were concerned about these new men, then he should be, too. Andrews decided to speak with Frame again in the morning.

Paxton Frame entered the cargo hold as the ship's first evening at sea was beginning. He wanted to settle this packing slip question quickly. If not, he personally would have to open the shipping container in front of the US customs officials to verify its contents. Then he would be the one who had to repack and seal the box.

With only three days in New York City, he didn't want to spend one extra minute on board the Peligroso. He was a career sailor who had been in ports around the world, but still loved the lure of a large city. Port calls had once been a time to blow off steam and drink himself into oblivion – and to get into trouble. Before his twenty-fourth birthday, Frame had been arrested in six different countries, each time for drunk and disorderly conduct. The last time, his captain had left him in a Manila jail for three days before getting him out. After that, Paxton Frame was a changed man. For the past three years, he had avoided bars and strip joints like the plague.

He had other plans for New York City. From Battery Park, it was a relatively short subway ride to Central Park. On the west side of Central Park was the American Museum of Natural History, and on the east side was the Metropolitan Museum of Art and the Guggenheim Museum. As corny as it seemed to some of his shipmates, Frame really enjoyed visiting these great galleries. He had seen all the greatest museums during his travels. Each city had a new place for him to visit.

It only took Paxton Frame five minutes to find the shipping container missing its packing slip. He looked around on the deck of the cargo hold, hoping against hope that it had been accidentally torn off and was nearby. It wasn't.

A closer look at the wooden container made him both furious and confused. There were marks in the wood where a screwdriver had been used to pull the staples out of the plastic pouch that held the packing sheet. This necessary package had been intentionally removed. Why and by whom Paxton couldn't even hazard a guess. It could have been anyone on the dock loading crew or anyone who had handled the container in the hold. The first mate wanted to believe it had to be a dock crew. "Those damn French," he muttered under his breath. "Those bleeding damn French!"

"Frame!" The sudden voice startled Paxton Frame. He recognized the voice immediately as the first officer, Miles Permi. Permi, second in command on board the ship, rarely came to the cargo area. He never said it, but most of the crew knew he felt it was beneath his dignity and position to come where the ordinary crewmembers were. He also was displeased when one of them came to the bridge when he was on duty.

A third generation Welsh sailor from Cardiff, Miles Permi had been with the Peligroso for two years. He suspected that it would be several more years before he got to command his own ship, a situation he blamed on Captain Andrews. Permi knew Andrews did not like or trust him as a first officer. His efficiency reports to the company had not been enough to have Permi fired, but they had been classic examples of damning with faint praise. "Mr. Permi has been a very good first officer. With experience, his judgment and difficulties in dealing with the crew should improve." Permi could quote the last paragraph from memory. If he could have switched ships or companies after that last report, he would have. Unfortunately, there are only so many positions available at any given time. He would have to bide his time here for the foreseeable future.

"Frame, what the hell are you doing prowling around the cargo containers?"

Permi's brusque manner chaffed at the first mate. "My job, Mr. Permi. I'm seeing after some missing paperwork for the captain. If I can't find it, I'll have to open this damn container, audit the contents, and have the company wire a replacement packing list to me before we reach New York."

"Well, never you mind about this box, Frame. I'll take care of it."

"Sir, with respect, you don't know what I'm looking for. Besides, the captain asked me personally to see about it. I don't think he expected me to have someone else, even you, carry out his wishes."

"Frame, you are not to open this case! That, mister, is an order." Permi's eyes bore a hole through the first mate.

"Mr. Permi, I am not about to argue this with you. I'm going to see the captain and have him settle it. Either I am to handle the cargo, or you are. We both cannot do the job."

Paxton Frame turned his back on the first officer to leave. He took one step when a blow from the right side crushed his temple. From the shadows a figure, dressed in black, stepped out. The killer's acne-scarred face was topped by a shock of black curly hair. He wore a vile, nasty grin on his face. In the man's hand was a two-pound sledgehammer.

"You talk too much, Permi. This worthless creature was about to get in our way. Don't let that happen again!"

"You idiot! Why did you kill him?" Miles Permi flared at the mysterious attacker. "I could have handled it! Now we have a body to take care of. A death on board ship is a serious matter. The maritime authorities will have to be notified. There will be an investigation for certain." A quiet panic began to overwhelm Permi. The killer smiled at him coldly. His crooked, yellow, tobacco stained teeth were protruding from a deeply tanned face.

"Your petty problems are of no concern, little man." The man pointed to a mound a few feet away. "Wrap one of these tie down chains around him and throw his body overboard. The mystery of his disappearance will remain just that – a mystery."

Together the men dragged the lifeless body of Paxton Frame to a hatch on the lower level of the cargo area. This hatch, normally only used in port to facilitate dockside access directly to the cargo hold, was lugged down for ocean passage.

Once the body was wrapped in a length of chain, the hatch was quickly opened. The two men slid the corpse through the opening letting it fall directly into the water twenty feet below, and closed the hatch. The whole thing had taken fifteen seconds.

The only flaw in their horrible plan was noticed on the bridge. In 1987, a ferry sank while leaving Zeebrugge, Belgium when the forward bow doors were left open allowing water to rush in. One hundred eighty-eight lives were lost when the ship capsized. Following that tragedy, all ships were required to have warning lights installed on the bridge that would give an indication of an open door. The owners of the Peligroso had taken that lesson to heart and installed sensors on every external hatch near the waterline.

When the two killers briefly opened the hatch to throw Paxton Frame's weighted body into the ocean, one of those safely lights illuminated on the bridge. It caught the eye of Second Officer Scott McQueen. He was in the process of deciding what to do when the light went out. This put him in a dilemma. The captain did not like to be disturbed when not on duty unless his presence was required. It was Captain Andrews' philosophy that his junior officers should make their own decisions when on the bridge. He wanted to be consulted only when an emergency occurred or when something totally unexpected happened. Did this hatch light justify a call to the captain? McQueen' problem was settled when Andrews strolled on to the bridge.

"Evenin', Scott. I trust you're having a pleasant watch. I just stopped up to catch a breath of fresh air before retiring."

"Good evening, sir. Yes, sir, it's been a lovely evening. The only thing out of the ordinary was the cargo gangplank hatch light came on for a few seconds and then went out a few minutes ago. I was considering sending a man down to check it out when you came in."

Captain Andrews thought for a second before responding. "It was on for how long?"

"Just a few seconds. Ten, maybe fifteen at the most."

"Did you check the circuit to make sure the bulb was still working?"

"Yes, sir."

"Well, it's probably just a sensor glitch. I wouldn't let it bother me. Tell you what; I'll take a walk down below to check it out. I wanted a little exercise anyway."

"Sir, wouldn't you rather have a mate go instead?
The captain's eyebrows rose noticeably. "Mr. McQueen, a word about command. When you get your first command someday, remember this. If there ever comes a time when you are too important to do a simple task, you are heading for a major problem. The men do not follow a captain because of his rank, but because of his leadership." Afraid he had sounded too much like an old professor, Captain Andrews punched his second officer on the shoulder and smiled. "I'll see to the door and then turn in for the evening. Call me if anything comes up."

"Aye, sir. Thank you."

* * * * *

The cargo hold was well lit when the captain entered. He walked to the hatch and checked the locking lugs. Satisfied that they were all fastened tight, he went to a phone box and rang the bridge. "Mr. McQueen, it is my privilege to tell you that the cargo gangplank hatch is well secured. Perhaps we have a gremlin aboard." He laughed.

McQueen responded, "I'll have him arrested and brought to your cabin in chains, Captain."

"You do that, Scott. Do that. Good night."

"Good night, sir."

Paxton Frame had been dead less than twenty minutes. His weighted body was just reaching the bottom of the sea floor thirty-eight hundred meters beneath the ship. Yet as his lifeless form plunged deeper into the abyss, the crush of water pressure had already turned his body into a pulp that was totally unrecognizable.

While checking the lugs on the hatch, Captain Andrews had no idea of the terrible crime that had just occurred within feet of him. He also had no indication that he, too, was seconds away from death.

Both Miles Permi and Lyndon Pearson were in hiding nearby. They had heard the sound of someone coming down the ladder into the cargo hold and had slipped silently into the shadows. Now, with the Berretta carefully held in readiness, they waited. When Captain Andrews entered the light, both men cringed inwardly. For his part, Pearson never minded killing, but to eliminate the captain would cause a myriad of problems that would hinder his assignment. If seen, they would have no other choice. If he came to the unmarked shipping container, they would be immediately visible, and he would die as the result.

Sure enough, Captain McLean Andrews started directly towards the box. He was ten feet away when another man shouted, "Captain Andrews!"

Turning around, the Peligroso's master replied, "Yes."

"Sir, Mr. McQueen asked me to remind you to sign today's log before you returned to your cabin."

"I would have remembered to do that about the time I crawled into my bunk. He saved me from having to get dressed again and come up there. Thanks." The two men walked from the cargo hold together to head for the bridge.

In the shadows, the smelly assassin released the safety on his pistol and placed it in a holster under his windbreaker. The bulge was virtually invisible.

The Peligroso was one day closer to New York Harbor.

Twenty-Two

Annu had made up his mind to contact the United States government. Such direct communication had never been made before in the history of Exeter. While the Elders had reluctantly accepted their King's recommendation, they were concerned for the security of the tribe. The King promised them he would not compromise his people. In his heart, he had serious doubts about his chances for success, but knew there were no other options.

* * * * *

Platte Janosek was sitting in the den of his home relaxing in front of a blazing fireplace. This was the first night in a week he had left his office before ten o'clock. The previous evening, he and Gale had been to the White House for dinner, and today he had spent his time infuriating the collective intelligence community. It had been a full day, and he was bone tired. All he wanted was a light workout on the treadmill, a hot shower, and perhaps some special time with his wife. His work schedule, and his wife's social obligations had affected even this facet of their life – much to his chagrin.

Janosek thought again about how much his job title was not really accurate. In most administrations, the Chief of Staff was a watchdog of the time and schedule of the President. No one ever got into the Oval Office without first seeing the CS.

This Chief of Staff had not been hired for his administrative skills. President McQueen had used Janosek in a way very different from his predecessors. In fact, Janosek's assistant generally handled the President's day-to-day calendar. Janosek was more that of an aide-de-camp. Instead of using Janosek as a true CS, President McQueen exploited his strongest attribute to the fullest possible extent, his expertise and skill dealing with Congress.

Janosek could walk into an openly hostile Senate or House committee hearing and leave a few hours later with them on his side. The President knew that his CS was the main reason so much of his proposed legislation got out of committee and on to the floor for consideration.

Just as Janosek was finishing a small glass of wine, he heard a ringing sound he dreaded. The distinctive chime told him that this was the special phone reserved for communication directly from the President. No one else even knew the number. Before it rang the second time, Janosek had the handset to his ear. "Yes, Mr. President."

"Mr. Janosek, I have some information for you that is of critical importance to the United States."

Surprise at hearing a voice other than the President's caused the Chief of Staff to pause for just a second before answering. "Who is this?"

"My name is unimportant. What I have to tell you is absolutely critical."

"I don't know how you got a hold of this phone number, mister, but whoever gave it to you is in deep trouble."

"Mr. Janosek, I have neither time nor inclination to debate this with you. I have access to any phone number I want to get. That is all you need to know. What I don't have is time. There is a nuclear device that has been stolen and is in transit. Right now I don't know its destination, but I suspect either the US or one of its treaty allies."

"This isn't funny, mister! What are you using as a source for this crap you're trying to pass off?"

"Mr. Janosek, I make no attempt at humor, and my source is not your affair. I am certain of its validity and reliability. Are you willing to listen, or do I need to call the President to request his involvement?"

Platte Janosek thought quickly before answering. "What makes you think you could get through to the President?"

"Just a moment please."

A few seconds later Janosek was given the most secret phone number in Washington. Less than twenty people in the world knew the private phone number to bypass the White House switchboard and directly call the President's residence. Whoever this man was, he certainly had prize material to deal with.

"Mr. Janosek, I know that the British government has given you the same information. I also know that our intelligence agencies have chosen to ignore it. I want you to understand that there is a real and viable danger to the stability of the world. If Azmud Salomi detonates that warhead in a, shall we say, sensitive area of the world, it will have global significance. World wars have begun with far less provocation."

"There are no super powers with the ability to wage a global conflict."

"Mr. Janosek, I also don't care to debate international politics. We both know that there are sufficient nuclear and conventional weapons in the hands of minor world leaders to bring this peaceful house of cards down. Now, I can get you hard evidence to present to the DIA or CIA to prove the allegations you made today, and the danger involved."

"Where did you get it?"

"That is not your concern."

"Mister, I don't even know who you are. I grant you that I'm impressed that you have access to some pretty restricted phone numbers, but how do I know you or your information can be trusted?"

"Mr. Janosek, I understand your skepticism. I thought about the ramifications before I called. That's why I contacted you on this phone and not at your office. Having access to your private number should give me some credibility. I thought of another way to prove my authenticity."

"I'm listening."

"For the past six administrations, each president has had access to a numbered Swiss bank account. The purpose of the account, I surmise, is to allow him immediate access to hard currency for emergency special operations in Europe. I am about to give you that number and the amount of Swiss francs in there."

"I will not confirm the existence of such an account."

"Mr. Janosek, I don't need confirmation of what I know for a fact. The account number is K1-5893-M98798-A09745. As of close of business today, there were $60,756,893 francs in the account."

Writing quickly, Janosek said, "Listen, I still refuse to admit the existence of such an account, but I need some time to check out your allegations. Where can I call you back?"

A quiet chuckle came over the line. "Mr. Janosek, you cannot call me. Check your watch, I will be back to you fifteen minutes from right now."

The phone line went dead.

Platte Janosek went straight into his study, unlocked a desk drawer, and removed a bright yellow phone from it. He picked up the handset. Immediately there was someone on the other line. "Put me through to the security officer on duty."

Janosek's mind was racing as he considered who the mysterious caller could be. It had to be someone in the Secret Service, the White House Communications Room, the CIA, the FBI, the National Security Agency, or any one of a dozen smaller specialized intelligence agencies. Whoever it was, he had some potentially devastating information. Janosek knew the Swiss account did exist. He also knew President McQueen hadn't even used it once. Even so, if the press ever caught wind of it, the President would be accused of hiding a slush fund or worse. They wouldn't care that the account was established almost forty years before by a president now long dead. As preoccupied as he was, Janosek didn't realize that only a few seconds had passed when a new voice came on line.

"This is Colonel Markham, sir."

"Colonel, I just got a phone call on my direct phone line. It's supposed to be used only by The Man himself. Do you have any explanation?" It wasn't a fair question, and Janosek knew it.

"No, sir, I don't know who else could contact you on that phone. If you want, I can have an agent check the line."

"Yeah, that's exactly what I want. Put a tap on it, too. Whoever the caller was, he's supposed to call me back in...," Janosek checked his watch, "twelve minutes. I want the call traced. Do not; I repeat do not, put a stop on the contact. I just want to know who's calling me."

"Yes, sir."

Janosek hung up without another word. He turned to the computer terminal on the credenza behind his desk and turned on his Macintosh computer there. Using a shielded communications line, Janosek called the computer in his office at the White House. There was a short pause then a password box appeared. Janosek typed in his code and waited. After two seconds, there was a rapid blink of the screen several times. Once that was accomplished, Janosek knew his data transfer was secure. He was using a sophisticated high-speed information scrambling modem that was developed by the NSA to transmit classified data to overseas embassies. Its code was modulated and altered by an algorithmic processor that changed several times a second. Both the transmitting computer and the receiving one had to be on the exact same transfer cycle. To accomplish the information download, the two computers had to be in perfect synchronization to "talk" with one another. That synchronization was accomplished immediately after the password was received.

Janosek opened several icons and soon reached a classified file. This file required him to type in a second password in order to open it. Janosek sat upright immediately. There before him was the secret account number for the President's contingency fund held in the Swiss Bank of Zurich. The account number was K1-5893-M98798-A09745. He noted the $60,756,893 franc balance. Three times he checked the numbers against the note he had written during his phone conversation. A cold chill went down Platte Janosek's spine. If this hacker can break into this file, there's no telling what other codes he's broken, and what else he can get his hands on, he realized. Janosek felt relieved that the immense United States nuclear missile arsenal had been disarmed. A launch code, while infinitely more complex, might well be within the ability of this man to decipher. A quiet terror gripped his mind – Armageddon – started not by a political decision, but by a computer genius and his $2000 microprocessor. The immensity of it slowly dawned on Platte Janosek.

Exactly fifteen minutes after he had hung up the phone, it rang again. "Yes?"

"Mr. Janosek, by now you've checked with the White House, and know my information is accurate. I've also proven I can bypass you and contact the President directly at will. Now, allow me to get to the point."

"I've been waiting for you to do that. Just what is it you want from me. Let me tell you I will not negotiate with you. The President has nothing to fear from the release of this bank account information. If you are planning to use it to blackmail the administration, you are sadly mistaken. He..."

"I have no sinister motives, Mr. Janosek." The voice broke in. "Blackmail is not my motive. The safety of the global community is my concern."

"I want to know who this is before I will talk with you further."

"Good night then, Mr. Janosek."

"Wait! Wait just a minute." Janosek yelled into the handset. He desperately wanted to keep the mystery man on the line longer. "How do I know you really have information I need?"

There was a barely discernible pause. "Mr. Janosek, it is a waste of time for me to tell you what you already know. As I said before, I understand your reticence. You either want to hear what I know or you don't. To be fair, I know this is difficult for you. So, I'll give you enough details to prove I deserve to be heard. Then you can decide if you have the time to hear more." The sarcasm was not lost on Platte Janosek.

"Mister, think about the position you're putting me in. You're asking me to discuss secrets of the highest level with someone who won't even identify himself."

"Life does give us difficult choices sometimes. I'm telling you I can help prevent a conflagration. It's up to you whether or not you want to respond. The blood, or rather instantaneous annihilation, of tens of thousands rests on your shoulders, Mr. Janosek."

Platte Janosek spent the next ten full seconds silently considering what the mystery man had just said.

Quietly and reluctantly he surrendered to the situation. "I'm ready to listen."

"All right. You already know that a nuclear warhead was acquired from an Estonian storage area. The Mossad, and consequently the British, believe Azmud Salomi is responsible for the act, but they can't yet prove it. No one knows where he plans on putting the bomb, how he plans on transporting the explosive, or if it's just a ploy to blackmail the world community."

Platte Janosek was amazed at what he had heard. This stranger had to be someone very high in the intelligence community. Why was he pretending to be an outsider? "You've conjured up an interesting scenario. I'm not admitting that this situation exists, but if it does, what do you know that would help us solve it?"

"Be in the Oval Office with the President at noon tomorrow."

"Why not now?"

"Tomorrow," the voice said firmly, "at noon."

"The President is not available at noon."

"The President's schedule is open for forty-five minutes after he meets with a United Nations delegation from eleven-thirty until noon tomorrow. I've already checked. Good night, Mr. Janosek." The line went dead.

Janosek did not hang up. Instead he waited. Whoever this man was, he definitely had some surprising information at his disposal. In a few moments Colonel Markham spoke. "Sir, I don't know how to explain this, but we couldn't trace your call. It appears to have come directly from the White House."

"There's only one person who can call me on that line from the White House, and this wasn't him, Colonel! I want a complete check of the security on this system, and I want it started tonight!"

Colonel Markham felt like reminding the Chief of Staff that the White House Communications Section did not come under the CS office, but thought better of it. "Yes, sir. We'll run a check immediately."

"In the meantime, if the President has anything classified to discuss with me, send a courier. I don't trust this phone line."

"Yes, sir. Do you want me to notify the President of this possible breach?"

"First of all, it's not a possible breach, it's a confirmed breach. Secondly, no, don't disturb him. I'll discuss it with President first thing in the morning when I give him your report on how someone could contact me like this."

"Yes, sir. Good night, sir."

"Good night, Colonel." Platte Janosek hung up. After all these years in Washington, very few things surprised him, and even fewer things dumbfounded him. This one did both. Everything in his mind told him that this phone call had come from a rogue intelligence agent. Why would he do it? What was his motive? Surely someone high enough in the security world to have access to this situation would also know he couldn't get away with trying to contact the President – especially using this line.

Platte Janosek almost never let a problem or situation bother his sleep. He didn't let this one either. He couldn't do anything until he had the Communications Section report, so there was nothing to ponder. Tomorrow perhaps he would have enough information to answer his questions.

Until then, there was his wife to consider.

Twenty-Three

Colin Johnson was at DI6 by seven o'clock in the morning. He and Geoffrey Singer had worked the previous night until 8:00 p.m. Then he had gone to Rimi's flat for his promised dinner. Around ten o'clock, much to Rimi's disappointment, he had left her to come back to The Centre. Singer had still been there, and they worked until midnight before quitting for the day.

Other than dinner, the only real break the two men had taken the previous day was the hour Johnson had required to see Kristi off from Heathrow Airport. The chartered Fencer V business jet had been ready to go the second she was there. Colin had been surprised to find an agent of Her Majesty's Immigration Service with the jet to bypass normal tourist exit procedures and hand-stamp Kristi's passport. Obviously King Annu's business associates had some influence with the government.

Kristi had called Colin's apartment from Exeter. It had taken her sixteen hours to get from London to her parent's home in Exeter. That time included almost two hours clearing customs and immigration at New York's John F. Kennedy Airport. She had left a message on Colin's answering machine that Ron's body would not be returned home for at least another day because of 'difficulties getting it out.' Johnson had interpreted that to mean smuggling the body from Russia into the United States. It had to be handled delicately to avoid raising questions and inquires.

The expected report from the Bundesnachrichtendienst, or BND, had taken far longer than Singer expected. It had been delivered to The Centre during the night. The reason for the delay had been simple; they had not been told exactly what to look for. They were simply told there was a critical need to have information on the cargo manifest of the train. To avoid any embarrassment at not performing a thorough enough search, the Germans had gone into extreme detail and followed up on every piece of cargo. They confirmed each parcel and container was received at its intended destination as scheduled. Everything was as expected. The only exception had been a relatively small wooden crate that had been taken off the train two stops prior to its original scheduled location.

A follow-up call to the shipping company revealed that the owners had contacted the company and said there was a change in plans. The crate was needed elsewhere. This sometimes happened, and no one really thought much about it. In fact, they only mentioned it because the BND had specifically asked about any cargo that had received special attention, and this one did.

Geoffrey Singer was reading the report when Colin Johnson entered The Centre. "Good morning, Colin. I trust you had a good night's rest, or did you go back to Rimi's place for a late night, all night, dessert?"

"We don't all think with that part of our anatomy, Geoff. But to answer your original question, I slept well – alone."

"What a pity, my friend, what a pity."

Changing the subject, Colin asked about the BND report. "Anything of interest?"

"No, I was just about to decide it was a waste of our effort, and trash it. But, I figured Sir Patrick would want to review it. That way he can tell his counterpart with our German brothers that he personally appreciated the effort they put into the work."

"Mind if I read over it?" For the next seven minutes, Johnson lost himself in the minutia of the report. "Interesting. This is about the most vanilla thing I've ever seen."

"Yank, forget for a moment that I'm a debonair man-of-the-world. Just what the hell does vanilla have to do with this report?"

Johnson responded humorously, "You ignorant, Englishman! Just where did you go to university, Geoff?"

In his best proper English tone, Singer answered, "I, sir, availed myself of an Oxford education. I, too, have attended lectures at Cambridge, Eton, Harrow, and Winchester. Unfortunately, none of them covered the topic of colorful colloquialisms of the colonists."

"Geoff, I'm gonna box you up, send you to Houston, and let you live with us Texans for a few months. That way you'll learn the proper way to express yourself," Johnson responded to his friend. "Vanilla means plain, untouched, unremarkable, unassuming. In other words, this thing is no help at all."

"That one crate is the flaw. I wish I knew for a fact that it was a routine matter to have a container removed early. I wonder how to check it out?" Singer thought aloud.

"Let's make a call to the shipping company. If the crate was off-loaded early, they must have had to lease a truck or lorry. From that information, we can see where it really went."

"You know," Singer said sonorously, "for a Yank you're not half stupid."

"Just trying to keep up with you, man, just trying to keep up."

"A noble goal. Now, I'll put a call into some friends and ask them to get this information. While I'm gone, please refrain from touching anything sharp or hot."

This time, it only took the German authorities two hours to send a telex with the information. The crate had been listed as containing auto parts. The lorry had taken it across Germany into France and to the port at La Havre. There were two unusual things about the crate that stuck in the driver's memory. When he crossed the border, the French customs inspector on duty only gave the transit documents a cursory look before clearing the truck through. Normally, they were pompous, ridiculously slow, and methodical. The second thing he remembered happened once he reached the port. The dock manager himself was at Le Havre to meet the lorry, and watched to make sure the crate was placed on the ship.

Singer and Johnson read the report together. "I can see why the driver remembered that crate. It seems an awful lot of high-level attention was paid to a single box of auto parts."

"I agree, Geoff. Is there a copy of the manifest in the transit documents?"

Singer leafed through several pages in the report. "None that I see. Why?

"Because it's my guess that we've struck pay dirt. They either have to create fictitious paperwork, or somehow get it off the ship without transit documents. Either way, we should be able to determine which ship has the box."

"Very good." Singer left the secure area of The Centre, walked down the corridor, entered a small sound dampened room, and pushed a button on the corner console telephone.

A moment later, Sir Patrick Baldwin himself answered. "Yes?"

"Sir, I think we've made an interesting discovery. Do you have a moment?"

"I'll be down in about ten minutes." The intercom light went out.

True to his word, Sir Patrick Baldwin walked into The Centre a few minutes later. "Sorry to keep you waiting, gentlemen." The distinguished intelligence chief smiled benignly. "What do you have for me?" He sat in silence while the two men gave a synopsis of their findings. After they were finished, he nodded thoughtfully. "If I may suggest one thing; check with the dock manager and see why he was specifically involved with that one crate. Surely someone encouraged his interest. Find out who that was, and you'll know who is responsible for the crate, and this possible terrorist plot. This is good work, gentlemen. Thank you."

Geoffrey Singer called the port authority at Le Havre. His request for information was quickly halted when he learned that the manager on duty, Julien Gauthier, had been killed in an automobile accident. "Tragic loss," the port authority spokesman said. "He simply lost control of his car and hit a tree."

It was immediately obvious to both intelligence officers that Gauthier had died within hours of his involvement with the shipping crate. They hated coincidences like that.

"One last question, please," Geoff politely asked. "Do you have a log of Monsieur Gauthier's activities before he left work that day?"

"One moment please."

A new voice came on the line. "This is the port manager. May I ask the purpose for your request regarding Monsieur Gauthier's work schedule?"

"Yes, this is Frederick Fleet with the British Admiralty Ministry. I had a question about a ship he was involved with. Tragically, it appears to have been the last ship he handled before his death. If you simply have the name of the ship, I'm sure I can get the information I require."

"All right," was the response. It seemed a logical request. "I will check the book. It will take a minute or two."

Colin Johnson whispered to his friend while they were waiting, "Frederick Fleet? Where did you come up with that name?"

Singer laughed quietly, covered the telephone mouthpiece, and whispered back. "He was the lookout in the crows nest of the Titanic when it hit the iceberg. It seemed like a fitting name."

The port manager was on the line again in about a minute. "According to the office log, Monsieur Gauthier was at dock 14 to check the loading of the Peligroso, a Panamanian cargo ship."

"Do you happen to know its destination?"

"It will be first in New York City, then Miami, and finally Corpus Christi, Texas. It is due back to Le Havre in twenty-nine days."

"That is most helpful. Thank you. Please accept my condolences on the death of Monsieur Gauthier. Au revoir."

As soon as the phone was hung up the men sensed they had the correct ship. It was just too much of a coincidence that Julien Gauthier had died in an auto accident immediately after supervising the loading of the Peligroso. It wasn't just intelligence paranoia that told them he had been murdered to keep him from talking about the ship when it exploded.

"Geoff, I recommend we listen to all communications to and from the Peligroso. We need to find out if any one on the ship knows exactly what they're carrying."

"Ok. I'll have to get Sir Patrick's authorization. We should be able to have a tap on all transmissions within the hour."

"Tell him also we know the target." A questioning look told Johnson that Singer didn't follow his reasoning. "It has to be New York harbor. If Salomi planned on detonating the bomb in Miami or Corpus Christi, he wouldn't risk having the bomb discovered by dock crews in New York. Obviously, he can't chance that, so the first port of call must be the target."

Both men felt good about their international detective work.

* * * * *

At 7:00 a.m., Second Officer Scott McQueen came to the captain's cabin and quietly knocked on the door. It took several successively louder hits to bring Captain Andrews from his sleep. "Come in," he barked. McQueen stuck his head in to the darkened cabin. "Yes, Scott. Have I overslept?"

"No, sir, but I have a problem, Captain. We can't find Mr. Frame. He was supposed to come on duty at 0500 this morning. When he didn't show up, I sent a man to his cabin. He wasn't there, and his bunk didn't even look slept in. We've checked the galley, the cargo areas, the showers, and the latrines. No one has seen him."

"I sent him to the forward cargo hold last night to check a crate. That should have only taken ten or fifteen minutes. Check all the crew areas a second time. I'll be on the bridge in five minutes."

"Aye, sir."

Miles Permi was on the bridge when the captain came in. As the first officer, it was his responsibility to brief the captain each morning on the previous night's progress and any message traffic. The missing crewman was the first item of discussion. "I've already started a stem-to-stern search of the ship for Mr. Frame. No one has seen him since about seven o'clock last night. It's my feeling he may have fallen overboard during a late night smoke or something."

"Mr. Frame did not smoke." Captain Andrews spoke tersely.

"Well, no one knows where he is."

"When you've searched the entire ship, speak with each and every crewman. I want to know exactly when he was last seen. We have those new men on board. They may not know Frame so take a picture of him to show them. I'll take the ship now and relieve you to head up the investigation."

"Yes, sir. But I think it's a waste of my time. I've already had the search done once."

Captain McLean Andrews glared at his first officer. "Mr. Permi! I don't give a damn if you've done the search ten times! If I tell you to do it again, you damn well better do it again!" Everyone on the bridge turned to look at the captain and first officer. Andrews rarely raised his voice. "Do it!"

Permi turned and left the bridge without another word. Captain Andrews waited a full minute to get his temper under control before speaking again. He picked up the bridge phone and called the communications room. "I need to send a telex to the company. Send someone up to the bridge to take the message, please."

While he was waiting for the admin clerk, the captain formulated his communiqué regarding Frame's disappearance. He decided also to have the company send a replacement shipping form for the crate in the forward cargo hold. That way he wouldn't have to be bothered with in it in New York.

An hour later, a mate came to the bridge. "Sir, Mr. Permi asked me to tell you that the entire ship has been searched without finding Mr. Frame."

"Very well. Thank you. Tell the first officer that I want him to have Mr. Frame's possessions inventoried, packed, and stored. Also tell him I expect a full report on the search at his earliest convenience." Captain McLean Andrews did not like having a junior mate report to him in place of the first officer. Andrews felt like it was insubordinate. He decided right then that he would replace Permi in New York. The company would just have to fly a replacement to meet the ship in the States, and fly Permi home.

* * * * *

A short time later, a message was sent to the company. Captain Andrews listed two of the three items he wanted the managers to know. His decision to replace his first officer would wait until he could call them via the satellite phone.

....

MESSAGE • MESSAGE • MESSAGE • MESSAGE

From: Captain: Peligroso (PA0852)
22 Oct, '09 • UTC 1045
Position: N48.46.9 W15.33.7

Item One: Crewman missing
As of 0700 this date, Paxton Frame, First Mate, (IMA No.137585) has been reported missing. A complete check of the ship has revealed no clues as to his whereabouts. Suspect he fell overboard during the night. The search will continue. We have transmitted per radio to all ships in the area and on reciprocal course to be on look out. Request guidance regarding possible return on course for rescue attempt. Details will follow as available. Please notify family with Captain's deepest regrets.

Item Two: Missing Cargo Manifest Packet
It has been discovered that one container in cargo area B-6 is missing its manifest packet. The container is labeled "Auto Parts", but lacks a shipping address. To prevent delay in first harbor (NYC), request a substitute transmittal sheet be sent via telex. The case is listed as pallet number B-6-3731E.
End message, signed Andrews, M., Captain

END MESSAGE • END MESSAGE • END MESSAGE
....

The message was received at the company hemisphere headquarters in Paris. The return communication was in Captain Andrews' hands an hour later. It generated no small amount of anger in the Peligroso's master. The ship was to presume Frame lost at sea. No change in course was to be made. Further, a transmittal slip for the cargo would be waiting with company officials in New York. Andrews, who had seen this kind of thing happen before, muttered, "Bastards. The loss of one of my men means nothing to these people. All they want is an on time arrival in the harbor. They don't care about anything except their profit margin. On top of that, I'll end up spending the better part of a day clearing customs because that bloody transmittal sheet will be no where to be found in New York!" He shook his head disgustedly. "Bastards!" he said again.

Twenty-Four

President Rogers and Platte Janosek were alone in the Oval Office. The First Lady, Charlene Rogers, had just left the men. She rarely came to the office, but wanted to remind the President, in the presence of his Chief of Staff, that she was planning a family reunion at the White House for July. Family reunions were very low on the President's fun-to-do list. Mrs. Rogers knew her husband could easily schedule himself to be out of Washington during the two days she was counting on. He wouldn't dare now - he had been reminded.

Janosek sonorously spoke to the President, "Maybe we should plan on invading some third world country next July in the name of restoring democracy there. That would keep you too busy to face the family. Let's face it; if that hillbilly predecessor of yours could use the military to distract the world from his childish behavior, you can use it to miss Charlene's family reunion.

"Wouldn't work. She would just tell me that Vice President Dickerson was going to be Commander In Chief for those two days." Both men laughed. "Besides, Roy will probably be our next nominee for this office. Charlene would just tell me he needs the experience of sitting in this chair."

The President was sitting at the same mahogany desk once used by President Wilson. On a credenza behind him set a bust of Abraham Lincoln. Both men were heroes to the current holder of the office. They, too, had faced overwhelming adversity in their administrations, and risen above them, just as he hoped to.

There are so many threats to the security of the world today, and so little that can be done to combat them. President Rogers often felt frustrated by the complexity of the international arena. So many dangers – so few options.

Earlier in the day, the President and his Chief of Staff had finished a working breakfast. Platte Janosek had briefed the President on his phone call from the previous night. The White House Communications section had performed every conceivable test on the security of the phone lines. Their conclusion was that somehow the person in question directly tied into the circuit and made the call. That was the only plausible explanation for the fact that the call appeared to come directly from the President. No one had ever been able to break the layers of protection around these communication lines before. This man seemingly did it with impunity. That fact alone made him dangerous. Added, of course, was the fact that he somehow knew about the possible nuclear warhead. If he chose to reveal to the press what he knew, this mystery man could cause the administration not just embarrassment, but a deep and sensitive public relations problem. The threat of a terrorist attack in the United States was a political situation as well a criminal one.

The President had decided to wait until noon to hear the man out. His Chief of Staff had one opinion. Whoever the mystery man was, he was dangerous. Both men also knew two other things. First, no one with potentially damaging information ever gave it away without wanting something in return. Secondly, this could be a clever and ruthless trap for the administration. Both thoughts were frightening.

* * * * *

King Annu was sitting with a cup of coffee. He had not slept particularly well. Once again, Maria was awake, too. She had joined him in the living area of the King's chambers. Annu looked at his watch and made a quick mental conversion. "It's a little after noon in London," he said to the old woman. "If you'll excuse me a moment, I have a short phone call to make." He called Colin Johnson's apartment not really expecting him to be there. Sure enough, after a few rings, the answering machine came on line. Annu hung up without leaving any message. He referred to the book on his desk, dialed a new number, and waited. After several seconds, he typed in another number and hung up.

Almost five thousand miles away, Colin Johnson was just sitting down to lunch in the upstairs cafeteria of DI6. He had a large salad and a chicken salad sandwich on his tray. Geoff Singer was a few seconds behind him. His tray contained a large, greasy plate of french fries and a hamburger. "Singer, I'll never know how you live on that greasy stuff."

"No problem, lad. It just slides through. Besides, I was wondering how you live on that green, leafy stuff."

There was no chance to answer because Rimi walked up just at that moment. In her hand was Colin's cell phone.

It was standard operating procedure (SOP) to leave all electronic equipment at the security desk before entering The Centre. Even non-transmitting equipment such as pagers were included. The SOP was part of DI6's communications security, and was supposed to be absolute. Colin Johnson didn't like the hassle of surrendering his cell phone each time he entered the building, and had found a solution that was acceptable to him. Since the device was not allowed in the secure sections of the building, he instead had Rimi keeping it in her cubicle. Besides Richard Nail thought he was on an indefinite assignment to New Scotland Yard, and no one else at the Embassy ever called him. Colin had not expected any messages, but he was wrong.

"Mr. Johnson, this better not be a call from any young lady!" Rimi said sarcastically.

"Rimi!" Singer responded with fake indignation. "Mr. Johnson is a man of character, integrity, and loyalty. I can't believe you would impugn his masculinity by insinuating he would court two women at once! It's both unseemly and audacious of you." He winked at Johnson. "Besides, Colin is much too smart to let you find out if he has another bird in the nest."

Colin wisely stayed out of the conversation until Rimi looked directly at him and tossed the phone into his lap. "Rimi, my dear, pay no attention to this troublemaker. There is no one else in my life. How could there be, when I'm already blessed with your company?"

"Mr. Singer is right – you are a smart man." Rimi gave Colin's cheek a pat and then turned away. She gave a credible bump and grind as she walked out. Both men watched with rapt attention – as did most of the men in the cafeteria.

It took Colin several seconds to remember his phone. He barely hid the surprise on his face when he saw the number. It was the return phone number for the Santa Fe, New Mexico telephone company customer service department, but Colin knew not to return a call to that number. "Geoff, I need a few minutes to answer this. I'll be right back."

Instead of calling from his unsecure cell phone in the cafeteria where anyone could listen in, Johnson went past the security station, out the front doors of the government building, and down to one of the few remaining red telephone boxes in London. He stepped in and used a twenty pence coin to call the secure phone number in his flat. There was no ring. Instead all he heard was a simple click. Johnson hit six numbers in rapid succession and he heard another click. Now the secure line would call Exeter and the King's chamber. Of course, if anyone had a tap on the line from this phone box, they could listen in on the conversation. Johnson didn't think that there was any chance of that.

The phone was answered on the second ring. "Yes?"

"Sire, this is Colin. I got your call."

"I don't have time to discuss this in great detail, Colin. I am about to call the President of the United States and need to know, with as much certainty as you can give me, just where the nuclear warhead is destined, and any details that might verify the threat."

For a moment Colin wasn't exactly sure he had correctly understood who the King was going to call ... the President of the United States? While the idea of hiding any information from King Annu never entered his mind, Colin thought for a moment before answering. He was concerned with separating concrete facts from the speculative ones.

Over the next several minutes, Colin revealed what details they had discovered of the transportation and handling of the weapon. He left out his theories about the dock manager at La Havre because he felt they were as yet unsubstantiated.

"Sir, did I understand you correctly – the President?"

"That's right. I'm hoping to convince him that the threat is real. Unfortunately, the ship you suspect is in international waters, so his hands will be tied to a certain extent. With enough hard facts, perhaps he can come up with a viable solution."

Colin Johnson took a chance with the King. "Sir, there are a lot of details still missing that could lead us down the wrong path. I would feel better with a few more hard facts to go along with my suppositions. You may be acting too quickly."

"You're right, but not acting quickly would be criminal. That's why the Elders have agreed to this contact."

"Will you place the call from Exeter?"

King Annu read John's mind. "Exeter will be safe. Our security section has blocked the National Security Agency's ability to trace my communication. They won't know who I am or exactly where I'm calling from."

"That will be quite a feat, sir. The NSA has a formidable arsenal of electronic tracking equipment."

Annu feigned disappointment, "Colin, you surprise me. In five or ten years they might be able to crack our protective systems, but by then we'll have something new."

"Yes sir. I'll let you know if we get anything else."

"Thank you, Colin. By the way, Kristi asked me again to tell you thanks for your help in getting her home."

"Sire, you deserve the credit for that. It was your wallet that made the trip possible. I merely made the phone calls."

Annu shrugged off the comment.

"Sir, I should get back. Good luck with the President."

"Thank you, Colin. I appreciate your counsel."

Returning to The Centre, Johnson found Geoffrey Singer pursuing a dispatch. The British agent's face was a mixture of both sadness and exultation. The yellow sheet in his hands was the facsimile of a maritime transmittal log. "It appears that our guess was accurate. The Peligroso's captain has reported to his company that the first mate has been lost at sea."

"That's tragic, but it doesn't tell us that the ship is carrying the warhead."

"There's more. The captain also told them he has container without the required packing slips. He's asked them to send the slips before he arrives in New York."

"And the response?"

"Basically they said too bad about the crewman and don't worry about the crate. It'll be handled at the port of arrival."

"Bingo!" Colin said with uncharacteristic enthusiasm. "I'd say we've got our transportation question settled." He grew thoughtful for a moment as he considered the information. "Obviously, by asking the company about the crate, the captain has shown he doesn't know about the weapon. We can also conclude, however, that someone in the company does know what's on board. Otherwise they would have tried to give him the information he requested."

"I agree, Colin. Perhaps a message from us directly to the captain is in order."

"Can we do that?" Colin asked surprised.

"Not officially, we can't. But, there are ways..." Singer responded cryptically.

Colin Johnson thought for a moment before answering. "I think contacting the captain may be premature right now. It's not likely he would believe a message that comes from outside his company. Plus it would be disconcerting to him to receive a telex that did not originate with his company. Most of all it might cause him to do something rash. That might be dangerous."

"How do you mean dangerous?"

It took Johnson just a moment to formulate his thoughts. "I still think the captain is in the dark about the nature of his cargo, but you can bet that someone on board the ship is involved. I don't believe for a moment Salomi would risk having the weapon unguarded. So if the captain believed the ship was carrying something dangerous, he might act. Salomi's men would then have to show their hand to stop him. The bottom line is that if the captain is unaware of the nature of the package, he may in fact, be safer."

"Yes. I see your point. How about..."

Singer's response was interrupted when Sir Patrick Baldwin entered the room. He had a thoroughly disgusted look on his face. "Gentlemen, the Prime Minister just called me. He has spoken again to President Rogers. The CIA and DIA have convinced the President there is no danger. They refuse to accept any of our evidence. They say it's too flimsy and circumstantial. Therefore, the PM has decided there is no substance to our concerns. He has asked me to end our work."

Both agents stood in disbelief. This was one of those times that caused men such as them to hate professional politicians. Singer and Johnson both detested men who made decisions based more on the way they wanted to see things instead of how they really were. These weak leaders usually found someone who would tell them what they wanted to hear. Then if later it appeared they made bad decisions, they had someone else to blame. More important, they had someone to publicly fire as proof that they were innocent.

Singer spoke with more sincerity than he really felt. "Sir Patrick, we have more information that may change his mind."

The old man sighed audibly. "Tell me what you have. Let me warn you that unless I have a handwritten note from Salomi detailing his plans, I doubt he'll listen to me."

The two intelligence agents shared everything they knew and suspected. Sir Patrick Baldwin listened without comment. The information from the ship's message caused Baldwin to nod thoughtfully. "Gentlemen, as solid as your research is, you still have just circumstantial evidence. However, while

I am convinced, that bureaucrat on Downing Street isn't, and won't be. I can't go back to him with these suppositions alone. He won't even discuss the matter with me."

"Sir Patrick, we can't just stop. There are millions of lives at stake here!"

Sir Patrick Baldwin believed in the two men before him. He wouldn't let them be stopped prematurely. "I told you the PM has directed me to stop work on this, but he doesn't run this operation. I do. Until he sees fit to replace me, I make the decisions about what work is or is not accomplished around here. I want you to keep up your effort, and bring me something I can change his mind with."

* * * * *

The phone rang in the Oval Office. The call had not been routed through the main switchboard, the communications office, or the Chief of Staff's desk. It was the private number used only by President Rogers. Even Vice President Dickerson never called his boss on this line. Rogers pushed the speaker button so that Platte Janosek could listen in. "Yes."

"Good afternoon, Mr. President. Thank you for answering my call."

"You didn't exactly give me any choice. Who is this?"

There was no hesitation. "My name, Mr. President, is Annu. I am King of a place called Exeter. My people, and there are almost fifty thousand of them, have been hidden from the world for almost over four hundred years. You will not have heard of us. Further, let me add, you will not find us."

The President and his Chief of Staff both sat in stunned silence. This preposterous introduction surprised them both. Together they came to the frightening conclusion that this mystery man was some deranged computer wizard with delusions of grandeur.

"Mr. Annu, I'm really pleased that you have seen fit to share your findings with us. Why don't you meet with me and let's talk face-to-face. You bring your staff and let them discuss this with my people here in Washington, or I'll meet you where ever you want to confer."

The voice on the other end of the conversation went instantly cold and angry. "Don't patronize me, Mr. President. We are discussing the annihilation of thousands of your people. Millions more will be affected."

No one talked to Rogers in that tone. "Now you listen here. I've played your charade longer than I want. I know all about this alleged warhead. It doesn't exist! That's all I'll say about it! Now, tell me who this really is, and how you've gotten the bits of misinformation you have. I give you my word you will not spend time in jail. I just want you to get the help you need."

"President Rogers, you're the one who needs help! I am well aware that the existence of my people is a difficult thing to accept. I am also aware that the President of the United States is often briefed on military secrets that would sound impossible to the average person on the street, but are real. You should be used to hearing preposterous yet totally accurate information." He let that settle for the moment. Rogers had been astonished by some of the top-secret material that had come across his desk as Commander-In-Chief. Annu continued, "Mr. President, I don't care what your advisors are telling you, this threat is real!"

"I refuse to listen to the ravings of a mad man!" The President was beginning to rant. He reached and slammed his hand down on the phone disconnecting the line.

Platte Janosek was quiet for a moment allowing the President to regain his composure. "Sir, I hope that was a wise thing to do. Whoever that was, he sure as hell has access to some highly classified information. We needed to know how he found out what he knew."

Before Rogers had a chance to answer, the phone rang again. This time, Janosek answered it. He listened for several seconds before responding. "I understand. Thank you, Colonel. Make sure this number is changed, but don't release the change to anyone."

The President didn't even need to ask about the call. "Don't tell me. They couldn't trace the call."

"No sir, they traced it. It seems the call originated from a phone in your residence upstairs."

"That's ridiculous! That call did not come from up there."

"No, it didn't. But it takes an awful lot of technological ability to make us think it did."

"Maybe that's the answer. This guy's probably broken into the CIA's computer system and stolen someone's notes. If he's that good, he probably can steal anything." The President pushed a button on the phone. His secretary answered instantly. "Tony, get Jace Pellicone on the line."

A soft and seductive voice responded, "Yes, Mr. President."

The President needed a little levity to break the tension.

"You know Platte, Tony's been my secretary since I was elected to Congress in 1970. That voice of hers hasn't changed in thirty years. It's a good thing that she's about the best secretary in Washington. Charlene has accused me for years of keeping her on the payroll just so I can hear her talk."

Both men laughed. Tony was in her mid fifty's, happily married to a Virginia state trooper, and the mother of three grown children. Her youngest had just received an appointment to the United States Air Force Academy in Colorado Springs. Rogers, a former fighter pilot, knew the young man would make a good officer. He was valedictorian of his high school class, a captain on the tennis team, President of the Student Council, and a volunteer with the Big Brothers program. Even with these credentials, Rogers didn't even try to pretend the boy's appointment was the result of a competitive application. He just felt it was a good use of his presidential powers to reward a faithful assistant, especially since the taxpayers would get a good officer in return.

Within a minute, Tony's sexy voice was back on line. "Sir, General Pellicone is on the line."

"Jace. How are things in Langley?"

"Still surviving, Mr. President. And how are things in the Center of the Universe?"

"We're also getting by. Let me tell you why I'm calling. It appears that someone over there has gotten a little careless with his or her communications security. I'm sending a transcript of a phone call I got a few minutes ago on my line here in the Oval Office discussing information that should be kept in the family, so to speak. Also I'll include the notes my Chief of Staff took on a call he got last night on his secure line."

"And you want me to find out who made the calls. Isn't that an NSA function?"

"No, I don't want you to tell me who made the call. Just find out where he's getting his information."

"I'll do my best, Mr. President."

"Before you go, Jace. I want you to verify the Company's position that there is no proof a nuclear weapon has been stolen and is being transported towards the United States or any of her allies."

"Sir, I have spoken again to my associates in the Mossad. They admitted to me that their initial information was sketchy at best. They place the probability at less than five percent. Also, the French secret service tells me that there is no way a nuclear device could possibly have moved under their noses. They are most offended that we didn't bring them in on our investigation immediately."

"I don't care what offends the French. They leak more information than we do, and at the moment that seems hard to believe."

Jace Pellicone responded indignantly, "That's not fair, Thomas!" The President and CIA Director had been friends more than forty years.

A heavy breath escaped President Thomas Rogers' mouth. "You're right, Jace. I apologize. Just try to get me some information. I really want to believe you're right. I'm trusting millions of lives on your information."

"Mr. President, I believe you can rest assured no nuclear weapon has been stolen."

"Thank you again, Jace. I sleep better knowing you're over there."

"Good bye, Mr. President."

The mood in the Oval Office improved dramatically with Jace Pellicone's assurance. He had never been wrong before when it came to something of this magnitude ... at least not until now.

Twenty-Five

Annu slammed the phone down on the instrument. Isha, standing nearby, decided not to say anything to his father immediately. The King rarely showed that kind of anger, and when he did, it was wise to stay away until he cooled down. Annu's temper was legendary.

His disposition was a source of personal frustration for Annu. He tried never to get angry when someone made an honest mistake, but he was unforgiving when someone was guilty of being reckless or irresponsible in his or her duties.

That was, he believed, the case now. Annu thought the President of the United States was a blind fool for refusing to even listen to him.

After a few minutes Isha ventured a comment. "Father, you know, I just don't understand the President." The Prince was deciding how far to go. "You merely asked him to believe someone who claims to be the king of a hidden tribe – the king of a lost civilization within his own borders. You simply asked him to take your word, a stranger, over that of his entire intelligence network. On top of all that, you broke into one of the most secure communication systems in the government and shared secrets that probably less than thirty people in the whole world know anything about." Isha smiled at his own gentle sarcasm, "I just can't understand why he's skeptical."

Even though he hated to, Annu laughed at himself. "I know, son. It's just so blasted aggravating that Rogers won't listen to me. Granted, in my heart, I understand. But it makes me feel so helpless. Here we have all this information, I risked a contact, and that damn politician won't listen to me."

A phone call from Colin Johnson interrupted the conversation between the two men. "Sire, I only have a moment. We've just intercepted a message from the Peligroso that confirms, at least in my mind, our initial assessment. I think you can confidently tell the President specifics about the ship."

"I've already talked to him, Colin. He's chosen to bury his head in the sand and ignore the facts. I don't think anything we tell him will change his mind."

"We've faced the same problem over here. The British Prime Minister has all but told us we are not to bother him again with this tripe. It's a frustrating battle, I know."

"Any suggestions?"

"None, sir. Perhaps the Elders would have some. I'll continue working here. If something comes in that you should know, I'll get back to you."

"Do that, Colin."

"One more thing, sir. If we aren't able to stop this, I'm planning to leave London and return to Exeter. I believe that if we're unable to prevent Salomi from his mass murder, you may have to recall the Protectors from around the world. I'm afraid we're headed for a crisis, and you may need us."

"How long before the Peligroso reaches New York?"

"Five days, sir. It should be arriving at 8:00 a.m. with the morning tide."

"All right, Colin. I'll have Prince Isha send the word to all Protectors to return to Exeter if they do not hear otherwise within four days."

"Sir, perhaps it would be best to tell them not to travel through any of the New York airports. We don't want to risk someone being stranded there."

Annu sighed. "Ok, Colin. Let's pray that won't be necessary."

"Good bye, Sire. I hope I don't see you in four days."

After hanging up the phone, Annu rubbed his tired eyes. The pressure and immensity of the problem weighed heavily on his shoulders. He was still frustrated at his inability to convince the President. "If the man would just let me give him the data, he could have the ship stopped and searched the moment it enters U.S. territorial waters. If he wants to avoid an international incident, that would do it. Unfortunately, the President only believes what he wants to believe. He's one of those people who makes up his mind and doesn't want to be confused with the facts."

Isha smiled at his father's play on words. "I know, Dad. But, there's an alternative that I think we must consider. It may be necessary for Exeter to act." Isha rarely used the term Dad to address his father. It was a very affectionate and personal term for him that was reserved for special moments.

Annu noticed. He put his arm around his son's shoulders. "Act? How? In our entire history, we've never involved ourselves in the political process of any country."

"That's not exactly accurate. Every time we permit some technological advance of ours to be leaked to the outside, we affect the lives of millions. This situation is far more critical to the people above than just giving them a new medicine or electronic gadget. The entire world will be devastated if that weapon is detonated. It's not difficult to imagine a world war as the result. Do we want that on our conscience? Especially if we have the means to stop it?"

"What means do you have in mind, son?"

"I want to take a team of Protectors to board the Peligroso and..."

"Board a ship in international waters?" Annu shook his head. "No, Isha. That's not an option."

"Father," Isha said gently, "we both know we can't stand by and allow this madman to kill innocent men, women, and children. I want to lead a team of five or six..."

"No!" King Annu interrupted.

"Father, we could do it. With a few Protectors we would at least have a chance to save thousands, perhaps millions, of lives. We can do it, I know we can!"

"Don't be ridiculous, son. You would never get on board undetected. And even if somehow you did, you have no idea who on the crew is involved."

"Colin is certain the captain isn't implicated. I could make contact with him."

"Making contact with the captain is exactly what I've been thinking about, son – but I'll do it not you." It was obvious to Isha that the conversation was finished. The king had made up his mind about how to handle the situation. "Ask the security chief to call me in thirty minutes." The king went into his chamber without another word.

Isha turned around to see Deidre standing by the door to her room. The sight of her made him feel so much better. They had been spending as much time together as possible the past several days. Now that Maria was strong enough, there was talk of the two moving back to her house. That thought caused Isha to appreciate each time he was with her even more.

In the past, love was not something Isha had ever really considered. He was the Prince. He was a Protector. He was too busy preparing someday to be King. Love would have to wait.

That was before Deidre. Now, every time he saw her, he was more certain that this young lady would someday be his queen. His years of training as a Protector had made him control his emotions when under pressure. Tomás had instilled in his young Prince the capacity to think clearly regardless of the circumstances.

Isha could control his feelings when threatened, but when he was near Deidre, he realized she was really in charge of his heart. It was an unusual internal emotional struggle to negotiate for the young prince. Isha didn't think he was handling it well.

He put on a forced smile. "Hi. Been standing there long?"

"Long enough." She crossed the room and looked up slightly into his deep brown eyes. "Isha, don't go to that ship. I don't want you to."

"And why not?"

"Because, your father is right. It's too dangerous. Listen, I know what's happening. The King told my grandmother, and since you were involved, she told me."

"Well, we have no secrets in this house. But, since you know what's going on, you obviously know we can't just sit back and let it happen. Ron was one of my Protectors. I won't let him die in vain."

"But does it have to be you? Isn't there another Protector who can lead this?"

"Can I take your concern as an indication that for some reason you care what happens to me?"

Deidre allowed a coy smile to escape. "No, Isha. I just don't want the future King of Exeter placing himself in danger unnecessarily. You have a responsibility to your people."

"I don't need you to remind me of my royal responsibilities," Isha said perhaps too sharply. "I've been the Prince of Exeter a long time. But more importantly, I'm a Protector of this tribe. I cannot – I will not ask one of my people to do anything I'm unwilling to do myself."

Deidre was unrepentant. "You're the Prince for goodness sake!"

"So? I'm also a Protector! At the risk of sounding immodest, I'm a damn good warrior!" Isha was feeling his anger rise, which surprised him.

Deidre's voice and expression softened noticeably. "I know you are, Isha. I've seen what you can do." The sight of a subdued attacker and two dead thugs were still very fresh in her mind. "My only concern is that something will happen to you."

She smiled at him and for just a moment Isha weakened. "I love you, too, Deidre." The look on his face betrayed his horror at having unintentionally said the words.

"Too?" Deidre replied alluringly. "I don't remember saying I love you first."

Isha waited at least ten seconds before answering. He knew her true feelings. He could feel them every time they were together. "Then you're saying you don't love me?" He sighed loudly, "I guess I have to go on the mission now. I have nothing left to live for."

Isha's attempt at humor to lighten the situation was totally lost on Deidre. "Don't you dare try and lay that on me, mister! I refuse to be the cause of you going on a suicide mission!"

Isha laughed gently. "I was joking, Deidre. All I was looking for was a chance to hear you say how you feel about me."

The young women answered immediately. She turned to face Isha directly and looked deeply into his chocolate brown eyes. "You know I love you, too. I've loved you since the first time I saw you in the Palace of the Governors. Every day since, I've realized just how much I care. Don't you remember what you told me on our first date?" Deidre thought for a moment, collected her memory, and quoted the short poem Isha had given her that night.

We are of one heart, you and I,
And nothing can ever end
The feelings that bind us.

"Isha, you told me that that poem was written by your favorite poet here. He said it for me, too."

"Well, that poem was a little cocky of me."

"What do you mean?"

He laughed out loud. "Deidre, I wrote that poem. I was really just making it up. I didn't think you would memorize it."

"Well, I did!" she said angrily.

Isha realized just how hurt Deidre was. He really wasn't sure how to placate her. "Listen, Deidre, you make me feel special. I'm not really used to that. Everyone, except Kevin of course, treats me differently because I'm the Prince. You treated me differently before you knew I was a Prince."

"That's how you treat someone you care about." Deidre took a long look at Isha. She wanted to hold him, but she didn't dare. "Does that mean you won't go on the mission?"

Isha didn't answer. He acted as if he had not heard the question.

Deidre just shook her head, turned on her heels, and stormed back into her room.

* * * * *

Isha was welcoming Exeter's security chief to the King's residence as Annu came out of his chamber. The three men talked for several minutes discussing the King's strategy. Once the plan and the message were agreed upon, the man left to carry out Annu's order.

With the advent of satellite relay technology, communications between ships at sea and land based stations are always available. In fact, every ship on an oceanic route constantly monitors two radio frequencies. First is a common frequency, a "party line", which all ships use to communicate openly with each other. Second is a discrete frequency that is only used to send messages to a particular ship. The security section of Exeter had already determined the discrete frequency for the Peligroso.

Within a half hour of the security chief's departure from the King's chamber, a secure message was sent directly to Captain Andrews. Annu had decided to contact the captain in a way that would make him think the company was sending the communiqué. This would assure Andrews' assistance without divulging too much. Annu realized the less he revealed, the smaller the chance of Salomi's assassins realizing they had been discovered.

....

MESSAGE • MESSAGE • MESSAGE • MESSAGE

To: Captain: Peligroso (PA0852)
    22 Oct, '09 • UTC 1800

CAPTAIN'S EYES ONLY *** CAPTAIN'S EYES ONLY
Regarding: Your msg of 22 Oct, '09 • UTC 0845

As of 0700 this date, Captain Andrews, it is believed you are carrying illicit cargo in the B-6 pallet number B-6-3731E. You are directed not, repeat not, to open the container. Instead, you are to continue to destination. Do not, repeat not, allow the cargo to be moved or unloaded from the hold.

Standby for further instructions. We are not certain, however we do suspect, that there are members of the crew who are involved. We recommend you do not discuss this message with any member of your crew.

Further, you are directed not, repeat not, to contact the company for further information. As you approach your port of entry into the United States, we will provide you with instructions.

CAPTAIN'S EYES ONLY *** CAPTAIN'S EYES ONLY

END MESSAGE • END MESSAGE • END MESSAGE

....

Captain's Eyes Only transmittals were used for sensitive messages. In theory, no one saw them except the ship's captain. In fact, that was never the case. The communications officer saw every message that came to the ship, as did the mate who manned the radios. Both men were sworn to secrecy in the case of confidential messages, but this one was extremely unusual. The two were discussing the communiqué when First Officer Miles Permi, entered the communications center. It was one of his responsibilities to check on incoming messages at the end of his duty watch.

"Anything new come in from the company about Mr. Frame?"

"No, sir, nothing about Mr. Frame. However, we were just about to send for the captain. We do have an Eyes Only message for him."

"What's it about?"

"Sir, we can't..."

"I'm the bloody first officer, mister!" Permi snarled. "The captain has no secrets from me. Give me the damn letter!"

The communications officer and radio operator both knew the captain kept all the classified messages from the first officer, but they feared the man and his legendary temper.

Miles Permi read the message twice. "I'll take this to Andrews. Don't mention it to anyone else."

"Yes, sir," the men answered in unison. Permi didn't hear. He was already out the door.

As he walked quickly down the passageway, panic drove Miles Permi. His heart was pounding, and a cold sweat poured from his brow. He had no idea what to do.

Instead of going up the ladder towards the captain's stateroom, he went instead down to the crew quarters deep in the bowels of the ship. Within a few minutes, he found the man he was searching for – Lyndon Pearson – one of the six new crewmen – the assassin who had killed Paxton Frame.

Permi shoved the message in his face. "What can we do? We've been found out." The fear and panic that surged through his body were obvious in his voice.

Lyndon Pearson glared at Permi in disgust. "Get a hold of yourself, you bastard! This possibility has been considered. We continue as planned."

"How can we do that? The captain will lock the hold down. We'll never be able to arm the bomb and then get away before it explodes." Permi was raving, and the pitch of his voice was going up with every syllable.

With snake like speed, the assassin's hand snapped out and caught the first officer's cheek. A red blotch marked the insult. "You're weak, Permi! Listen to me! You can fear your captain or work with me. But remember, he and the rest of this crew are going to die. With that fact in mind make your choice."

Miles Permi tried to recover his composure. "I brought the message to you not him, didn't I? That should prove who I'm loyal to. This captain and this company have both stepped on me for the last time. When the Peligroso explodes in New York, everyone will blame her owners and Andrews. With the money I get from Salomi, I'll be able to live very comfortably on any South Pacific island I choose to buy. After all, everyone will figure I'm dead, and no one will ever be able to tie me to all this."

"Just remember who's the founder of your feast. Salomi doesn't tolerate fools."

"You know I'm loyal to Salomi. I guess I'm just concerned about the discovery of our cargo."

"You fool!" The disgust in the voice of Lyndon Pearson dripped off his tongue. "If your company really knew what we're carrying, they wouldn't order us to continue. They would have us stop where we are while every U.S. Naval vessel in this hemisphere came to board us."

The realization that Pearson was right slowly ebbed through Permi's mind. He had allowed his panic to override common sense. He felt a rush of relief.

"What should we do?"

"Who else has seen this message?"

"Just the communications room. Why?"

Pearson didn't answer the question. "I want you to call my associates to your cabin in fifteen minutes. Tell them to bring their tools. Everyone will understand. In the meantime, do nothing out of the ordinary. Understand?"

"Yeah, I understand," Permi replied, but he didn't really. It angered him that this ruffian was ordering him, the first officer, like an underling. There was really nothing he could do about it. Permi was terrified of Lyndon Pearson. He was a cold-blooded killer, a true sociopath. The first mate vividly remembered the ruthless way Pearson had crushed the skull of Paxton Frame. There was no pity, no remorse, and no mercy.

Pearson turned without another word and walked away leaving Permi standing there.

Five minutes later, both the communications officer and communications mate were dead. Neither man had the time to spread the alarm. Silently and almost instantly, Lyndon Pearson killed them.

Leaving the communications space, Pearson locked the door behind him and left the Do Not Disturb sign clearly visible. Other crewmen knew not to enter when the sign was up. The delay in discovering the dead men would give Salomi's men time to carry out their backup plan.

Captain Andrews was a creature of habit when it came to his working ritual. Most captains used the prerogatives of their position to work during the day, but he always scheduled himself for the evening bridge watch. When at sea, he took an afternoon nap, awoke at precisely the same time, showered, and then shaved with an old straight razor his father had given him thirty years before. His practiced hand quickly removed the shaving cream and stubble from his face. No matter how rough the seas or how much the ship was affected, he rarely nicked himself.

Andrews was standing at the washbasin when there was a knock at his stateroom door. "Come in," he yelled. He looked back into his mirror to finish the last of his shaving. He used the mirror to see who was coming in. Miles Permi and a man Andrews barely knew entered. They left the door open slightly.

The captain was immediately uncomfortable. He didn't know why, but there was no doubt in his mind that this was a dangerous situation. "Yes, Mr. Permi?" The tension in the cabin was palpable. "Is there a problem?"

Instead of the first officer responding, the other man did. "There is no problem unless you make one. I'm afraid your service is no longer required, and Mr. Permi is now in command of this ship."

"Is this some kind of sick joke? Mr. Permi, I want an explanation."

Permi was enjoying his position of power over Andrews. He allowed all his frustration to vent. "You don't deserve an explanation. Since I've been on this crew, you've kept me from having any chance at command. I've simply decided to make my own opportunity."

"You're mad! The rest of the crew will never follow you in this mutiny."

"Actually, you're probably right. However, my associate here has friends among the crew who possess very powerful incentives. They may not follow happily, but they will follow or die instead."

Andrews looked the other man in the eyes. "You head the six men I hired in France. Mr. Frame raised questions about you just before he disappeared. I see his concerns were justified."

Pearson puffed up noticeably. "Unfortunately he won't be able to gloat at his astute observations. He's now resting in about six hundred fathoms of water."

Up to this time, Captain McLean Andrews had been standing at his washbasin. He took a towel from the rack and dried his face. While drying, he used the towel to cover his razor and fold its blade into the handle. With the skill of a master magician, Andrews carefully palmed the razor. Stalling for time to think through the situation, the captain walked to his bed and sat down. He reached down and pulled out his shoes. "It's safe to assume that you and your men are armed?"

The nine-millimeter Parabellum Berretta materialized from inside the man's jacket. "It might interest you to know that I'm by far the least armed man in my group." For a second, all three men were looking at the handgun. The distraction gave Andrews the chance to carefully slide the straight razor into his sock. As he stood up, his pants leg dropped to hide the razor.

"What do you expect to gain from this?" The question was rhetorical, but Andrews was desperately trying to give himself time to come up with solutions. "As far as I know, there hasn't been a successful mutiny anywhere in the world during my lifetime." The comment had no effect on either of the men. "You can't possibly run this ship and guard my entire crew with only six men."

A chuckle slipped from the man's twisted smile. "Well, actually, you started this trip with a crew of twenty six. If you subtract me, my five men, and of course, Mr. Permi here, you now have nineteen. Mr. Frame got too nosy. He's proof that curiosity does kill. Plus, your two communications men have just had a terrible accident. That brings you down to sixteen living crew members, including yourself, of course."

"What the hell happened to my communications team?"

"You don't listen well. For two very good reasons, they are not your communications team. First, you are no longer the captain of this vessel. Second, they're dead." Pearson was pleased with himself for this sick attempt at humor.

"You've already killed three of my men?" Andrews could not believe what he was hearing.

"Again, you're not listening. You are no longer the captain of this ship. Mr. Permi is."

McLean Andrews fought to maintain his composure. "What is the purpose for this mutiny, and what makes you think you can get away with it?"

"Our purpose for the commandeering of the ship is not of your concern." Miles gave Permi a knowing smile. "You, however, may be interested in knowing that history will forever regard the name Peligroso along side that of the Enola Gay."

Andrews could not fathom why his ship would be associated with the airplane that had dropped an atomic bomb on Hiroshima. It sickened Andrews to realize the thug standing before him was right. They could guard his whole ship with just seven men. The only areas that required constant watch to keep the ship operating were the bridge and engine room. He was worried about his men, and silently prayed for their safety. Andrews was certain that, for the time being, only God could help his crew. He felt suddenly weak and powerless. For a man of action like McLean Andrews, these feelings were overwhelming.

While Miles Permi and Lyndon Pearson were with the captain, the other men in Salomi's hire were taking control of the rest of the ship. Two men with automatic weapons entered the engine room. They forced the four men there into a corner with their hands over their heads. Then they took the youngest man, a twenty-one year old from Toronto, put a gun to his head, and told the others they would see his brains be splattered over the entire room if they didn't obey. They obeyed. The engine room was under the control of the Salomi's men.

The only immediate concern for Lyndon Pearson was the off-duty crew. Seamen are, by the nature of their work, a hearty group. The last thing Pearson wanted was for several of them to get wind of the mutiny. They could easily sabotage critical functions on the ship, or even try to retake the ship by force. Pearson doubted there were any weapons on the ship, but he couldn't be sure. More importantly, he couldn't afford to have anyone injured or killed in a fight. It was absolutely crucial, therefore, that he have all the crew in one place. Captain Andrews was his answer to that problem.

Second Officer Scott McQueen was on the bridge when Captain Andrews, First Officer Miles Permi, and another man entered. As was the custom, McQueen started to give the captain as status report. "Sir, we're just..."

The third man interrupted him. "We don't care! Everyone leave their stations and move to the bulkhead." At first, no one moved. Then the bridge crew noticed the large handgun held at the captain's back, and they did as they were told.

Miles Permi picked up the microphone for the ship's intercom. "Do it just the way we told you. Don't forget, you're the most expendable member of the crew. We already have a captain, so you're just another person to guard. If you say one thing besides what I told you, I will kill you."

A look of hatred poured from McLean Andrews' eyes as he took the microphone. "Gentlemen," he began, "this is the captain speaking. I want all off-duty crewmen to meet in the mess immediately. I repeat I want all off-duty crewmen to meet in the mess immediately."

All over the ship, the intercom message had an instantaneous affect. Never before had Captain Andrews issued such a command. Men who had just gotten in their bunks after an exhausting day of work, still quickly pulled on their clothes and hustled to the mess. It was the largest room on the ship, and the only place the captain could have a face-to-face meeting with virtually his entire crew. Something big must be happening.

Twelve minutes later, there were eight men waiting in the mess. They constituted the entire remaining off-duty crew. Almost every one of them had served in the Navy. Military training dies hard, so when the captain came in they began to get to their feet. These men had not been able to break the habit drilled into them by the service. McLean Andrews waved them back into their seats.

"Gentlemen, I want you to listen carefully to what I'm about to tell you. There can be no misunderstanding here. Mr. Permi has assumed command of the Peligroso." A murmur of disbelief erupted from the small group of men. "Quiet! Mr. Permi and his associates are now in command of the bridge and engine room. They have already killed three of our crew. They will not hesitate to kill more."

A stunned silence filled the room.

Andrews took a deep breath and continued. "Men, I don't want any of you to attempt a foolish struggle against them. They are heavily armed, and they've already proven a willingness to eliminate anyone in their way."

Miles Permi stepped in front of Andrews and looked around the room. "Men, welcome to my crew. I trust you will give me the fine service you gave your former captain. If you do, there will be a very nice bonus when we get to New York. If you don't, you'll never see your families again." He paused briefly. "Do I make myself clear? Do your jobs as normal and you will be rich men. Screw with me, and you will be dead."

Three men, each with an Uzi machine gun, walked in. One of them spoke to Lyndon Pearson and confirmed the bridge and engine room were now being guarded. They stood by as Pearson informed the crew of his plans. "As of now, this room is your quarters. When you are not on duty, you will be here."

The ship was now completely in the control of the mutineers. Pearson turned to Miles Permi. "Captain Permi, why don't you head up to the bridge and take command of your ship." He handed over the nine millimeter Berretta handgun. "I doubt you'll need this, but it is an effective way to assure they are cooperative up there."

Over the next several hours, shipboard life became a hellish nightmare for the crewmembers. At shift times, an armed guard escorted them to their posts.

McLean Andrews, the proud man who for almost thirty years had been a captain of an ocean going ship, now found himself working in the engine room. The backbreaking work was a far cry from being at the helm, but he realized that he was a liability to the mutineers. If they decided he wasn't pulling his own weight, he quite probably would be executed as an example to the rest of the crew.

Andrews was not the type of man to allow his ship to be taken from him without a fight. Already he was forming a desperate plan for getting the Peligroso back.

Twenty-Six

The funeral of Ron Warren was a day of mourning in Exeter. Annu and the Elders had declared it. Ron was the first Protector in almost sixty years to die while living above, and Exeter honored his memory.

Robbie Marcus, a Protector who had trained with Ron, spoke for the brotherhood at Ron's funeral. "From the earliest days in their training, Protectors are indoctrinated with the old French adage noblesse oblige. It means in essence, that those who have much are responsible to care for those with less. Ron understood noblesse oblige and lived his life accordingly. His life was an inspiration for those of us who follow him." The young man paused to gather his thoughts and control the emotion he was feeling. "When a warrior dies, it leaves all other warriors a little diminished. With our loss of Ron, the Protectors are all diminished greatly. He lived his life to keep Exeter in peace. Now our brother has gone to the ultimate peace. Requiescat in pace – rest in peace, Ron."

As Robbie walked back to his seat, a hand reached up to touch his arm. For a moment he stopped and looked down. The face of Kristi peered back at him. Her cheeks were damp from her tears, but the strength in her eyes was undeniable. She spoke barely above a whisper. "Thank you, Robbie. I think Ron would have appreciated your words."

"Kristi, I wish I could have said more," he whispered.

Her tight smile was all the reply he received.

King Annu ended the service for his Protector. "As we go, we will finish the work of this young man. He will not have died in vain." He looked down at the casket that was before him. Placed carefully on the cover was Ron's sword, a symbol of his position. Annu could think of no other appropriate words. "Requiescat in pace, my Protector. Rest in peace, Ron."

The funeral ended and Annu spent several minutes alone with Ron's parents. Up until this time, they had thought their son was the victim of a robbery. Annu told them instead that their son was a hero. He gave them a brief explanation. After hearing the circumstances of his son's death, Ron's father had one simple request from his king. "Highness, don't let my son's death be in vain. He gave us the warning. Please stop this madness before others, so many others, die, too."

"You have my word, we will use everything in our power to prevent it. Your son lost his life to give us the warning. We will stop it. I promise."

Even as he walked from Ron's parents, Annu felt the pressure of his words. He knew they had to keep the Peligroso from carrying out its horrible mission. Seeing the distraught parents of his dead Protector gave him even more resolve. Annu simply had no idea yet how to accomplish it and still protect the secrecy of Exeter.

Waiting at the royal tram were Isha, Kevin. Isha had also asked Robbie, Jackson, and Cody to join them. The king paused for a moment and looked intently into the eyes of the young warriors. "Gentlemen, we have some planning to do. We can't expect any help from Washington. It's up to us."

"Yes sir," they responded in unison.

Within an hour King Annu had called a council of his Elders. Isha and Kevin spent twenty minutes giving them a complete briefing on the situation. After the briefing, Kevin left to sit with Celia, Deidre, Robbie, Jackson, and Cody. Isha returned to sit with the King.

The Elders were divided. Some were adamant that it was none of Exeter's business. They argued that the sovereignty of the tribe was absolute. The fact that Exeter was located deep beneath the United States did not require them to protect the country. Further, they added, involving themselves would be a dangerous precedent. Exeter would be safe if the entire surface of the Earth was destroyed. The climate system would continue to provide untainted oxygen. The underground rivers would continue to give pure water. Life in Exeter, they argued, would continue unchanged even if a worldwide conflagration occurred above.

Annu and Isha sat quietly while Elders with other opinions argued their positions. It appeared they would not be able to reach any kind of consensus when the oldest man in the room raised his hand. Annu nodded in the direction of the man. "Yes, Maurice?"

Maurice Grolier, who had been an Elder far longer than any man in the recorded history of Exeter, slowly and painfully, rose to his feet. "Sire, with respect I wish to address my friends and colleagues here."

Isha noted that Maurice still used the more formal protocol of Elders long ago. The king recognized the circumstance and responded appropriately to his most senior Elder. "The King requests the counsel of Maurice, of the Grolier clan."

Grolier cleared his throat. The room fell totally silent. Grolier was treated with an almost worshipful deference. Everyone knew he rarely spoke when the Elders debated. He chose instead to listen to the thoughts of his younger colleagues. When he did speak, they listened with dutiful respect. "Sire," he paused and looked around the room, "and my peers, we are faced with a challenge unlike any I can remember before. In my youth, while those above killed each other in what they called the war to end all wars, we recalled all Protectors to the safety of Exeter. We did the same thing a generation later when that mad man ran loose in Europe. Even in the conflicts of Korea and Vietnam, we were able to prevent any Protector from being conscripted. Our rationale has always been that Exeter owes allegiance to no nation above. Therefore, our young men and women have not gone to war." There was a murmur of agreement from the Elders who were arguing for isolation. Grolier raised his hand and they quieted. He continued, "Now I think perhaps we were wrong." A stunned silence came over everyone. He waited for several seconds before going on. "We were wrong, and I was a part of every decision that was made during those years so long ago." He stopped and pointed at Robbie. "This young Protector here made me realize my error. When he eloquently eulogized our fallen warrior this morning, he reminded me of something. Something I should have never forgotten in the first place. Noblesse oblige, my friends. Exeter has the greatest minds living any where on this planet. We live with technology on a daily basis that those above will probably not have for another thirty or forty years, and then only if we allow them to have it. This utopia is ours because of those in our history who have been willing to die for it. God has blessed us and our people. Noblesse oblige. We are responsible before God and each other for those above who need our help. If we had not discovered this murderous plot, we would not have been placed in the situation of having to protect those above – but we do know – and we are responsible. Noblesse oblige."

The old man sat down. Annu sensed immediately a change in the attitude of the Elders. The most persistent of those opposed to intervention realized that if Grolier, a long time isolationist, felt the need to become involved in this dangerous situation, then perhaps there was merit.

Annu spoke quietly, "Maurice, thank you for reminding us that our gifts and abilities also bring responsibility with them." He looked around the room. "Is there further discussion?"

The Elder who had spoken before Grolier stood and addressed the group. "Sire, I remove my objections to the action."

Annu nodded. He knew the retraction was an honest admission that the Elder's mind had been changed. He had not been bullied into retracting his objection. The king answered him, "It is noted with my appreciation." Again he scanned the room. "My friends, I will protect the sanctity of Exeter. Whatever is required to remove the scourge of this threat above will be done in such a way that our home will not be compromised. You have my word."

Maurice Grolier slowly raised his hand and was recognized by Annu. "Sire, I recommend we now consider this to be a council of war." A council of war had not been called in almost four hundred and fifty years. The last one had come as Conquistadors entered their lands. The ensuing conflict had led to the moving of the tribe to the caverns they now called home.

"With the consent of the Elders, this is now a council of war. We will adjourn for now and meet again in two hours." The king stood. The Elders also stood as Annu and Isha left.

Maurice Grolier met his sovereign at the door to the chamber and offered his hand, "Sire, I served your grandfather, and your father. We often disagreed with each other, sometimes loudly. They were great kings, and you learned well how to rule. They would be proud of you." The old man smiled at Isha. "Prince Isha, I will look forward to serving you when you become King someday."

Annu laughed, "Maurice, my old friend, please allow me to live a few more years before giving the throne to my son. After all you have been an Elder for what, seventy-five years? I've only been king twenty-five years."

"Yes, sire," the old man joked, "but the Elders need someone who can remember a long way back. I was hoping you would allow me to be around for your grandson to reign."

The King laughed. "I grant that wish. As long as there is Exeter, you have a place with our Elders." The king gently hugged the frail body of Maurice Grolier. "And when my grandson rules Exeter, he will be fortunate to have your council." All three men knew that no matter how much they desired it, Grolier would never serve another King. The cancer raging throughout his body might even prevent the celebration of his birthday in two months.

"I will stand at their command, as I have yours, Sire," the old man responded warmly.

* * * * *

The ride back to his chambers was a long one for Annu. His kingdom flashed by the tram, and yet he took no notice. The king knew his son was right—the ship had to be stopped while still at sea, but how?

Isha and Kevin sat quietly in the tram. Both knew they would soon be planning and hopefully executing the most difficult and dangerous mission any Protector had ever faced. The Elders had approved an unprecedented intervention in an event above. Their authorization gave the king permission to use the worldwide reach of Exeter to intercept the Peligroso and prevent the use of her deadly cargo.

Now came the challenging part—determining how to accomplish it. Each of the three men on the tram was lost in his private thoughts. King Annu broke the spell first. "Well, there is one good thing about this situation. We won't have anyone looking over our shoulder to tell us we're doing it wrong, because no one has ever done anything like this before." The slight wrinkles around his eyes were deepened by the smile he showed.

"We'll figure something out, Father. I know we'll come up with a plan."

Annu considered his son for a moment. He had grown and matured into a handsome man with a gifted intellect. There was no doubt in Annu's mind that somehow they would be able to handle the situation. For the moment, however, he couldn't fathom how.

As the tram entered the King's chamber the three men inside stood to exit. There waiting for them was Deidre. Her dark hair was tied back up into a tight bun, and her regal pose was striking. She had the look of someone who was on a mission. There was an intensity to her face that was noticeable even from the tram.

Isha was especially glad to see her. When they had parted earlier in the day, she was still angry about his decision to lead the Protector team on its raid. He didn't entertain the hope that she now saw things his way. He did hope she would eventually understand his sense of responsibility and commitment. As much as he loved her, duty to Exeter was still his first priority.

Deidre ignored Isha completely confirming his fear that she was still upset with him. Instead she looked at Annu. "Sir," she began, "my Grandmother may have a solution to your situation." Deidre waited for a moment before continuing. The blank look on the three faces before her betrayed the disbelief in the minds of Annu, Isha, and Kevin It irritated her that they were so obviously skeptical, and that irritation reflected in her tone. "Of course, she's just an old woman and not a famous warrior... ."

Annu immediately attempted to soothe her indignation. As they walked into the royal chambers he put his arm around her shoulder and spoke apologetically. "It was not doubt in our minds, Deidre, just surprise. I'm ready to listen to any suggestions that may help." No one thought for a moment that the king was being condescending or demeaning in his response. His tone and attitude were sincere.

"I think she would rather share her idea with you personally. Besides, neither she nor I know if her idea is practical or even possible."

"Well, let's find out then. Where is Mrs. O'Leary?"

"In your study, sir."

Maria Rodriguez-O'Leary was sitting in a large overstuffed chair in the middle of the room. On her lap was a legal size yellow pad of paper. On a desk beside her was the 2006 volume of *The Whole World Catalog of Ships*. The annual research volume was considered by most scholars to be the most complete reference book on commercial ships. While individual ships were not discussed, great detail on each type of vessel was available.

Maria stood as the king entered the room. Annu had already told her several times that it was not necessary, but she insisted standing as a show of respect. The king had decided that trying to get her to stop was a useless endeavor, and so simply accepted it.

"Please, sit down, Mrs. O'Leary." As she settled back into the chair, he noticed that she still moved with difficulty. She's not ready to go back to her house without someone to help her there. She needs to stay here until her recuperation is farther along. "What do you have for us?"

"Well, I knew when you left here this morning that you wanted to get approval from the Elders to intercept that ship at sea. So, I figured that you might need to know some details about its lay out. I took the liberty — and King Annu I have to ask your forgiveness for using your name — to have your library system research cargo ship design. They didn't have anything like that available, but a very nice lady named Mary Lois brought this book instead."

Annu, of course knew that Mary Lois was the Royal Librarian and was responsible for the sixteen libraries in Exeter. He could only imagine the high-level attention that took place in the library system when someone from the King's house called requesting information on ship blueprints. Considering the subterranean location of Exeter, he doubted there was much call for specific details regarding ocean-going ships. He could only imagine how the librarians must have scrambled to find the information they thought the king himself required. The Whole World Catalog of Ships was probably the closest thing they could come up with.

Annu doubted her investigation would help, but did not want to discourage Maria's initiative. She obviously wanted to assist, and it was true he had no idea how to proceed.

"Maria, thank you for your research. Let me know if you come up with a suggestion." The king hoped his sounded more sincere than he felt.

"Perhaps it would make it easier if I knew what you were needing to do."

King Annu never for a moment thought Maria was being nosy. Instead, he realized she was only wanting what she felt was necessary in order to make honest suggestions. "Our problem is two-fold, Mrs. O'Leary. First, we have to come up with a way to secretly board a cargo ship while it is moving on an open ocean. Secondly, once on board we have to figure out who on the crew is involved and how to stop them without endangering the rest of the men." The king saw understanding in the eyes of the old woman and continued. "As far as we know, nothing like this has ever been attempted before."

"Can you actually get on a ship while it's moving?"

"Well, obviously it would be easier if the ship was stopped, but I can't think of a way to do that."

The brow of Maria's forehead furrowed in thought. "Then our real problem is figuring out how to get on the ship. Right?" Pointing at a diagram of an ocean going cargo ship with its large flat superstructure. "Could you use this area to land some kind of plane?"

"No, this picture makes it appear flat, but there are cranes, hatches, and a thousand other obstacles that would keep a plane from landing there. Besides, it's way too short."

"Could you parachute on to the ship?"

All three of the men were secretly embarrassed that this old woman had so quickly and succinctly cut to the heart of the situation. They had been trying to figure out how to board the Peligroso. It was almost humorous that they had ignored such an obvious possibility.

Actually parachuting was out of the question. There was another solution, however. It only took an hour to get a rough idea formulated.

Twenty-Seven

Exeter had been screening and jamming all communications to the Peligroso since King Annu's first transmission to her. Routine company messages had been allowed through in order to keep the mutineers unaware that their plot had been discovered. Annu did not want them the least bit suspicious.

The planning of Exeter's interdiction of the Peligroso was going full stride. It was decided that having the ship stopped would greatly improve the team's ability to get on board safely. How to accomplish this required a careful ruse that demanded a second contact with the ship.

Early the next morning a new a discrete message was sent to the Peligroso. Exeter's technical expertise once again made it appear that it had come from the company.

....

MESSAGE • MESSAGE • MESSAGE • MESSAGE
To: Captain: Peligroso (PA0852)
    23 Oct, '09 • UTC 1300

*** OPERATIONAL IMMEDIATE ***
*** OPERATIONAL IMMEDIATE ***

As of 0800 this morning (UTC), a nighttime collision between two freighters at the entrance to New York harbor has operations into the docking area stopped. Currently, there are thirty-three ships at anchor outside the harbor awaiting the damaged ships to be raised and moved.

The Harbor Master's Office has directed this line to have the Peligroso hold your current position until the harbor is cleared and the backlog of ships are moved.

We estimate a twenty-four to thirty-six hour delay at your current location. This directive is applicable only to those ships en route to NYC.

If there are changes to this directive, we will immediately pass them to you.

Jonathan McKelvey,
Managing Director, Operations

*** OPERATIONAL IMMEDIATE ***
*** OPERATIONAL IMMEDIATE ***

END MESSAGE • END MESSAGE • END MESSAGE

....

A great deal of discussion in Exeter resulted in the message. The warriors felt the Peligroso would take the telex at face value and not attempt to contact the company for clarification. This delay would give Exeter the time it needed to act.

Isha and Kevin knew time was not on their side. To avoid interference with the U.S. Coast Guard, it was crucial that the entire operation take place in international waters.

The planning team estimated they needed at least thirty hours. That would allow time for planning the mission, for assembling equipment, pinpointing the Peligroso's location, and for rendezvous with the ship. This would permit them to intercept the Peligroso a full two days outside United States territorial waters.

* * * * *

In the hours since Miles Permi and Lyndon Pearson had taken control of the ship, they had continued to keep crew members sequestered when not on duty. This assured that none of the Peligroso's regular personnel learned about the deadly cargo she was carrying. Since Pearson had killed the ship's two communications crewmen, he had kept the knowledge they had from being passed along.

Now Pearson had the communications shack under his constant scrutiny. Relief shifts of guarded crewmen monitored incoming messages. Nothing except general status and position reports were transmitted back. They did not want anything to appear out of the ordinary to the company.

When the fake message from the company came in ordering the Peligroso to maintain her position in the middle of the Atlantic Ocean, Lyndon Pearson read it with uncontrolled anger. The timetable for completion of his horrible task was tight. He could not afford any delay.

He decided to ignore the directive. His decision was instantaneous and irrevocable. The Peligroso would continue straight into New York harbor without delay. If necessary, he would deal with getting past the damaged ships when he got there.

* * * * *

In Exeter, the planning team was going ahead unabated. In the final proposal, it was decided to assault the ship using six Protectors. Prince Isha directed Kevin to personally choose the Protectors who were to accompany them on the raid. Kevin surprised everyone by deciding to take David and Robin Marcus' three sons—Robbie, Jackson, and Cody. He had also selected Skye, who was another man from Cody's class of new Protectors.

Kevin's rationale was simple. All four were inexperienced, but no senior Protector had any real experience with this kind of mission either. Each of these men, however, had a distinction that made them desirable for the operation. During the planning, it was apparent that getting on board the ship would be the hardest facet of the operation with the most "unknowns".

As Protectors-in-training, Cody and Skye had helped develop an experimental team transport system. To gather enough data during the testing of the system, Cody had checked out his brothers in its use. As a result, these four men were the most experienced Protectors when it came to operating this specialized transportation system. Since it was the key to getting on board undetected, their practical skill in using the equipment offset their actual inexperience as Protectors.

For Annu, there was one delicate matter to be handled carefully. Kristi wanted to go on the mission. She felt a moral obligation to avenge her fiancé's death. For that very reason, Isha did not want her along, and the king agreed. The Prince explained to Kristi there was absolutely no question about her skill as a Protector, but she was too close to the event and might have trouble with her objectivity if on the operation.

Kristi came close to telling her Prince where he could put his "objectivity", however, the fact that she had that initial response made her realize Isha was right.

In the end, Annu found a solution that would keep Kristi in Exeter, but allow her to remain a crucial part of the team. She would be in charge of communications during the mission. Everyone seemed satisfied with the situation—everyone except Deidre. She wanted Isha to run the mission from the safety of Exeter instead of actually going on the trip.

Deidre had convinced herself that if Isha left on this mission, she would never see him alive again. No amount of reassurances would comfort her. She wouldn't even kiss him good-bye as he left Exeter.

Maria did not share her granddaughter's fears. She hugged Isha warmly and whispered into his ear, "Come home to Deidre, Isha. She needs you – and you need her, too."

"The plans are coming together, Mrs. O'Leary. She has nothing to fear, I'll be home in a few days," Isha responded.

Maria O'Leary did not tell the Prince of Exeter that there was plenty of justification for Deidre's fear. Instead, she just hugged him.

* * * * *

As Isha returned to the planning team, Exeter's electronics section was calling the king with bad news. They had been monitoring NSA and CIA satellite imagery over the past several days. Outside the intelligence community, it was a little known fact that the entire North Atlantic was under constant scrutiny by geosynchronous satellites.

These intercepted satellite pictures showed the Peligroso had not stopped. It was still moving at approximately twenty-two knots. At that speed they would enter U.S. territorial waters in less than two days. Plans had to be moved ahead as quickly as possible. More importantly, it meant that the interception and boarding would have to be accomplished on a moving ship instead of a stationary one. Annu could not understand why the ship had not followed the fictitious company message. Why the ship had ignored instructions was not the critical matter. The team was now committed to landing on a moving deck at night.

* * * * *

Isha and Kevin calculated conservatively that landing on the ship while underway reduced the chance for success by fifty percent. They tried not to dwell on the difficulties of getting on board. Instead they concentrated on modifying their plan to respond to this latest development. It was better to keep busy instead of giving their minds a chance to mull over the bleak prospects.

Everyone worked a little faster to make the plans come together. A scant eight hours after the Elders gave permission for the attack, the team and all their equipment boarded a jet for a flight from Santa Fe to Islip, New York. The six passengers on the plane used the flight time to finish the planning for their mission.

Waiting for them in Islip was a specially prepared transport plane with extended range fuel tanks. The plane had been leased to an international mining company, and made regular trips from the United States to Iceland, Greenland, and the Azores. For today's flight, the regular pilots were told to stay home today, and were replaced by special contract pilots (from Exeter). This was not a totally unheard of arrangement for this type of leasing company. They had a contract guaranteeing the total cost of the aircraft in the event of an accident; they got a premium price on the lease; and their pilots were free to fly other trips.

Today, the replacement pilots had filed a flight plan to Reykjavik, Iceland. They had arranged a somewhat circuitous route with aviation authorities on the ruse that they were conducting over water surveys on the way to their final destination. For the authorities, this was not an unusual occurrence. Several industrial research projects were ongoing in the Atlantic and airborne inspections were commonly associated with them. The aircraft would also be flying well below the usual high altitude commercial airline routes to and from Europe. Because of this, no one would pay particular attention to the plane unless it failed to land at Reykjavik on time. To the authorities, this plane was simply one more to be tracked until landing—just what the Protectors on board were hoping for.

The required cargo and passenger manifest did not list the Protectors or their equipment. This was not an oversight. They would not be on the plane when it touched down in Iceland.

U.S. customs officials made their mandatory inspection of the cargo manifests and passports of everyone aboard. Since the plane was leaving the United States, they did not actually come on board—as they would do on an inbound flight—that would be accomplished in Iceland.

The plane took off just as the sun was going down in the West. The golden glow at the horizon gradually darkened to give way to a crystal clear black sky. As the plane started on its easterly heading, it was over the Atlantic Ocean within minutes.

Isha, Kevin, and the four young Protectors were belted into web seat harnesses in the huge cargo bay of the plane. The Prince looked at the faces of the five young men with him. He knew that there was a pretty good chance that some of them would not be coming home alive. They weren't just his subjects, they were his friends. Kevin had been like his brother. Isha had also known the other four Protectors their whole lives. He and Kevin had helped train all of them.

The tallest of the group was Robbie. He was a handsome man with a chiseled face and very pale blue eyes. Robbie was one of those men who seemed to thrive on stress. His strongest attribute, however, was as a tactician. He was a natural leader and was very popular among the other Protectors.

Robbie's partner in the assault was Skye. He was a stocky, red headed, and freckled face young man who looked all of sixteen. His baby-like face camouflaged the fact that he was by far the most dangerous member of the Protector team. He was an expert in six different martial arts. While in self-defense training, he held the record for the fastest knockout in Exeter's history. Unfortunately, it was an instructor he knocked out. The remainder of that class had been tough for Skye as the embarrassed instructor used his ill-advised student to demonstrate every kind of hold and takedown possible. At the end of the day, Skye was black and blue, but proud of his recognition as a fighter.

Jackson Marcus was three years older than his brother, Cody, and had been a Protector for that long. Both brothers were electronic and engineering specialists, but were also masters at devising and setting traps. Jackson and Cody were blessed with compact athletic bodies, sandy hair and a devil-may-care attitude that made them extremely popular with the young ladies ... much to their mother's chagrin.

All six Protectors were supremely trained warriors. They knew the odds were against them, but none doubted for a moment that Prince Isha would bring them through.

The flight would be a long one, but the Prince decided to decline the pilot's offer of the cockpit jump seat. He believed that a leader should endure whatever hardships his men were forced to suffer. Isha knew that soon the web seat would be making a permanent indentation on his butt. After about an hour, he thought perhaps he needed to reconsider the pilot's generous offer, but by then it was too late.

The Protectors were all wearing similar clothing. A thin rubberized outer jumpsuit covered their clothes. The jumpsuit had an impregnated wire matrix that would operate from a small battery to warm the men. The design allowed the warriors to stay in forty degree temperature for two hours without the danger of hypothermia, yet was thin enough to allow them complete unrestricted movement. The head covering was also heated, but the gloves were not. This was a design problem Exeter had not had time to remedy. Gloves had to be so flexible that the wires usually broke after being worn just a few minutes. This mission demanded the suits, but there wasn't time for any modifications to the gloves. The men would have to be careful to protect their hands.

The eager, and perhaps apprehensive, faces of the young Protectors before him were enough to keep Isha in the back with them. The web seats would soon seem comfortable, almost luxurious, to them. Within three hours, these men would be jumping from this airplane over a pitch-black ocean to land on a moving target.

Anyone who missed landing on the darkened deck of the cargo ship would be lost in the Atlantic with absolutely zero chance of rescue or survival. That fact was well known to all six men.

The Whole World Catalog of Ships was before them on the floor of the airplane. Each man had memorized the expected layout of the Peligroso. Everyone had specific responsibilities. They knew the details, but no one felt totally confident. There were too many unknowns.

The worst thing they had to deal with was the lack of complete blueprints for this specific ship. Like most ocean going cargo ships, the Peligroso had her bridge and control areas on the aft part of the superstructure. The Peligroso was certainly very similar to the information in *The Whole World Catalog of Ships*, but there were obviously differences. How much those differences would affect their plans was a huge question mark.

One of the biggest concerns was the crew. With twenty-six men on board the terrorists had to be holding the off duty crew somewhere. There are only a couple of places big enough, the ship's mess and the engine compartment. The engine room would have too many areas for sabotage. They wouldn't trust keeping the crew there. So Isha felt it had to be the ship's mess – it was a best guess, nothing more. Nothing was set in concrete.

"Just remember, flexibility is the key to success." Isha kept telling them with a huge smile on this face. Flexibility had been his motto for the past several hours. He kept telling the team over and over that they had a great plan on paper. When it came to actually carrying it out, however, they would have to use good judgment to alter and adapt it to the actual situation.

"Flexibility is the key to success," had become almost a humorous cliché. Whenever the Prince started to say it, the rest of the team would laughingly finish the pronouncement. It had become a humorous way to handle some of the pressure they were under.

Again and again they recited their individual and group responsibilities. They wanted the mission to go smoothly, but they weren't naive enough to believe it would.

Isha and Kevin both tried to rest. They believed if they napped, the other four would also. It was hopeless. Their adrenaline was pumping through their systems, and their minds were racing to try to find solutions to problems they hadn't considered before.

As the two leaders looked at the young band of warriors, they realized that one, Cody, was fast asleep. His head was propped back against the aircraft bulkhead; his mouth was wide open and a loud snore escaped with each breath.

Skye looked at his friend with undisguised disgust mixed with admiration. "He's always been able to do that. He can sleep anywhere." He paused for a second then punched his friend in the side. "Cody, wake up! Your snoring is louder than the engines!"

Everyone laughed as the young man looked around in surprise and bewilderment.

The bit of humor was enough to break the tension for a moment. Isha added to the levity, "Cody, I would appreciate it if you would pay attention when I'm speaking. I was telling the team to try and get some sleep."

The young Protector responded instantly, "Yes, sir. I'll try."

* * * * *

Thirty-five minutes later, the pilot called back. "Sire, Exeter is calling on the secure channel. They want you to test the system."

"Thanks. Ok, everyone, let's see if we can talk to Mother."

Each of the men placed a small receiver in their ear. Attached to it was a small microphone that barely stuck out of the ear canal. One by one, each man checked in with Exeter. The calm voice of Kristi answered each one by name. Mother was with them.

A tiny, yet extremely powerful transmitter attached to each man's belt enabled the team to have constant communication with each other. The signal was also monitored in Exeter by way of borrowed satellite transmissions. There was some question as to how effective the satellite communication would be once the Protectors were within the bowels of the ship, but that was the least of their concerns. There were too many other things to worry about.

Sooner than any of the team expected, the pilot called back. "Sire, we have a lock on the ship. Your drop will be in six minutes. We need to go on oxygen so that I can depressurize the aircraft."

As everyone on board put on portable breathing systems, a strange calm suddenly filled the back of the airplane. The waiting was over. Finally the warriors would be able to act. Their concentration was so intense that none noticed that the pilot had slowly begun opening a valve to lower the atmospheric pressure inside the aircraft to that outside. This had to be done in order to open the exit the team would use.

Before putting on his mask, Isha looked into the eyes of the young men in front of him. "Gentlemen, millions of lives depend on what we do in the next few hours. Be strong." He held out his arm. Each Protector placed his hand on that of their Prince. "Remember, we belong to each other."

"We belong to each other." The men repeated solemnly. There was nothing else to be said. This stoic promise, repeated in various ways through the centuries, was the basis for the principles and dogma that bound all Protectors.

Kevin took over his role as operations director. "Ok, everyone strap in, and check each other's equipment." He yelled forward to the pilot, "Kill the lights back here."

"Yes, sir," the aircraft commander replied. He reached to the overhead lighting panel and flipped a toggle switch. At the same time, the copilot closed the door to the cockpit to stop any instrument panel lights from penetrating the blackness of the cargo compartment.

The darkness was staggering. As each man's eyes adapted to the dark, they calmly took the time to prepare mentally. Silently each one prayed for wisdom to handle the unknowns ahead. They knew the danger and also prayed for courage to face it. They were Protectors, trained to a degree unknown to those who lived above, but still mortal. It was not a fear of death that bothered them; it was a fear of failure.

Looking at an indicator mounted on the aft bulkhead of the cabin, Kevin announced, "Two minutes. Put on the masks."

One-by-one the men donned form fitted night vision goggles. These were nothing like the bulky goggles worn by conventional military forces. These were customized to withstand the windblast that would accompany a parachute jump.

Instead of darkness, now the men could see clearly their surroundings and friends. The eerie darkness now gave way to a ghostly greenish light.

Each man looked at the equipment of the man next to him. Every strap and connection was double-checked for security. When Isha checked Kevin, he discovered his inflatable life preservers on the floor pushed under his seat. "Missing something, my friend?"

"No. I've decided not to take anything with me that's extra. If I get on the ship, I won't need a life vest. If I miss the ship, it'll only prolong the inevitable. So, to my way of thinking, I don't need to take it." Isha just smiled at his best friend. They had been through much together. The Prince knew once Kevin had his mind made up, nothing would change it. Besides, he was right.

"Thirty seconds." The door to the outside electrically slid upwards into the fuselage of the plane. A blast of freezing air momentarily took everyone's breath.

"Twenty seconds." The men stood in their places.

"Ten seconds."

"Five..."

"Four..."

"Three..."

"Two..."

"One..."

"GO!"

Isha was the first man to jump out the door into the darkness beyond. The other five Protectors followed him immediately. Kevin was the last one to dive out.

The mission was on.

Twenty-Eight

The Protectors were now scant seconds away from either landing on the Peligroso or in the cold Atlantic waters. The ocean meant certain death, and the ship held only slightly better odds.

The night's weather worked in favor of the assault. A high overcast cloud cover blocked any glimmer from stars or the new moon. There were no lights at all that would give warning to anyone on the ship. Here, far at sea, they were about to be boarded by a band of warriors with a unique transportation system.

Even with the night vision goggles, the men could see only a few of the other team members and a barely detectable image of the ship far below. The Protectors were spread out. Their clothing and equipment were designed to make them almost invisible in the darkness. Each man was wearing a black form-fitting jumpsuit with a tight head and face covering. The few weapons they carried were flat black. There was nothing polished that would reflect any light source to give away their presence.

Ten agonizingly long seconds after he jumped from the airplane, Isha knew everyone was in a free fall towards the shadowy waters below. He yelled into his microphone. "Now!"

Instantly the Protectors pulled what appeared to be a normal parachute "D-Ring". From a pack on each man's back unfurled a chute very similar in design to one used by precision parachute demonstration teams all over the world. The rectangular canopy, which was really a parasail, was attached to shroud lines that gave the individual great control over both direction and speed of the descent. The canopies were made of a solid black material that was almost invisible against the ebony sky.

What made this parachute from any other in the world was a small ducted fan engine attached to the control lines above the men's heads.

The fan and power pack gave everyone an instant source of thrust. In effect, the team now floated under miniaturized ultralight parasails. Their ducted fan engines could propel the men at speeds approaching thirty knots. That was more than enough to overtake the Peligroso if necessary.

These self-contained parasails had huge possible military applications if Exeter ever decided to release them. Large numbers of troops could easily be dropped over secure terrain and then transport themselves almost silently to enemy controlled positions for surprise attacks. The soldiers would be almost invisible on radar, and yet could carry weapons and ammunition for a sustained attack.

The closest Protector in the package was twenty or thirty yards away from Isha. Beyond him, the Prince could barely see a second man. From there, even with the night vision goggles, the darkness swallowed the remaining team members.

As soon as Isha looked up and saw a full parasail above his head, and felt the thrust of the small quiet electric ducted fan motor, he really believed for the first time they would make it. There was no doubt in his mind.

The Prince needed to know the condition of his team. He spoke tersely into his attached tiny microphone, "Team check!"

"Kevin's on!" Kevin responded immediately.

"Robbie's on!"

"Skye's on!"

A chilling silence filled the air. Finally a voice called in, "Cody's on!"

Since the men could only vaguely see the shapes of the other individuals in the group, no one knew for sure if all six parasails had opened. A second check in resulted in the same responses.

The Prince waited for what seemed an eternity, but was really only a few seconds, "Jackson, check in!" No reply.

Isha could now see the moving ship a thousand feet below him. With the aid of the goggles, he could easily see the moving deck.

Finding a spot to land where the warriors could avoid the many cables, hatches, ventilation shafts, and cargo winches was Isha's first priority.

After he landed, each man would then home in on the Prince's signal and fly over the deck to match the speed of the ship. The Protector would have to quietly land on a moving and pitching deck using the minimum of light provided by the goggles.

The moment each Protector had secretly feared for the last twenty-four hours was now scant seconds away.

In Exeter, four anxious faces peered at the monitor before them. Transmissions from the team had been crystal clear so far. Kristi expected it to be for the entire descent. Annu told Maria and Deidre that the men were still within range of the airplane that had brought them from New York, so that it was relaying their radio signals. Shortly, as the airplane got farther away, the clarity would deteriorate significantly.

* * * * *

Even as the Protectors were parasailing to the Peligroso, Colin Johnson was on the phone to Exeter. He had just received information he felt Annu should know immediately.

Someone, and Johnson did not know who, had broken into the port authority at Le Havre, France. Files had been ransacked and a small amount of money from a petty cash drawer was stolen. Before leaving the office in a total shambles, the files on a ship called the Peligroso had been photocopied. The rest of the chaos had been a smokescreen to hide the true reason for the break in.

Geoffrey told Colin about the photocopied files, but claimed he had not ordered the illegal entry of an office in a foreign country. Johnson didn't believe his friend. The ends justifies the means was one of Singer's central beliefs. Johnson didn't agree, but had to admit that the information had been very helpful.

Just hours prior to setting sail, Captain Andrews had called the office to say he might have to delay his departure while he found replacements for six of his crew. The port authority made note of the call since there was a chance he would hold up other departing traffic. The note then continued that the captain had called back two hours later to say he had hired replacements and would leave on schedule.

Immigration officials required each ship to document crewmembers. Geoff's stolen file contained a copy of the mandatory crew manifest for the Peligroso's entry into the harbor, and the one for its departure. Comparing the two lists provided Johnson and Singer the names of the six new crewmembers.

On a hunch, Geoffrey Singer ran the names of the six men through the files of Interpol. One name, Lyndon Pearson, brought an immediate response. He was wanted as the main suspect in the assassination of a Turkish army general two years before, and had a long dossier on file covering more than a decade. Several governments, including the United States wanted him. Lyndon Pearson was the quintessential terrorist.

* * * * *

Jackson's failure to check in was a source of real concern. The team was minimum strength already. The loss of even a single warrior would be disastrous and a personal tragedy for the King. Isha had purposefully kept the number as low as possible. Redundancy was not as big a worry as was secrecy. The Prince believed the key to accomplishing his mission was stealth which equated to a minimum attack force. The fewer people they landed on board the ship, the less chance of being discovered too early.

Isha was the first to reach the deck of the ship. He quickly judged the ship's vertical movement to be no more than three feet. That would be easy enough to compensate for in the landing. Matching the forward speed of the ship, and hence, the landing area was also going to be tricky.

Neither Isha nor Kevin had much experience with the powered parasail. They both were more than a little worried about this part of the mission. If the warrior came in with too much speed, he would hit the deck, be thrown forward, and end up with the canopy possibly entangling itself.

If the landing were too slow, the deck would be moving faster when the man touched down. This would cause him to be violently thrown backwards.

The bottom line was the landing had to be made as close to the actual ship's speed as possible. No one, not even the young Protectors on the team who had helped develop the system, had ever tried this type of thing before.

Isha came over the ship from the left, or port, side. He was careful to avoid being anywhere near the bridge of the ship. Other than required navigation lights on the ship, the bridge had the only lights on the ship. The landing area was dark, but still visible from the bridge, high above the aft section of the ship. The chances were that no one could see the darkened figures coming aboard. However, if someone on the bridge was to see anything suspicious, they could flip a single switch. Instantly the entire deck would be bathed in bright lights used for nighttime loading and unloading. There would be nowhere to run or hide for the team.

Isha was only ten feet above the port rail of the ship when he made a hard left pull on the shroud line of his parasail and throttled back on the fan engine. The turn and power reduction both eliminated some of the lift generated by the canopy and he landed, a bit too hard, but safely on the deck.

"I'm down," Isha said as he pulled in on the lines to cause his parasail to collapse. This had to be accomplished immediately, because the ship's movement was creating a fifteen to twenty knot wind across the deck. If the canopy was not deflated, the Protector could very easily be pulled off his feet and dragged by the parasail.

"Hit your beacon, sir," Kevin responded almost immediately.

Blast it! Isha harshly said to himself. He had forgotten the homing signal all the other Protectors would use to find him on the large deck. "Transmitting," he said tersely.

The remaining team members could all plainly hear a low steady tone in their headsets. The receivers gave slightly different tones to guide the warrior left or right towards the beacon Isha carried. These rough directions would get the men close enough to their leader until they could see him with the night vision goggles.

Within forty-five seconds five men were on the deck with Isha. Everyone crowded around Jackson who explained that his transmitter was out. He could hear everyone else, but could not check in.

Isha quickly took stock of their situation. Everyone was safe. Two men were bruised by hard landings, but no one was seriously injured. Jackson was given the one spare radio. There were two settings on each radio. On the first power setting, the men would be able to talk with each other. On the higher setting, they should be able to talk via satellite connections with Exeter. Isha put his radio on the second setting.

"Hi, Mom. We're home," Isha transmitted. This was the first chance to see if the team would be able to talk with Exeter.

No reply.

"Mother...?" he tried again.

After several seconds Kristi's voice came through. It was scratchy and difficult to understand, but there. "Hi, boys!" she said cheerfully. "How are the sea breezes?"

"Chilly," was the Prince's answer. "Listen, Mom, you're a little difficult to understand."

"Just a second – let me check on that."

Twenty seconds later Kristi was back, this time much clearer. "How do you hear now?" Isha looked around at the rest of his team. Each man gave silent but enthusiastic thumbs up signs.

"That's much better!"

"Good! Now, don't ever call me Mom again." The men all smiled and Kristi continued, "Guys, the King has something to tell you."

Annu took about a minute to inform the team about Colin Johnson's phone call. "It looks like you have at least six bad guys. I still think someone one on the crew has to be involved. It would have been too difficult to get everything set up without an inside man already on board before these guys were hired."

Jackson asked if there was anyway to distinguish the new crewmembers from the old. "If everyone looks alike, how will we know who to take out?"

"I would think you should go for anyone with a weapon, Jack", the King joked back.

The young warrior rolled his eyes and smiled at the logic. He had opened himself up for that one. "Good plan, sire," was his only retort. "Good plan."

Quickly the team carried their parasails and attached fan engines to the railing. The engines, while not particularly heavy, would be enough to slowly sink the chutes to the bottom of the ocean. There was no place to hide six parachutes, harnesses, and engines, so they had to be discarded.

"Wait a second," Cody thought of an alternative. "We can store them after all."

"Where?" someone said disbelieving.

"There," Cody said pointing to a covered lifeboat mounted in it's launching crane. It was so obvious that everyone stopped for a moment in disbelief.

Isha broke the spell, "Well, what are we waiting for? Let's hide this stuff and get to work."

A women's voice, obviously not Kristi's came over the radio. "Be careful, Isha. I love you."

Isha's team all pretended not to hear Deidre's call.

"I will – and I do, too," was the only response.

Then, predictably, Celia's voice came in over the headsets, "Love ya, Kev."

Hearing his wife's voice from so far away made Kevin stop for a moment. Kevin, who didn't really like public displays of affection, was uncharacteristically responsive. "I love you, too. When I get home, are you interested in starting a family?"

Everyone in Exeter's communication room laughed … except Celia.

King Annu took the microphone from Kristi. "David and Robin just asked me to tell their sons how proud they are of them."

None of the Marcus sons said anything, but each of them nodded silently. Everyone on the mission and everyone in Exeter realized the personal communications were just a way of saying, "come back", but it was now time to get to work.

Isha took control of his team. "Okay, guys, no more mushy stuff. Let's get our heads in the game."

It took less than five minutes to completely conceal the equipment. "Ok, team. Now's the time."

Jack looked around in feigned bewilderment. Kevin scanned the deck trying to figure out what was confusing his friend.

Jack simply said, "This doesn't look like any floating nuclear bomb I've ever seen before." His failed attempt at humor, which sought to ease a little tension, in fact just reminded the team what they could not forget. They had just successfully landed on a moving fifty kiloton weapon.

Twenty-Nine

Salt spray fell as a fine mist on the deck of the Peligroso making it as slippery as ice. Everyone was concerned that they might fall and give away the group. There was an eerie aspect of the darkness that amplified the vibration and unnatural movement of the ship. It seemed as if the ship itself resented the unorthodox way Exeter's men had come aboard.

The freezing wind mixed with the sea mist chilled each man. As good as the warming jumpsuits were, they couldn't withstand the power of the cold October North Atlantic. Each breath the men took made their lungs ache and drained their strength. Their hands hurt and stiffened making all movements difficult. Even the Protectors, as healthy and remarkable as they were, would only last a short time in the unforgiving cold before their effectiveness was lost.

Isha and his team quietly knelt behind a large cargo hatch cover, opened their packs, and quickly unloaded the specialized equipment they had brought from Exeter. Nothing was broken, which was a relief. From all obvious appearances, they had landed their parasail transports undetected. No floodlights had come on to bathe the cargo deck and give away their hiding place. Surprise still seemed to be on their side, but it couldn't last for long.

The six men on the assault party had planned to be separated into two teams. Each group had a specific target to reach. Things were going smoothly, but Isha knew that could change instantly. While he was not by nature a pessimist, the Prince was a careful warrior. This attack had too many unknowns, too many critical details that were just guesses on the part of the planners. Isha was uncomfortable with it, but he was on the deck of a moving ship three hundred miles from land, so options were limited.

The first and crucial target was the bridge. Once there, that team would control the ship. The Peligroso could be stopped here if necessary. No one wanted to disarm the weapon while in the harbor. It was far better to handle it this far into international waters.

The team slowly moved aft along the superstructure. The main hatch from the upper deck into the structure was sealed against the forces of nature. Isha loosened the lugs as quietly as possible, but the heavy metal latches scraped loudly against the jams. The Protectors tensed, preparing for an unseen threat. If someone were in that passageway, they would certainly see and hear the team.

After the lugs were loosened, the hatch then opened silently on well-oiled hinges. Robbie rolled quickly through the opening and came up inside the passageway with his gun ready to protect the rest of the team. They followed in an orchestrated pattern. Once inside, the team removed their heated jumpsuits.

"Damn!" Isha cursed quietly. "We should have thought to bring work clothes like those the crew would wear. That way we might be able to blend in a little better."

"Why?" Kevin responded. "By now, they've got the entire crew guarded. They couldn't let that many men run free."

Skye spoke what he was thinking, "If they're being kept in the ship's mess, that's also probably where the greatest number of bad guys are." He looked quickly around. "Are those the stairs we take?"

Kevin shook his head in disgust. "Skye, this is a ship. On a ship, these are called ladders—not stairs—ladders."

Skye smiled at the gentle rebuke. "My apologies, sir. Is this the ladder we take?"

Kevin answered, "Much better, my son. You are definitely trainable. To answer your question, my young Protector—I haven't got a clue."

Isha considered the situation and decided his flexibility speech might be appropriate right now. "Ok, we have the first change to the plan. I want to take the bridge first and the engine room second. We'll get the crew after we control the ship."

There was no disagreement.

Using the outer passageways they slowly moved up towards the command level of the ship. They expected at every turn and ladder to meet armed guards. Instead the ship was as quiet as a tomb. Only the distant drone of the engine and the constant vibration under their feet disturbed the stillness. It was as if the Peligroso itself was warning the Protectors of a danger ahead.

"Where are the guards?" Jackson, the youngest Protector asked.

"Why should they have guards in the passageways? As far as the terrorists are concerned, they have all the threats being kept together. Not seeing anyone is a good thing. It means we're still unexpected."

Slowly, painfully slowly, they worked up the ladders. At each corner the lead man in the group would slide a miniature fiber optic line unobtrusively around the bend to check for sentries. The actual fiber was only ten times the diameter of a human hair, but it was connected to an eyepiece that gave the Protector a wide-angle view. The fiber was an almost invisible way to see without being seen.

The process of checking each spot made moving a slow routine, but before anyone really believed it possible, they could hear the sounds of men working.

Isha and Kevin moved soundlessly to both sides of the door. The Prince slid the optic fiber into the room and looked into the eyepiece.

There were three men in the control area of the bridge. One at the control panel, one at a chart table, and one standing away from them a short distance where he could see the rest. There might be more, Isha couldn't really tell. The wings of the bridge were hidden. If anyone were there, the team would deal with him as necessary. Isha and Kevin would be the first two in followed immediately by the four remaining Protectors.

On Isha's hand signal Kevin moved silently away. Back around the corner he whispered instructions to the rest of the team. "I think there's only one guarding the rest of the crew. I'm going to take him out." He looked around at his team. "Robbie, you follow me in and watch my back. If we've missed any bad guys it's your responsibility to eliminate them."

Everyone knew his assignment. Isha and Robbie moved in absolute silence to the bridge hatch. Without a sound the Prince of Exeter entered the command bridge. For a second no one moved. Then, almost in slow motion, the man at the back of the bridge lifted a small submachine gun and pointed it directly at Isha. "Who the hell are you?"

Isha stared back with his hands in the air. In a quivering fearful voice he answered, "It's just me. I was sent up here to replace the helmsman."

For a moment, the guard was confused by the unexpected response. That fraction of a second was all it took for Isha to move his hands down at lightning speed. Instantly a razor-sharp throwing knife flew from a sheath strapped to Isha's right wrist.

The muzzle of the guard's gun dropped a fraction of an inch as the man looked down at his chest. Just to the left of the sternum the hilt of the knife was sticking out. A look of bewilderment was on the man's face. "It doesn't hurt," he said quietly. "I can't believe it doesn't hurt." Those were the last words he spoke before his perforated heart quit beating.

Kevin quickly scanned the room looking for anyone who appeared to be a threat. There was none. The three remaining men were frozen in shock. No one spoke for several seconds. Finally, one of the men whispered, "Who are you?"

"We're friends." The rest of Isha's team came on to the bridge. Two of the Protectors dragged the lifeless body into the chart room.

The stunned crewman stared at the six warriors before him. The oldest was Isha at twenty-six. None carried heavy weapons. They were not an intimidating sight.

Isha totally ignored the man's skeptical looks. "How many men are holding the ship?"

"We don't know for sure. They have two different men who stay up here on twelve-hour shifts. They do the same thing, we think, in the engine room. Plus they have one or two always with the crew in the ship's dining mess. We figure that they must have seven or eight men."

"How often do they check on you?"

"Someone calls every hour or so."

"And how long has it been since the last report?"

"I don't know. We got here maybe thirty minutes ago, so it could be any time now."

Isha made a quick calculation. "Ok. Here's what we're going to do. You two stay here and keep doing your work. If anyone questions where this man is, tell them he left to whiz or something. They won't believe you, but it'll give us a little more time."

The man's apprehension got the better of him. "Are you military?"

"I said we're friends." Isha understood the crew's concerns but time was critical. These men had crucial information, and he had to have it quickly. "Who leads their group?"

"The first officer, a man named Permi, Miles Permi, has taken command of the ship, but we don't think he's really in charge. There's another brute who tells Permi what to do. He's a big guy, a real mean SOB named Lyndon Pearson. Watch out for that one. He's a sadistic bastard. He likes hurting people."

Isha made a rapid decision. "Ok, here's the plan. Skye, you stay on the bridge. If anyone comes in that shouldn't be here, you handle them."

"Yes, sir."

"Just one guy? That's all you're leaving? Listen, maybe you don't understand, these guys are killers."

Isha looked at the three frightened men and then at Skye. He quietly answered, "No, it's you who doesn't understand. This young man is more than able to handle anything or anyone who walks through that hatch. As long as he's here, you're safe."

Isha noticed a cross-section drawing of the Peligroso mounted on the aft bulkhead. It gave a fairly detailed schematic for the different levels of the ship's design. He took it down and laid it on the charting table. Using the diagram, Isha got directions from the crew for the quickest way to the engine room. The plan remained the same - capture the engine room - then release the crew.

Isha, and the rest of his assault force, quietly worked its way down to the engine room. The sound of their padded shoes seemed unnaturally loud on the metal deck. They really didn't expect to find any threats. Salomi's men had very little reason to expect an assault in the middle of the ocean, and they had firm control over the crew.

From the bridge crew they had learned the mutineers kept a strict regimen. The crew was tightly controlled, and living under a constant threat of sadistic killers with automatic machine guns. By now, everyone knew three of their crewmates had been viciously murdered.

Every man did exactly as he was told. No one wanted to risk any retribution from the bloodthirsty executioners. It was all simply a matter of survival, but survival was still a challenge. Day to day life was difficult in the cramped space of the ship's mess. Sleeping was almost impossible because the lights were always on. Round the clock shipboard life also meant that someone was always awake and moving in the area. The result was that no one, not even the captors, slept well. Lack of rest made the guards even more cruel.

A sense of helplessness permeated the Peligroso. No one would have even thought of trying to retake the ship. If the crew had had weapons, they would still have been at a disadvantage. These six men were all trained killers. As a final coercion, Miles Permi and Lyndon Pearson had made it plain they would shoot the captain at the first sign of resistance from the crew.

The five Protectors knew there was little chance the rest of their rescue would go as easy as the bridge had. Every moment brought them closer to being discovered.

Kevin was the first to break the silence, "Isha, if you're going to keep me out past regular work hours, I need more money."

"You don't get paid anything, Kev." The Prince waited a moment. "On second thought, I'm doubling your salary."

"Sire, two times zero is still zero."

"My math is excellent. Therefore, the offer stands. As of right now, you're on double pay."

"Thank you, Sire. You are most generous."

"Think nothing of it. Now, that we've settled the compensation issue, let's get the bad guys."

"Your command is my wish, Highness. Besides, someone has to be the adult supervision around here." Kevin smiled and continued, "That, as usual, is my responsibility."

"Yeah, right. Take the point, Mister Adult Supervision."

As Kevin moved to the front of the team, he suddenly froze in his steps. Coming the opposite direction were four men. The last one was wearing a yellow rubberized slicker and holding a shotgun that he used to goad the other men forward. He was cursing loudly at his prisoners, and threatening to kill them all if anyone gave him any reason. Kevin guessed this was a replacement crew for the engine room. The gaunt and haggard faces reflected the fatigue and stress they had been living under. One man had a black eye and a large bruise on the right cheek. They moved with slow methodical steps as if life had been drained from their legs.

Kevin made a sweeping motion with the palm of his hand back to the rest of the team. Instantly the Protectors backed into an open hatch, and slid as close to the bulkhead as possible. As the guarded men and their abusive sentry passed, Isha stepped out behind the group.

The Prince knew disarming the guard would be dangerous. In the close confines of the passageway, if the shotgun accidentally discharged, some or perhaps all of the hostages would be injured or perhaps killed.

Again, at least for the moment, surprise was on Isha's side. In total silence, he moved behind the sentry and tapped him on the shoulder. By reflex alone, the young man looked around. In that fraction of a second, Isha grabbed the barrel of the shotgun and pointed it straight up. He used his other hand to squeeze a pressure point on the man's forearm. Everything below the man's elbow was paralyzed preventing him from pulling the trigger.

Isha ripped the gun from the man's grip, rotated at the hip, and used the wooden stock as a club. Everyone in the passageway heard a sickening thud as the gunstock hit the man squarely in the middle of his forehead.

The engine crew turned around just in time to see their former captor smash against the bulkhead and slide to the deck. A stranger wearing a black jumpsuit was reaching down and feeling the man's neck for a carotid pulse. Finding it strong and regular, the man looked up. He tossed the gun to the nearest man from the Peligroso's crew. "Here, if this jerk wakes up, use this to keep him quiet. Try not to fire it unless you have to. We really don't need to advertise that we're here."

The grizzled old mate who was now carrying the gun answered incredulously, "Advertise. Advertise? There isn't any advertising to do. Mister, I don't know who in the hell you are. They'll know something is wrong when we don't show up in the engine room right away. These people keep real close ties on us."

"Then we better act fast. Bring this trash along with us."

* * * * *

Two minutes later, four men entered the engine room. The last one was carrying a shotgun, and wearing a bright yellow slicker. A winter stocking cap covered a large portion of his face. The guard on duty in the engine room looked up as his accomplice came in. " Where the hell have you been? I was about to call Pearson about you."

The guard looked up and shrugged silently. Before he spoke, the prisoner at the front of the group grabbed his stomach and doubled over in pain. His agonized cry distracted the engine room guard for a second. That was all the time the man in the yellow slicker needed.

He moved beside his associate and whispered, "Hey buddy, is this guy Pearson the one in charge?"

The old guard looked around in bewilderment. "Who are you?"

A young man smiled back menacingly at the guard, and responded, "At the risk of ruining your whole day, we're not friendly. Now you've got just two seconds to decide whether or not you want to make this easy on all us." He didn't even get a chance to start counting.

The guard started to swing his pistol towards Isha. Before it moved two inches, Kevin reached from the man's blind side, grabbed the barrel and wrenched it up and in the opposite direction. This ripped the gun out of the man's palm and trapped his finger in the trigger guard. By twisting the gun barrel down, the man's finger snapped and was broken at the knuckle. Kevin looked down at the man who was holding his hand in agony. "That was a bad decision, Mister. I think you should have listened to my boss."

"You bastard! You broke my hand!" He lunged madly at Kevin who sidestepped and caught the attacker with a sidekick to the knee and an immediate roundhouse kick to the side of his head. The man fell like a sack of concrete.

"These people aren't overly troubled with brains are they? On top of that, they just can't handle the slightest constructive criticism," Kevin said sarcastically. "On top of all that, I'm supremely disappointed in the training their mothers gave them."

Isha shook his head silently at Kevin's total disregard for the danger of the situation.

"Cody, I want you to stay here with the engine crew and our two guests. We're going to try to reach the rest of the crew before everyone knows we're here.

One of the crew released in the passageway was a crusty old seaman. His gnarled face revealed an almost unconcerned demeanor, and he seemed to be taking the rescue attempt with uncaring detachment. "Listen," he growled with a raucous voice, "We've got a bunch of psychopaths up there in the mess. They've got the men packed into one area of the room opposite from the hatch. You'll never be able to sneak in there unseen."

Isha and Kevin got the men to draw floor plans of the area where the crew was being held captive. The schematic revealed what the old man had said was true.

The mess was an elongated room, twenty feet wide and almost thirty long, with the kitchen at the far end. Five dining tables were mounted to the floor right inside the hatch. The sailor said that Permi and his cronies used them as barriers to keep the prisoners from direct access to the exit. Unfortunately, it appeared the tables would also act as obstructions to keep Isha's team from rushing the mutineers.

* * * * *

It took the four Protectors only five minutes to reach the mess hall on the ship. Isha slowly moved the fiber optic lens around the corner to check out the room.

From what he could see, Isha knew surprise would not be on their side. Kevin's assessment was right to the point, "There's no way to keep the crew out of the line of attack as we go in. If the bad guys fire, they'll take out a lot of innocent people, too. I don't think we should try and get in there."

"Then we'll have to find a way to make the mountain come to Mohammed," Isha responded. "We have to come up with a way to make them want to take the prisoners and leave the mess hall. According to the guys in the engine room there are eight of the crew and four bad guys still to go. The question is how do we get them to out in the open?"

Robbie looked around the passageway. "Sir, can you tell if there are portholes on the far side of the mess?"

Isha used the fiber optic lens to look into the room. "Yeah, I can see five or six portholes. Why?"

"I was thinking that a kitchen must have vents to the outside. Vents that aren't cleaned regularly have a certain propensity for fire hazards. If you catch my drift."

"Can you make it happen?"

Robbie looked at his brother, Jackson. "Ready to make Smokey the Bear mad at us?"

Jack thought a moment before answering, "Yeah, I've kind of felt left out of the fun so far."

* * * * *

Within fifteen minutes, the brothers were on the upper deck of the Peligroso. Looking down the port side of the ship, they discovered a small scuttle vent that stuck out ten inches. "Looks like we struck oil – or at least grease," Robbie joked quietly.

Jackson tied a rope harness around his waist. Robbie was there to belay the loose end of the harness. The brothers had the utmost trust in each other, but Jackson had to get one jab in. "Hold tight, Bubba. If you get slippery fingers, I go for a very long, very cold swim."

"Not to worry. I spit on my hands first."

Despite the joking, Jackson knew that if Robbie actually did let the rope slip, his life would be over in seconds. He didn't let that stop him for a moment and silently slid over the side of the ship.

Eighteen feet below the upper deck was the kitchen vent. It had a scoop design that created a low-pressure area outside the opening as the ship moved. This caused the air inside the mess to be drawn out of an exhaust tube while simultaneously drawing fresh sea air back.

Easing slowly down the side, Jackson spoke quietly into his microphone. "Rob, I need to come about two feet forward. That will put me just in front of the vent."

Even though Robbie's muscles were aching from the strain, he slowly inched the rope along the railing.

"Perfect! Stay right there!"

At that moment, the hatch the two Protectors had just used opened with a loud creak. Out stepped a rough looking, six-foot man. A black knit watch cap barely hid an abundant supply of unruly hair. Lyndon Pearson had chosen the worst possible second to have a moment of fresh air. If Pearson looked to his left, there was a good chance he would spot Robbie twenty feet away.

The exertion and strain of holding his brother made Robbie's breathing rapid and heavy. Each time the young warrior exhaled, he produced a small, but very visible cloud of condensation. Both of his hands were straining to grip the rope that was his brother's lifeline. Discovery meant almost certain death. There was no place on the deck to tie off the rope quickly enough to fight if necessary. Remaining hidden was Robbie's only hope for his and Jackson's survival.

Light from the open hatch dimly illuminated the area. Luckily, a few shadows cascaded across the deck, and Robbie, in his black jumpsuit, was partially concealed by the shade. Despite the cold, he avoided making even the slightest movement.

For a very long thirty seconds, Pearson stood and deeply breathed the cold night air. His lungs hurt as the frigid wind cut its way inside. Finally, a shiver passed through his body, and he went back in closing the hatch.

Hearing the lugs close down, Robbie quickly whispered to his brother. "Hurry, Jack! We might not be as lucky next time."

Below him Jackson was struggling to control himself while hanging along the hull. From a small knapsack where he carried his survival kit, he brought out a package and poured the contents into the vent. A small pile of gray metal shavings filled the opening. On top, Jackson put several half dollar sized cinnamon colored plugs from his bag. There was no way the wind would allow a match to light, so Jackson placed a small spark generator next to the pile. Immediately Robbie pulled his brother up to the deck. Two seconds later, the mound erupted in a brilliant flame that lasted less than fifteen seconds.

Jackson's survival kit was designed for use in a wilderness situation. The package he emptied contained magnesium shavings. When ignited, they burned with a white-hot flame. The heat was enough to kindle even damp wood. The magnesium, combined with cork packing chips created a brief, but very smoky blaze.

Heavy white smoke billowed into the vent and back drafted into the mess. Kitchen area smoke detectors suddenly screamed out their shrill warning.

The panicked guard on duty woke up his sleeping partner. Neither man knew exactly what to do. The seven prisoners in the mess stated yelling in fear.

* * * * *

Permi and Pearson had taken Captain Andrews to his cabin. They needed him to open his safe containing the transit documents.

Pearson pushed Andrews into a chair. "Tomorrow morning, we enter New York harbor."

Andrews was still trying to be master of his ship. The proud captain's eyes flashed. "I know all about our time table, you bastard!"

"Please be careful there, old man. Tomorrow a port authority pilot and a customs official will come out on the harbor tug." Andrews started to respond, then thought better of it. Pearson finished, "The first thing they'll ask for will be those documents, and the papers had better be in order."

The captain thought he might have a trump card. "And, what if they're not? One word from me and every police boat in NYC will be on your butt."

Pearson didn't seem at all worried about that happening. "That would be true, but neither you nor any member of your crew would live to see it."

All three men in the cabin knew Andrews would do nothing to make the officials feel anything was out of the ordinary. Holding the crew hostage would assure Andrews' service. Shortly afterwards, he would be killed, along with hundreds of thousands, perhaps millions, of others when the nuclear device was detonated.

Suddenly, the sound of fire alarms echoed through the passageway. The warning seemed to reverberate down the metal bulkheads growing louder and louder. Permi picked up the captain's phone and dialed the two-digit extension for the bridge. When there was no answer on the second ring, he and Pearson looked at each other warily.

"Andrews, if this is a trick by the crew, I swear you will be the first to die," Pearson hissed.

"My men are not stupid enough to advertise anything to you by setting off a fire alarm. Has it ever crossed your cretin mind that the ship might really be on fire?"

Pearson answered him with a backhand across Andrews' face. "Be careful, old man. I took your ship. I can have your life as easily."

Captain McLean Andrews wiped a small spot of blood from his lip. He stared fearlessly into the eyes of the man who had just struck him. "Pearson, if you touch me again, I'll either kill you or die trying." Lyndon Pearson thought for a second, but said nothing. He needed Andrews' expertise to get into New York harbor.

Permi walked to the door of the captain's cabin and looked back. "Listen, I'm going up to the bridge. I'll find out there what's happening with the fire alarm, and I'll call you if there is anything to it."

* * * * *

Three levels below the captain's cabin, smoke was rapidly filling the mess. The frightened guards roughly pushed their prisoners into the passageway to escape the feared blaze. Even though they were convinced there was a fire, the guards were not going far without talking to Lyndon

Pearson. He was not one to reward initiative, and every man he brought on board was afraid to do anything that might make him mad. The consequences usually meant death.

Little did they know there was no fire, and the smoke would begin dissipating within seconds.

One guard led the men while the second followed the pack. They were working hard to control their panic, but it was a losing battle.

All of the Protectors, connected by the radios they carried, knew exactly what was happening. As a result, Isha and Kevin were waiting in the corridor outside the mess.

Surprise was still on the side of the Protectors. As the group moved quickly down the passageway they did not expect to find anyone else there. The first man to step around the corner was totally confounded at the sight of a stranger standing there. So shocked, he didn't even move his gun. "Who are you?" he sputtered.

"Good night," Kevin answered as he landed a quick right jab squarely on the guard's jaw. The man's knees buckled and he fell into the arms of the crewman directly behind him.

The startled crewmember looked at Isha, who raised a finger to his lips. Amazingly, the man didn't say anything, but nodded in understanding. He and Kevin dragged the unconscious man with him down the passageway. Each prisoner in turn coming around the corner could see what was happening. A combination of the shock they were in and the hardships they had endured for the past several days were enough to dull their senses. No one made a sound.

Around the corner, and fifteen feet behind, the other guard was unaware of anything that was taking place in front. He simply kept yelling at the prisoners over the sound of the fire siren. The moment Isha saw the sights of the submachine gun, he reached around and grabbed it, pointing the barrel up. The guard, completely taken by surprise, pulled the trigger.

A quick chop from Isha's right hand dropped the guard instantly. By then, damage had already been done. Even such a short burst from the gun had fired eight bullets. Seven of the bullets went harmlessly into the ventilation ducting. The eighth bullet hit a metal strap and ricocheted back. Isha felt himself spun halfway around as the slug smashed into his right thigh.

The lead went cleanly through his muscle half way between the knee and hip. Fortunately, it missed the femoral artery. Otherwise, the Prince would have bled to death within a few minutes.

Isha fell to the metal deck. At first there was no pain, then a spasm in the muscle created a wave of agony that rolled over Isha. Within a second, Kevin was by his best friend. He stepped over the unconscious guard, grabbed Isha's backpack, and removed the first aid kit. Kevin put a heavy gauze pad over both the entrance and exit holes and held them there tightly with a three inch elastic bandage.

"Are you ok, Isha?"

Through his pain the Prince took a deep breath and answered, "Are you looking at the same leg I am? I think I'm a shade less than ok."

Kevin flipped the switch on his transmitter and went to high power. He spoke into the microphone as calmly as possible. "Exeter, can you read me?" No response. "Exeter, damn it, listen up!" Only silence. "Robbie, are you guys still outside?"

Robbie and Jackson had just come in from the arctic air outside. "No, but we're just inside the hatch."

"Get back out there. Prince Isha has been shot, and my transmitter won't reach through all this metal. I need you to relay messages to Exeter."

"Is he alive? Where are you?"

"Right outside the mess hall. Yeah, he's alive, but I need some help."

Robbie spoke quickly, "I'm ready to pass along your transmissions. Do you want Jackson down there?"

"No, keep him with you for now. Go ahead and make contact with home." Kevin then gave Robbie the information he wanted passed.

"Exeter, this is Robbie."

Kristi answered instantly. "What's going on, Robbie? We've missed you guys." The cheery sound in her voice was forced.

"Kristi, we have a hard situation here. I need you to patch me through to the King's physician."

"He's already here, Robbie." There was a cautious tone to her voice now. "Everyone is here, Robbie." The young Protector knew she was telling him that King Annu, Maria, Deidre, Celia, David and Robin Marcus were all listening.

"I'm relaying messages for the guys below. Kevin wants me to tell you Prince Isha has been shot." Totally unnecessarily he repeated, "I say again, Isha has been shot. He has a single wound in the upper right leg. Kevin says it's a clean wound that went completely through the muscle of his leg. He has a pressure bandage in place, and says the bleeding is almost stopped."

In Exeter, the King's personal physician, Doctor Frank Pullen, listened quietly. He felt a personal as well as professional involvement. Pullen had delivered Isha, and felt a strong father-like love for the Prince. The doctor silently cursed in frustration, and looked at his old friend. "Annu, why didn't they take a biomedical transmitter? I can't treat what I can't see."

The King took a deep breath. He would not let worry for his son take priority over the mission. "They weigh too much, Frank. We couldn't afford to carry one."

The doctor nodded in resignation. He asked politely to sit in Kristi's chair. She got up and handed him her headset. Only then was he aware of a quiet sobbing in the room. Pullen looked around to see Deidre with her head against Annu's shoulder. The King was whispering something to her and gently stroking her hair.

Doctor Pullen started asking for information. Robbie relayed both the questions and the responses. The doctor's biggest initial concern was blood loss. Once he was assured that the bleeding was controlled, he began breathing slower. He ordered Kevin to give Isha a shot for pain. Since he didn't know the Prince's blood pressure or other vital information, the doctor really didn't like prescribing a strong pain medication.

When the message was relayed to Kevin and Isha, the Prince shook his head at the idea. His response was simple, "Kevin I'm not going to be sent into dreamland by some pain medication. So, if you try and stick me with that hypo, I'll shove it up your... ."

Kevin interrupted, "I get the message, sir." He carefully picked up his friend and carried him thirty feet back into the mess. The rescued crewmembers followed silently. They dragged the unconscious guards with them. Kevin gave the two nearest men cord from his pack. He ordered them to take the guards into the kitchen and tie them up there.

The smoke had almost totally dissipated inside the mess. "Robbie would you please pass the word to Doctor Pullen that Prince Isha has respectfully, but rather emphatically, declined pain medication."

Robbie, who had heard the entire dialogue, used a less expansive vocabulary in his relay to Exeter, "Doctor, The Prince doesn't want to take the shot. Furthermore, I think anyone here who tries to administer it will need pain medication themselves, if you catch my drift."

All Doctor Pullen could do was shake his head in disbelief. "Sire, if your son refuses my help then all I can do is sit here as a spectator with you."

Annu nodded. "He doesn't want to risk being incapacitated. We'll get him off the ship as soon as possible."

"There is always the danger he may bleed to death."

The King continued to hold Deidre to his shoulder. "I know. For now, all we can do is wait and pray."

On the Peligroso, Isha had Kevin take some pulpy gray mixture from a sealed pouch in his bag. The prince forced the poultice into both the entry and exit wounds. "Tell my father I'm using some of Grandpa's stuff. It'll stop the pain as fast as morphine, and should keep the muscle from cramping."

Kevin was skeptical. "You and your homemade remedies, Isha. You should be in a hospital right now, not stuffing your new holes with a concoction like that."

"Do you see a hospital anywhere nearby, Kevin? This will work until I can get some help. My Grandfather knew his stuff."

* * * * *

In Exeter, Annu and his doctor listened to Robbie's relay of the information. The king nodded his head in approval. The doctor nodded his head in disbelief.

Nearby, Maria took Deidre's face into her wrinkled hands, and spoke gently to her granddaughter, "Sweetheart, he'll be fine." Maria hoped her words sounded more confident than she felt. "He's got a lot to come home for."

Thirty

All of the Protectors were listening intently to the transmissions between the ship and Exeter. On the bridge, Skye was sitting in the captain's chair and was focused on the conversation. Allowing his attention to be distracted proved to be disastrous.

When Miles Permi strutted onto the bridge, Skye was preoccupied with adjusting his earpiece to better listen to his radio.

One of the crewmen saw the first officer and called his name as a discrete warning to Skye. Permi looked around the bridge and instantly realized the man in black shouldn't be there. Without taking time to consider who the intruder was, Permi raised his gun and aimed it at the stranger's head.

Fortunately, the crewman's warning gave Skye the second he needed to react. He rolled off the chair just before a bullet cut the air and shattered through a window across the bridge. Cursing loudly, Permi quickly got a second shot off at the fleeing figure.

Skye made his escape by diving through a hatch on the opposite side of the bridge. Even with finely honed reactions, he was too late. It wasn't immediately obvious to Permi or the crew, but the second bullet had created a quarter-sized hole in Skye's right shoulder. As the young man tried desperately to get away, blood began spilling out through his jumpsuit and on to the metal deck.

Skye knew he was seriously hurt. The nine-millimeter slug from Permi's Berretta had shattered the young man's shoulder blade and collarbone. His right arm hung uselessly at his side. A wave of nausea and numbness flowed through Skye's body and threatened to overtake him.

The injured Protector flipped on his transmitter. "Prince Isha or Kevin, this is Skye." He tried to sound calm. "I'm sorry to add to you problems. I've been shot, and could use some help." A strange silence answered back. Slowly, painfully, Skye looked down at his shoulder. He knew from what he saw that his fate was sealed. The bullet that had torn through his shoulder had also cut the thin wire from his headset to the transmitter pack on his hip. There was no way to communicate with the rest of the Protectors.

Permi held his gun on the bridge crew while he dialed the captain's cabin. Lyndon Pearson answered on the first ring. "What is it?" he asked curtly.

"We've got guests. I shot one of them. The crew here in the bridge told me that four or five men took out your guard about an hour ago. They claim that they're not military, but I don't know who the hell else they could be."

Pearson's mind quickly considered his options and they were limited. All that mattered was that he bring his deadly cargo into New York harbor. Salomi would accept nothing less, and Salomi held all the aces.

If the bomb was detonated on schedule, a million dollars would be deposited in a numbered bank account in Zurich. If the mission failed,

Pearson's wife and two children would disappear. Salomi used that kind of leverage to assure unflinching loyalty from his followers.

"Call the mess and the engine room. Make sure they are still under our control. Then call me back here – and stop that damn alarm!"

Permi found the master fire detection panel. From the lights, he could tell that the detector in the kitchen had activated the system. A sinking feeling coursed through his veins as he called there.

Below decks, Kevin had left the Prince long enough to hide the remaining crew members. Isha was alone when the phone attached to the bulkhead rang. With great difficulty, he moved off the table and staggered over. His right leg felt like it weighed a ton and every nerve ending was on fire. He snatched the receiver from its cradle and listened.

A rough, deep voice exploded in the earpiece, "This is Permi, who's there?"

Isha had studied the crew list well enough to know the name. Despite the pain, Isha worked hard to sound in control and strong. "Well, hello Mr. Permi. I was told you were the bad apple on the crew, and you've just confirmed it."

"Who is this?"

"Not that it matters, but my name is Isha. My friends and I have taken the ship back. We know about your toy, and we've decided not to let you kill all those people with it."

Permi hung up and dialed the engine room. No one answered there. Finally he dialed the captain's quarters. Pearson answered on the first ring. Permi tried unsuccessfully to sound calm, "Listen, some guy in the mess hall picked up the phone and said his team controls the ship. I can't get any one in the engine room."

"We need to find out where our people are."

"The bridge crew said your guard was killed when these people came up here."

"Find out how they got on board. If there was a helicopter, then they must have a ship nearby that's large enough to launch it. Check the surface radar for any contacts. They didn't materialize out of nothingness. Find out where they came from!"

"I'll get on it, but listen!" Permi was desperately trying to control the fear in his voice. "Pearson, whoever this guy is that I talked to in the mess knows about the cargo!"

Pearson felt a cold chill throughout his body. For a split second even this hardened terrorist felt a wave of nausea.

There were only a handful of people in the world who knew what they were carrying. Pearson knew that if the United States government had knowledge of his mission, it was doomed. They would never allow the Peligroso to enter New York harbor. A sense of dread washed over Pearson and he took a couple of deep breaths and forced himself to think calmly.

Suddenly Pearson felt a surprising composure. He realized that the U.S. government must not know about the bomb. He was sure if they did, there would be an armada of naval ships surrounding the Peligroso. The absence of those ships meant that these men, who ever they were, were not military commandos. Pearson decided he would worry about who they worked for after he killed or captured them. Until then, he didn't care who paid their salaries or would pay for their funerals.

* * * * *

With the crew safely hidden and the two captured guards tied up, Kevin came back into the mess hall where Prince Isha was laying down with his leg elevated. The bleeding had stopped, but the muscles had begun cramping. Anytime he moved at all, a painful spasm took the Prince's breath. He was beginning to have second thoughts about passing up the morphine.

It was time to consider his flexibility philosophy. "Kevin, if it looks like I'm out of the picture, I want you to take my place."

"Isha," Kevin protested, "you're not going to win any kick boxing competitions for a while, but you're certainly not going to die."

"Die? Who said anything about dying? I mean if I have to take that damn morphine."

Kevin was embarrassed. "Sorry, sir. I just thought..."

"Forget it, my friend. You can't have my job that easily." Isha smiled despite the pain. "Besides, if I wimp out and die, you'll have to face Deidre all alone and explain how you let me 'buy the farm'."

"Sorry, I don't have the guts to do that. You just have to keep breathing." Kevin carefully checked the pressure bandage that he had tied around Isha's upper leg. "This looks like it smarts a bit."

"That, old buddy, is a masterful understatement," Isha responded carefully. "How long has it been since we did a check on everyone?"

"Fifteen, maybe twenty minutes."

"The plan calls for a check every thirty minutes. Since they obviously know we're here now, go ahead and do another one."

"Ok." Kevin went to high power on his transmitter. "Team check Kevin's on."

"Robbie's on."

"Jackson's on."

"Cody's on."

Silence. Everyone listened carefully to the deafening silence.

"Skye, are you there?" Kevin questioned.

More silence filled everyone's headsets.

Isha looked carefully at his partner. In spite of the pain from his wound, Isha was still in command of this team of Protectors. He pressed the switch on his transmitter. "Skye, come in." He waited for a moment. "Team, listen up. They know we're here. Cody, I want you to remain in the engine room, but stay alert for guests. Robbie, you wait above decks to relay messages home. Jackson, meet Kevin one level below the bridge. I want you two to find Skye. There's a chance that we don't own the bridge anymore, so be careful. From now on, I want all of you checking in every ten minutes. No exceptions."

* * * * *

Three levels above, Permi was in control on the bridge. He was working to contact the rest of Salomi's men. It was a fruitless effort. Permi decided he needed to stay on the bridge and not to follow the man he had shot. The amount of blood he found in the passageway led Permi to believe the wounded man was dead, or would be shortly.

He was close to being right. Hidden in a storage locker one level below the bridge, Skye was weakening from the loss of blood. He was too weak to travel farther, and was determined to stay hidden until he was rescued or was dead. Skye's blood starved brain was too clouded to consider the fact that his wound was providing a direct path to his sanctuary for anyone.

The bare bulb in the storage locker illuminated the small room with a bright, unyielding light. Skye felt his life slipping from him. The brilliant glare was becoming a faint and distant glow. All Skye wanted to do was go to sleep. The pain in his shoulder felt detached; a dull throbbing ache. Strangely, instead of fear, a sense of peace surrounded the young man. He thought about Exeter and the girl he had hoped to marry soon. He knew he wouldn't live to see that day. A gray fog came over him, and Skye passed out.

Kevin and Jackson joined up in a central passageway. The Peligroso, like most ocean going vessels, had both port and starboard passageways. Under major structures, like the bridge, there were smaller lateral corridors that connected the main two passageways.

Kevin decided to send Jackson down the port side while he searched the starboard. This would give them a quick way to cover each level. They were expecting a sustained search, but it didn't take long.

Twenty seconds after they split, Jackson called over the radio, "Kevin, I've found him! Get over here."

As soon as Kevin came around the corner, he saw the blood that had so quickly led Jackson to the storage locker. He then saw Skye. The wounded man's face was almost totally devoid of color. Kevin was certain Skye was dead. The sheer amount of blood in the corridor and storage locker was enough to confirm his assumption.

As Jackson rolled his friend over, a faint groan escaped from the pale lips. "He's still alive," Jackson exclaimed.

Skye barely opened his eyes and smiled weakly. "Of course I'm still alive, you dweeb. You sure took your sweet time getting here, though."

"We were held up in traffic. Sorry."

"No sweat. Just see if you can find your way to the nearest doctor. I seem to have sprung a leak here."

"Yep, It's a good thing this is covered by your warranty."

" That guy named Permi may be on the wrong side, but he sure can get a shot off fast." Skye was trying hard to control his fear. "How bad is it, Kev?"

"We have Doc Pullen on the phone. He'll have you on the mend before you know it. Just hold on."

"Yeah, sure. I'm not going anywhere, at least nowhere fast."

* * * * *

Doctor Pullen didn't like what he heard from Kevin about Skye's condition. Frustrated at the lack of options he had, Pullen gave his best first aid instructions over the radio. In less than a minute, the two Protectors were wrapping Skye's shoulder with a pressure bandage. This stopped the steady flow of blood for the time being. Kevin and Jackson gently picked up their friend, and carried him gingerly to the mess hall.

Neither Protector thought he would survive the move, but they couldn't leave him to die alone. We belong to each other was more than a motto to the Protectors; it was a pledge, a solemn promise between warriors.

* * * * *

The Prince was waiting for his three subjects in the mess hall. From the conversations he had been hearing over the radio, Isha knew how bad Skye's wound was. He was prepared for the worst.

Once they laid the hurt man down, Isha hobbled over and felt Skye's wrist. The pulse was almost nonexistent. Skye's breathing was slow and forced. He was lapsing into a deep shock. Perhaps if he were in a modern trauma center, they could save him, but here, Skye was dying. The only blessing was that because of his deepening shock, he was in no pain.

Kevin relayed to Isha that it was Permi who had shot their friend.

Isha held Skye's hand tight so he would know he was not alone. The Prince spoke quietly into the young man's ear, "Rest for a little while, Skye. If we get into a bind, I'll come and get you."

A very faint movement of Skye's head told the Prince that he had been heard. Within seconds however, Skye slowly took a deep breath and released it. The muscles in his face relaxed and a peaceful calm settled over the boyish, freckled features.

Isha released the hand of his fallen Protector. He glanced over to Kevin and Jackson then spoke quietly into his microphone, "Robbie, pass the word to Doctor Pullen that Skye has just died." Isha looked down at the pale face below him. A silent rage pulsed through his veins.

Jackson spoke angrily, "We'll revenge your death, Skye."

Without raising his eyes to Jackson, Isha answered with a tired voice, "Skye wouldn't want that, Jack. Revenge is never an acceptable motivation. It takes a piece of you. Revenge makes you loose your objectivity and ability to think under pressure." The Prince then glanced at the two Protectors standing above him. There was coldness in his eyes. "Having said that," he continued, "When we get Permi, I want him myself."

"Yes, sir," both men answered simultaneously.

In Exeter, King Annu closed his eyes in pain when Robbie passed the report. He had been the one to approve each Protector on the mission, and he felt personally responsible for Skye's death.

* * * * *

In the captain's cabin, Lyndon Pearson's fury was gaining intensity. He knew his well-planned scheme was falling apart at the seams. All the evidence forced him to that conclusion, but he still found it impossible to believe.

Pearson quickly considered his situation and resources. Other than Miles Permi, none of his team could be found. The bridge was again under his control, but no one answered in the engine room. Of most concern for Pearson was the stranger Permi said had answered the phone in the mess. That seemed to indicate the crew had been released and his guards neutralized.

Given the circumstances, a lesser man might have been considering giving up. Lyndon Pearson wasn't such a man. He was accustomed to facing overwhelming odds successfully. He believed that ruthless determination and execution would almost always even the odds.

The ship was still his, and the captain was his prisoner. Most important of all, he alone knew the code that would arm the nuclear warhead. That kind of knowledge gave him incredible power.

* * * * *

In about twelve hours, the Peligroso would power between Fort Hamilton and Fort Wadsworth. Those defensive positions, which once protected the entrance to New York harbor, would fail to stop the greatest threat ever to pass between them. Within minutes, the Peligroso would proceed under the Verrazano-Narrows Bridge and enter into the Upper New York Bay. She would then slow to pass the Statue of Liberty and Ellis Island. At this point, the Peligroso would stop her engines so harbor tugs could take over and carefully maneuver the vessel into her dock.

In a perverse way, Pearson found it humorous that both the Statue of Liberty and Ellis Island would soon afterwards be molten contaminated masses of rubble when the Peligroso's deadly cargo performed its mission.

* * * * *

As long as he held Andrews, Pearson believed the rest of the crew would do his bidding. *The fools admire their captain. All I have to do is threaten him and they'll line up to do my bidding,* he thought.

Andrews seemed to be reading the terrorist's mind, "My men will never let you get away with this, Pearson."

"Sure they will. Otherwise, they'll get to watch their captain thrown overboard." Pearson smiled benignly, showing his yellowed teeth. "Who knows, maybe you can avoid being turned into chopped meat by the ship's screws. If you do, perhaps you can swim two hundred miles to the U.S. coast. I wouldn't bet on it, of course."

Andrews stared fearlessly into the terrorist's bloodshot eyes. "My men will never allow you to use this ship. I'm not sure what your objectives are, but don't plan on making the crew a part of them."

"That may be unfortunate for you, Andrews."

The conversation was cut short by the shrill ring of the phone. Lyndon Pearson grabbed the handset from its cradle. "Yeah! Talk to me."

"It's Permi."

"You idiot! Who else would be calling me? Have you found the man you shot?"

Permi resisted the urge to yell back at Pearson. "No, but he's bleeding heavily. He's probably dead by now. Do you really want me to leave the bridge and find him?"

Permi was obviously right to have stayed on the bridge. "No, stay there. I'll come up in a few minutes." Pearson turned to face McLean Andrews. Pearson forced his fury under control. With feigned politeness he explained, "I've got to walk around. Unfortunately, I can't take you with me. So I must ask you to have a seat here at my desk."

McLean Andrews sat down behind the mahogany desk that was bolted to rails on the deck of his cabin. Lyndon Pearson then used leather bootlaces to tie the big Scottish man to the arms of the chair. The straps cut into his flesh, but Andrews did not complain. He refused to give his sadistic captor the satisfaction.

Once Pearson believed Andrews was securely tied, he left the captain's cabin and headed straight to the bridge. It was the situation McLean Andrews had been waiting for. He lifted his leg up to where his tied hands could reach the straight razor hidden in his sock. Carefully, he moved his fingers into the sock and slid the razor against his leg.

When exquisite care, McLean Andrews twisted his fingertips to grasp the folded blade. Finally, the captain was able to cup the razor in his secured hand. Using the edge of the chair's arm as a contact point, he rotated the blade from its handle.

Now came the truly difficult part. "Damn," Andrews muttered to himself. His arms were so tightly bound that his fingers were becoming numb. *If I drop this razor I'll never be able to get it again!*

The captain carefully manipulated the blade with his bound hand until he was able to use the open razor to cut the leather binders on his right hand. Once that was accomplished, he quickly released his left hand.

Captain McLean Andrews knew his first priority had to be the release of his crew in the mess hall. From hearing one side of the conversation between Pearson and Permi, Andrews was aware something was happening, and that perhaps one of his men had been shot.

As Lyndon Pearson and Miles Permi were meeting on the bridge, Captain McLean Andrews was quietly slipping out from his cabin. He knew he couldn't reach the communication's shack without being detected, so he opted for the mess hall. Andrews knew that being discovered would mean certain death at the hands of the psychopath who now controlled his ship. He forced that thought to the back of his mind.

Andrews moved in total silence stopping at every crossing corridor to listen for the sound of steps. The tomb like quiet was unnerving. Only the slight sway of his ship's deck and the inaudible low frequency drone of engines far below betrayed the fact the Peligroso was moving at eighteen knots towards New York City.

She was twelve hours from the harbor and fourteen hours from annihilation.

Thirty-One

On the bridge, Lyndon Pearson and Miles Permi confirmed, much to their disbelief, that all five of their men were either dead or captured. They were the only members of the squad not already eliminated by this unknown assault team.

Even Pearson, who was generally prepared for any eventuality, was unable to accept the team's eradication. His men were the best money could buy for this kind of operation. To him, it was impossible to imagine a force so small could have decimated them.

As Pearson anticipated, Permi was clearly having trouble controlling his panic. "Who the hell are these guys?" he gushed. "How did they get on board?"

"I don't really care," Pearson said contemptuously. "How they got here doesn't matter. What we have to do is dispose of them."

"How?" was the response. "They've taken all your men!" Permi was practically yelling.

Pearson grabbed Permi's arms, and dug his fingernails into the man's muscle. He whispered quietly and menacingly, "Don't you ever raise your voice at me again." He let his words sink in before continuing. "I don't care if they walked across the water to get here. This is my ship, and my mission."

Permi started to remind Pearson that he was the Peligroso's acting captain, but decided against it. No one, not even Permi, really believed that he was in charge of the ship.

Pearson released his grip on Permi. He glared at the frightened man with an ice-cold stare. Permi tried hard to return the gaze, but after a moment found himself looking down and away.

Pearson spoke loud enough so everyone on the bridge could hear him. "Permi, I'm going below. Stay here and keep this ship heading to New York. I don't care if you have to kill these men and pilot the ship yourself." He then walked over to the bridge crew. "Don't make him carry out that order," he threatened them.

The crewmembers nodded in compliance. They had no choice but to do as they were told. Maybe later they would have options, but for now, there were none.

* * * * *

Three levels below the bridge, Captain McLean Andrews was still slowly working his way down to the mess hall. He soundlessly moved from corridor to corridor.

Andrews wasn't sure what he would do when he reached his crew. All he carried as a weapon was his straight razor. That wouldn't be very effective against the automatic weapons he knew the mutineers were carrying.

Finally Captain Andrews was only one deck away from his men. He was hoping to surprise a solitary guard and take his weapon. He figured if he got that far without dying maybe he could get everyone else free.

The Earl of Cardigan would really love me, Andrews thought to himself sarcastically. *Let's just wander on down to Balaclava, guys. Trust me.* The captain knew he had about as much chance of succeeding as the light brigade had in that famous Crimean battle.

Despite the odds, Andrews knew he had to try. Freeing his crew and getting the Peligroso safely to New York were his responsibility. To McLean Andrews, a captain's obligations were sacred and irrevocable. He would rather die than willingly capitulate his command to these mutineers.

You better be ready to back up that philosophy, Andrews said to himself. At that moment, he slipped around a corner and found himself face to face with Lyndon Pearson.

"Well, well, hello there." The blue steel of a silenced pistol was aimed at the captain's stomach. "I expected to find you tied up in your cabin. Imagine my surprise when you were missing." Pearson moved the pistol to signal Andrews to turn around.

This is it. He's going to shoot me in the back, the captain thought. Instead, Lyndon Pearson pressed the muzzle into Andrews' spine, and pushed so hard that the older man almost fell forward.

"Now, if you would be so kind as to return with me to your cabin." Pearson spoke as if to a backward child. "I really have more important things to do than to continue rounding you up."

The veneer of defiance that had covered the old seaman was cracking. Being recaptured so easily had crushed his self-confidence. Perhaps there really isn't any way to beat these bastards, he thought sadly.

It only took a couple of minutes for Andrews and Pearson to get back to the cabin. The leather restraints that had tied the captain to his chair were lying on the floor. Lyndon Pearson still pressed the barrel of his gun firmly into the captain's back. The older man knew at any moment a slug would explode from that barrel, sever his spine, and end his life. The waiting for that moment was excruciating.

"Andrews, I generously let you live, and this is how you repay me?" Again, Lyndon Pearson used his condescending and degrading tone to further demoralize the captain. "How am I supposed to react?"

Instead of giving Andrews a chance to answer, the assassin used his pistol as a club and hit the captain at the base of his neck. The large man dropped into a heap. Pearson quickly searched the unconscious man and found his straight razor.

Twenty minutes later when McLean Andrews woke up, he felt like his head was twice its normal size and bursting. If he could have touched there, he would have found a knot the size of an egg on the back of his head. Movement was impossible, however. Lyndon Pearson had bent the unconscious captain's legs at the knees and tied his ankles tightly together. Then he had pulled the remaining length of rope up Andrews' back to tie the man's hands behind him. This binding painfully bowed Andrews back and caused his muscles to cramp and spasm.

Every time Andrew's back had a spasm or he moved either his arms or legs, it tightened the rope and the pain intensified.

Andrews knew that his captor had used this restraint before – probably very effectively.

The proud Scotsman did not want to admit defeat, but already the pain of the contortion on his body was becoming unbearable. His legs were quivering from the stain of being bent backwards so far, and with each involuntary spasm of his muscles, the rope was cutting tighter and tighter into the his wrists. Andrews' hands had already become a raw pain. Andrews knew his only chance to prevent additional agony would come from staying as still as possible, and that was getting more difficult by the moment.

* * * * *

With the captain secured in his cabin, Lyndon Pearson was ready to meet the threat to his mission. He was determined to destroy the men who were trying to thwart him.

Pearson's passionate hatred for his adversaries was reaching fever pitch. On an uncharacteristic impulse, he removed a handset from a wall phone and dialed the mess hall. It rang only once before Kevin picked up.

"K.T.'s Bar and Grill. Half price drinks until six. How can I help you?"

"This is Pearson. If that sort of humor is supposed to impress me, you've failed miserably," Pearson responded sarcastically.

"And I had such hopes that you would like me."

"Are you in charge?"

"In charge of what?" Kevin answered innocently.

"Let me make myself clear. Since you're on this ship it means you know what my mission is. I have no intention of letting you get in my way."

"Well I appreciate your honesty, Mr. Pearson. Now, to answer your question, I'm not the one in charge, but my boss can't come to the phone right now. Allow me to present you our position instead. By now you know that only you and that slime of a first officer are running free. The rest of your merry band is either dead or our guests. Considering that, why don't you two just consider your little escapade at an end?"

"I have no intention of altering one detail because of your intrusion. I don't care where you guys came from or who pays your salary, but I'm going to kill each and everyone of you."

"I appreciate the warning, Mr. Pearson. Just today my boss doubled my salary because of this little adventure," Kevin answered calmly. "I guess in light of your comments, I ought to ask for hazardous duty pay, too." Kevin's apparent unconcerned demeanor was more than Lyndon Pearson could handle.

Unable to control his temper further, Lyndon Pearson screamed into the phone, "You'll never see another sunrise! I'll sink your bodies to the bottom of the ocean!"

Pearson slammed the phone down. His hands were shaking in rage. To calm himself, he took two slow, deep breaths. The terrorist waited for his hands to stop trembling, then removed an envelope from a flat pouch dangling on a chain around his neck. He had been carrying the case for almost three weeks. In that time he had not allowed the file out of his possession even for a moment. Pearson broke the seal on an envelope, and read the short message inside carefully.

He had made his decision. Even for someone as familiar with death as Pearson, it was a difficult one. The unrepentant murderer of dozens of men straightened himself and took yet another deep breath. In his mind the die was cast and nothing could cause him to set another path in motion.

Lyndon Pearson silently opened the door, looked both ways, and headed towards the nearest hatch leading to the cargo holds.

Thirty-Two

Isha and Kevin looked at each other with undisguised concern. Lyndon Pearson's threat was real. He did have the capability to destroy the Peligroso and everyone on it.

Isha, despite his painful leg, was still the careful commander. He took quick stock of the situation and said to Kevin and Jackson, "We've got Cody in the engine room guarding it and the men there. We can't afford to leave that area unsecured. Robbie is on the deck relaying messages to Exeter. Someone has to do that. Communication home is too critical. That leaves the three of us to guard these men and handle Permi and Pearson."

Jackson thought out loud, "Don't forget we have to take care of Skye, too." The dead Protector was still lying on a serving table, carefully wrapped in a blanket.

"Ask a couple of the crew members to put his body in the ship's cooler, please."

Jackson simply nodded. Instead of getting help from strangers, he walked over to his dead friend, and picked up the man. Effortlessly, he carried the body into the kitchen area.

Neither Isha nor Kevin made a move to help. Both recognized that this was something Jackson needed to do alone. He was a close friend of Skye. As far as Jackson was concerned, the philosophy - We belong to each other - didn't end at death. It was his responsibility to care for Skye.

The young man returned after a couple of minutes. No comment was made about the redness of his eyes.

Isha made some quick decisions. "Jackson, you stay here with the crew and these two guests." The Prince looked at his best friend. "Kevin, you and I are going to meet with Pearson and Permi."

Jackson spoke up, "Sir, you're hurt. Why not let me go with Kevin. Or maybe you could relieve my brother on the deck."

Kevin quickly answered for the Prince, "Thank you for the suggestion. When King Annu places you in charge of a mission then you can assign people where you want. Until then..."

Isha jumped in, "Jackson, I'm sore, but ok otherwise. I appreciate your recommendation, but if we fail, no one should be blamed except me. I feel like I need to be there when we deal with the weapon." The Prince did not want to be too harsh with his young companion. "However, if there is any doubt about my ability, the rest of the team will be the first to know."

"Sire, I didn't mean anything by that. I wasn't trying to run your mission. I promise."

Through his pain, Isha smiled. "Don't worry, my friend. If you offend me, you'll know. Until that time, I expect you to give me your suggestions and any ideas that might help the mission."

* * * * *

Miles Permi was getting anxious. He had not been able to contact Lyndon Pearson in almost an hour. His apprehension was growing by the minute. There was no conversation on the bridge to break the tension and tedium. Permi felt like his head would soon explode.

Finally, he couldn't take it anymore. "I'm leaving for a few minutes. If I so much as suspect any change to the course or speed of this ship, I will come back here." Permi used the barrel of his gun to point to the outside wing of the bridge. "I will personally take each of you out on that wing and blow the top of your heads off. Do I make myself clear?"

The wide-eyed expression of the men told Permi they believed him and wouldn't do anything to risk making him carry out his threat.

* * * * *

Lyndon Pearson was moving inside the forward cargo hold with great difficulty. The ship, going at flank speed, was pitching with each swell of the ocean. In about eight hours the ship would be inside New York harbor. Pearson had decided that even if somehow he were killed, the ship would still carry out its lethal objective.

To accomplish that, Pearson was going to arm the weapon with a time-delay to assure its detonation inside New York waters. Once he inserted the arming code within the weapon's electronic brain, nothing could stop it except the disarming code. Pearson didn't even have that code.

Pearson's trump card was still to be played. Even though the bomb could not be disarmed, the timer could be altered to allow for an earlier, or even instantaneous, detonation.

It only took Lyndon Pearson ten minutes to get to the crate. Twenty feet away was a storage locker with a fire extinguisher, several pry bars and an array of tools inside.

Working quietly, it took fifteen minutes for Pearson to expose the control panel on his deadly cargo. He studied the unfamiliar Cyrillic (Russian) letters on the face of the panel. Since many of the Russian letters look so similar, he spent a great deal of time making sure he selected the correct ones. Comparing the alphabet against those in his message, the calloused hands of Lyndon Pearson moved sixteen rotary dials to specific characters. Then he pushed a heavy blocking collar away from a recessed bright red button.

After just a moment's hesitation, Pearson pressed the button. A firm snap confirmed it was actuated. Immediately the blocking collar slid back and locked to cover the button. As a final step, Pearson reviewed the chart on his message sheet, and reset the arming dials. This second setting placed the detonation sequence for exactly ten hours later.

This self-destruct timing had been designed as a method to prevent weapons from falling into enemy hands if a storage facility were over run in battle. Russian engineers had never intended the procedure to be used to set a booby-trap, but it would work that way all too well.

Every contingency had been anticipated. Holding the arming code sheet by his fingertips, Pearson touched the corner of the page with a flame from his cigarette lighter. The chemically treated page disappeared almost instantly in a flash of fire.

The nuclear device was now armed. In ten hours, the Peligroso would vaporize along with everything in proximity to her. Since the warhead also had a vertical movement sensor, it would also instantly explode if lifted one hundred feet out of the cargo hold. This detonation sequence was automatic even if the ten-hour arming cycle were not completed.

Lyndon Pearson now knew destruction was inevitable. With the only copy of the arming code now destroyed, there was no turning back. His only concern was living long enough to escape.

Pearson carefully restored the crate to conceal any evidence of tampering. The weapon, control panel, and battery package were now sealed inconspicuously. Salomi's plan was now in its final stage.

Pearson lugged down the watertight doors of the cargo hold as he left.

* * * * *

In Exeter, Dr. Pullen was not pleased with Prince Isha's decision to move. He complained to the King, "Sir, for now, your son's bleeding is under control. If he tries to walk on that leg, he could easily hemorrhage."

Across the room, Maria was still holding Deidre's hand. The color was gone from the young woman's face, but she was stoically holding back her tears.

"You can tell him that, Frank. I don't think he'll listen, but you can tell him," Annu responded. There was, in the King's mind, no way to prevent his son from doing whatever he thought was necessary. Once the situation was settled, then Isha would listen to reason. Until then, his sense of duty and honor was far stronger than his personal welfare. No command from a doctor, or for that matter, a king, would force Isha to lie there in relative safety while his men put themselves in harm's way.

The doctor wisely decided not to push the issue.

* * * * *

Lyndon Pearson and Miles Permi met each other outside the captain's cabin. Pearson chose not to tell the first officer that the device had been armed. There's no reason to panic Permi he decided. Pearson was certain the man would be terrified if he knew fifty kilotons of explosives were already ticking away towards detonation nearby.

"Are you certain the bridge crew will continue to do what you told them?"

"They believe I'll kill them on the spot if I so much as suspect they're changing course or speed."

"Well, for a while, we just have to go on the assumption their fear will overcome their common sense. That won't last long."

Permi answered automatically, "I think it'll last long enough. I saw the look in their eyes." After a second, the first officer realized something was wrong. "What exactly do you have planned, Pearson?"

Without a moment's hesitation the assassin answered, "My strategy is very simple. You and I will search this ship. We will kill everyone we see. As long as there are enough crew members left to man the bridge and engine room, we don't need anyone else."

The horror of Pearson's scheme flooded Miles Permi's mind. "You're mad! I won't shoot my own men in cold blood. There has to be another way. I'm the captain, damn it!"

"It's a little late to be developing a conscience, Permi. Besides, things have gone too far, and you can't stop it."

"Can't stop what?" A sudden look of apprehension clouded Miles Permi's face.

"You weak little man," Lyndon Pearson spit the words with total disgust. He savored his words with relish enjoying their effect on Permi. "Thirty minutes ago I set the bomb to explode automatically."

"What! Are you insane? You can't do that!" Permi was screaming. His eyes were wide open with fear.

"It's done. Nothing or no one can stop it now."

"How could you do that without consulting me?"

"Consult you? Why would I do that? You, Mr. Permi, are a coward who could never be trusted to handle such a decision."

"I'll show you who's a coward." Permi raised his gun and aimed it at Lyndon Pearson, but the killer had anticipated the move. He grabbed the gun barrel and jerked it upwards and away from his body.

Lyndon Pearson's pistol materialized out of nothingness. "Permi, you've screamed at me once too often." With that, Pearson pulled the trigger on his Berretta three times in quick succession. Two of the bullets ripped through Permi's body and ricocheted down the corridor. The third bullet, the fatal one, ended up lodged in Permi's spine.

Miles Permi was thrown against the bulkhead by the force of the bullets tearing through his body. A small fountain of blood squirted from the wounds for several seconds, and then seemed to stop completely.

* * * * *

In the mess hall, Isha was trying out a walking stick loaned to him by a crewmember that collected them. It was made of gnarled diamond willow from the Yukon, and carved to expose the beautiful grain of the wood. The stick was about forty-eight inches long, perfect for helping the prince move with much less pain. Even though his leg was very stiff and becoming even more tender, he was forcing the discomfort from his mind – at least for the moment.

As they left the mess hall, both Protectors were carrying weapons they had removed from the guards. Neither man wanted to use guns. They would prefer to employ the ancient arts they had learned as Protectors. Unfortunately, their adversaries were carrying automatic weapons and would not hesitate to shoot in the ship's confined corridors. This meant Isha and Kevin would have to be prepared to defend themselves with guns if necessary.

Suddenly, three sharp explosions echoed through the corridors. Both men recognized the sound of gunfire.

Isha spoke first. "Find out where everyone is."

"Ok." Kevin went to high power on his transmitter. "Team check Kevin's on."

"Robbie's on."

"Jack's on."

"Cody's on."

"Sound's like everyone is all right. Kevin, have everyone stay where they are for a while. I don't want our guys out being where they can be shot accidentally."

Kevin carried out his Prince's orders. "Isha, how about you and I? Do you want us to split up or stick together?"

"For now, we'll stay together. That will make it harder for them to get behind us."

From then on, the two Protectors moved from corridor to corridor. Each man carefully guarded his partner's back from surprise attacks.

After an hour of virtually silent movement, the warriors from Exeter had checked the Peligroso's entire second level. Kevin noticed his prince was limping more and more noticeably. The stiffness in Isha's leg was becoming a problem, but Kevin decided not to mention it. It would do no good, and would only make the prince mad.

Finally, the Protectors slid around a corner. There in front of them was a man on the floor. A small pool of blood was around his abdomen. He appeared dead. Kevin quickly checked the carotid pulse and found it very weak.

Slowly, as if wakened from a deep sleep, Miles Permi opened his eyes. He tried to focus his vision on the men above him. "Pearson shot me. I can't believe he shot me," he whispered hoarsely.

Isha and Kevin realized they were looking at First Officer Miles Permi. It was also obvious he was near death. "Permi, where is Pearson?"

Suddenly Miles Permi remembered through his foggy mind the last words from Lyndon Pearson. He reached up and grabbed Kevin's arms in desperation. His eyes were wide open in terror. "He's armed it. The son of a bitch armed it. He didn't ask me. He just armed it." As his words gushed out, Permi exhausted the last of his energy. He slowly released his hold on Kevin, and his arms fell limp at his side. The creases on Permi's contorted face eased as he released his final breath.

The weight of the dead man's last words was not lost on Isha and Kevin. The bomb was armed. When had he set it? When was the weapon scheduled to detonate? Could they disarm it? There were too many questions, and no answers to be found.

For now, the Protector's only priority was to find Lyndon Pearson.

"Everyone listen up," Isha spoke tersely into his transmitter. "Pearson has armed the weapon." He waited to see if anyone would ask him to repeat his comment. No one did. "We have only one job now. Let's find that madman and fast."

Kevin quickly began making assignments. He spoke quickly and decisively. "Cody, stay close to the engine room, but check out the lower level of the ship. Jackson, I want you to relieve Robbie outside. He's been in the cold long enough. When you get up there, search the upper deck. Pearson may be trying to get off the ship somehow. Robbie, when you come down, make sure the rest of the crew stays in the mess hall. I don't want any of them getting shot."

Cody jumped in, "Kevin, I want to bring my prisoners up to the mess hall. I think it would be easier to watch all of Pearson's people in one place. Plus they have enough people up there to take the load off our team."

Jackson spoke immediately, "The ship's crew would be happy to baby sit all of Pearson's kids. I don't think they like them very much."

"Ok, good thinking. Be careful that only guarding goes on down there. I don't want a vigilante action. Understand?"

"The second officer, a man named McQueen, says he'll take care of everything," was Jackson's answer. "I think he'll curb the other men's enthusiasm."

Robbie finally also spoke, "Kevin, if it's all the same to you I'll stay up here. I've got my thermal suit on, and I'm staying pretty warm now. I've already checked the upper deck several times."

"Ok, Robbie. Let us know if you need a replacement. Remember, hypothermia is not a good thing."

With the assignments parceled out, Kevin looked at Prince Isha for further instructions.

"Let's find out where the captain is, my friend. Chances are he has some information we can use. Since he obviously is not with the rest of the crew, it's my guess he's been kept in his own cabin."

"That sounds logical." Kevin closed his eyes in thought for a moment visualizing the ship's layout in his head. "The closest passageway to the captain's cabin is up one level and forward."

"Ok. Everyone listen up. I still want check-ins over the radio every fifteen minutes."

"Yes sir," the Protectors responded almost in unison.

* * * * *

In Exeter, King Annu had the brightest of his specialists attempting to break into computer files around the world. Each person had only one goal—to gather information about the arming codes on nuclear devices of the former Soviet Union. It would be a challenging, if not impossible, task. To compound the difficulty of their work, the researchers lacked specifications of the individual warhead they needed to narrow their search. Hopefully that would come when Prince Isha could actually see the weapon and give them details.

As the Protectors slowly approached the door to the captain's cabin, both men silently wondered what they would find inside. Lyndon Pearson had shown no hesitation to kill.

Isha took a small slender instrument from a small pouch strapped to his leg, and slipped it into the door lock. The tool expanded inside the lock to push the tumblers and release the mechanism. Isha quietly turned the doorknob a fraction of an inch. Another slight turn of the knob, and he felt the door come ajar. An almost imperceptible nod from the prince told Kevin to get ready.

Both men shoved the door open simultaneously, and expected a burst of gunfire to answer their attack. Instead, only silence replied. Isha quickly glanced inside the cabin. There was no assassin inside. Instead, Isha saw a large man hog-tied on the floor.

The man spoke with a distinctive Scottish accent, "I guess you're the gentlemen who have been playing havoc with Mr. Permi and Mr. Pearson. Welcome aboard the Peligroso. I don't know who you are, but I'm sure as hell glad to see you. Now would you be kind enough to cut these blasted cords off? I'm more than a bit uncomfortable here, and it's damn near impossible to maintain any sense of dignity in this position."

As Kevin quickly sliced the bindings, Isha helped McLean Andrews to his chair. The captain looked curiously into the eyes of his rescuers, "Gentlemen, may I assume you're with a Special Forces unit?"

The two men looked at each other for a moment. A friendly smile and chuckle answered, "We're just friends, Captain. We're just friends."

Thirty-Three

Captain McLean Andrews was becoming painfully aware that the numbness in his hands was being replaced by an excruciating tingling sensation. He was sitting at his desk gingerly rubbing his sore and chaffed wrists in an attempt to force blood back into the tissue. The muscles of his back were still cramped and aching from the strain they had been under. He knew tomorrow he would have trouble even walking because of the stiffness. Actually, he hoped there would be a tomorrow in which to be sore. Prince Isha had filled the ship's master in on the events of the last twelve hours. He finished with Permi's deathbed confession.

Andrews didn't seem too surprised that his ship was carrying a nuclear device. "I had sort of figured it was something like that. Pearson was too proud of his plan to keep it quiet. He kept making comments that couldn't be interpreted any other way."

"We have to try to end Pearson's madness here. Captain, do you know where the bomb is?"

"Let's say I have an educated guess. There's an unmarked cargo container in the forward hold I found suspicious. Someone has gone to great care to prevent its contents from being readily known."

"Can you take us there?"

"This is my ship again. I can bloody well take you any bloody place I want!" the old seaman bellowed.

"Not exactly. There's the small matter of a nuclear warhead a few hundred feet from here. This may be your ship, but I think that bomb is really in charge – at least right now."

Andrews showed no fear. "Then let's take care of it. I never want anyone or anything to take command of my ship again!"

After a quick check with the team, Prince Isha, Kevin, and Captain McLean Andrews started towards the forward cargo hold. The three men moved cautiously. They knew Lyndon Pearson still had free access to all areas of the ship. The Protectors realized Pearson enjoyed killing, and didn't fear dying himself. That combination made him a dangerous predator to deal with.

As they moved, Kevin took the point with Isha following and the captain in tow. This system allowed each man to protect the other from surprise attack. After what seemed hours, but was really only fifteen minutes, Kevin loosened the lugs around a watertight door. On the other sided was the forward cargo compartment.

The only light in the darkened cargo hold came from an emergency beam at the far end of the area. It cast an eerie shadow over the cargo crates. Isha looked at Andrews, "Captain, where's the power switch for the hold?"

"Here," McLean Andrews said, "but it's not going to help." He pointed at a waterproof switching box on the bulkhead.

Isha and Kevin recognized why immediately. The electrical cable going from the top of the box had been severed by a fire axe that was lying nearby.

"Well, if Pearson has gone to this much trouble I'm sure we're in the right area," Isha commented. "Captain, I recommend you stay here and guard the door while we search the hold."

Andrews started to protest, but recognized the logic in Isha's suggestion. These two men were professionals and trained for what they were facing. Andrews knew he wasn't. "Alright, I'll stay here. You men take care. This bastard's a real work of art. He won't bat an eyelash before sending you to your grave."

Kevin glanced at the older man, "Burial at sea isn't in my plans."

Isha just shook his head. "Call out to us if you see Pearson. We'll be nearby."

"Just see that Pearson doesn't blast my beautiful ship all over the North Atlantic," Andrews said protectively.

"That order is at the top of our priorities list. Both men handed Andrews their captured weapons. "Hold on to these guns until we get back."

"Aren't you gonna need them when you find Pearson?"

"Kevin never was a good shot," Isha responded. The two Protectors began moving into the hold. Suddenly, as an afterthought, Isha looked back. "If the situation arises and you decide to take a shot at Pearson, please be careful. I don't think having a lot of lead flying around the warhead would be too healthy – if you catch my drift."

McLean Andrews replied sternly, "That would never happen. I hit what I aim at. You two be careful out there. I know this man. He'll kill you."

"Staying alive is the second item on our list of priorities," Isha said. No one mentioned the slightly growing red stain on the pressure bandage around his upper leg. It wouldn't have mattered what either Kevin or Andrews said. Isha had to be in great pain, but he wouldn't admit it.

* * * * *

In Exeter, Annu warily looked around the chamber. He was nearly exhausted. The last several hours had been difficult on everyone there. Kristi was using her communications responsibility to stay busy, but for everyone else present, it was just a waiting game.

The waiting was doubly difficult for Deidre and Celia. Their beautiful faces seemed to have aged years. Maria was holding her granddaughter's hand and occasionally patting it affectionately, and Celia was sitting with David and Robin Marcus.

Unexpectedly, the old woman got up and walked to Annu. She put her arm around him and spoke quietly, "Your son will be home soon. He's an extraordinary young man. I know he'll be fine."

"From your lips to God's ears," Annu answered. At the moment, he was a father, not a monarch.

* * * * *

At that exact moment, Isha and Kevin had split up and were slowly moving from shadow to shadow on opposite sides of the hold. The cargo was stacked higher than the Protector's heads. Tie-down chains held the wooden containers in place to prevent them moving from the ship's passage on rough seas.

Both men knew their martial arts skills would be severely limited in the tight constraints of the boxes. They were equally sure Pearson would have a difficult time shooting in the same environment.

Fifty feet inside the hold, Isha was silently inching his way towards the location Andrews had said held the wooden crate. Suddenly a pained cry filled the cavernous cargo hold.

"Kevin," Isha spoke quickly but quietly into his microphone, "check in!"

"That wasn't me, Isha."

"Get to the captain!"

The men quickly found McLean Andrews crumpled on the deck. Blood was cascading down the right side of his face. The old man was barely conscious. "He slid up behind me and hit me with some kind of pipe. Damn it all!"

"Kevin, take the captain to the mess. They can take care of him there."

"I can make it on my own," Andrews protested.

"We need you to bring this ship into the harbor. I can't risk losing you. Kevin, do as I've said."

"Yes, sir. I'll be right back."

The old Scotsman outweighed Kevin by fifty pounds, but the young Protector easily helped him down the passageway. Andrews was leaning on Kevin for support and stumbled every few steps. It would be a long trip to the mess.

Isha moved back into the hold, and melted into the maze of cargo containers. *I should have had Robbie bring me one of the low light goggles from our hiding spot on the deck,* Isha thought, *but there wasn't time for that now.*

Out of the darkness, a voice echoed through the vast hold. "So, it's just you and me now. Good! I've been looking forward to killing you."

"Well, if that little bomb of yours goes off, I'll be dead anyway."

The words of both men reverberated around the boxes and made it impossible to discern their origin.

"Tell, me Pearson, how much time do we have?"

"It doesn't matter. There's nothing you can do. We're all as good as dead."

"I'm sure you'll understand if I still try."

No answer.

Isha moved in total silence. Even the sound of his own breath seemed deafening to the Prince.

Isha never saw the attack coming. From atop a double-stack of cargo, Lyndon Pearson dropped a two-pound sledgehammer on Isha, and the Prince fell to the deck.

Pearson jumped down beside the comatose prince. He reached down and felt Isha's neck for a pulse. He felt none. The young man at Pearson's feet was obviously dead. Lyndon Pearson stepped back and viciously kicked the fallen warrior.

Picking up the hammer, Pearson stepped over the dead man and walked twenty feet to his container. Unconcerned about discovery now, Pearson quickly exposed the warhead control panel.

As Pearson walked by the lifeless body lying on the deck, he impulsively kicked it again. That's what you get for trying to interfere with my plans!

* * * * *

In the mess hall, Kevin had McLean Andrews sitting on the edge of a serving table. The older man had an egg sized bump at the hairline above his right eye. There was also a small cut on his right cheek that happened when Andrews fell to the deck after being hit.

"The bugger played me like a school yard thug. The bastard slipped up behind me, whispered my name, and smashed my bean when I turned around." He shook his painful head side-to-side disgustedly. "I can't believe I let him sucker me like that."

"Don't worry about it. Isha will take care of him."

"No he won't!" a voice boomed in. "He's quite dead, you see." There, standing in the entryway to the mess hall, was Lyndon Pearson. In his hand was an automatic pistol. It was leveled at Kevin. "I had the pleasure of killing him in the cargo hold a few minutes ago."

Stunned silence filled the room. Kevin, particularly, couldn't believe what he had heard. Isha was indestructible. He couldn't accept that the Prince of Exeter was dead.

Pearson continued, savoring each word, "It seems you've been watching my crew. Now, it's their turn to return the favor."

Kevin now regretted his decision to guard all four surviving members of the terrorist group in the mess. Now Pearson was freeing all them simultaneously. He spoke harshly to the thugs, "Get your weapons back from these people. Move!" Instantly, the four men grabbed their guns from the hands of the Peligroso crewmembers that had been their guards.

Andrews glared fearlessly into Lyndon Pearson's uncaring eyes. "What are you going to do to my ship?"

"Nothing," Pearson lied. "Since our mission has been discovered, there is no chance for success. I'm not spending the rest of my life in prison. Before we enter the harbor, my team and I will launch a lifeboat and escape to shore. You will then be free to bring the ship in. I don't care. The authorities will never catch us. We will be out of the country before they can react." Yellowed teeth showed wickedly from Pearson's twisted smile.

"You are a lying bastard. My men will never take this ship into the harbor."

"Yes they will. By my estimation, we're only four hours from landfall. You and I will be soon go up to the bridge and encourage your crew to do as I say."

"Never. I'll never help you."

Moving his gun a fraction of an inch, Pearson pulled the trigger once. Captain McLean Andrews' face showed instant shock - then pain as the bullet tore through his knee.

Kevin reacted instantly and lunged at the cold-blooded killer in front of him. Even with his lighting reflexes, Kevin could not prevent Pearson from simply moving his pistol a few inches and firing.

This second bullet struck Kevin just above his left ear. The projectile took a few millimeters of hair and scalp as it grazed the side of Kevin's head. The impact was sufficient to stun the young man, and he stumbled backwards against a bulkhead.

Lyndon Pearson looked around at the shocked crewmembers in the room. "The next person who disobeys me will find himself at the bottom of the ocean."

The heartless assassin looked down at McLean Andrews, writhing in pain on the deck before him. "Now, are you ready to help me?"

"You bastard!" Andrews spoke through the pain.

Pearson took a single step forward and put his boot heel on the captain's shattered knee. With exquisite pleasure, Pearson slowly leaned forward and pressed all his weight straight down.

Captain Andrews screamed out in agony, and then went limp as unconsciousness released him from the pain.

* * * * *

Robbie knew more than thirty minutes had passed since the last check in. He hesitated to ask about it over the radio. He didn't want to remind Prince Isha or Kevin of their own orders. When they're ready for a check in, they'll ask for it, he decided.

In the engine room, Cody had arrived at essentially the same conclusion. He had completed his search for Pearson and now was guarding his critical area of the ship.

There was no way for Robbie or Cody to know how badly things had gone for the rest of the team. They were in the dark and hesitant to try and communicate with anyone else.

Kevin woke up with an excruciating headache. He was suffering from double vision and a loud ringing in his ears. Jackson was doctoring his wound. "How bad is it?"

"Fortunately he hit you in the head."

Kevin ignored the jab. There were too many things racing through his mind. Kevin was well aware that he was second in command. With Isha dead, the weight of the mission fell on his shoulders.

Isha   dead. Pearson's words came flooding back and forced itself through Kevin's pain. The enormity of that realization was almost beyond his comprehension.

For the moment, Kevin forced himself to ignore his grief and concentrate on the immediate situation. There would be time later to avenge his best friend's death.

* * * * *

On the bridge, the crewmembers there were still carrying out Miles Permi's last order. They had been sailing the Peligroso at flank speed on a direct path for the entrance to New York harbor.

The men looked in fear as Pearson, and his accomplice, dragged the bleeding hulk of their captain on to the bridge. They dropped his comatose form behind the chart table. "Gentlemen," Pearson spoke softly, "Andrews' life, and yours, depend on how well you answer the next question." He paused for effect. "Where are we, and how long until the Peligroso enters New York harbor?"

The three men stared in disbelief at McLean Andrews' crumpled body. "Sir," one of them answered, "we're right here." With a shaking finger, the man pointed to a spot on the navigation chart.

"Are you sure?" Pearson bellowed.

A barely perceptible nod was the only response.

The time estimation Lyndon Pearson had given in the mess hall had been wrong. The Peligroso was not four hours from the United States. She was just shy of two hours. The bomb would explode three hours later.

Damn! That's too much time. In three hours, the crew can have the authorities all over this ship. We'll be able to escape, but maybe they'll have time to disarm the weapon. Pearson knew the plan had to be altered.

Out of the recesses of his twisted mind, Pearson developed a new plan. He ordered his accomplice to keep the ship moving, and quickly jogged back to the mess hall.

"How many men are on your team?" he screamed at Kevin and Jackson.

"Just us and the one you killed."

"I don't believe you."

"I don't really give a damn what you believe. We expected you to be acting alone or maybe with one other person," Kevin lied. "We were wrong not to bring a larger force."

"I'm afraid that will soon prove to have been a fatal mistake."

"What do you mean?"

"I originally planned on killing the captain once he docked the ship. That way he could bring the ship in, and then be eliminated," Pearson said without feeling. Your interference means that we can't afford to have any witnesses left."

"Mass murder? You plan on killing everyone on board? Why? You still need someone to bring the ship into the harbor."

"Not true. I would need someone to bring the ship into the dock. But if I were to simply ground the ship on say, Liberty Island, it would give me lots of options. For example, finding the entire ship's crew murdered would occupy the authorities a long time. That would give us opportunity to get far away before the weapon detonates. Brilliant, if I say so myself."

"You wouldn't dare murder the whole crew," Jackson exclaimed, knowing he was wrong.

"On the contrary, I'm doing them a favor. Every one of you is going to simply evaporate when the bomb goes off anyway. I'm saving you all from the dying in a thermonuclear detonation."

"You can save that sick convoluted logic. It's wasted on me."

"Doesn't really matter. I'll just make you one of the first to die," Pearson hissed.

* * * * *

A short time later, in the operations center of the New York Port Authority, a lone controller named Weldin Pouncy was working the arrival sector for the harbor. He had been watching the surface radar return on an unknown ship for the past hour. Ships normally followed certain standard procedures when entering the harbor. This one had failed to make any of the mandatory radio contacts required by the Port Authority. Pouncy checked the timetable and verified no ships were scheduled to arrive for several hours.

Even an unexpected arrival wasn't that unusual. Sometimes captains pushed their ships at flank speed instead of normal cruise in order to reach port early. However, since ships were sequenced for arrival to ensure dock space was prepared, this practice was discouraged.

Pouncy's calm demeanor and attention to detail were just two of the many reasons he was the top controller on the entire Eastern Seaboard. The other reason was his amazing intellect and intuition. He could just look at the radar scope and somehow "feel" something was wrong or needed immediate attention. Other managers had asked him to teach rookie controllers how he did it, but it was nothing he could teach. It was an innate gift and one Weldin Pouncy used to its highest level.

Pouncy was confused, but not especially alarmed by the lack of communication from the ship. Like with modern airliners, total radio failure on ocean going ships was extremely rare—but it did happen. This was quite probably just such an event. It was not a major emergency because there were standard international maritime rules and procedures to handle such occurrences. The captain would know what to do, and Pouncy would be sure the Port Authority was ready also.

He reached for a two-inch thick binder from the cabinet behind his desk. Using tabs on the cover sheets, he quickly found the appropriate procedural section. Systematically, Pouncy started notifying the necessary individuals and agencies on the checklist.

Ten minutes later, with five phone calls completed and the checklist accomplished, Weldin Pouncy continued with the rest of his duties. The silent ship was still thirty minutes out. A harbor tug was scheduled to rendezvous with her. Things should go smoothly, and in an hour the unknown ship would be safely at dock.

* * * * *

On the Peligroso, Lyndon Pearson was quickly implementing his new plan for escape. He gathered all of his men except for those required to guard their prisoners. "Listen up," he said tersely. "We will soon all be very wealthy men." He waited to let the words sink in. "You have done an excellent job. I would not be surprised if Salomi himself will be there to congratulate you when we return home." He stared proudly at the men before him. "Soon, you will be heroes at home. Your families will be proud to speak your name. Your countrymen will honor you."

Broad grins erupted from the men. They were far more excited about the money than the recognition. None of them believed they would really ever meet their leader, but they didn't care. They did believe they would soon be rich men, and that was all Pearson really wanted. He just needed them another thirty minutes or so.

Lyndon Pearson had no intention of sharing the reward from Azmud Salomi with his men. Even this close to the goal, they still had no idea about the true extent of the mission. Their ignorance also meant they would believe whatever Pearson told them.

Not only would there be no money, in reality his secret plan meant that none of them would be allowed to live.

Pearson's plan was exquisitely unrefined. First, he replaced the Peligroso's bridge crew with two of his own men. While they were competent to steer the ship into the harbor, they lacked to skills needed to enter the dock.

That didn't matter. Pearson had a less demanding end to the voyage planned. Directly in the path of the Peligroso's bow was his target – Frederic Bartholdi's magnificent work Liberty Enlightening the World   the serene and magnificent Statue of Liberty.

"Put the bow of this ship straight into the middle of that island, mister!" he ordered. "I want the Peligroso sitting directly under that statue."

The two men were completely confused and stared at their leader for a moment in surprise. "Do you have a problem with that?" He yelled.

"No sir," they answered in unison. Neither man wanted to comply with the order, but they knew it wasn't healthy to question Lyndon Pearson.

For his part, Pearson was certain they would follow his instructions. He watched in satisfaction as the helmsman made a small correction to the ship's course.

After his men had the ship headed directly towards the Statue of Liberty, Lyndon Pearson stepped to the hatch. He reached inside his windbreaker, removed the nine-millimeter Berretta there and calmly shot both men at point blank range. They were dead before they hit the deck.

Pearson's plan was now irreversible. He allowed two minutes to go below to the mess hall. Once there, he would order his men to use their automatic weapons to quickly execute everyone on the crew. Again, he was sure they would carry out his orders. Once the crew was dead, he would then kill his remaining people, too.

Finally, Pearson's plan was to rush down the remaining three levels to the engine room. There it would only take a few seconds to kill the three crew and one guard.

That would make Lyndon Pearson the last living man on a floating mausoleum named the Peligroso. The final part of his escape would be the trickiest. He would brace himself for the ship to crash into Liberty Island. He knew it would be violent, but decided he could avoid injury by being prepared.

Once the ship hit, he would use the confusion and pandemonium that was sure to follow and escape into the crowd. Finally, even using the ship that shuttled tourists from Battery Park out to Liberty Island and back, he would have more than an hour to escape New York City before the bomb exploded. That would be plenty of time.

* * * * *

On the bridge of the harbor tug, Symmetry, Captain Fredrick Gunn watched in fascination as a large cargo ship steamed under the Verrazano-Narrows Bridge and entered into Upper New York Bay. He had been expecting the ship since being notified an hour earlier. He knew the ship was not in radio contact with the Port Authority, but he was still confused about it.

"I wonder what that captain can possibly be thinking," he said to no one in particular.

The helmsman looked up to see what the captain was looking at. His eyes grew wide in bewilderment. "Oh, God," he whispered in disbelief.

Five hundred yards away, the bow of the Peligroso was cutting through the water at what Captain Gunn estimated was at least five times the maximum speed for the harbor. A large wave was cascading off the bow leaving a powerful and dangerous wake behind the ship.

"There's no way she'll be able to stop." Gunn's mind was racing as he picked up his microphone and flipped a long, black toggle switch on the transmitter. This switch put the radio instantly on Channel 16, which was set to 156.8 megahertz, the emergency channel monitored by all Coast Guard ships. "Mayday, mayday, mayday! This is the NYC harbor ship Symmetry transmitting on guard." Gunn waited only a moment before continuing. "There is a freighter just inside the upper bay that appears to be out of control. She is at flank speed and does not respond to radio. Pass the word for all ships, to be aware of extremely large wake danger."

The Coast Guard immediately responded and said a cutter would be dispatched asap.

Gunn's helmsman was busy moving the Symmetry away from the runaway ship's path. Suddenly he stiffened and grabbed his captain's arm. "Sir, she's headed for the Lady!"

Fredrick Gunn's nineteen years experience as a harbor tug captain had given him a keen eye for projecting a ship's path. He used that ability on a daily basis to join up with ships and attach lines to them. Then he used his powerful tug to gently push those huge ships into relatively tiny docking areas. In all his years, Gunn had never had a single ship or dock damaged by an error on his part.

Gunn had been too busy transmitting the warning to pay attention to the mystery ship's path, but he recognized immediately his helmsman was right. What was more, he realized it was already too late to prevent the ship from grounding herself violently on Liberty Island. He grabbed his microphone again. "Mayday, mayday, mayday! This is the NYC harbor ship Symmetry again transmitting on guard. All ships in the vicinity of Liberty Island - danger, I say again - danger." Gunn used his bridge binoculars to look across the harbor to identify the rogue ship. "The cargo ship Peligroso is headed directly towards Liberty Island. She shows no indication of trying to alter course. Unless something changes within the next couple of minutes, I see no hope for her to stop. I expect her to ground within five minutes."

Gunn's dire transmission and warning was monitored at a dozen locations within the port area. One of the quickest to respond was the National Park Station located on Liberty Island. Two rangers dressed in their characteristic green uniforms and wide brimmed hats raced out to the precipice of the island.

Both had been assigned to Liberty Island for more than five years, and in that time had seen literally thousands of ships pass by. This ship was definitely coming straight at them, and fast.

The senior ranger made a quick decision. "We better get everyone to the other side of the island right now! Get on the P.A. system and make an announcement. I'll stay here and start rounding up everyone I can."

Within a minute the first of several announcements had been made. Dozens of tourists, who seconds before were staring up in rapt fascination at the copper clad statue, were now running for their lives in fear. The entire ranger force began to organize and funnel everyone away from the apparent point where the ship would hit. The professionalism and bravery of the quick-thinking rangers was responsible for the safe evacuation of everyone around the monument.

The combined quick reaction of the Symmetry's captain and of the National Park Service rangers ensured the immediate safety of everyone on the island. It was, however, a momentary reprieve. None of them realized they were standing at ground zero for a thermonuclear explosion. From the opposite side of the island, everyone watched as if in a trance as the immense hull of the Peligroso grew ever closer. Some were already thinking of the great stories they would be telling once they got home from their trip. Watching the crash of a large ship certainly wasn't on their itineraries.

* * * * *

On the Peligroso, things were moving figuratively and literally too fast for Lyndon Pearson. The couple of minutes it took him to get from the bridge to the mess hall seemed like an eternity. He rushed into the room and began to shout hurried orders to his men.

The room was empty.

Pearson froze for a moment trying to figure out where everyone could possibly be. Then from the pit of his stomach a realization struck him. "The bomb," he suddenly thought to himself.

An unfamiliar feeling - panic - immediately seized Pearson. Knowing he only had a few minutes before the Peligroso rammed at breakneck speed onto the rocks surrounding Liberty Island, Lyndon Pearson ran blindly to the forward cargo hold.

Breathlessly, he got to the container. Emergency lights still produced the only illumination in the area, but they were enough for him to see clearly. The box that contained his terrible cargo was still open with the control panel was exposed.

Pearson stared at it for a moment. From the shadows behind him, a voice from the grave spoke, "So that's what a nuclear bomb looks like." Pearson whirled around and stared disbelievingly at the man he had killed.

Thirty-Four

For a moment Pearson was dumbfounded and peered into the shadow. "How," he stammered, "how are you alive? I... ."

"I know. You killed me. Well, things aren't always the way they seem." Lyndon Pearson continued to stare at Isha. His mind raced as he tried to make sense of what he was seeing. "When I kill someone they stay dead."

"Sorry to break your record."

"I don't know how you came back from the grave the last time, but you won't do it again."

"I only had to do it once, Pearson. I just want you to remember, we know about the bomb."

"So what? This ship will so be blown to hell and back, and there's nothing anyone can do about it."

"Maybe, but you'll be dead, too."

"So? My family will be well cared for, and I will resting in a very special place."

"Well, I won't argue with that. But if you kill all those people there will be no place on Earth where your name is not hated."

"Small price for immortality. Don't you think?"

"That's not immortality, that's infamy."

"I refuse to get into an argument of semantics because I intend to be far away from this ship when it explodes. Unfortunately, for me to escape, you have to die."

"Well, that remains to be seen. Your guards thought they would get to kill us, too. Right now, they're guests of mine. Next time tell them to expect the unexpected. They never even saw me walk into the mess hall."

"No matter. They'll be dead, too." Pearson reached into his windbreaker and removed his gun. He looked at Isha's wounded thigh and smiled. "I think I'll start with your other leg." Pearson pulled the trigger of his Berretta. Nothing happened. For the first time in his professional career, Lyndon Pearson had failed to count the number of times he had fired his weapon. The clip and chamber of his gun were empty.

"Darn, looks like I get to live," Isha said sarcastically.

"No, it just means I get to kill you another way," the furious Pearson responded. From the deck, he grabbed an iron pry bar and, his face contorted in anger, Pearson moved towards Isha.

The prince knew he was weak from the wound to his leg. His grandfather's poultice had done its job and relieved much of the pain and muscle spasms, but he had lost a lot of blood. Isha realized he wouldn't last long in an extended battle with Pearson and he had to end this fight quickly.

Isha taunted Pearson to make the man react in anger. "I'm warning you. If you come at me with that bar, I will kill you."

A wicked laugh escaped from the terrorist. "You fool. You're in no position to threaten me. You're already half dead. I'm just gonna take care of the other half." He slowly moved forward menacingly. Pearson was too experienced to swing wildly. Instead, he made short hammering motions with the claw end of the bar.

Unexpectedly, Isha dropped to the deck and used his good leg to sweep Pearson's knee. The larger man was caught off guard and fell hard. He rolled to his side and lashed out with violent kicks towards Isha who easily eluded them. It only took Pearson a moment to jump back to his feet. He rubbed his left elbow which had taken the brunt of his fall.

"That'll cost you."

"What? You plan on killing me twice? You haven't even been able to kill me once," Isha taunted.

Pearson's face flushed red with anger. Isha's belittling insult had its desired effect. In a fury, Lyndon Pearson raised the pry bar and rushed Isha.

This time, Isha stood his ground and called on every ounce of training and skill he possessed. At the precise moment when there was no other course of action available, the prince used the last of the strength in his wounded leg and leaped straight up.

Pearson tried to react, but there was no time. As if in slow motion, he watched as the man he intended to kill jumped. With incredible precision, the man's opposite leg folded at the knee then exploded out into a powerful kick. Pearson could see the foot approaching his face, but there was nothing he could do to stop it.

The man's kick plus Pearson's forward momentum created a deadly contact. Lyndon Pearson, the man who was willing to kill hundreds of thousands and harm millions, was defenseless to stop Isha's assault. He felt the force of the prince's kick for only a second, and then his head seemed to erupt into a flash of bright lights. His legs buckled, and he started to fall. Before Pearson collapsed completely to the deck, Isha reached down and grabbed the man's shaggy hair.

Pearson stared up through blurry eyes into the face of the young man who had kicked him.

"I'm going to save your life so you can have a very public, very humiliating trial," Prince Isha said contemptuously.

Lyndon Pearson still had fight remaining inside his hideous existence. He suddenly reached for the knife he carried strapped on his forearm. His reflexes were too slow. Isha reacted with a single karate chop into Pearson's temple. Then with a slow, deliberate action, he grabbed both sides of the man's head and twisted.

A loud crunching snap signaled the end to Lyndon Pearson's life.

"So much for a public trial," Isha remarked to the corpse in front of him.

"Kevin," Isha yelled into his radio. "Where are you?"

"I'm on the bridge, Isha. Standby." He moved control levers on the bridge that signaled emergency reverse power to the engine room. The response was instantaneous from the Peligroso's engine crew.

A second later, Isha was almost thrown off his feet by the power of the Peligroso's engines reversing her propellers. The screws churned feverishly at the water, but there was no hope for the ship.

Kevin grabbed the ship's microphone and shouted over the intercom to every section of the ship. "Everyone grab hold of anything you can. We're about to hit. We just have a few seconds. Brace yourselves for a collision!"

All over the ship, men began reacting. The crew, who were guarding Pearson's men in different cabins around the ship, did exactly as told and prepared for the inevitable impact.

In the cargo hold, Isha was in a vulnerable position. The tons of freight surrounding him were tied down to withstand ocean storms, but not the stress of a grounding. He knew there was a real danger that he would be crushed under their weight when the boxes fell forward. There was nowhere to hide, and no time to escape.

With scant seconds left until the ship's forty thousand tons smashed into Liberty Island, Isha sprinted to a bulkhead next to the external watertight hatch. He threw his body behind the bulkhead, and balled up as small as possible there.

* * * * *

A loud scraping and grinding noise marked the last seconds of the Peligroso's final voyage. Her bow plates were smashed and crumpled like cardboard sheets by the violent forces.

The Peligroso's brutal crash resulted in the first thirty-eight feet of the ship being twisted and torn. Only by the grace of God did the forward cargo hold not flood.

Isha was completely stunned by the force of the impact. It took several moments for his head to clear enough for him to look around. While many of the crates were scattered and broken, Paxton Frame's skill had survived him. His loading and tie-downs had endured even the destruction of the ship.

"Isha," Kevin yelled, "are you ok?"

"Yeah, I am. Do you call that a docking?"

"Not bad for my first time don't you think? Where's Pearson?"

"In hell, I expect." How's the rest of the team?"

A quick radio check showed everyone bruised but alive. "Kevin, assemble everyone down here in the cargo hold immediately." He paused for a moment to decide how to phrase his next order. "Bring Skye with you," was all he could think of saying.

"We'll all be there in five minutes," Kevin responded.

The Peligroso had been aground for less than five minutes, but already rescue personnel were climbing all over her. Captain McLean Andrews was sitting on the bridge with his wounded leg resting on the chart table. He was directing the evacuation of his crew with his typical gusto. Kevin had asked the captain to refrain from mentioning Isha's men to anyone. Andrews still assumed that a secret military group had been on his ship. He could keep his men quiet, at least for a while.

* * * * *

Isha knew he only had a short time with the weapon before NYC Port authorities were swarming the cargo hold.

Suddenly help spoke in his ear. "Sir, I think we may have a solution for your little problem." Kristi's voice sounded sweet to the Prince.

"Welcome to New York. How is it I'm able to hear you inside the ship now?"

"It's not a problem when you're just a couple of miles from a relay tower, sir. We've been listening to you for the past hour. The king figured you didn't need any distractions from us, so he ordered radio silence from Exeter."

"You said something about help. I could sure use it," Isha said. "From what I could gather from the late leader of the pack, we don't have much time."

Over the radio, Isha described the control panel in great detail. At first Kristi was doing all the talking. Soon, however, other voices started asking the prince questions about the different switches, the Cyrillic letters, and the indicators. The biggest problem Isha had was describing the letters so that there was no question in the minds of the scientists exactly what characters he was seeing.

Isha could tell that specialists in Exeter were digesting everything he was saying. It gave Isha some comfort knowing that the finest minds in the world were at work deciphering the code to disarm this weapon. There was only one concern in his thoughts – Will they be in time?

At one point King Annu's voice came over the radio. "Son," he spoke calmly, "how far can you get from the ship if we can't solve this?"

"Not far enough. Father, I don't think I should leave if there's any chance I can stop this by being here. I am sending my team away though."

Just at that moment Kevin, Robbie, Jackson, and Cody came in. Cody was carrying a heavy canvas bag that obviously contained the body of his friend, Skye. The team had heard Isha's last comment and didn't agree with him.

Robbie said what they were all thinking. "Sire, we came here as a team, and we want to leave as a team. We belong to each other. Remember?"

"Sir," Isha spoke to King Annu, "the team will be staying together until we handle this situation."

"I understand, Isha. Tell your team we'll do everything possible to bring them home soon."

Robbie looked at his brothers and whispered, "That's assuming we don't get blown to Exeter by that little thing over there."

Everyone chuckled, but the laughter was insincere. The men all knew that it was a real possibility that they were in their last few minutes of life.

A new voice came over the radio. "Prince Isha, see if you can find a metal plate on the bottom of the weapon. It should be about fifteen inches aft and below the control panel, and should have three letters and five or six numbers."

If he knows the serial number's location that precisely, he must be looking at a diagram or schematic of the weapon, Isha thought hopefully. "Just a moment. We've got to take more of the box apart." Isha reached over and picked up the pry bar next to Lyndon Pearson's body. He used the bar to carefully break away two more boards from the crate. The emergency lights were too dim to see the small numbers on the bottom of the casing.

Robbie looked over at the dead man and thought out loud, "I'll bet that jackass smoked. Let's see if he's got a lighter." A quick check of Pearson's clothes produced a butane lighter.

"Good thinking, Robbie!" Isha praised.

The flickering flame in the semi-darkness was plenty bright enough to see the characters on the three-inch metal plate riveted to the bottom of the control casing. Isha described the characters carefully then the numbers.

"Alright, sir. We copied that. Give us a few minutes to try to get some information back to you."

"We're not going anywhere," Isha said.

"We hope we're not going anywhere," Kevin chimed in.

* * * * *

In Exeter, scientists, computer experts, and security analysts had indeed broken into a highly classified computer system. They now had access to a huge encrypted file listing serial numbers and arming codes for most of the nuclear devices from the former Soviet Union.

The encrypted file would take time to decode, but time was the one commodity they had the least of.

Exeter's finest computer experts were stymied. King Annu was understandably interested in their work. "Where did you get this file?" he asked.

One of the men looked up from his computer terminal. "We had difficulty with the old Russian technology, sire. So, we broke into the CIA's files."

Annu was incredulous. "The CIA had a list of the soviet arming codes?"

"Well, yes sir. I expect they got it when things started going crazy."

Another analyst clapped his hands together in excitement. His broad grin seemed to encompass his whole face. "That's it!" he exclaimed.

"Did you find the code?" Annu asked.

"No sire, maybe something just as good." He looked at the analyst who had been talking to the king a second before. "You gave me the answer – the crazy man's code."

Most of the faces reflected confusion, but one or two nodded in agreement. "What's the crazy man's code?" someone asked.

"Twenty odd years ago, someone got concerned that a crazy man might get access to the codes for our nuclear arsenal and somehow bypass all the security to set one off. As unlikely as that seemed, they decided that someone crazy enough to do it might find a way. So, they then built into the unified nuclear control system a code that would instantly disarm all of our warheads simultaneously. What's more, individual warheads could be disarmed if they were autonomous from those weapons on the network – like attached to alert aircraft for example."

Everyone sat in rapt attention, but no one seemed to understand. The scientist in frustration decided to be blunt. "If the President of the United States went off the deep end, the military wanted to be able to stop him from unilaterally starting a nuclear war. They felt like civilian control of the weapons had to have some kind of military override."

"Congress and the President have gone along with this?"

"No, I don't think they know about it."

"Who in the military has access to the – what did you call it – the crazy man's code?"

"I don't really know. It would be my guess, however, that the command post in Cheyenne Mountain would certainly have it, and probably a few others. It would have to be a very few. No one would dare reveal that the code even exists. You can imagine what would hit the fan if word ever got out to the government that someone in the military could override their arming codes."

"Ok, we know that the U.S. arsenal has an override code. Does that mean the former Soviet Union had one?"

"Well, the fact that the Soviet military distrusted the civilian authorities has never been a dark secret, and warriors are usually the last ones who want war. I wouldn't be surprised if our military didn't give the technology to their Russian counterparts ... or vice-versa."

"Okay," Annu decided, "everyone keep trying to break the code we have right now." He turned to the scientist who had advanced the new possibility. "Pick three others and do your best to find out if this override code exists, and what it is."

"Yes sir," was the terse response. The man was already moving towards a man and two women in his cluster of analysts. "These three are the best I know. If the code exists, we'll find it," he said with more confidence than he felt.

* * * * *

On the Peligroso, a phone in the forward hold rang. Robbie picked it out of the receptacle and answered. Captain McLean Andrews was on the other end. "You might want to tell your boss that they want to take me to some damnable hospital. I don't know how much longer I'll be able to stay here."

Robbie realized Andrews had been keeping everyone away from the hold. That wouldn't last long after they took him to the hospital.

"Sir, I'll tell him."

Isha reached for the phone. "Captain, what have you told the authorities?"

"Nothing. So far, all we've had were some people with badges that say Park Ranger, whatever in blazes that is. I do know that the Coast Guard and Port Authority will be here within a few minutes." He waited for Isha to say something. When he didn't, Andrews continued, "Do I understand that you were never here?"

"That is our preference. You don't know anything about who we were or where we came from."

"That'll be easy. I bloody don't know who you are or where you came from!" His tone softened, "My crew and I are grateful to you for saving our butts, lad."

"You are a brave man, Captain. I promise to see you again under better circumstances."

"We'll go look for girls together," the old Scotsman kidded.

"I've got one at home I plan on marrying," Isha responded.

"Too bad, Laddie," Andrews said. His tone went from forced jocularity to serious, "Don't let anything hurt my ship worse than she is already. Ok?"

"Have a safe trip to the hospital, Captain," was Isha's only reply.

"I've got everyone running around here looking like bloody chickens with their heads cut off. It will be quite a while before you have interruptions where you are."

"Thank you again," Isha spoke. "Don't worry. We'll do our best here. Have a nice life, McLean."

People rarely ever used the captain's first name. He was touched. "I don't even know your name," he responded almost sadly.

"Isha. My friends call me, Isha. I would be honored to have you in that group."

"Thank you, Isha." The line went dead.

* * * * *

In Exeter, things moved faster than anyone expected. On their third attempt to find an override code, the analysts hit pay dirt. In a top-secret mainframe computer buried deep inside the Pentagon, was a file that described exactly what the analyst had articulated to Annu fifteen minutes before. In that message file was a complex sequence that would disarm any weapon of the type Salomi had acquired. It seemed too simple an answer to so complex a problem.

"I guess my Mom was right," the analyst pontificated. "Live a good life, and good things will just happen to you."

Another scientist laughed. "Why weren't you so pure when we were pouring over those endless codes two hours ago?"

* * * * *

It took Isha three tries to follow the complicated procedures being radioed to him. Each time something wasn't quite right. Finally, as he moved the last dial, the heavy locking collar slid back and away from the cherry red button that popped up. The locking collar then slid reversed to prevent the button from being activated.

The bomb had been disarmed, and everyone on the team felt like the weight of the world had literally been lifted off their shoulders.

"Thank God," one of the Protectors whispered.

Isha took in a deep lungful of air and quietly responded, "Amen. Okay, we get to celebrate later. Right now, let's use that hatch and get out of here."

"What about the parasails we hid in the lifeboat on the main deck?" Jackson asked.

"Well, we would have let the military have them soon anyway," was Isha's response. "There isn't time to retrieve them."

"Good call, son," Annu spoke. "When you and the team can get out, there will be a local news helicopter landing in a few minutes. Get into it and tell the pilot that you are his cargo. He'll understand."

"Thanks, father."

"See you soon, son. Well done!"

* * * * *

Isha, Kevin, Robbie, Jackson, and Cody easily slipped through the chaos without any problem. Tourists and authorities were too busy to notice five men, one carrying a heavy canvas bag, as they worked through the crowd to a television news helicopter. The men quickly climbed aboard, and lifted off immediately.

Thirty-Five

Over the next week, coverage of the mystery ship grounded beneath the Statue of Liberty dominated the national and international press. The discovery of a disarmed nuclear warhead less than two hundred yards from the symbol of America's freedom had shocked and angered the entire nation.

Every crewmember of the Peligroso had been interviewed at length by various agencies of the United States government, each of which was convinced they had jurisdiction. These interviews had done nothing to shed light on the mysterious team who had rescued the crew, disabled the weapon, and prevented the holocaust it would have created.

Captain McLean Andrews, questioned from his hospital bed, reported that the men had merely said they were friends. He refused to say anything beyond that.

Andrews was released from the hospital a week later. That night he was in a front row center stage seat to watch his daughter, Liddie, perform in an off Broadway play. It was the first time she had ever seen him cry.

Only two of Salomi's men were still alive. They were taken into federal custody directly from the Peligroso. They were both surprised when they were told about the bomb they helped to smuggle. Neither man was exceptionally smart, but they understood that they had not been told about the warhead because they were expected to die in the blast. Once the new U.S. terrorism laws were explained to them, the men decided to cooperate fully with officials.

It took the journalistic bloodhounds a very short time to backtrack the terrorists and Lyndon Pearson to Azmud Salomi.

President Rogers used the averted crisis to call for the worldwide dismantling of all weapons of mass destruction. He carefully sidestepped questions about any military teams that might have been involved in the Peligroso's rescue. "I can't comment on that because of national security," he said tactfully. Within a few days, over the heated objections from the Pentagon, news reports of an actual top-secret anti-terrorist military squad would be leaked to the press. Rogers knew the journalists would assume this team was the one involved.

Politically, the attempted nuclear attack on the U.S. had been a blessing for the Rogers administration. He was now seen as the President whose decisive actions in sending in the anti-terrorist team had saved millions of lives. Neither he nor Platte Janosek ever admitted otherwise.

* * * * *

In Exeter, the team was welcomed with mixed feelings. The thrill of averting the greatest calamity to ever face the United States was diminished by the death of Skye. He was buried in the ceremonial robe of a Protector. His younger brother, Rowe, who would soon be a Protector himself, spoke the eulogy. "My brother believed that Exeter has a responsibility that goes beyond our borders. He died because of that belief. I will miss him, but I know his death helped save more lives than he could ever have imagined."

King Annu threw the first handful of dirt into the grave. He looked into the faces of Skye's family. "Your son," he said emotionally, "died because I sent him on a mission. He helped prevent a disaster of the highest order, but I want you to know I feel a burden that has never before rested on my shoulders. Please accept my deepest apology. I ask for your forgiveness." Words failed the ruler of Exeter at that point.

Skye's father stood next to his king. "Sire, you also sent your son on that mission. Skye loved you. He would not have wanted anyone else to go in his place. As a father, I will miss him. As a citizen of Exeter, I'm proud he was able to do what no one else could have done. There is no forgiveness required."

The two men hugged for a moment. Annu then regained his voice enough to continue, "Requiescat in pace – rest in peace, Skye."

That night, in the king's chamber, Isha, Deidre, Kevin and Celia relaxed. Isha's damaged leg would take several weeks of physical therapy to regain its strength. The white gauze wrapping and a noticeable limp were all that reminded everyone of the Prince's injury. He refused to mention it. Deidre refused to ignore it.

Kevin had a simple bandage on the side of his head that covered his wound. The only permanent damage he faced was a small groove through the hairline. He said it would always give him something to start a conversation with.

Everyone else was asleep, and the four young people were sitting in front of a rock fireplace enjoying the warmth and the quiet. The flickering fire danced off their faces. No one had spoken of the mission. They were lost in their own thoughts.

Slowly a spontaneous tiny smile grew on Deidre's face. Isha and Kevin both noticed it and looked at each other. Celia knew what was coming.

Isha finally decided to ask, "Where are you, Deidre?"

"Remembering a conversation I listened into from the Peligroso."

"Really? And what conversation was that?" Kevin continued.

"It seems that the captain wanted to corrupt our prince here, but Isha said he wasn't interested because of a girl back home." She had an innocent look on her face, but the gentle smile was still there. "He also mentioned something about wanting to marry her."

Kevin looked at Isha with delight. Isha simply said, "First, the captain wanted me to enter into a life of debauchery that I couldn't handle. Second, I didn't know my private conversation was being monitored. Third,..."

Celia jumped in, "Third, you got caught."

Everyone laughed and Kevin asked, "Just what did you mean, my friend?"

Prince Isha thought before answering. "I guess I meant that I'd like you to be my best man." He took Deidre's hand, "and if you'll have me, I'd like to make you the princess of Exeter."

King Annu and Maria were awakened from a sound sleep in their chambers by a loud shout of "Yes!"

Epilogue

Azmud Salomi was desperately trying to hide his involvement in the attempted attack on the United States. Earlier in the day he had ordered the execution of anyone associated with the planning or implementation of the assault, but it was already too late. Salomi was being denounced around the world.

His state controlled newspapers and television stations were vehemently denying any involvement with the foiled nuclear detonation. The world press, for the most part, was ignoring his protests.

Economically his country would soon be paying the price for the failed attack. The United Nations Security Council had officially condemned him and was debating instituting an international boycott of his oil. Saudi Arabia had already agreed to cover any loss of supply on the international market. Salomi loudly cursed the Saudi King as a puppet of the United States.

Salomi also cursed the situation he personally was in. Had the nuclear weapon detonated, the entire Arab world would have been looking at him as the central leader of the region. Instead, he had lost face. To Salomi, losing face was the worst thing that could happen.

There was no doubt in his mind that this was a relatively short-term setback. He figured it would take five years before the economic and political pressures were eased. He could wait that long.

An international boycott would mean shortages. Salomi really didn't care that the citizens in his country would suffer. He knew he could use his people's suffering to his advantage. Blaming the shortages they endured on the United States would be an effective propaganda ploy with the uneducated masses.

Patience was the key. Five years was all he had to endure. Until then, his day-to-day life would hardly change at all. Regardless of the hardships the poor endured, he would still live like a king. If he had to wait for world opinion to change, he would still do it in luxury.

Azmud Salomi walked through the palace towards his private residence. He curtly acknowledged the bows of several servants along the hallway. A discrete distance away, still close enough for instantaneous action, were Salomi's four bodyguards. Each man had a compact submachine gun slung from his shoulder. All were prepared to use their weapons at the first indication of danger to their leader.

As usual, no attendants were around as Salomi entered his mansion. He always wanted this time of solitude to pray. When in public, Salomi was a religious zealot. When alone, he avoided the practice of any religious teachings. In this private room Salomi had a customary, yet strictly forbidden, daily ritual. He enjoyed a snifter of brandy every evening. His privacy was certain. The servants knew not to enter when Salomi was in what he told them was his private meditation.

The blinds were pulled against the bright afternoon sun. Salomi savored the coolness of the darkened room for a moment. He walked to a cabinet along the south wall and opened a hidden panel. Inside was a bottle of his favorite brandy. He rolled the snifter between his hands to warm the crystal before pouring his drink.

Suddenly, he was aware of someone in the room. Quickly he turned and started to shout a warning to his guards stationed outside. A lightning chop to his throat cut the sound off instantly. The blow was not hard enough to kill the man, just to prevent his shout.

Azmud Salomi found himself staring into the coldest eyes he had ever beheld. They belonged to a young woman, no older than twenty-five years old. They lacked any emotion, but they frightened the man.

In his country, women were treated as second-class citizens who were totally ruled by their husbands. Salomi was not accustomed to seeing any woman assert herself.

"Who are you?" he croaked through his hurting larynx.

"Who I am is not important. All you have to know is that your plan to destroy millions of lives caused both the death of my fiancé and a good friend of ours." She stepped even closer to Salomi until her face was right in front of his. "They died because of you. Now you will die by my hand."

Desperately Salomi's mind raced. How could this woman have entered into the most secure place in his kingdom? He turned to run to a hidden door behind a wall tapestry.

Two men, about the same age as the woman stood silently by this exit. Trapped, Salomi again tried to yell for help, but his damaged throat would only produce a hoarse whisper.

The men did not speak nor interfere. The woman was obviously in charge. She grabbed and turned the frightened leader around roughly. Again he found himself staring into her eyes. He knew he would soon die, and he knew she would be the executor. A cry of anguish escaped from his lips.

Azmud Salomi, the man who had calmly ordered the murder of thousands in his own country and tried to kill millions of others, was terrified at the certainty of his own death. He wanted to beg for mercy, but he knew it would be futile.

The last words he ever heard were those of the young woman who simply said, "Ron, this is for you and Skye."

Prince Isha, Kevin, and Kristi knew that now their fallen Protectors would finally rest in peace.